"Packed with charm, wit, and a thoroughly satisfying romance, *Jane of Austin* made me want to pick up and move myself down to Texas. Dear reader, put the kettle on, mix up some scones, and be the heroine of your book club by bringing *Jane* to this month's meeting."

—KIMBERLY STUART, author of the Heidi Elliott series
and *Sugar: A Novel*

"*Jane of Austin* offers readers a fresh and contemporary take on a beloved classic. What a delight to enjoy Austen in this new modern way and find the characters and story as approachable, relevant, and engaging as the classic that has captured our hearts and sensibility for more than two hundred years. Heroine Jane's quirky brightness brings this rich tale of love, life, music, and tea to life—and leaves you yearning for more!"

—KATHERINE REAY, author of *Dear Mr. Knightley*
and *A Portrait of Emily Price*

"Quirky and charming, *Jane of Austin* goes down like a perfect cuppa. I was enchanted!"

—TERI WILSON, author of *Unleashing Mr. Darcy,*
now a Hallmark Channel original movie

"I love a story that I can savor, and this delicious charmer has it all—a swoon-worthy hero, unrequited love, quirky and loveable secondary characters, and a heroine you want to root for! (Not to mention many delicious recipes!) When tea-shop owner Jane and her sisters move to Austin looking for a new future, she has no idea that love is waiting for her too. The only problem is, she'll have to get her heart broken to find it. Beautifully written, a keeper of a story, and the perfect beach read!"

—SUSAN MAY WARREN, *USA Today* best-selling, RITA
Award–winning author of the Montana Rescue series

Jane of Austin

A Novel of Sweet Tea
and Sensibility

Jane of Austin

HILLARY MANTON LODGE

WATERBROOK

JANE OF AUSTIN

The characters and events in this book are fictional, and any resemblance to actual persons or events is coincidental.

Trade Paperback ISBN 978-1-60142-934-6
eBook ISBN 978-1-60142-935-3

Published in the United States by WaterBrook, an imprint of the Crown Publishing Group, a division of Penguin Random House LLC, New York.

WATERBROOK® and its deer colophon are registered trademarks of Penguin Random House LLC.

Library of Congress Cataloging-in-Publication Data
Names: Lodge, Hillary Manton, author.
Title: Jane of Austin : a novel of sweet tea and sensibility / Hillary Manton Lodge.
Description: First edition. | Colorado Springs, Colorado : WaterBrook, 2017.
Identifiers: LCCN 2017005491 (print) | LCCN 2017012219 (ebook) | ISBN 9781601429353
    (electronic) | ISBN 9781601429346 (softcover) | ISBN 9781601429353 (e-book)
Subjects: LCSH: Man-woman relationships—Fiction. | Life change events—Fiction. | Sisters—Fiction.
    | BISAC: FICTION / Romance / Contemporary. | FICTION / Family Life. | GSAFD: Love stories.
Classification: LCC PS3612.O335 (ebook) | LCC PS3612.O335 J36 2017 (print) | DDC 813/.6—dc23
LC record available at https://lccn.loc.gov/2017005491

Printed in the United States of America
2017—First Edition

10 9 8 7 6 5 4 3 2 1

In loving memory of Helen Law Rounds, my grandmother
and a great reader who loved Jane Austen best.

1916–2016

Prologue

But indeed I would rather have nothing but tea.

—JANE AUSTEN

San Francisco, CA
2009

"Well, girls," our father began, "it's been a good run. And I'm not saying it won't be again, but we're going to have to . . . economize."

"Economize?" I repeated, exchanging glances with my sister Celia, seated next to me, and our kid sister, Margot.

At least, I would have exchanged glances with Margot, but she was toying with the edge of her Powerpuff Girls Band-Aid.

The three of us sat together in a row on the sofa that had belonged to our grandmother. Everything in the old house seemed to have come from one family member or another.

Three years ago, Celia and I had sat on this same sofa when we were told about the car accident that ended our mother's life. It was tragic and ironic all at once. Tragic because we'd lost our mother and because five-year-old Margot was in the hospital with scrapes and a cracked rib.

Ironic because our father had just been hired on as the CEO of a car company.

Since then, the house and its contents had felt more important. Dad had worked, as he usually did, but even though I was in college and Celia had just graduated, we remained at the grand old house on Pacific Avenue. Near to Margot; near to memories.

Dad's work responsibility had only increased over the last few years, what with being the CEO of Edison Motors, and while he and Celia had the finance and business world in common, they rarely discussed it. Neither did he and I discuss botany (my passion) or the finer points of Nickelodeon programming (Margot's current passion, which we hoped might develop into a love of film down the road). As it was, the three of us seldom saw him when his family man image wasn't in need of some spit and polish.

"Did something happen?" Celia asked. "At Edison?"

"In a manner of speaking," he hedged.

Celia and I both waited, silent. Margot folded her legs until she could rest her chin on her knees.

"I've been ousted by the board," he finally said, his words coming out in an awkward rush. "The recall and all that, well, they're shortsighted. Shortsighted and malicious, if you ask me."

My back straightened in alarm. "Malicious?"

"They set the SEC after me," he continued, his face drawn but resolute. "There were some accounting issues, and while that's not my responsibility, I'm the fall guy in their little corporate drama." He paused, wincing. "Things are going to be a little rough for a while, but it'll shake out. In the meantime, we're going to decamp."

"Decamp?" Celia asked, frowning, but it was the other word he'd used that gave me pause.

I leaned forward. "We? How do you mean?"

In most ways that mattered, our nuclear family had ended in the car accident. Dad worked, and Celia, Margot, and I looked out for each other. There hadn't been a *we* that included our father in our family for a very long time.

"Yes. My assets have been frozen, pending investigation."

"Frozen?" Celia squeaked out.

He nodded. "Frozen. And there are debts. At any rate, the house will be on the market shortly."

I jumped to my feet. "The house? You can't sell mom's house!"

Celia rose and tried to place a soothing hand on my arm, but I shook her off. "This house has been in the family for generations."

Margot scowled. "It's my house too."

Dad lifted his chin. "It's also worth a great deal of money, young lady. And it was our house, your mother's and mine."

"No!" I tried to fill my lungs with air. "You can't sell it!"

My voice sounded strange to my own ears, sluggish and overloud. My face flushed in panic and embarrassment.

"There's no discussion," my father said, the calm in his voice only increasing the shame and anxiety knotted in my chest. "I'm leaving for the Caymans until the whole thing blows over."

I narrowed my eyes. "But—aren't your assets frozen?"

"The ones the SEC knows about," he amended, waving a hand casually. "You know how it is."

I didn't, actually. But then, I was just a college student, not a CEO.

"What about me?" Margot demanded.

"You'll come along," he reassured her. "It's sunny. You'll like it. There are . . . boats. You like boats, don't you?"

Margot's lip curled with disgust. "I get seasick."

"Is that even legal?" Celia asked. "Leaving the country?"

"It's what my lawyer advised," he answered, his chin lifting higher.

Celia and I exchanged dubious glances.

"And as I said, the three of you can come with me," he said. "I'll be able to access my offshore accounts."

"But . . . we're in school," I said, working hard to keep my emotions in check. "Margot and I, anyway, and Celia just started her new job." My brows knit together. "Next week is midterms."

Celia nodded.

"We can't just pick up and go to the Caymans," I said. Even the words felt strange in my mouth.

"I hate school," Margot said, sitting up. "I'll go."

Celia shook her head. "You have to stay in school. And you'd miss your friends, wouldn't you? Isabelle and Kaitlyn?"

Margot conceded with a shrug.

"If you stay here," Dad said, his voice stern, "I won't be able to pay for your tuition. I won't be able to pay for your dance classes, either," he said, looking at Margot. "The money you have is the money you'll have, until the rest of you turn twenty-one and can access your trust funds, the way Celia has. Because those were set up by your mother and grandparents, the government can't touch them."

I swallowed, fighting to keep the panic down.

"Nothing has to be decided tonight," Dad said. "Think about it. Take your time."

Celia nodded.

"I'll need your answer the day after tomorrow though," he finished, "in order to secure plane tickets."

I spared a glance at Celia, my mind churning. She said nothing, and we dispersed shortly after for bed.

The next morning, the *San Francisco Chronicle*'s front-page above-fold headline featured our father. I snuck the paper off the front steps and read it in the privacy of the upstairs library.

Most of it sounded like what our father had described, but other words jumped out as well. *Fraud* and *embezzlement* being the most notable.

He'd assured us everything had been a mistake, but . . . but had it?

Beneath the fold was a picture of Dad and Celia. Sure, her back was turned, but it still listed her by name. I wasn't an expert in the field, but I didn't think that was a good thing for Celia.

By the end of the day, my fears came true.

"They let me go," she said, her face pale and shocked. More shocked, somehow, than after Dad's news the previous day.

"There's no way to fight it?" I asked, my voice low as we sat together on the unfashionable yet blissfully comfortable sofa stashed in our favorite attic nook.

She shook her head. "No. I mean, I could. But what if it didn't work out? You saw the paper. I'm"—she sniffed—"unemployable. In finance, trust is *everything*."

I wrapped my arm around her shoulders and held tight. "I'm so sorry."

"I had to take my stuff out and everything."

"Did they give you severance?"

She nodded. "If I agreed to go quietly."

And she would. Anyone who knew Celia would know that.

She sniffed and laughed. "The only bright side is that I think I have a date."

"What?"

"It's a coworker. He was hired on the same time as me. Teddy Foster. He helped me put my stuff together, gave me his briefcase so that I didn't have to do a walk of shame with a cardboard box. Walked out with me so it just looked like we were leaving for a meeting."

"And then he asked you out?"

She laughed again, disbelieving. "I think so. He asked for my phone number."

"Did he text?"

A nod.

I laughed and shook my head in disbelief. "Look at you. Getting fired and getting a date, all in the same day."

"You can laugh, but it won't be funny for long. Not—not with everything else. I needed that job. Nobody else is going to hire me."

"I know," I said. "I have a plan. Well, it's the beginnings of a plan." I held out my hand, preparing to count off with my fingers. "First, I quit school."

"Jane, no!"

"Yes. My trust fund won't kick in for another two years, and yours won't cover my tuition and Margot's—and rent. So I'm going to quit school, and we're going to start a business."

"A business? Jane, be serious."

"I am being serious! You'll work your magic and open a shell corporation, and we'll use it to get a lease. Nobody will know it's the infamous Woodward sisters. We'll get a lease, open a shop, and . . . I don't know, sell soap."

Celia goggled at me. "Shell corporation? Soap?"

"I *have* learned a few things listening to you and Dad over the years. But it doesn't have to be soap. We could sell, I don't know . . . antiques. You love antiques."

"I know nothing about antiques."

I racked my brain for ideas. "Tea. A tea shop. I learned all about tea when I was studying abroad."

"I know," she said dryly. "It's all you've been talking about. And why I want you in school—you and botany."

"I'll finish school later. This is an emergency."

Celia sighed. "What's sad is that I know you're not being hyperbolic." She pulled her chunky cardigan closer. "A tea shop?"

"A tea shop. Something quaint, tourist-friendly."

"You hate tourists."

"Desperate times." I met her gaze. "Dad taking Margot to the Caymans is a terrible idea."

Celia winced. "I know. But I want what's best for her, and . . ."

"It's not her fleeing the country with Dad," I said firmly. "She needs us. We need her."

Celia hugged her arms to herself. "A tea shop?"

I nodded, my mind full of tea leaves and steaming water. "A tea shop."

"Small business ownership is hard. Most small businesses go under in the first year."

"But it's us! You and me. Your brains, my winning personality—"

Celia said nothing, but her raised eyebrow filled the silence.

"Okay, fine," I conceded. "Your brains, *your* winning personality, and my expertise in the kitchen."

She gave a rueful laugh. "That sounds more plausible. I just—I don't know."

"Do you have any other ideas? We can't let Margot go. We . . . we almost lost her once."

My eyes began to fill with tears; Celia reached to hold my hand tight.

"You're right," she said, her voice steadier. "If she wants to stay, we'll find a way to make it work."

1

You can never get a cup of tea large enough or a book long enough to suit me.

—C. S. Lewis

December 2016
San Francisco, CA

"So you see," Jonathan explained, "what you've been paying as a lease for your little tea shop—it's well beneath market value."

"I'm aware of that," I said, though until now I hadn't known *quite* how far below. I hadn't had to. But I didn't let on; I didn't like the condescending tone of our landlord's nephew's voice.

Well, ex-landlord. Because the owner of our building, Atticus, had passed away the week before. Atticus had passed, and there was no way we could pay his nephew the number on the paper in front of us.

"You've been leasing the space for six years now?"

"Seven," Celia corrected softly.

"Right. And the market, you know, has increased in the area exponentially. Which was fine for my uncle, but for myself as a businessman . . ." His voice trailed off, leaving us to infer his thoughts on not exponentially increasing our rent.

"Do you think," my sister Celia asked carefully, "that there could be some room for negotiation?"

"Well," Jonathan started. But his wife, Phoebe, laid her hand over his to stop the flow of words.

"My uncle-in-law was quite the philanthropist," Phoebe said, drawing out the last word. "But the recession is over." She smiled, or at least gave her best facsimile of a smile. "Our son's tuition won't pay for itself."

I opened my mouth to protest, but Celia kicked my foot and shook her head slightly. I looked out the office window and counted to fifty.

Backward.

If Celia didn't want me to point out that Jonathan and Phoebe's son was all of three years old, I wouldn't. If she didn't want me to remind Jonathan that since he'd inherited his uncle's real estate holdings, we could use the tea salon space for free and he'd hardly miss a penny, fine. We were hardly standing between his son and whatever lower-tier private university Jonathan Junior wouldn't attend for another fifteen years, and everybody in the room knew it.

"You could speak to your father," Jonathan suggested.

My hands clenched into fists.

Celia spoke first, saving me from trying to string together a civil sentence. "We've chosen to keep our business interests completely separate from our father, thank you."

Phoebe's smile edged into a smirk. "That's probably for the best."

I rose to my feet, struggling to remain calm. "We'll be out in the thirty days stipulated in our lease agreement." It would be a thin, sad holiday season, but at least we could spend it at our home before relocating.

Jonathan clapped his hands. "Excellent. You'll find something else; I'm sure of it."

I wasn't but didn't say anything.

"Could you make it fifteen?" Phoebe asked.

My spine straightened. "Excuse me?"

"Jon's uncle simply rented without making improvements to his properties, and many of them need major repair and updating. I have a list of clients waiting to look at the space," Phoebe continued. "The remodels will have to be completed before they see it."

"Fifteen days," I said, barely controlling my temper, "is Christmas Eve."

"Oh," Phoebe said. "I hadn't realized. I apologize. How about twenty?" She clasped her hands together and gave us a benevolent smile. "Start the new year somewhere fresh."

"Twenty is fine," Celia answered quickly, before I could tell Phoebe where she could shove her fresh new year. "Thank you."

And before I could say another word, she grabbed my hand and dragged me from the office.

We stayed silent as we walked down the hallway, but once the elevator doors closed, I whirled to face my sister. "What were you doing, agreeing to twenty days? What they're asking is illegal!"

"Of course it is, Jane." Celia pressed the *L* button to take us back to ground level. "But you and I both know that they can make life miserable for us if we disagree, and we can't afford a legal battle."

"It wouldn't come to that. You're dating Phoebe's brother; she wouldn't take it to court. Speaking of, does Teddy know about this?"

"He would have told me if he'd known. We'll figure it out."

I faced the elevator doors and crossed my arms. "I don't like it. I don't know how we're going to get the three of us *and* the business moved out in twenty days. And"—my anger redoubled—"the building *isn't* out of repair."

"I know," she sighed.

"How are we going to tell Margot that Christmas just got canceled?"

"It's not canceled, just . . ."

"We can take a break from packing," I said dryly, "to hold hands and sing carols. That's our very-best-case scenario. Let's not pretend it's a good one."

Celia sighed again.

I shook my head. "We're Valencia Street Tea. What are we going to do if we're not on Valencia Street anymore?"

"I suppose we'll just be Valencia Tea. Or something."

I wrinkled my nose. "Mmm. I like Valencia Tea Company better."

"That's perfectly fine."

My stomach twisted with the thought, though. "Are you sure you couldn't say something? To Teddy?"

Celia lifted a resigned shoulder. "Phoebe's always gotten her way. If she says jump, he jumps. And tries not to get hit."

"But he—"

"No," Celia said.

I scowled and leaned against the mirrored elevator wall. "You've been seeing each other for how long? The two of you are practically engaged."

"His hands are full enough at work; he doesn't need to get tangled up with Jonathan and Phoebe's issues."

"Atticus would be horrified." I shook my head. "I took his favorite scones to the memorial."

Celia sighed. "You're right. He would be shocked."

I tried to take a deep breath, but it came out ragged. "How are we going to find another space in twenty days," I asked, quieter, "much less move? What about the tea plants? And Margot?"

"I won't tell her you thought of the tea plants first." Celia's mouth settled into a firm line. "We'll figure something out."

∞

For the last seven years, we'd leased the downstairs of the row house—not Victorian, like the Painted Ladies, but built after the 1906 earthquake. Diverse and eclectic, our neighborhood on Valencia Street had gentrified over the years, with shops and restaurants springing up around us.

The upstairs of the house had been remodeled into an apartment, and when the tenants left three years ago, Atticus had offered it to the three of us. We'd been living on borrowed time, I now realized. Atticus didn't raise our rates as the neighborhood changed, always telling us that he valued us and our tea shop.

In exchange, we kept him in tea and all the scones he could ever desire. The arrangement pleased us all—our old apartment had been cramped and a longer commute for Margot to get to ballet. After we moved in upstairs, she'd been able to walk to school and back, take BART to ballet, and have her homework supervised by Atticus in exchange for company and croissants.

Having the second floor also meant I had room for a secondhand piano and access to the rooftop, which is where I grew my personal tea plants.

The tea plants, like all *camellia sinensis* plants, grew slowly. I harvested them occasionally for our personal use and practiced making white, green, and black tea from the leaves, but I wouldn't be able to use them on a commercial basis until I had more mature plants. Atticus had treasured my tea, and I'd always set aside the best of the harvest for him.

Atticus's death meant that those days were now at an end. Our home, our business, and my plants—all would need to relocate.

"Maybe we won't have to move far," I said to Celia upon returning home. "We can go inland. Pleasant Hill, Walnut Creek . . ."

"Maybe," Celia answered.

Margot wouldn't like it, but neither of us would say so. As a junior in high school, Margot would likely find a move to the farther-flung burbs a fate worse than death.

"When is Teddy picking you up tonight?" I asked, reaching for something positive in my mind.

"When he gets off work, so . . . around eight or so."

I squeezed her hand. "Maybe he'll have a brilliant idea."

"That would be nice," Celia agreed.

We found Margot on the balcony, practicing her dancing and using the rail as a bar. Celia gestured her to the small kitchen table, and the three of us sat down.

"We're going to have to move, aren't we?" she asked, her face resolved. "Because Atticus died?"

"Yes," Celia said. "But we'll find something else."

"I saw a For Rent sign two blocks over," she offered.

"Oh." Celia nodded. "Good. I'll look into it."

I knew my older sister. She would look, just as promised. But if the owners wanted what Jonathan and Phoebe wanted, there was absolutely no way we'd be able to afford it.

"We should start packing," I told Margot. "Even if we don't know where we'll land yet, we can still get ready."

She wrinkled her nose, but nodded.

Margot and I spent the evening in our apartment; the two of us made a pile of items that needed to be put away and another pile to be donated. I was asleep on the sofa when Celia returned later that night; Margot had long since retreated to message friends from the privacy of her room.

"Did you have a good time?" I asked, though the rosy glow in her cheeks gave away the answer. "Did he have any genius ideas?"

The glow faded, just a little. "No," she said, removing her jacket before taking a seat beside me. "But he does hope we find somewhere nice and close by."

"He doesn't think he can influence Phoebe?"

"Phoebe is un-influenceable."

"I highly doubt that, for a series of reasons it would be petty to mention."

The corner of Celia's mouth turned up in a smile. "No?"

"Also, I'm tired."

"That makes more sense."

"It is strange, when you think about it, that we're being evicted by your boyfriend's sister and her husband."

Celia sighed. "Not evicted, exactly, but I know what you mean, and yes. But don't worry. We'll start looking for new places tomorrow."

∞

Every night, Celia closed out the till and we examined the numbers.

We had a little money, but not enough.

When I turned twenty-one, I gained control of my trust fund. My mother's family had money, but not limitless wealth. The fund meant we had enough to pay off debts and tuck an appropriate amount into an emergency fund. The rest went into long-term investments to ensure that Margot could go to college. At the time we'd toyed with trying to buy a location rather than lease, but even then the price of purchasing property in the city was simply out of our reach.

Certainly, we couldn't afford a place that could compare to where we were, especially after moving into the second-floor apartment.

With the investment money inaccessible, we had enough to keep the business going, to keep Margot in toe shoes, to make sure we all had medical coverage. Over the years, we'd gotten good at creatively making ends meet.

But the more we looked for a new space for Valencia Tea and a new growing space for the tea plants, the more my worries became real.

We'd had no luck finding anything in any of the adjacent neighborhoods; the For Rent sign had disappeared by the time Celia set out to inquire. Nothing across town, and so far Celia had been reluctant to examine the farther-flung suburbs, wanting to stay close for Teddy and Margot's school, no doubt.

I just worried that close wouldn't remain an option.

On day seven, we holed up after hours in the shop with the Oh Hellos playing over the speakers.

"Maybe if we tried something new with the Internet business," I suggested as I wrapped yet another teapot up with packing wrap and placed it in a box. "Like a tea subscription box. Right now, most of our sales are local, but that kind of hook could take us national. Or maybe we do a pop-up shop from time to time or a food cart. What do you think of that?"

"We could," Celia answered, looking up from packing her frilliest teacup. "But we make good money off the pastries. I'd want us to come back to this model. And I'd miss all this—the cups, the customers. This place has been special."

I looked around at the space, with its original windows and vintage wallpaper. "It has."

A rap sounded at the door behind me. "We're closed!" I called without looking up.

"Just me," came a familiar male voice.

"Teddy!" Celia set her packing aside and jumped up to unlock the door and let him inside.

He'd obviously come from work, his suit perfectly cut but a little rumpled from the day's wear. He and Celia looked good together, like a Zales diamond ad. His hair was dark, like Phoebe's, but where Phoebe's was viciously straight, his was thick with a bit of curl.

Speaking of diamonds, I wondered—and not for the first time—when he'd get around to putting a ring on it. After all, they'd been together for ages.

"Sorry about leaving you in the cold, Teds," I said, sitting up and taking notice of the bags in his hands. "Whatcha got there?"

"I brought Indian," he said, lifting a plastic bag full of containers.

Celia gave him a chaste peck on the cheek. "You're so sweet."

"I'll get plates!" I called out. "What's in there?"

He began to pull plastic tubs of curry out, one by one. "Lamb *rogan josh,* chicken *tikka masala, baingan bharta,* and dal curry."

I cocked my head to the side. "But what will the rest of you eat?"

Teddy gave a warm laugh. "There's *palak paneer* too and samosas for Margot. Is she upstairs?"

"Only until the scent of food finds her nose."

Sure enough, seconds later Margot's head, surrounded by a soft halo of curls that had escaped her ballerina bun, appeared in the doorway. "Teddy! You're here!" Her eyes lit on the food on the table. "And you brought Indian!" She looked up at him, her large dark eyes hopeful. "Did you get samosas?"

He lifted the brown paper bag. "Just for you."

She threw her arms around his middle in an impetuous, classically Margot hug. "You're the best."

The four of us set up the containers at one of the café tables and filled our plates with rice, naan, curries, and samosas. As we ate, I looked around at the tea shop, struck by the realization that we wouldn't be here, in this space, much longer.

After everything that had happened, Valencia Street Tea had become our home. It had provided a living for the three of us, a rewarding one that provided us the flexibility to take care of Margot.

And while I'd taken a class here and there, working toward finishing my degree, this home had given me the space to lean into one of the great loves of my life—tea. Here, I had space not only to grow my own tea but also reason to buy bulk tea and mix it with herbs, citrus peels, or flower buds to create my own specialty flavors. I loved experimenting with those blends, not just to brew as tea but to season food.

All this I could have done on my own, without the restaurant part of the tea salon, but that was Celia's favorite part. Aside from keeping the books, she'd left the world of finance behind, embracing the hospitality side of running a tea shop. She loved serving tea in her eclectic collection of teapots and teacups, loved serving shortbreads and pound cakes, loved meeting customers and hearing about their day.

Every single good Internet review mentioned Celia, usually by name. The few bad ones?

I believe one former customer referred to me as a "termagant," which if memory served me was actually code for "someone who will insist on people keeping their hands out of the loose-leaf tea jars, thank you very much."

Margot sighed contentment as she ate. "I don't want to leave," she said. "I want to stay here forever, eating Indian takeout with Teddy."

"We'll find something close," I said, sounding more confident than I felt. "Close to our customers. Close to Teddy." I passed the container of rich green *palak paneer* to Celia. "I promise."

∽

On day ten, Phoebe called. "I'm going to come in," she said, "to take some measurements. Could you or your sister unlock the door for me?"

"It's open," I said.

"Oh," she said, surprised. "You're still open?"

I looked around the dining room at the regulars clustered around tables and bit back a dozen sarcastic retorts. "Yes, we are," I said instead.

"Do you have any of those green-tea macarons?"

"The matcha macarons?" I reached into our pastry case and removed the tray. "No, I don't believe I see any in the case."

Phoebe made a noise of disappointment and hung up. I set the phone down and raised the tray. "Matcha macarons, anyone? They're on the house."

Within seconds, the macarons were gone.

"I can't believe you're leaving," one of the customers said. "And over the holidays, no less. You're Valencia Street Tea. You belong here; it's in the name. You're an institution."

I gave a sad, wry smile. "We've only been here since 2010."

"In this neighborhood? Institution."

I smiled a thank-you and put on a brave face, knowing that Phoebe could walk in at any moment.

"It's just so dated in here," Phoebe said with a sigh after her arrival, as if the vintage interior made her tired.

I watched as Phoebe took in the original paned windows, the floral wallpaper, the crown molding, and tiled stone floors. If I could have taken the lot of it with us, I would have. I loved our tea salon, from the sign on the front to the potted plant in the back, and my heart broke at the thought of what she might do to it.

"Yes," she said finally. "A lift is just what it needs."

I physically clamped my tongue between my teeth.

Her vulture-like gaze swung to the bar, and her eyes lit up. "That's nice though," she said. "That can stay."

"Actually," Celia said, coming up behind me, "the bar is ours."

Phoebe's eyebrows, which managed to be at once massive and manicured, furrowed low over her eyes. "What's that?"

"The bar," Celia repeated, placing a hand over the marble top. "We bought it on craigslist."

Phoebe considered this information.

I knew why she wanted it. Even if she wanted to turn the row house's interior to something minimalist and Scandinavian, the bar was something special. A solid wood base, with scrolling and flowers carved into the richly finished wood, and a thick marble top.

"Are you sure?" Phoebe asked, her head tilted with considered condescension.

"Our accountant has a copy of the receipt," Celia replied sweetly.

Sweetly, but with a hint of steel. My sister was nobody's dummy.

"It will be very heavy to take with you," Phoebe pointed out.

"I've been working out," I deadpanned. "And my baby sister, Margot, is a ballerina. Calves of steel, that one."

Celia snorted, but being refined and ladylike, she covered it with the gentlest of coughs.

Phoebe sighed. "It's just as well. You'll be out on the twenty-ninth as we discussed, yes? I have workmen coming to replace the windows."

"The windows?" I repeated, dumbly.

"Your energy bills must be sky high with these things," she said, reaching out and tapping the paned glass.

"We boil a lot of water here," I said. "It helps."

"I suppose." Phoebe looked the place over and sniffed. "It'll be a lot of work," she said, "but so rewarding it in the end."

One of the customers asked something of Celia, and she stepped over to assist.

I reached for a rag to wipe down the bar top and changed the subject. "We've enjoyed getting to know Teddy over the years," I said to Phoebe as I cleaned the crumbs and tea spills from its surface. "I never had a brother, so it's been fun having him around."

Phoebe's expression turned smug. "Both of my brothers *are* special: Rob with his app start-up and Teddy with his success at the firm. He's up for partner, you know."

I nodded. "I do."

"He has a bright future ahead of him. Our parents have high hopes for his career, you know."

My mouth quirked into a wry smile. "How Camelot of them."

"With his skills, his family connections, Teddy—Theodore, I should say—could go far."

"Yes," I said. "It's too bad he's not doing anything with his life."

I was being sarcastic, but Phoebe didn't catch it. "He should have been made partner last year," she said, and as much as I disliked her, I could read the sisterly anxiety on her face. "Everyone said he would be."

That I hadn't heard. "Oh?"

She lifted a shoulder. "This year should be the year. As long as the firm can overlook . . . you know."

"I don't."

"You know," she said, searching for words. "The . . . association."

I squinted. "The mob, you mean?"

"No!" She huffed out a sigh. "The association. With your father. Where is he?"

"We don't speak much," I said. "He travels. I'm not sure where he is." I tried to be casual, but something cold lodged within my chest. Dad had enjoyed his extended vacation in a variety of nonextradition nations over the years.

"At any rate," I said, "I don't see why my father should be a factor. We have very little contact with him, and he's never met Teddy."

"Doesn't matter. The name, you know."

I wished she'd stop saying that I knew. I didn't. At least, I hadn't, but this time I was getting a very bad feeling that perhaps I did.

"You're saying that Teddy's been passed up for partner because he's dating my sister."

Phoebe released a breath, looking grateful that she didn't have to be the one to say it out loud. "Yes, exactly. It's not her fault. But the association . . ."

I was beginning to hate that word.

But what did it matter? Teddy? Being manipulated by his work, his family? Giving up Celia?

He would never.

I met Phoebe's gaze. "Yes, well, shame that Teddy's never given a dry tea leaf about our father."

Celia returned, a cautious smile on her face as she took in both of our expressions. "Could I offer you a cup of tea while you're here, Phoebe?" Celia asked.

∞

On days eleven through thirteen, we met with banks. We applied for loans and looked for anything that would give us the liquid cash to see us into a space within the city.

The experience reminded us why we'd opened the tea shop through a shell corporation in the first place.

After Dad left the country eight years ago, the name Woodward was splashed across every Bay Area newspaper as investigators and journalists worked to figure out if our father was corrupt or merely inept. To this day, nobody could be sure. The Valencia Street Tea gamble had, until now, provided a fairly stable living. Dad had offered to send us money now and again, but we'd declined. Sure, we'd had our lean years, but we were together, the three of us, and that was all that mattered.

But memories in this town ran long, and no bank wanted to give Walter Woodward's daughters a loan.

2

A Proper Tea is much nicer than a Very Nearly Tea,
which is one you forget about afterwards.

—A. A. MILNE

On day fourteen, I spent the day baking. Margot tried to join me after school, but I shooed her out of the kitchen after she dropped a bag of flour and set a dish towel on fire.

I baked extra scones, croissants, and Danishes, and they flew out the door. It seemed that our customers, knowing about our impending uncertainty, decided to do what I would do under threat of a favorite shop closing; they stocked up. Our books were in the black, but nowhere near the numbers we would have to hit to stay.

So I kept at it, consoling myself that at least we'd have extra moving money.

Celia left early for a date with Teddy that night, and Margot wouldn't be dropped off by her best friend's mom until the late hours. I closed up, turning up the music—*La Bohème*—as I wiped down the tables, mopped the floors, washed the dishes, and got everything ready for the following day.

Being alone, I startled when I heard the back door open and slam shut. I turned down the music to investigate, and my shoulders relaxed when I saw Celia.

"Oh, it's you. I didn't expect you back so soon."

"I'm sorry; I didn't mean to scare you," she said, her tone strained.

My eyes widened once she stepped into the light. "You've been crying! Celia, what's wrong? What happened?" I threw my arms around her. "Don't be sad about moving away from Teddy. I'm sure he'll find a way to see you."

"No he won't," she said, her voice thick with tears.

"Of course he will," I assured her. "He'd go to the moon and back for you."

She placed her hands on my shoulders and stepped back to meet my gaze. "We broke up, Jane. Teddy and I broke up."

My eyes flew open in shock. "You broke up? How?"

She shook her head and wiped her nose with the back of her hand—a very un-Celia-like gesture. "I . . . I'm sorry, I . . ."

"You don't have to talk about it if you don't want to," I assured her.

Except . . . it just didn't make sense. Because I knew Celia and I knew Teddy, and I'd seen them just a few days before, looking as happy and relaxed and cohesive as ever.

I hadn't experienced it myself, the kind of togetherness I witnessed between the two of them. My own relationships—though few and far between—tended to be short and fiery and marked with plenty of bickering. But Celia and Teddy shared the same sense of calm and warmth. While they weren't at all the same person, they complemented each other.

So the fact that they broke up? My brain tried and failed to comprehend the news.

"Did something happen?" I asked, my eyebrows furrowing as I tried to wrap my head around it. "Is he joining the Peace Corps? Taking a job in"—I racked my brain—"Antarctica?"

Even as I said it, I thought, *No, that's not true. They'd still be together if he left for Antarctica.*

And then it hit me. "Phoebe. Was Phoebe a part of it?"

"I'm sorry," Celia said, her gaze dropping to the floor. "I really can't talk about it."

"Okay," I said. "That's fine."

It wasn't. It wasn't fine, not in the slightest. Had Phoebe really managed to work her will? Was Teddy—our Teddy—*really* willing to let his family dictate his dating life?

But Celia was my sister, and she was hurting. I put my hands on my hips.

"What do you need? I can put the kettle on. There are a couple pumpkin scones left. I can order a pizza. Tell me what to do."

"I just want to go to bed."

"Bed. That's good. Bed. Okay. You head upstairs; I'll bring you a cup of chamomile."

She looked as though she thought to argue but decided against it. "Fine. Bring me a cup."

I brought her a scone for good measure.

The morning of Christmas Eve, I awoke to find Celia holding her phone in my face.

"It's a phone. I see that," I said, rolling over to the opposite side.

Celia tugged on my shoulder. "It's not the phone. It's what's on the phone. Look!"

I took it and held the screen close enough for my tired eyes to focus on the text. "It looks like an e-mail."

"It is! Read it!"

"You're strident first thing in the morning." But I did as she said, sitting up to read aloud. "'Dear Celia.'"

"Shh! Don't wake Margot."

I raised an eyebrow and returned to the e-mail in a softer voice. "'Glad you wrote. Of course I remember you—you're the spitting image of your mother.'" I looked up at my sister. "That's true. You are."

"Keep reading."

"'You asked about what the market looked like for small-business owners and tea in the Austin area. I've got good news for you. The Austin business scene is eclectic, and the tea salon you described might fit right in. And I can do you one better: you and Jane and Margot are welcome to come stay in our guesthouse for as long as you like. Bring your plants with you. We have three acres in Barton Creek, so pick the one that you like best and put it to good use.'"

I shot a look at Celia. She grinned and nodded for me to continue. "'There are some nice spaces for a tea salon not far from us, and you may find the prices more reasonable than the Bay Area. Yours sincerely, Ian Vandermeide.'" I looked up. "Wait, Austin? And who is Ian Vandermeide?"

"Mom's cousin Ian. You've met him."

"I don't have your talent for remembering faces. Or names." I pulled my tangled hair from my face. "So you wrote? To ask him about us moving to Austin?"

"Look, we need somewhere to go, Jane. I started writing friends and family around the country, just asking if they thought their city might be a good fit for our sort of tea salon."

"But . . . *Austin*?"

"Yes!"

"Austin, Texas."

"Yes, Jane."

"Celia. Darling." I placed my sister's phone in her hand and wrapped her fingers around it. "We are California girls. We are not Texas girls. Texas is . . . it's essentially a whole other country. It actually *was* a whole other country."

"Yes, but Texas also has a guesthouse and a place for Margot and a place for your tea. And"—she paused—"people are less likely to know who we are."

I lifted a cynical eyebrow. "I wouldn't be too sure about that. And anyway, Margot's halfway through the school year. I don't think she'd be thrilled about moving."

"She was probably going to have to transfer anyway or have an hour-long commute to classes. That's two hours every day that doesn't go to homework or ballet."

"Fair enough. I just don't know. Does tea even grow in that part of Texas?"

"Austin is still zone 8. Zone 8b, to be precise."

"You looked it up."

She sat back on the bed. "I know you worry about your plants."

"And Margot? How are the schools?"

"Westlake High is well rated. At least, according to the Internet."

I chewed my lip. "Texas."

Celia nodded. "Texas."

"But . . ." I shook my head. "There has to be something closer. I know the real estate around here is sky high and the cost of living is higher than New York, but *Texas*? Surely there has to be some kind of middle ground. Like, Oregon or something." I sat up straighter and shoved my hair from my face. "Vandermeide . . . isn't that the weird, oil-money side of the family?" My eyes widened with recollection. "Ian's the ex–naval officer who retired to breed hunting dogs or something."

"I think they're pointers? Or some kind of spaniel? I don't remember."

I lifted an eyebrow. "What about you and Teddy?"

Celia looked down at her lap. "I told you. We broke up."

"Yes, you told me," I said, squinting.

"You don't believe me," Celia stated in disbelief.

"I thought you were going to get married!" My brow furrowed low. "Seriously, Celia, what happened with you guys? Phoebe was talking about you two and his job, and I thought it was crazy talk, that you guys were solid, but—"

"Please. Don't make me talk about it. I just . . . I can't."

"So if he wasn't pressured by his sister or his job, what? He joined a cult? The CIA?"

"No. He's . . . he's fine. He's still Teddy."

"He didn't get accepted onto *The Bachelor* or anything like that? Because he's too even tempered to make good ratings. No offense."

"Jane, I love you. And I get it. Teddy and I have been together for a long time, and I thought . . ." She stopped herself from continuing. "Relationships are hard, and they have to be right for both people on a lot of different levels."

"That makes no sense."

"I know. And I'm sorry. I just . . . I don't want to talk about Teddy. I want to talk about Austin, and how we might want to move to a place where Dad's reputation doesn't follow us everywhere we go."

"Did Teddy break up with you because of Dad?"

"No," Celia said in an exhale. "He did not break up with me because of Dad. Jane"—she sighed—"please."

That last *please* did me in.

"I'm sorry," I said, reaching out for her hand. "I'm sorry about you and Teddy, and . . . I'm sorry I pushed."

I didn't like a lot of people, but Celia?

She knew as well as I that if we wanted to stay on the West Coast, we'd find something. It wouldn't be in San Francisco, it wouldn't necessarily be glamorous, but we had options.

For Austin to suddenly be the only recourse—it wasn't about our finances as much as a need to get away. Far away.

But I loved her. If my sister needed a change of scenery, I knew my answer wasn't *yes* or *no*. It was *how far* and *when*. I leaned forward. "So Austin, then?"

Celia's face relaxed into a smile. "Austin. It's a fresh start."

Cranberry Vanilla Scones

7 tablespoons cold unsalted butter

¼ cup milk, plus more until the dough just holds together

1 tablespoon vanilla extract

1 3/4 cups frozen cranberries, roughly chopped

¼ cup white sugar

1 ½ cups whole-wheat pastry flour, divided

1 cup all-purpose flour

1/3 cup brown sugar

3 teaspoons baking powder

½ teaspoon sea salt

Zest of two oranges

2 tablespoons turbinado sugar

Position the oven rack in the center, and preheat the oven to 400 degrees. Prepare a large baking sheet by lining it with parchment paper.

Cut the butter into small pieces; refrigerate. Stir together the ¼ cup milk and vanilla extract in a measuring cup. Set aside.

Toss the cranberries together with the ¼ cup white sugar and ¼ cup of the whole-wheat pastry flour and set aside.

In a large mixing bowl, stir together the remaining 1 ¼ cups of whole-wheat pastry flour, along with the all-purpose flour, brown sugar, baking powder, sea salt, and orange zest.

With your hands, work the chopped butter into the flour mixture, pressing the butter pieces into dime and oatmeal-sized flakes. Add the dried cranberries, and toss to mix. Pour the milk in a spiral around the mixture. Use a fork and then your hands to mix and press the ingredients together, turning them within the bowl and adding more milk by the tablespoon until a dough just forms.

On a lightly floured surface, press the dough into a circle about $3/4$ to 1 inch thick. Use a biscuit cutter or drinking glass to cut circles from the dough. It's okay to press scraps together gently for the last scone or two. Place the scones onto the baking sheet, and sprinkle liberally with the turbinado sugar.

Bake for 15–20 minutes, until the scones are lightly golden on top. Allow to cool 5 minutes before serving. The scones are delicious warm or at room temperature.

Makes 6 scones.

3

If a man's from Texas, he'll tell you. If he's not, why
embarrass him by asking?

—John Gunther

Callum

When the plane landed, I unbuckled my seat belt and tried to stretch, using all
of the two inches between myself and my fellow passengers. My left leg ached,
but that was nothing new.

In the midst of a plane full of people, the flight attendant wove her way to
me, then leaned over solicitously. "Do you need any assistance deplaning today,
sir?"

"No, ma'am," I said. "But thank you."

Deep, deep down, I knew that carrying my rucksack would be an exercise
in persistence and balance. But the day I asked a tiny thing like her to carry my
bag for me—well, that would mean I was probably dead.

I had the window seat, and while my row mates offered to let me out first,
I waved them on. While the crowd thinned, I turned my phone back on to
check for messages.

There were ten. Every one from Ian.

I got here early—less traffic than expected. Parked in the waiting lot.

*Are you hungry? I can't imagine what they fed you on the plane. Pilar
made oatmeal cookies, but we can stop for tacos if you need a real meal.*

I also have Dr Pepper with me. Do you still drink Dr Pepper?

And so on. I smiled, and sent a quick text to let him know I'd landed before I pocketed the device and scanned the plane. Just families with children

looking under seats to make sure they'd gotten every last bit of child detritus. I took a deep breath and planned my next move. With the armrests shifted upright, I could scoot down the row and get to the end where I'd have more room. I planted my right foot, using my cane on the left and pushing up with my right arm to get myself up before finding my balance on my right foot and the new, unfamiliar prosthesis that took the place of my left knee, calf, and foot.

A brief glance up revealed the petite flight attendant, watching with worry in her eyes.

I'd worn my uniform, thinking it was its last hurrah as I left the life I never thought I'd leave. With the flight attendant's eyes on me, I began to regret my decision.

"I'm all right, ma'am," I said. Aware that she was watching closely for any sign of weakness, I reached inside the open overhead compartment and wrestled my bag down.

While it met the airline's size requirements, it probably weighed as much as she did.

I used my left hand to steady myself with the cane and chose not to react to the painful pressure of the additional weight of the bag. *Suck it up, Beckett.*

I maneuvered myself and the bag down the narrow aisle, where the flight staff waited. "Thank you for your service, sir," said the gentleman in the captain's uniform, reaching out his hand to shake mine. With the bag slung over my shoulder, I shook his hand, the copilot's, and the two flight attendants' with the petite attendant last. She looked up at me, her eyes huge and dewy. "You're an inspiration," she said. "Merry Christmas."

I was many, many things, but I was pretty sure an inspiration wasn't one of them. But I nodded to be polite, thanked her, and made my way down the jet bridge. Inside the terminal, I texted Ian.

On my way out. Need to stop at checked baggage.

My phone buzzed back a second later.

Cool, man. Need a hand?

I typed a quick reply. *Nah, it's just a couple bags. I'll be fine.*

Those words sank in deeper as I approached the baggage carousel and saw my two camo-print bags and green duffle float once and then twice around.

Thirty-three years old, and everything I owned was in those bags.

I put in the required quarters for a luggage cart; there was a time when I didn't need one, but I wasn't a masochist. With a deep breath, I wrestled the bags and duffle off the conveyor belt without tipping over. Then I pushed the cart out into the Austin, Texas, air. I tucked my cane into a bag, and so help me, I used the cart as a support.

Ian's white Cadillac Escalade rolled around a split second later, the passenger-side window rolling down even as he leaped from the car. "Beckett! You made it!"

He hugged me with his boundless, Ian-like enthusiasm, his hand pounding me on the back. Ian was a giant who played football with me at the Naval Academy. I was a midshipman fourth class when he was second class—what other colleges would have termed freshman and junior years—and in the two years we played together, he was the tallest and broadest player on the team. He earned the nickname "Blond Fezzik" and wore it with good humor.

After graduation, Ian served as a navy officer, and two years later, I continued in my intention to join the marines. We stayed friends though, even after Ian decided the military wasn't ultimately for him; with his family's oil money, he didn't exactly need the job. So he'd been discharged honorably before focusing on other pursuits. His wife, Mariah, for one and his love of dogs, for another.

My first two years at the academy were not easy ones. But somehow, we hit it off enough on the practice field for him to decide we'd be friends for life. Oddly enough, it seemed to have stuck. So when I knew I was returning to Austin, staying with Ian was my first thought.

As he greeted me like he would a long-lost brother, I knew I'd made the right decision. "It's good to see you!" he said, grinning from ear to ear. "You've got to be exhausted."

I gave a slight shrug and slid my carry-on from my shoulder. "Reagan to Bergstrom isn't a long flight."

Ian used his key fob to open the back of his SUV and energetically tossed my bags inside. "Still, air travel takes it out of you. Every few years, Mariah suggests getting a time share on a private plane, and every time I think it's a waste of money, and then I fly and reconsider it." He paused and held his arms out. "Look at me. Do I look like I fit on a commercial plane?"

I chuckled. "Mariah and the kids good? Thanks for picking me up today. I'm sure the traffic was a nightmare."

"Happy to do it, and glad you can spend the holidays with us." Ian said, and I believed him. He'd offer his right arm and consider it a pleasure to do so. "Mariah's great, the kids are . . . spirited." He closed the back and unlocked the car doors. "You know how kids are at those ages. I know how I was." He chuckled. "So I'm probably getting off easy."

"Haven't spent any time with kids for a while, not American ones, anyway," I said, climbing inside. "I wouldn't know."

I thought of the village kids who had followed us, alternately trying to beg candy and possibly pick our pockets. "How are the dogs?" I asked, opting to change the subject.

"The dogs!" Ian's face lit up. "Well, Miriam just had a new litter, and I think it's her best yet."

He continued on in that vein, detailing the number and health of the puppies and offering me one, which he'd done with nearly every litter, even while I'd been overseas. After several moments, his face sobered, and he glanced at me before returning his focus to the road. "I'm sorry about your dad. Sounds like it was sudden?"

"As far as I know."

"Is there going to be a service?"

It was my turn to shrug. "There was a small service, no family present."

Ian set his chin. "If I'd known, I would have been there."

"I know you would have. I didn't know until it was over."

That was the thing. My accident and my father's death had occurred within hours of each other. I was medevaced to Germany before being transferred to Bethesda, in Maryland. There had been several surgeries—surgeries to try to save my leg, surgery to remove it when the earlier ones failed. I'd spent so much time unconscious that they didn't tell me about my dad.

Roy, my dad's best friend and executor of his estate, finally tracked me down. He visited me at Bethesda and gently broke the news.

We hadn't been close, my dad and I. There were a lot of reasons. And looking at Roy, with his weathered brown face and kind eyes, I felt like I knew him better than I'd ever known my father.

Roy had told me about my dad's will too.

There was the house, for starters, the one I'd grown up in. But the one that took me aback was the news I'd inherited his chain of barbecue restaurants, the one that my father had devoted himself to for his entire adult life. The one he'd planned to leave to my older brother, before Cameron died when he drunkenly crashed his Corvette into a tree.

When I lost my leg, I figured that I'd get my new leg and do my best to content myself with a desk job. I'd been within spitting distance of promotion to major. Going back to Austin hadn't ever been in the plan. Too many memories. But as Roy detailed what had happened with the restaurants and the number of jobs on the line, I knew. I was done. I had a whole new set of responsibilities.

So I pursued a medical discharge, which was granted without a fight. And just like that, I was a civilian for the first time in twelve years, home for the first time in ten.

"That's a raw deal," Ian said. "But I know it's been a raw deal for a long time."

I nodded, not knowing what else to say.

"Well, you're welcome to stay at the house for as long as you like."

"Technically," I said, "my dad's place is mine now. But Roy said it looked like it needed some work."

If Roy had said so, it was true. Under normal circumstances, I wouldn't care. I'd stayed in enough places without electricity or running water—or any water, for that matter. So the idea of being in my dad's ramshackle house didn't present a practical challenge. But the truth? I wasn't ready to darken that door. Not yet.

"You stay as long as you need if you want to fix up your dad's place, find a place of your own, or both. We're happy to have you. Now," Ian continued, "I've had Pilar make up one of the guest rooms for you. We do have the guesthouse, but I've promised that to my cousins."

"Oh?" I asked, conversationally. If he wanted to put me on the roof, I didn't care. "Which cousins are these?"

"They're my cousin Rebecca's girls. Rebecca died in a car accident, some years back. Drunk driver."

I worked to stifle a grimace. That was the one bright spot in Cameron's death; he'd driven drunk, but managed to only harm himself. He hadn't taken anyone with him.

"Anyway, Rebecca's husband . . . let's not get into that. But her daughters were always real nice, and they've just lost their lease in San Francisco, and the oldest one e-mailed to ask if the Austin market might work out for them. I told them to come on out and find out."

"How old are they?"

Ian paused to think. "I dunno. You're going to make me drive and do math at the same time? Let's see. Rebecca was fourteen or fifteen years my senior, and I was about eight when Celia was born—I guess Celia, she's probably about twenty-eight or so, and Jane is a couple years younger. And then Rebecca had a surprise baby when she was older, and she's still a teenager."

"So they're all coming out from San Francisco?"

"Once they're all packed up. You don't mind, do you?"

"It's your property, Ian. You can do whatever you like."

"I haven't seen them in years, but they've always reminded me of Rebecca, and Rebecca was my favorite cousin."

I could see the wheels turn in Ian's head as he shot me a sidelong glance. "That side of the family is the good-looking side too. If you don't have a girl, you know . . ."

"You sound like you're setting me up with your sister," I said dryly. "That's just awkward, man."

"Suit yourself."

But I knew, deep down, that wouldn't be the end of it.

4

There are few hours in life more agreeable than the hour
dedicated to the ceremony known as afternoon tea.

—HENRY JAMES

Jane

Christmas passed in a haze. We paused for a candlelight service and a gift exchange for Margot's benefit. Still, the mood from behind the handheld candles was grim. Packing to the dulcet sounds of "God Rest Ye Merry Gentlemen" didn't take the edge off of the fact that we were soon leaving home.

We threw a party the night before we closed, three days after Christmas. Our neighbors helped us carry all twelve tea plants from the balcony to the tea salon, where Celia strung twinkle lights among their leaves. We played music, Margot invited friends over, and we danced with our customers—well, Celia did, and I danced with Celia. Secondhand dancing.

It felt like the Christmas ball in *Meet Me in Saint Louis* but without the happy ending.

Celia didn't mention Teddy. I wondered if he'd come by; we were all friends, after all, before he and Celia began to see each other seriously. But in the sea of familiar faces, his remained absent.

At the end of the night, we crowded around the vintage bar and carried it carefully, slowly, out the front double doors.

Patrick, one of the stylists from next door, shook his head. "I feel like we're pallbearers," he said, "carrying the spirit of your business away."

Carly, the candy maker from two doors down, gave a grunt of dismay. "If this were a spirit, it wouldn't weigh so much."

"I'm just glad it's going with you," Patrick said. "I don't want *her* to have it."

Patrick had been at the shop the day Phoebe made an appearance, and the impression hadn't been favorable.

"I'd take it all if I could," I said, as we passed very slowly through the doors toward the trailer waiting on the street.

We quieted as we got the bar into place. Heaven knew how we'd get it out, but that was a logistical problem for another day.

"Did Atticus know?" Patrick asked, as we gazed out at the street from the mouth of the trailer. "Did he know Jonathan would practically evict you over the holidays?"

Patrick put voice to a question that had certainly come to my mind in the previous weeks. While ours was a business relationship with Atticus, it had been a personal relationship as well. We knew when he had surgery on his knee and sent bouquets of macarons on his birthdays. He helped Margot with her homework, delivered soup when we were sick, and brought his chess-club members to the salon on the third Tuesday of every month.

Were these the actions of a man planning to leave his holdings to a nephew?

A nephew like Jonathan, married to a woman like Phoebe?

The person with the answers now resided at the San Francisco National Cemetery.

None of the questions meant I loved him less; I just hadn't expected events to turn out exactly as they had. But what *had* I been expecting, really? We'd been living in a bubble for too long, and now we were on to our next chapter.

Margot spent the night at a sleepover with her friends. I stayed up way too late putting together playlists for the drive.

The next morning, Celia and I loaded the plants into the back of my pickup truck, with the canopy over the top to protect them from being whipped by the wind.

"You okay, Jane?" Celia asked as I yanked on the tie-down straps.

"I can't look at it," I told her. "I can't look or I'll cry."

"It'll be okay. The leasing agent I told you about says there's a great property in a vintage neighborhood that's perfect for us. We'll start up again, and next year we'll go all-out for Christmas, you'll see."

"It's just . . . we've already started over. This was the do over. This was supposed to be our version of smooth sailing from here on out." I held up a hand before Celia could placate me. "I know. It's a small business, and things happen, and we're lucky to have even made it this long. I just thought we'd already been through the wringer and could coast a bit longer. Apparently," I said, glancing up at the sky, "that is not the plan. But I wanted it to be the plan."

Tears filled my eyes, and I swiped at them quickly with the back of my hand.

Celia wrapped an arm around me. "It's a big change."

"We just weren't supposed to have more change. The next change was supposed to be Margot going off to college and, you know, getting her nose pierced."

Celia just rubbed my arm while I tried to wrestle my feelings to the ground.

Because the truth was we'd been so close. I'd felt close to my dream of being able to go back to college and finish a botany program.

But now? Those dreams were on the back burner. Again.

I shook my head and patted Celia's hand, the one that rested on my arm. "I'm okay, really. It's just an emotional day."

Celia rubbed my arm. "What do you think? Are we ready to go get Margot?"

"And tear her away from her friends?" I leaned against the trailer. "Let's give her another fifteen minutes."

∞

I hated pulling Margot away from her friends. There were tears and promises to connect over social-media platforms I was only vaguely aware of. To keep the mood light, I plugged my phone into our ancient, non-Bluetooth stereo and began one of the most important discussions we would have.

Road-trip music.

"So," I said. "I've got the necessary soundtracks downloaded, so we don't have to worry about data—*Elizabethtown, Almost Famous, About a Boy,* and *You've Got Mail.*"

"*Hamilton?*" Celia asked.

"Cast recording and the mixtape."

"*High School Musical?*" Margot asked, her voice still sounding a touch weepy.

"Because I love you, we've got the full suite, if you will. I also went mad with power and put in the soundtracks to *Frozen, Enchanted,* and *Moana.* Also, there are playlists."

Celia, behind the wheel, patted my leg. "You wouldn't be you if there weren't."

"We have our Norah Jones playlists, our upbeat indie mixes, the flat-out pop mixes—whatever flavor you're in the mood for, I've got."

Celia widened her eyes innocently. " 'Free Bird'?"

"There is a Lynyrd Skynyrd mix."

"How about we drive around the block and call it good?" Margot asked.

"We can drive around the block," Celia said patiently, "but we still have to keep going."

"Okay, if you guys can't decide, I'm making an executive decision." Three taps on my phone screen, and the stereo speakers released the opening bars to the Jackson 5's "I Want You Back."

"There," I said, turning to look at Margot in the backseat while shimmying my shoulders. "I dare you to be sad while this song is playing."

Margot gave a valiant effort, but I danced in the front passenger seat, waving my arms and hands until she couldn't fight the smile any longer.

And that's how we left—singing along, waving our hands, trying not to let the heartbreak get to us.

∞

As it turns out, driving across the country while towing a trailer takes a long time. Even longer if you're transporting a teenager with a bladder the size of a walnut.

"We're going to cut off your liquids, Margot," I threatened as we pulled into yet another dilapidated gas station in the middle of Nowhere, Arizona. "I mean it."

We drove long days. Although we made an educational stop at the Grand Canyon, much of the drive was long and grueling. By the time we reached Roswell, New Mexico, we were thrilled to find an actual city with places to eat dinner and a Starbucks for the drive ahead.

While the baristas made our drinks, Celia pulled out her phone. "I finally got pictures from the agent I've been in contact with," she said, flipping through before holding the phone out to me. "This is the property that I told you about, the vintage one. It's in Hyde Park. I guess that's a good neighborhood for small, idiosyncratic businesses."

"That might be us," I said with a straight face, taking the phone. "Unless we started serving coffee."

"You should serve coffee," Margot said, planting her elbows on the table and resting her chin on her hands. "Coffee is yummy."

"When did you drink coffee?" I asked, amazed.

She shrugged. "Harper's house. I liked it."

"You're allowed to like it," Celia said.

"I don't think so, no," I retorted just as the barista called out my black tea latte. Margot's cocoa and Celia's americano came up next, and I carried them all back to the table.

"Come look at the rest of the pictures," Celia said, passing me her phone. "I think they're perfect."

Scrolling through, I had to agree. It was a vintage house, one story, with a front porch that we could use for outdoor seating. The inside had old wood floors, like the ones we'd had in San Francisco, and a long bar. "It looks good. Did the agent say what it used to be used for?"

Celia took a sip of her drink. "I think he said 'hipster tacos.'"

"Fair enough. And it's still available?"

"It is. I thought we could go take a look the day after we arrive."

I handed the phone back to Celia. "Let's do it. Do we have backups though?"

Celia tapped at her phone again. "We do, which is smart, because apparently it's a tight market right now. Not a lot of new things are coming up."

I looked through the other options. They weren't as flat-out charming but could be serviceable. "What's the foot traffic like in these areas?"

"The first is best, apparently, but the downtown one is good. Not sure about the last."

Foot traffic was essential for us. Aside from the die-hard tea enthusiasts who used search engines to find us, most of our customers were lured in with charm and pastries. Some were pre-existing tea drinkers; others we turned to the dark side.

"I think they look good," I said. "The sooner we get into something new, the better."

"Agreed." Celia tucked her phone away, and we sat and enjoyed our drinks and the feeling of not being cooped up in a vehicle.

I drove the last leg of the trip, and by then we were all feeling rough around the edges and deeply, desperately tired.

For the last hour, I'd been driving through a steady stream of Texas rain. Texas rain, I had figured out within minutes, did not mess around. Celia had finally fallen asleep, and not even the rain's racket could rouse her. Margot had been watching YouTube videos on her phone ever since we'd returned to cell service.

At least I-35 was straight and flat. Trying to negotiate such weather in the San Francisco hills would have ended all of us.

Just straight. Straight ahead, I told myself. We were still in the hinterlands, only a few miles out of town near Buda, and soon enough we'd be . . . well, I'd never been to our cousin Ian's home, but I liked to think we'd at least be snug and dry.

We'd be fine.

The sudden *bang* startled me almost as much as the way the truck lurched and then shimmied across the road.

Margot shrieked. Celia sat up with a start. "What happened?"

I clutched the steering wheel hard, not daring to take my eyes off the road, "I don't know yet," I said, guiding the truck to the shoulder. I didn't know, but I had my suspicions.

I climbed out of the truck without my rain jacket, and the rain instantly soaked through my hair and clothes. But I hardly noticed, because what I saw was so much worse.

Margot stayed inside, but Celia followed and together we surveyed the damage. The canopy, with its rusted clamps, had detached and must have struck the hitch in its descent. Now, the trailer lolled against the shoulder twenty feet away, and the fallen canopy lay in the middle of the road.

"No!" I shouted, my words drowned out by the heavy downpour. "No, no, no! How are we going to fix that?" I turned to look at my plants; two of the planters had tipped and all of them were being pelted with heavy rain. "My plants!"

Through the closure and the moving, I'd held it together. But right now, with the darkness and the rain and my plants under water siege, I felt tears of panic escape my eyes and mix with the rain.

A white Toyota Tundra honked as it passed, but rather than speeding forward, it pulled over to the shoulder, several feet away from the truck. A tall male stranger emerged from the cab and strode toward us. He called out, and I shook my head as his words disappeared in the wind and rain.

Without waiting for an answer, he walked straight toward the canopy and pulled it from the freeway to the safety of the shoulder. He released it before approaching us.

My breath caught as I took him in.

He was even taller than I'd thought. He wore jeans, a plaid shirt, and a Stetson that sent raindrops flying. The face beneath the hat? Not an ordinary face. It was the kind of face usually spotted on stages and screens.

He was beautiful, he was here, and he wanted to help.

"I'm Sean," he said, striding close enough for me to hear. "Sean Willis. Where are you headed?"

Celia introduced us, explaining that we were on our way to our cousin's when the canopy had given way.

"I can hook your trailer up to my truck, no problem," he said.

I cast a worried glance at my camellia plants. It was one thing for them to be rained on. It was another thing for them to be rained on at freeway speeds.

Sean read my gaze and nodded at the plants. "Those were under the canopy?"

"They were. They're . . . they're a bit delicate."

He nodded, no trace of condescension in the gesture. "I've got a tarp; I'll see what I can do. We'll have to come back for the canopy."

The tarp came first, whether by accident or because of a sensitivity to my plants, I didn't know. But we tied it on, and then he backed his truck up to secure it to the trailer.

Once both vehicles had been settled—Sean's glossy white truck hitched to our shabby moving trailer, my elderly truck topped with a cerulean blue tarp—Sean tossed me his truck keys.

"That tarp is going to give it extra wind resistance. You take my truck; I'll follow you."

I stared down at the keys and then back at him, this man I'd just met with the most extraordinary blue eyes.

It wasn't fair. Because he looked really, really good, and I knew that between the stress and the rain, I looked somewhere between half-crazy and three-quarters drowned.

"My sister's in the back of ours; I'll have to get her. You trust me with your truck?" I asked, squinting up at him.

He winked. "You trust me with yours?"

Thinking about the truck's touchy clutch and the ignition that required a mix of affection and persistence to start, I raised an eyebrow. "That's a good point," I said, nodding toward my vehicle. "You may not be able to handle it."

"I'm not worried," he said dryly.

I wrangled Margot and her backpack out of the backseat, explaining in as few words as possible about the plants and the truck and the guy who was loaning us his truck to get the rest of the way to Austin.

Sean waved at her as she climbed in, and her eyes widened as she took in his face. "I know," I told her as she climbed into the back of the cab. "He's very pretty."

Celia gave him Cousin Ian's address, and our strange caravan was ready, with Sean in our truck and the three of us in his. I started the ignition, enjoying the quick response and subtle growl of the engine. And then I checked the rearview mirror, waiting on Sean.

"Spying on him?" Celia asked.

"Waiting to see if he can start the truck," I answered, but by the time I finished speaking, the vehicle had already begun to creep forward. I sighed. "I guess he really is that handy."

Celia cut a glance at me. "He seems very helpful."

"Really hot, you mean," Margot offered.

I pulled out onto the road, my face flushed and my heart beating fast in my chest. "What was that?" I asked, stealing another glance in the rearview mirror. "I feel like I hardly got a decent look at him, but—"

"Feeling better about the prospect of Texas, are you?" Celia asked.

"Did you see how he moved the canopy? Like it was nothing." I shook my head. "And this truck? Drives like a dream."

∞

Celia called ahead to Cousin Ian to let them know where we were, and more importantly that we now had an extra vehicle in our party.

"I reached the housekeeper," she said. "She promised to pass on the message."

"Did you try his cell number?"

"That was his cell number."

My eyes widened. "Fair enough." I checked the rearview mirror again. I couldn't make out Sean's face, but the truck was still there, the air whipping the tarp over my plants.

"He's still following, I take it?" Celia asked. "He hasn't turned in the opposite direction with your tea plants?"

"That's a terrible thing to say." I cautiously changed lanes. "And I could overtake him in this truck if need be."

Celia wedged her elbow against the door and rested her head against her hand. "I've heard Texan men are still chivalrous." She cast me a glance. "It'll be interesting to see how this one shakes out."

5

I shouldn't think even millionaires could eat anything
nicer than new bread and real butter and honey for tea.

—DODIE SMITH

Jane

The lights of the house blazed as we drove down the very long, very circular
driveway up the hill from Barton Creek. Without knowing what exactly to do
or where to go, I pulled the truck and trailer in front of the house.

"Ohh!" Margot exclaimed as she took it in. "That's the biggest house I've
ever seen!"

"I feel we ought to go looking for the servant's entrance," I said as I slid the
gearshift into park. I removed the keys and patted the dash. "You're a good rig,"
I told the truck as I unbuckled my seat belt.

"It has been nice," Celia said, looking around. "The rain's stopped too.
Things are looking up."

Sean pulled my own truck along a short distance away.

I climbed down from the tall seat in time to see a giant of a man open the
front door and step outside.

"Welcome!" he crowed, his long arms outstretched. "Welcome, welcome
to Austin. I'm Ian—I know it's been a long time." He pointed to Margot.
"You were this high when we met. Come on inside. We were just fixin' to eat
dessert."

"Dessert?" Margot chirped, clambering quickly from the truck.

We exchanged hugs awkwardly, at least I did. Celia's the sort of person capable of being reunited with a relation we'd met once, in the nineties, and handling it with an easy grace.

Naturally, I let her go first.

"This is my wife, Mariah," Ian said. "And my mother-in-law, Nina."

Mariah nodded toward Sean's truck. "Very nice," she said.

I gave it a rueful glance. "It is. It's not mine; it's Mr. Willis's," I said, finding myself unable to call him by his first name in front of my relatives.

"Mr. Willis was kind enough to loan us his truck," Celia elaborated. "Jane's truck is the one with the tarp."

"Tarp," Mariah repeated woodenly.

"To protect my tea plants," I added, though I didn't imagine it would make any difference. Mariah, I supposed, had visions of rusted cars covered in bright blue tarps behind her eyes and the sound of neighborhood sighs in her ears.

I shot a glance at Celia. Mariah probably would have also preferred if we'd entered around the back. At least we'd met her halfway, arriving under cover of darkness.

"What an adventure you've had," said Nina, and I could tell from her tone she meant it. "Rescued on the road by a stranger . . ."

At that moment, Mr. Sean Willis ambled toward the group and tipped his hat. "Evening, folks," he said before introducing himself.

Ian shook his hand heartily. Mariah stopped frowning at the tarp, her features settling into a more welcome expression.

Nina fanned herself.

"Come in!" Ian insisted, having never released Sean's hand. "There's dessert on, and my housekeeper makes a cup of coffee that will warm you straight through."

"Not tonight," he said. "I need to get back. I'm staying with my aunt," he continued, "less than a mile from here."

I turned to him in surprise. "Are you really?"

He grinned at me. "Hello, neighbor."

"Huh."

His eyes twinkled. Literally—they were twinkling away, and I couldn't string two words together.

Ian led us all to the *casita,* which stood about two hundred feet from the house itself. He rode with Sean in Sean's truck while I drove behind, happy to be reunited with my plants.

The casita wasn't charming, not exactly. It had been built sometime in the nineties; the materials were not shabby but dated. Tile, oak, striped wallpaper with a sunflower border along the ceiling.

I hated it on sight.

Its saving grace was a good view of the grounds and a patio with a brazier. "Plant what you like wherever you like," Ian told us as Sean untied the tarp. "Make it your own; we're very glad you're here. Your mother was a good woman." His eyes grew misty. "My favorite cousin, always kind, easy to talk to. And your father . . ." He paused. "Your father had a dog I liked."

I nodded. "You're very kind," I told him.

"You're Rebecca's daughters; you'll always have a home here." He put his hands on his hips and turned to Sean. "You must come back. Join us for dinner tomorrow? Or Friday? Anytime. It's the least I can do," Ian insisted. "Rescuing my cousins. And you're a neighbor after all."

Sean's gaze twinkled at me before returning to Ian. "Yes, sir. I'll come for dinner Friday."

Celia shot me a wide-eyed look. I didn't respond, on account of having a severe case of the heart flutters.

Satisfied, Ian gave him instructions on a back lane to the main road, and we thanked him heartily before he drove away.

"Good man, that one," he said. "And he has a good hat. You can tell a lot about a man by the hat he wears."

I could only nod.

Celia and I begged off dessert, much to Margot's chagrin, citing extreme exhaustion and residual dampness. But Ian could only be dissuaded so far, and we found ourselves agreeing to brunch the following morning.

Ian helped us carry our bags in, taking them upstairs as if they weighed nothing. The guesthouse was smaller than our apartment in San Francisco, dispelling the notion that everything might truly be larger in Texas. There wasn't a bedroom as much as there was a bedroom loft.

"Umm . . . ," Margot said as she took in the sleeping situation.

I wanted to chime in with her, but being one of the grown-ups, I made up my mind not to utter any of the snarky comments that had immediately sprung to mind.

The bedroom featured a twin-sized bunk bed on one side and a queen-sized bed with another twin bed lofted above it.

"I'll fight you for the top bunk, Margot," I told her, knowing she'd likely want the lower bunk anyway.

I sighed on the inside. Twenty-six-years-old and sleeping on a rickety-looking bunk bed. I hadn't slept in a bunk bed since summer camp. But my sacrifice was rewarded by a slightly less sullen Margot, who clambered up to the loft and tossed her backpack onto the lower bunk. "I can take the bottom one," she said, sounding at peace.

Crisis averted.

The loft hung over the sitting room and looked out over the kitchenette. Thankfully, the bathroom featured a large enough counter that we had a fighting chance at fitting our various toiletry items on it, if we were judicious about space.

"Mariah doesn't use this place," Ian said, surveying the space with his hands on his hips. "But it's clean and the A/C will go to near subarctic in minutes. There's wood outside if you'd like a fire, and," he continued conspiratorially, "marshmallows in the cabinet that I hid from the wife. Now, if you need anything, don't hesitate to call the house." He pointed at the corded telephone that hung on the wall next to the refrigerator. "Pilar will have it for you in a jiffy."

We thanked him and waved good-bye; Celia sank into a chair and took everything in.

"It'll do," she said, looking at me.

"Until we find a place of our own, I suppose."

Celia laughed under her breath, and I narrowed my eyes. "What?"

"We've just driven across country, and I can tell you're itching to get back to your teas."

"I'm Mary Lennox, I guess—just give me a bit of earth for a garden." I sat down next to her and wrapped my arms around my knees. "I wonder if there's a piano at the big house that Mariah would let me play." I looked up at Margot, still perched at the edge of the loft. "Do you think that rail will do for a bar?"

Margot shoved against it experimentally before taking it and stretching her leg out into a *grand battement.* "It'll do."

"Maybe you need to make Mariah a cup of tea," Celia suggested, "in exchange for using the piano."

"Mmm . . . chamomile for calm, lemon balm for clarity. Just a touch of honey."

"There you go." She yawned. "I don't think I need any chamomile to sleep, not tonight."

"You take the big bed," I told her as we climbed the stairs. "I'll take the bunk above Margot."

"Are you sure?"

I gave a small grunt. "Just take the bed before I change my mind."

∞

"So we're going over for brunch, then?" I asked Celia as the three of us crossed the lawn to reach the great house. "And then dinner tomorrow. When are we going to go look at those properties? The ones you showed us?"

"In between," Celia answered. "I know, it's a lot of socializing for you. I think we're the shiny new playthings."

"Well, I didn't come to be the floor show. I came to open a tea shop.

Although," I added ruefully, "I shouldn't complain. Sean's supposed to come tomorrow."

"You look especially nice today."

I felt my face flush. "I suppose."

I had showered that morning and towel dried my curls, which had decided to behave. And perhaps I was also wearing eyeliner and lipstick, rather than strictly mascara and a touch of tinted lip balm.

No matter what Celia said, I couldn't remember having met these family members before, and the impression I'd made the night before was certainly more disheveled than usual. I tended to favor the "start as you mean to go on" approach, but I figured that a little extra primping this morning would cancel out the lake creature who'd appeared in the driveway the night before.

"Why do you have your purse with you?" Margot asked, squinting at me.

"Oh, you know. I've got a heavier cardigan in there. My phone. Cash if I need to tip the staff. I don't know."

"I might put my phone in there," Celia said. "If that's all right." Soon enough, she and Margot emptied their pockets and stashed the contents inside. "You have tea in your purse," Margot stated, eyes accusing.

"I always have tea in my purse."

"You're weird."

"I'm idiosyncratic," I retorted. "That's different."

We made an effort to curb the sisterly bickering as we climbed the steps to the front door and knocked. A uniformed housekeeper answered within seconds.

"They're in the dining room," she said, pointing, but the information was hardly necessary. Shrieks of laughter and chatter came from the left corner of the house.

"It sounds like a bingo parlor," I murmured to Celia, who shushed me discreetly before we stepped through the french doors.

"There they are!" Mariah's mother, Nina, waved an arm in greeting before setting her plate down to envelop us in hugs. She wore a flowing caftan in bright orange; her hair was pinned up into a dark chignon. "Just look at the three of you, pretty as a picture. Add a cup of water to the soup, Pilar!"

"We're not having soup with brunch, Mother," Mariah chided before turning to us. "You must be so tired from your drive. Did you hit any snow?"

"No snow," I started to say, but nobody was listening to me.

"It's just an expression," Nina told her daughter. "You need to relax. Go get a massage." She turned back to us. "You poor dears, moving over the holidays like that. I hope you got to stop somewhere fun during your drive."

"We stopped at Roswell," Margot answered. "They have aliens painted on the windows of restaurants."

"That is exciting." Nina grinned at us.

"Also the Grand Canyon," I added. "Remember?"

"Yeah, that was cool," Margot admitted.

Mariah stepped between us and her mother. "There's a breakfast buffet on the sideboard. Please do help yourselves."

I cast a discreet glance at Mariah and her mother. Nina's figure was lithe yet curvaceous, where her daughter's was tall and ruthlessly slim. They shared the same wide gray eyes and, I suspected, might once have shared a nose, but despite the faint similarities, I would never have placed them as relatives, much less mother and daughter.

Nina nodded toward the plates at the end of the sideboard. "Yes, get a bite, chickadees, and then come sit down. I want to learn all about you."

∞

Two hours and a second helping of quiche later, I began to wonder if brunch would ever end. I itched to get out and start looking at properties; if the market was as tight as the agent had described, we needed to hit the pavement.

We discussed, in no particular order, the health and education of Ian and Mariah's children, their other houseguest, who was running or riding or otherwise athletically inclined, and ultimately my sisters and myself. Our time at Stanford, our sainted mother, and the currently street-less Valencia Street Tea.

Over our father and his legal foibles, the Vandermeides drew a veil, though I didn't trust its longevity. It was too good a story to remain discreet about forever.

Dad's scandal, though, didn't seem to affect Ian's opinion of us. "My financial man just retired," he told Celia, "and I need someone to keep watch over my books and my investment profile. If memory serves, you did that in California?"

Celia sputtered for a moment before recovering. "I did, yes, several years ago."

"Interested in getting back into it here?"

Her eyes widened. "I'd have to become licensed," she said. "Take the tests . . ."

"Perfect! Well, it's perfect if you're interested."

"Yes, of course!"

"See?" Nina said, pouring herself another mimosa. "It's nice to see that women in this day and age can be smart *and* pretty. You have to have left broken hearts behind in San Francisco."

I shook my head and hoped that if I answered quickly and thoroughly enough, my answer might satisfy for all of us. "The salon kept us busy. I hardly ever date."

Nina's eyes widened. "You? With that hair and those legs?"

"If I'm in the shop or my rooftop garden, I'm not out on dates," I answered. "It's as simple as that."

Nina's gaze slid to Celia. "What about you, Miss Celia?"

Celia shifted uncomfortably on her chair. "I'm not seeing anyone currently, no."

"California men." She rolled her eyes. "You're here now, at least. You'll both be engaged in a year; mark my words."

"Celia had a boyfriend," Margot said. "California men aren't all stupid."

"Margot!" I shot my younger sister a sharp look with a quick shake of the head.

Margot slumped in her seat. "Well, she *did*."

"Oh!" Nina fixed her gaze more sharply on Celia. "Do tell!"

And I watched as Celia, poised and collected Celia, froze.

That was it. Me interrogating my sister at home was one thing. Even if it was friendly fire, it was still friendly fire in a room full of strangers, and I didn't like it.

"Can I make anyone a cup of tea?" I blurted, my face flushing pink.

"Pilar can make tea," Mariah said, lifting a hand to signal her house-keeper.

Celia shook her head. "Not like Jane."

"What kind of tea?"

"Green tea," I said. "From my own leaves. They're from my plants, from seeds I brought back from Japan."

Celia's eyes widened. She knew I kept that supply dear.

"They let you do that?" Nina asked. "Bring in seeds?"

I shrugged. "I had to get a permit; it wasn't so bad. Anyway, I raised these plants from seedlings, and I've been able to harvest them the last few years."

"Don't spend your best leaves on us," Nina said. "We wouldn't know good tea from bad tea if it were speaking aloud and telling us what's what."

"What about the Dragonwell?" Celia suggested, regaining her voice. "That's really nice."

"I've got that one in my bag," I said.

Mariah goggled at me. "You keep tea in your purse?"

"Occupational hazard." I said, over the sound of Margot's soft snickering. "May I borrow a few things from the kitchen?"

Gratified that the room's attention had shifted from our personal matters—and any questions that would cause Celia to turn even paler than normal—to the subject I felt most comfortable with, I followed Mariah into the kitchen, and the others trailed after us. Pilar found a teakettle, teapot, sieve, and thermometer.

I found bottled spring water in the fridge and used it to fill the kettle. I brought the water to a boil and then used hot tap water to heat the cups that Mariah set out. I calculated the ounces of tea for the pot—two grams per serving.

While we waited for the water to heat, I used the tap water to preheat the teapot as well. I measured the temperature before pouring, and waited until I was sure of a 180-degree reading before blanching the leaves through a sieve.

They unfurled just a little, and the color brightened.

"What's that for?" Mariah asked.

"It cleans the leaves," I told her, giving the sieve a gentle shake. "And they begin to unroll, so they'll infuse better. In a proper tea ceremony, I would do this with every serving and pour the water into the cups to warm them. But today we'll focus on making a larger pot of tea."

I poured hot water into the teapot, discarded it, and then placed the tea leaves inside with a pair of silver tongs.

And then I poured. For those moments, the chatter stopped, and all eyes were on me as I poured the water over the leaves in the teapot. "There," I said, closing the lid. "It steeps for three minutes.

Mariah eyed the teapot suspiciously. "Do you use spring water in your shop?"

Celia nodded. "For an extra fee, and always for the premium teas."

"We're getting the very best then," said Nina. "I can't wait to taste it!"

I waited and then sniffed the teapot before pouring, using the sieve to catch any leaves. The tea had turned the perfect shade of very pale green, and I flushed with happiness to see it.

That was my tea; my hands had harvested the leaves and spread them onto drying racks back home.

I handed Mariah the first cup, then poured tea for Nina, Ian, Celia, and Margot.

Celia gave me a smile over her cup, one I couldn't quite read.

Mariah peered into her cup. "Does it need sugar?"

"No," I answered flatly. "It does not."

I raised my own cup to my lips, letting the crisp, buttery taste wash over my taste buds. My eyes closed as I let the flavors work their magic.

Perfection.

"Tea party?" came a low voice from the doorway.

My eyes flew open.

"Beckett! There you are," said Ian, setting his cup down long enough to give the other man a clap on the back. "Come meet my cousins! They're the ones I told you about. They've just moved here from San Francisco. This is my old friend," he said, slinging his arm around the other man. "Captain Callum Beckett."

He was tall, this new man. Tall with dark-brown hair, gone silver at the temples. A nose just shy of hawkish. I couldn't quite tell how old he was. But then, from my post in the kitchen, I couldn't see him well.

Callum stood next to Ian and gave us a nod. "Hello. I apologize," he said, gesturing to his exercise-wear. "I was out on a walk,"

Ian introduced each of us by name. Celia gave her warmest smile and extended a hand. "It's very nice to meet you."

He shifted his hands then to shake her hand. And that's when I noticed. He held a cane in his right hand, and of the legs visible beneath his shorts, one was a jointed prosthetic. His left leg had been amputated above the knee.

A Perfect Cup of Tea

4 heaping teaspoons tea leaves
4 cups water (ideally filtered), plus more for preparation

Set a kettle of water to boil. When hot, use the heated water to preheat the teapot and cups. To preheat, fill each vessel about a third full, wait 30 seconds, and discard the water.

Add the tea leaves to the teapot—about one heaping teaspoon per cup of water. If you choose to use a tea infuser, use the largest size that will fit in your pot. You want lots of space for the leaves to unfurl.

Pour a splash of hot but not boiling water over the leaves to blanch quickly; discard the water but retain the leaves. Note: most high-quality teas will come with a recommended water temperature. You can use a clean food-safe thermometer to gauge the temperature of the water.

Once the leaves have been blanched, they're ready to be steeped. Heat the water to the temperature recommended for your tea; 185 degrees will suit most teas. Pour 4 cups of that water over the tea leaves; allow them to steep. For green tea, allow 3–7 minutes. For black, 3–5. Be careful not to oversteep! If the leaves steep too long, the tea becomes bitter and tannic.

Decant the tea liquid through a fine mesh strainer or remove the tea infuser.

Pour the tea into the cups, and savor with friends.

Serves 4.

6

Out on these Texas plains you can see for a
million lives
And there's a thousand exits between here and
the state line.

—CAEDMON'S CALL

Callum

Walking toward the kitchen, I thought it was Lila. Not Lila as she was when
I'd last seen her—the Lila who existed in my deeper memories, the days before
Cameron. The woman in the kitchen had the same energy, the same kind of
focus that made you want to pay attention because whatever it was she devoted
herself to was worth your time.

As I got closer, reality and rationality won out. This woman stood taller,
her features more delicate, her curls a deeper shade of chestnut.

And she hadn't been broken by life. That was the biggest difference.

Even when I knew it wasn't, couldn't be, Lila, I still couldn't take my eyes
off her. She was flanked by a fair-haired woman with the same fine features,
and a teen with a mop of gold curls—sisters, I guessed. Ian, Mariah, and Nina
stood nearby and watched as she made tea like a chemist in a lab. She measured
the water temperature and everything.

My mom used to put a handful of Lipton teabags into a Pyrex measuring
cup and microwave it until the water turned nearly opaque. Casual inference
told me that this woman wouldn't consider that to be tea.

I smothered a laugh when Mariah accepted her cup of tea and glared at it
with suspicion. I knew Ian's wife liked her tea iced and sweet.

The leaves were aromatic, and the scent pulled me deeper into the room. I wanted to meet her. When I stepped forward, Ian saw me and greeted me like his long-lost best friend. Which . . . I supposed I was, before making the introductions. "This vision is Celia," he said, introducing the blond sister.

Celia offered her hand, but the instant I couldn't shake it, I felt my broken parts illuminate. I watched as the women looked lower, but not in a flirtatious way. No—it was clinical. That's what happened when most of your leg wasn't your leg anymore. And today, there wasn't a possibility of coolness. I was leaning hard on my cane because the walk around the grounds had my leg, hip, and back aching.

Oblivious, Ian continued with the introductions. "This young lady is Margot, and this is Jane," Ian finished, finally gesturing toward the woman I was most interested in meeting. "She's making us tea."

Such an old-fashioned name, but it suited her. She had a level gaze, a small but stubborn chin. Not the sort of person who tolerated idiocy. But she was clearly passionate about tea, so she had to have a whimsical streak.

But maybe that was just me projecting, thinking of Lila.

I hoped that maybe there was still a chance to make a good impression though. I drew myself up, squaring my shoulders, but as I saw her face, I knew it was too late.

I could already see the pity in her eyes.

7

My dear, if you could give me a cup of tea to clear my
muddle of a head, I should better understand your affairs.

—Charles Dickens

Jane

I gathered myself as quickly as I could. The last thing Ian's guest needed was me standing and staring like an idiot. "Hi," I said. "Would you like some tea? I just made some for everyone else; it's no trouble to make you a cup."

"Retired captain," he said, amending Ian's introduction. "And that would be nice, thank you."

Like every other southern man, he had lovely manners. "I'll resteep the leaves; it'll only take a few minutes." I reached for the teakettle. "The great thing about using good-quality tea leaves is that you easily get three steepings from them without a loss of quality."

He didn't answer, just waited.

Callum. Callum Beckett. He seemed nice, just . . . serious. Older. And injured.

I took extra care with his tea.

Nina asked about my plants, and I obliged, explaining how and when I picked the leaves and buds, how many plants I had, that they didn't flower like camellias.

I watched Callum's tea closely and presented it to him when done.

He lifted it to his lips immediately. "That's very good," he said after a moment. "Tastes like . . ." He smiled. "Not like I expected. But good."

I found myself smiling back.

∞

Mariah suggested taking our tea to the living room and called the au pair to bring down their oldest son to play the piano for us, but Celia gave our regrets—we were meeting our leasing agent shortly.

"We might be staying for free," I said once we got into the truck to go meet Chad, the agent, "but that doesn't mean the rent isn't high, not if we're looking at a number of mornings like that."

"The Vandermeides are very kind to let us stay," Celia said as she buckled her seat belt. "It won't be for long."

"I mean, Ian's super generous, but Mariah isn't what I'd call *warm,* and Nina is nosy."

"*I* like Nina," Margot said, fastening her seat belt. "She's funny and nice."

"Yes she is," Celia agreed, before turning back to me. "Shall we go look at some spaces?"

I pressed my hands together in exaggerated supplication. "Yes, please!"

We met Chad at the edge of Shipe Park, at the corner of East 44th and Avenue F. "I've got good news and bad news," he began. "The space on Duval? They accepted a tenant just this morning."

"No, really?" Celia's face fell.

"That was the one you showed me, right?" I asked, looking from Celia to Chad.

"Yeah, the cool vintage one. That's . . . man. That's really too bad," she said, running a frustrated hand through her hair.

"Are there other spots? Close by?" We'd met him down here, after all. There had to be something else.

Chad nodded. "There are two more spaces, but I have to warn you, they're not as strong as the Duval space."

I grimaced. In my experience, if a leasing agent said anything negative about a space, it usually meant that now was the time to tie on your running shoes.

Sure enough, one had such a tiny kitchen that I would have had to look at renting a separate commercial kitchen space. The other was just a few blocks from the capitol building, yet too far from the main foot traffic area to justify the higher price tag.

Discouraged, we stopped at Torchy's Tacos, after Internet research convinced Margot that we had to go.

One bite in, and I offered my younger sister a high five. "Good find, kid. This is the most amazing thing I've eaten since we left the Bay."

Celia nodded in agreement, a dollop of avocado crema at the corner of her mouth.

I finished my first taco before turning to Celia. "So, today was a bust."

"It was. I really wanted that spot on Duval."

We'd driven by it on the way to the first alternative, and I'd recognized it immediately. Without looking inside, I knew it probably would have been perfect.

"We'll keep looking," Celia said.

"We're getting steady orders with the online business. I need to fill a bunch tonight. With Valentine's next month, I thought about blending a new tea—something with hibiscus, that will brew up pink—and promoting that. Make an event out of it."

"Sure," Celia said, distracted. "That sounds great."

I suppressed a frown at her lack of interest, deciding it wasn't worth commenting on. Instead, I drowned my sorrows in another taco.

Back at the casita, Celia caught my arm. "Thanks for making tea earlier for everyone."

"Oh." I had to think for a moment and shift my mind back to that moment. "You just looked uncomfortable. I'm sure there were better ways I could have, I don't know, redirected things, but it was the first idea that came to mind."

Celia's lips quirked upwards. "Of course it was. At any rate, it was very kind of you."

"Of course," I answered. "Though Mariah looked at me as if I were crazy."

Celia's mouth eased into a sideways smile. "Not everyone has your passion for dead leaves."

"The global tea industry was valued at $38.2 billion last year," I retorted with a shrug. "She's missing out."

"True enough."

"I'm putting the kettle on," I said, glancing upstairs after Margot, who seemed to have disappeared into the loft.

I filled the kettle with water, glancing over my shoulder at Celia. "I know it's been a hard time for you too. And I'm still curious about what exactly happened with you and Teddy. Everything seemed fine, at least from my spot in the cheap seats."

Celia looked at the ground, looked at the boxes, looked everywhere but at me. "We broke up."

"I mean, were you expecting that? Which one of you, I mean . . ."

"There were a lot of factors," Celia said, her face a careful mask. Even from where I stood, I could tell she was choosing her words carefully, examining each one for appropriateness. "We were starting to want and need different things, and it became clear that we needed to go down different paths. There were . . . factors. It was complicated."

Nope, that still didn't jive, not with every other observation I'd ever made about those two. "How can it be complicated? You either want to be together, or you don't."

Celia shook her head. "Sometimes it really is complicated. But it doesn't matter; none of it matters. We're here; we should unpack."

I cast my gaze around the small, cluttered guesthouse. She was trying to distract me, but she had a point.

It was a redirection, but I'd allow it. "All right. How much should we unpack? How long are we going to be here?"

"We shouldn't leave until we have a new space," she said. "We can't afford rent and utilities on the Internet business alone."

"If we promoted it a bit more, we might get there. We've got our nest egg—"

Celia shook her head emphatically. "It's too risky. Let's wait. More spaces will come up. Chad said that things will pick up in the spring."

My eyebrows flew upward. "Spring? I missed that part. You mean we might not even be able to sign for a place until spring? It could take us months to get the permits going. You're planning to have us stay here that long?"

Celia's delicate blond brows furrowed. "Of course that wasn't the plan. I should have committed to the Duval location sight unseen. I just thought we had time. It's my fault."

"There's no fault. You didn't know," I said, though I felt the seed of resentment burrow into my heart. "I just . . . I guess if I'd known we weren't jumping straight into a place, I feel like we should have stayed in California."

Celia crossed her arms, stung.

"Look," I said. "I'm not saying we should go back. We can't afford it. I just . . . I don't like it. I don't like limbo."

"I know you don't."

I turned away and looked at our belongings, packed and piled along the walls, and then back at Celia. "Can we talk about the food-cart idea?"

"Let's hang in a little while longer," she suggested, a note of pleading in her voice. "Food carts still cost money, and I feel like we should consider all of our options before we sink money in that direction. Chad said there were more spaces."

"I thought he said there wouldn't be more until spring."

"Better ones in the spring, but we can still look."

I hugged my arms to myself. Numbers weren't my thing; they were Celia's. Trying to figure out a balance sheet created a headache from behind my eyes, like my brain was trying to retreat from the source.

But there were a lot of things about the situation that weren't adding up.

Were we here because Celia was running away from the situation with Teddy? I opened my mouth to query my sister, and then closed it.

Right now? Even if it was true, she wouldn't tell me. And what did it matter? We were here now, and like it or not, we were stuck in this guesthouse in Texas.

I took a deep breath. Finding a café-type space, finding an apartment—those things took time.

Maybe she was telling me the truth, but I didn't for a moment believe that she had shared the whole story about Teddy. Not even close. I'd *seen* them together, and I knew my sister. They were head over heels in love with each other.

Something happened, and now we were in Texas.

I looked up at Celia, her face shadowed as she looked out the back window.

She'd talk to me when she was ready.

I turned my attention back to the stove. "I've got an appointment to take Margot to the high school tomorrow, to get her registered," I said as my tea water began to boil.

"Oh. That's good. Thanks for arranging that."

I shrugged. "Just doing my part to keep Gogo literate."

"Do you want me to go with you?"

"Of course, if you want," I said, reaching for the mug I'd unpacked, the one with a watercolor llama on the side.

"I told Mariah I'd go with her and the children to the park tomorrow."

The park. I cleared my throat. "We'll be fine," I avoided her gaze, fishing in my tea bin for a sachet of my favorite chai blend. "But I'll text if anything goes awry."

"Yes." She squeezed my shoulder. "I'm sure it'll be fine."

She climbed the stairs to the loft, leaving me with my tea and my thoughts.

∞

Margot climbed beside me in the truck, a sullen expression fixed firmly to her face. "I don't want to go to a new school."

I pulled the seat belt across my chest. "It's this or homeschooling, and if I were in charge of your education, all you'd learn would be the Latin names for plants and how to play four different instruments."

"Not how to brew tea?" Margot asked archly.

"You're funny," I said. "You're learning that no matter what."

"I won't fit in there. I'd rather stay here. Nina could teach me."

"I bet Nina could teach you many things," I said, putting the truck into reverse before starting down the long driveway. "And she still can. After school."

Margot grunted a reply.

"It'll be a change," I told her. "I'm not telling you that you'll love it off the bat. But I think that if you give it a chance, if you smile at people, if you put a little energy into meeting people and making friends—"

"Like you?"

I cleared my throat. "I had friends at school."

"But now?"

"It's different when you're an adult, when you're running a business. I was friends with Atticus, and we had our neighbors. And Celia, of course, and you." At the stoplight I turned to smile at her. "That's a lot."

Margot seemed mollified, and we cranked up the Ramones for the rest of the drive.

In short order she was registered at Westlake High School, where the counselor enthusiastically encouraged her to try out for the dance program.

Naturally, Margot groused the whole way home. "I have math in the mornings. That's the worst."

"But the rest of your day will only get better. Unless, of course, you discover that you really like algebra. Cool women like Katherine Johnson really like algebra."

Margot wasn't biting at my attempts at positivity. Instead, she crossed her arms and stared out the window. "The dance team is dressed like cowgirls."

"I don't think actual cowgirls dress like that," I said, though when I saw the team picture, I had a hunch Margot might not go for it.

"Cowboy boots. I'm not trading pointe shoes for cowboy boots."

"Nobody said anything about trading, hon. We'll find you a dance studio next, it's just that it seemed as though your formal education might take precedence." I snuck a glance at her. "You might just try for the team. It's other girls who dance, a new kind of step. I'm sure you could do it."

Margot's arms crossed tighter. "Cowboy. Boots."

"You know we're in Texas, right?"

Margot grunted. "That's hard to forget."

"Think of it this way. You're learning about a new culture, and the boots represent their cultural dress."

Silence.

"We'll find a dance studio for you soon. I promise."

"I want to go back."

We drove in silence for the next several blocks. "It's a new adventure," I said at last. "Let's listen to music, okay?"

I let the Ramones take over before we had any chance at continuing. Because the fact was, I wanted to go back too.

∞

After herding Margot through the high school to enroll, an afternoon spent unpacking and organizing felt like child's play.

Sean would be coming to dinner at the Vandermeides' and even a cursory glance in the mirror told me that a shower would be in order before dinner if I wanted to be presentable.

So after getting enough of the kitchen put away—enough that I felt like I'd actually done something more than just make a bigger mess—I retreated to the bathroom for a long, hot shower. I scrubbed my face, washed my hair, and after toweling off, twisted my hair up and jabbed a pencil into it. As I stepped into the bedroom, Celia eyed the coif and sighed. "I wish my hair would do that."

"I've always wished I had your hair," I reminded her, turning to tuck a piece behind her ear. "If I get crumbs in mine, they might hold for a week."

"You got Mom's hair, you and Margot."

I pressed my lips together. "I've missed her, especially of late." Life felt so turned around. I missed the days when I could go to her and let her untangle things for me. And if she couldn't, she could at least reassure me of my ability to untangle it on my own. I needed that reassurance about now.

Celia placed a hand around my waist. "I miss her too."

"I still like your hair."

She laughed, and I realized then how rarely I'd heard it since we left. Since Teddy.

I smiled at her "I like hearing you laugh."

"I laugh!"

Not like you used too, I thought.

Margot tromped up the stairs in a rush. "Can I borrow some lip gloss?"

I gestured to my open makeup bag. "Have at it."

"You look pretty," she said. "But you need mascara. You look weird without it."

I wrapped an arm around her. "I'm so thankful for you," I told her. "Without you, I might be at risk for thinking too highly of myself."

I shrugged into a cardigan before we left, though the evening wasn't overly chilly, with the temperature hovering around seventy. "Grab your jacket," I told Margot before we closed the casita door behind us and left for dinner.

As the three of us trekked back across the Vandermeides' immaculate lawn, I felt my stomach churn in anxiety. Thinking of Sean gave me the butterflies. But what if my memory had been messing with me? Sure, in my recollections he'd been tall and golden and perfect. Did the fact that he recovered my tea plants and tossed me the keys to his pickup cause my memory to sharpen his cheekbones? Did my response to his ability to start the truck cause the cleft in his chin to appear from nowhere?

It wasn't just his looks though.

Really.

I'd have been impressed with an average-looking guy who took charge like that. A guy who didn't mind stopping to help in the middle of a rainstorm. The fact that he was thoughtful *and* good looking? He just seemed too mythic to be real.

Maybe the real Sean Willis, in the light of Mariah's chandelier, would be smug or overbearing. I didn't know. All I knew was that he'd taken care of me, my sisters, and my tea, and the past forty-six hours had built him into Captain America with a Stetson.

We crossed the lawn to find Ian, Mariah, and Nina on the back patio, strings of lights reflecting their glow in the swimming pool and a fire pit at the center taking the edge off of the slight chill.

Also, there were dogs.

Half a dozen dogs.

Ian waved when he saw us. "There you are! Seemed too nice out not to eat outside. Come meet my dogs—there's Sam and Margaret, Sally, Frances, Adele, and Lucadia."

"All named for a President or First Lady of Texas," Nina told us, beaming with pride.

I knelt down to pet the one passing closest. Sally, I thought. Or Lucadia. "What kind of dogs are they?"

"Springer spaniels. Excellent hunting dogs; they can spot a bird a mile away," Ian said, chest puffed out as he reached into his pocket.

All six dogs sat immediately.

He tossed out treats and called commands, and they obliged. Maybe not as quickly as they'd sat, but still they watched and tried to follow in a series of rolls and jumps. Mariah ignored the furry fracas, choosing to give instructions to Pilar. Once the exhibition ended, Lucadia—or perhaps Frances—returned to my side for pets.

We'd had a golden retriever when I was young, but I hadn't had a dog in my home since I was sixteen. Now, rubbing the ears of Ian's dog, I could see the appeal.

When the clock said ten after seven, I began to think that maybe, just maybe, my memory had been overgenerous on the subject of Sean Willis.

"It's a pity," Nina said. "He seemed like the sort of young man who would show up for dinner. And we're having Frito pie, so he's missing out."

I frowned. "Frito pie?"

"Yes!" Nina confirmed enthusiastically.

"What's that?"

In my head, I was trying to picture some kind of savory crust made of the salty, fried chips, but Nina set me straight.

"It's chili," she explained. "Served over Fritos, with sour cream and cheese on top."

"Fritos?" Margot looked up at me. "What's a Frito?"

Ian laughed. "Poor girl doesn't know what a Frito is! Is that what San Francisco does to you?"

"It's possible," Celia agreed.

"Frito pie was your mother's favorite dish," Ian said. "Talking about this is making me hungry. Let's serve up, y'all."

"We're still waiting on Jane's young man," Mariah protested.

"He's not my young man," I countered. "Especially if he doesn't show up."

Ian sprinkled a layer of Fritos into his bowl. "If there's no chili left," he said, ladling chili over the top, "he'll learn an important lesson."

"It's true," Nina said as the rest of us reached for bowls. "Muscles like that need protein, mark my words. Oh well. There's always Beckett. He's a catch." She turned and brightened as the man himself entered. "Beckett! You're just in time; you have no idea."

This morning, Callum had been dressed in workout clothes. Tonight he wore pressed chinos, a button-down shirt, and a sport coat. His shoes bore a military sheen, and once again I felt sorry for him. He seemed too stiff, too polished. I wondered if he'd ever be comfortable as a civilian.

"Did you have a nice afternoon?" I asked, having no idea what else I could ask about, besides the weather.

Or how well he knew the dogs' names.

"I did, thank you," he said with a nod.

A pause, long and ungainly, inserted itself between us.

"Tea," he said after that moment. "How did you start growing your own tea?"

"Oh," I said, brightening. "I studied abroad for a year, in college."

"Your major?"

"Music," I said with a wry grin. "But the time overseas made me want to switch to botany. I went to Japan, and the family I stayed with took their tea ceremony very, very seriously. So when I took an interest, they introduced me to friends of theirs who owned a tea plantation."

"And you were hooked?"

I grinned. "I was hooked. So my first plants are ones I brought back as seeds."

"You made green tea. Do different plants make different kinds of tea? Is there a black tea plant?"

"Well, yes and no," I answered. "All tea—all true tea—comes from the same sort of plant. It's what you do with the leaves that changes what kind of tea you can make. But some plants are cultivated more for use in black or green, not unlike wine grapes."

I was about to explain the differences between oolong and black tea, when an elaborate chime sounded.

"He's here!" Nina said, sitting up and finger-combing her hair. "I knew he wouldn't miss dinner, not with forearms like that."

I caught Mariah's eye roll, but noticed that she stood taller in anticipation as well.

Ian hastened into the house for the door, and the rest of us waited. Moments later they stepped outside, the strung lights glinting off Sean's hair.

"Sorry I'm late," he said, his voice warm, and the hair on my arms stood up. "I wanted to bring something nice, and it took more work than expected."

The dogs rushed to greet him, swarming around his feet and jumping on his legs until Mariah called them off.

He patted them before walking toward me and Celia, hat in hand, and I saw that my memory had been truthful. If the Austin Chamber of Commerce put him on a poster to promote tourism, I had no doubt of their success.

In his hand he carried flowers, and my eyes widened as I realized what they were. He held them out to me. Well, me and Celia, but he looked directly into my eyes. "Texas bluebonnets and California poppies." He leaned close. "They might not be California poppies, but they were the only poppies I could find in the city."

I beamed up at him. "They look awfully Californian to me," I said.

"Welcome to Austin," he said.

The way he looked at me felt like the best day at the beach and Christmas morning, all rolled into one.

But Ian interrupted. Naturally.

"Glad you could make it! You remember my wife, Mariah, and my mother-in-law, Nina."

"Of course," he said, with a friendly, polite nod.

"And this is my friend Callum Beckett, who's staying with us. Callum recently retired from the United States Marine Corps."

Sean shook Callum's hand. "Thank you for your service, sir."

Callum didn't answer, only nodded back.

We took our seats around the patio table, and I found myself seated with Sean on my left and Celia and Margot on my right, Callum across from me, and Nina next to him, with Mariah and Ian holding up the ends of the table.

"What do you do, Sean?" Celia asked as Pilar rolled a cart across the patio, telling the dogs to scatter in Spanish.

I watched, fascinated, to see that the cart bore plates of food. Pilar set one plate in front of each of us efficiently; I looked down to find a salad composed of avocado slices and grapefruit, crowned with arugula.

Sean picked up his fork. "I'm a musician," he said. "Musician for love, sound engineer for money."

"Jane studied music in college," Celia offered.

Sean turned to me. "Did you? I should have majored in music, but I stuck with business instead. Just wanted to get in and out. Would have been harder if I'd actually cared." He shook his head. "I'm in a band now; it's going well. Booking lots of gigs."

"Are you now!" Nina folded her hands. "Who are your influences?"

"I like to say we're what happens if you mix the Foo Fighters with the Frames," he answered. He started to explain who the Frames were, but Nina waved him off.

"Glen Hansard's band. Yes, I know them. I've had a passing interest in music over the years."

Ian cackled. "This lady," he said, pointing at Nina, "toured with the greats. There isn't much about rock and roll that she doesn't know."

Nina wasn't paying attention; her gaze was fixed on Sean. "You play guitar? Drums?" She squinted at him. "Sorry, I'm losing my touch. You're lead guitar, aren't you?"

He gave a bashful grin. "Lead guitar, guilty."

I speared a piece of grapefruit with my fork. "You're getting good gigs?"

"We've kept busy. We'll be at South by Southwest come March."

"That *is* exciting!" Nina exclaimed. "Good for you."

"I'm so ready for real rock to make a comeback," I said, reaching for my glass. "I like pop as much as the next girl, but there aren't enough electric guitar riffs on the airwaves."

"I can't dance," Sean admitted wryly. "So pop was out."

Everyone laughed, myself included. Everyone except Callum, who seemed to be paying more attention to the dog at his feet than the rest of the dinner party. If I wasn't mistaken, he'd been slipping pieces of avocado to Frances. Or maybe Sam.

If we were going to stay any length of time, I was going to have to learn the dogs' names.

"What did you listen to? As a kid?" I asked Sean.

"Garth Brooks," he admitted. "My mom loved her country ballads, and my dad liked Johnny Cash."

"And you started playing rock guitar, how?"

"A kid's got to rebel somehow," he said with a wink. "It would have been okay with my dad if it had been southern rock, but . . ." He shrugged.

"And you're a sound engineer as well?" Mariah asked.

"It pays the bills." He reached for his glass of iced tea and took a long drink.

The conversation shifted to Celia and myself, our tea shop in San Francisco, our plans to open a salon in Austin.

Sean asked after Ian and Mariah's children, and Mariah happily discussed her pleasure in finding a good preschool for their daughter, whom she believed to have extraordinary artistic talent.

Celia and I exchanged glances, both of us thinking of Jonathan and Phoebe. We'd had enough of overzealous parents.

Ian spoke some of his business, but waved the topic away after a few sentences. "I inherited my money and used it to make more; it's nothing noble. Nothing like Beckett, here. A true American hero."

Callum shifted uncomfortably. "That's overstating it a bit, Ian."

Ian gave a good-natured splutter. "Hardly. You saved six men before the second explosion took you out of action."

I found myself sitting up straighter.

Ian pointed at Callum. "Beckett assisted a squad with a building sweep, but come to find out it was rigged. First blast took out half of it, but Callum dragged six of them out to safety while they waited for backup."

Callum shook his head. "That's the bedtime-story version. Yeah, I saved four men—well, three men and a woman. But six others were killed in the blasts, and two more died waiting for a medevac." He drew a deep breath. "I did save four marines that day, but I also lost eight. To me, that doesn't quite add up to heroism."

"That's how you hurt your leg?" Margot asked, her voice girlish and innocent.

Callum's voice softened. "Yes. The second blast. Brought the rest of the roof down."

Ian shook his head at his friend. "They gave you the Bronze Star with a Combat V," he said. "It should have been a Silver Star."

Callum waved his hand. "A parting gift to go with my medical discharge."

Ian narrowed his eyes and pointed his fork at Callum. "Say what you will, you're still the best man I've ever met, Beckett."

An awkward silence would have descended over the table if Celia hadn't changed the subject. She asked about the upcoming South by Southwest festival and the way it had grown over the years. Nina, in particular, was more than happy to share her knowledge.

Little by little, Callum's shoulders relaxed.

I couldn't imagine what he'd been through. I'd lost my mother, an event with its own violence. But to live in a war zone, for everything to go wrong, to walk into a building with twelve people and leave with four living—it shifted things in my head. It made the conflict and its aftermath real.

I was inclined to agree with Ian—Callum was a hero. Maybe one of the truest signs of heroism was a sense of disbelief in the title.

Why was he staying here with Ian, I wondered. Didn't he have family? Loved ones?

I was lost in those thoughts when Sean nudged my elbow. I turned and gave him a bright smile.

"Tell me about the music you studied in college," he asked, his eyes fixed on mine.

And we were off again.

Backyard Frito Pie

For the chili

2 tablespoons olive or grapeseed oil

1 medium onion, chopped fine

3 cloves garlic

2 pounds ground beef

2 teaspoons salt

1 ½ tablespoons chili powder

1 teaspoon cumin

¼ teaspoon chipotle chili powder (optional)

1 tablespoon cocoa powder (optional)

1 teaspoon liquid smoke

1 28-ounce can crushed tomatoes

3 15-ounce cans black beans, drained and rinsed

1 can fire-roasted chopped tomatoes

To serve

Fritos or tortilla chips

Sour cream

Grated cheddar cheese

Sliced avocado (optional)

Chopped jalapeño (optional)

Heat the oil in a large sauté pan over medium heat. Add the onion, stirring and cooking until softened. Add the garlic, and cook for another 2 minutes. Add the ground beef, and cook until thoroughly browned.

Transfer the ground beef, garlic, and onion mixture to a slow cooker. Add remaining chili ingredients and stir. Cook for 10–12 hours on low.

Serve chili in bowls, ladled over the chips, and top as desired.

Serves 8–10.

8

While her lips talked culture, her heart was planning
to invite him to tea.

—E. M. FORSTER

Jane

"Sean Willis likes you very much," Celia said as we walked back across the lawn to the guesthouse.

"Normally I'd argue," I answered, feeling my face flush pink. "But he asked for my phone number and sent a text before he left."

"Smitten. Although he doesn't seem to be alone in that."

"You're so lucky, Jane," Margot sighed.

"And for one evening," Celia continued, "you've done pretty well. You know where he stands on Led Zeppelin and Aerosmith, and he admires the Oh Hellos and Darlingside as much as you do, but doesn't think too highly of Coldplay. Your disagreement about Jars of Clay made me think your love could die on the vine, but you managed to come to an accord. I'm glad he came around."

"You're very funny."

"Take it slow, dearest, or you'll run out of conversation topics."

I gave her arm a swat with the back of my hand. "He asked; what would you have me do? I still think Muse is overrated."

"I know you do."

"But he's also heard of Balmorhea. And Peter Gregson."

Celia poked me gently with her elbow. "If I could have conjured a man out of thin air for you, he would look and sound an awful lot like Sean. I was only saying that . . . it could . . . there might be wisdom in holding back."

"Holding back?" I repeated. I tested the thought in my mind, and my mind rejected it. "We've just met. But if we like each other, there's no reason to hold back."

"But you don't know that you like him."

I raised an eyebrow. "Um, I'm pretty sure I do. Wait—let me think on it. He's tall and blond and handsome and kind, and he's quick to help strangers and has good taste in music."

"You like who you think he is."

"I think most of us like each other for who we think the other is," I said, dryly.

"You know what I mean." Celia sighed as we reached the guesthouse door.

"It's just good to get to know people slowly sometimes," she continued. "Because it takes a while to unpack who someone really is."

"You're right," I said. The way she said it made me believe she was really talking about Teddy. Rather than ask about it, I changed the subject.

"Sean mentioned he has a spare truck hitch," I said, kicking off my shoes. "He offered to swing by tomorrow to put it on the truck, so we can use the trailer again."

"That's very kind of him." Celia gave a careful smile. "I do like him, Jane. I don't mean to give you the impression that I don't."

"Good. I'm . . . I'm glad." I looked around. "Do you want tea? I think I want tea."

"Moroccan mint?"

I nodded. "Moroccan mint."

9

You must remember that space is large; it is even larger than Texas.

—Dr. Wernher von Braun

Callum

I'd walked around Ian's property again that night, feeling the prosthesis chafing against my stump. No amount of sock and padding could change that. But the night cooled enough to keep me in the moment, just enough that it softened the memories for a little while.

Later the nightmares visited again. When I woke up enough to focus on the digital clock beside the bed, I discovered I'd at least made it past 3:00 a.m., an hour longer than the past two nights.

An extra hour of seeing the faces of the eight dead marines. Lt Harris, Cpl Leight, Cpl Cruz, LCpl Reuben, LCpl Keathley, PFC Esposito, PFC Reyes, Pvt Washington.

Their faces before, their faces after. Their families at the memorial in DC. Reuben's mom, Keathley's twenty-one-year-old fiancée.

I wasn't a hero. I was a cripple who couldn't save all his marines.

Once again, I sat up in bed and ran my hands over my face. This had to stop.

But I wouldn't sleep, so I attached the prosthesis, retrieved my swim trunks from where I'd hung them the night before, tossed on my bathrobe, and crept out of the house. The air had cooled significantly since dinner, hovering a few degrees below fifty. It felt bracing, staggering.

It brought me back to the moment.

I dragged one of the lawn chairs to the poolside ladder on the deep end and then sat to remove my prosthesis. The last thing I needed was a rusty leg; I felt enough like a Cylon as it was.

Once I'd detached my titanium leg, I braced myself on the ladder rails. With my toes just touching the tile that rimmed the pool, I closed my eyes and focused. I focused on my body, its alignment, the muscles and joints where my weight rested. I breathed deep as my back straightened, my abdominal muscles firmed.

When my body found its center, I began to count.

One. I sucked in air and rocked forward.

Two. Taking another breath, I flexed my knee.

Three. I used my hands and leg to propel myself into a dive, my arms finding their place over my head a split second before they hit water.

The water was just this side of bitterly cold, but still wasn't as cold as some ocean swims from my past. My hands cupped, pushing the water away. My shoulders worked, and my body complained at the task of a freestyle stroke without the benefit of two legs to scissor kick.

Before, I could swim laps until morning. Now? Three laps, the last with my body screaming at me.

But the screaming distracted, strengthened.

Afterward, I rested at the side of the pool, submerged to my chin, arms stretched wide. In the distance I could see the guesthouse, and my mind recalled the dinner party on the patio.

I'd liked Jane, pretty much from the moment I saw her. The way she stood, the way she spoke. It wasn't just her resemblance to Lila. She had a candid quality I responded to. Trusted. And a smile that could make a man forget things.

But that smile? Hadn't been directed at me. Nope, it'd been directed at Golden Boy.

I wouldn't have liked him even back when I had two legs.

Nope. I'd gone to school with guys like him, had to suffer them at the Naval Academy. Too much charm and good luck, too little hardship. Or if there had been hardship, he certainly hadn't learned from it.

And he'd turned Jane Woodward's head. Why wouldn't he, though? They'd told the story of her truck's broken hitch. He'd saved the day when she'd needed a hand.

If I'd been there that night, I would have struggled. It wouldn't have been pretty. The frustration sent me across the pool one more time.

Truth was, Jane Woodward had no reason to look my way.

In the morning, I slipped into the kitchen in search of a light breakfast. But Pilar stopped me before I laid a hand on the fridge door.

"Plate for you," she said, pointing to the warmer.

I opened it up to find a plate piled high with *migas* and a side of black beans. "You're too good to me," I told her, using a towel to remove the plate.

"You swim too much, exercise too much." She nodded. "I gave you extra cheese."

My face reddened; I'd tried, really tried, to be as discreet about my nocturnal swimming as possible.

Pilar didn't miss a beat. "You are the only person in the house with swim trunks wet at night and dry during the day."

"I can't sleep," I told her.

"Neither could my daughter when she came back," she answered, giving me a pat on the back. "Eat up."

Ian found me twenty minutes later, scraping the last of the cheese residue from the plate. "Beckett! There you are."

"Just getting an early start," I said.

"Still not off military time?"

I gave a rueful shake of my head. "Not yet."

"Are you sleeping?"

"Some," I hedged.

"Fair enough." He leaned back as Pilar wordlessly set a plate in front of him. Ian thanked her, spent a moment in prayer before tucking in, and then ate while I drank deeply from my coffee mug.

"I'm going to the house this morning," I told Ian. "Checking in with the builders."

Ian nodded. "Good, good. You want company?"

"I'm fine."

Ian took another bite of breakfast, squinted, and shook his head. "I'm going with you."

"Don't trouble yourself," I started, but Ian waved a hand, interrupting.

"You spend too much time alone."

"But—"

"You need a dog, is what you need."

As if on cue, one of Ian's pack of hounds padded into the kitchen, eyes wide and hopeful.

"This is not a place for the dog. Get out of my kitchen!" Pilar called out, waving a tea towel at the dog.

"She doesn't mean any harm," Ian protested to his housekeeper.

She narrowed her eyes at him. "Her hair will be in my food, and Mrs. Mariah won't be happy."

Ian winced. "You have a point." He cleared his throat. "In that case, Pilar, I take full responsibility for any dog hair Mariah might find."

Pilar scowled but said nothing

"You're a brave man," I told him before I tipped my mug back and finished the last of my coffee.

"Eh," he said. "I'll wipe the kitchen down myself. You still need a dog."

"I'll think about it," I said, setting my cutlery down. "Like I said, I'm headed to the house today. I want to make sure the finish work looks okay."

"I'll come along, give you a second opinion. How's it coming?"

I shrugged. "It's coming. Electrician went through last week; all of the light switches work now. I'm meeting Roy afterward to talk about the restaurants."

"Separate cars, then." Ian rose from his seat, and the dog at his feet sprang up to join him.

"Separate cars," I agreed with a nod. There was no fighting it, once Ian had set his mind to be helpful. "If you take your A7, I expect you'll beat me there."

∞

The house sat on the corner of 42nd and Avenue G, one of the largest lots and largest houses in the neighborhood.

And it was mine.

"Always was a fine place," Ian said appraisingly as I climbed from my car; he had beaten me there, as expected. "You'll have it shipshape in no time."

I nodded and slammed the car door shut as the memories flooded back.

I hadn't planned on returning. My brother Cameron had attended Trinity University in San Antonio and majored in business. He'd made it clear that he planned to join the family business, running Dad's family of barbecue joints.

For many people, it wouldn't seem all that lucrative, but Smoky Top Barbecue enjoyed a lot of success. The flagship location in Hyde Park was the kind of hole-in-the-wall that insiders loved and celebrities sought out.

There were two reasons why. The service was second to none. The staff weren't just efficient; they were the kind of friendly you could only find in the south. The host would welcome you in like you were late for a family dinner and take you to a table like they'd been saving it just for you. And if there were no available tables? The host checked in frequently, giving diners updates about when they could expect to be seated.

As for the second reason, that was all Roy. Dad's best friend was a barbecue alchemist, a pit master in the truest sense. He could smoke a side of ribs until the meat could hardly stand to remain on the bone. Dad provided the restaurant; Roy provided the barbecue that made your eyes roll backward. The server would bring a tray with seven different sauces.

The flagship restaurant put Dad and Roy on the map. After graduation, Cameron helped Dad expand across Austin, with plans to continue into San Antonio.

Dad and Cameron—they were a club. There wasn't room for me.

How did I know? Cameron told me so.

So I left. I made it into the Naval Academy and went overseas as quickly as I could after receiving my commission in the Marine Corps. There was no place for me in the business, and I wouldn't have wanted it even if there had been. I made a life for myself, traveling the world.

I wasn't the worst son and brother, or at least, I tried not to be. I stood next to Cameron when he married Lila. Lila, my high school girlfriend, who started dating him when they were both at Trinity.

But I was in Germany when I got the e-mail from Cameron that he and Lila had divorced, enabling Cameron to date a string of leggy waitresses working their way through medical school. He may or may not have been seeing half of them before the divorce, but I didn't want to know.

I was in Iraq when Cameron died in a car accident, drunk out of his mind at the moment of impact. My father hardly spoke to me during the funeral, and after that I spent all my leaves with my friend, Lt Reggie Harris, and his family.

My father sent a few e-mails after that, but not many. I knew he was busy managing the restaurants, but I also knew he'd lost Cameron and that I was a poor substitute.

I was in Afghanistan, on a routine mission, when a bomb tore through the retaining wall. I'd been able to help several marines reach safety before the second explosion tore through my leg. They airlifted me to Germany, where surgeons tried to save my leg before ultimately deciding to amputate. I remained in a postsurgery haze until my arrival at Bethesda.

It took me finally getting my phone back and calling a dozen friends to find out what had happened to Reggie Harris. I finally called his brother, who broke the news gently that Reggie had died on the ground, waiting for the medevac.

Two days later, Roy found me after traveling to Maryland to give me the news about Dad.

Roy informed me that I was the heir not only to Dad's house in Hyde Park but also all five Smoky Top locations. And the restaurants, he noted in his gravelly voice, needed my help.

The thing about Roy is that if he asks for help, you listen.

In the weeks that followed, I understood why. Cameron hadn't done a bad job with the expansion of Smoky Top. I had to give him credit. But after Cameron's death, Dad hadn't been able to keep up with five locations. He'd hired an extra manager who had skimmed funds and inflated the ordering costs. By the time he was arrested, Dad had his hands full trying to keep tabs on all five locations himself.

"We need the help," Roy told me as he sat beside my bed. "There are a lot of jobs on the line."

So I came home. Came home to lawyers, trust agreements, and five restaurants that needed . . . I didn't know what.

And the house? Just this side of habitable. Looking up at it, I still didn't know if I'd hang on to it or sell it. At twenty-seven-hundred square feet, it seemed like a lot of square footage for a guy like me.

Either way, it was on its way to having a new air compressor and a new roof. Ian's favorite contractor was assisting in the repairs. And while those were going on, I had begun to organize for an estate sale.

It was coming together, which meant decisions lurked around the corner.

A thought pinged in my mind. If I shared the house with someone . . . someone like Jane . . .

I saw her face again, focused on her tea, and later at dinner, eyes glowing at Sean.

Ian's thought process must have explored a similar trail. "It's a lot of house for a bachelor," he said, his voice heavy with meaning.

"Mmm," I answered, squinting as I looked up toward the new roof.

"You had to have noticed my cousins," Ian continued, undeterred.

"Celia's not interested in me," I told him, my voice frank. "Unless I miss my guess, there's a man back in California."

"You think?"

"Just a hunch."

A strong hunch. I knew what it looked like to be pining. It was the way my face had looked for three years.

"Jane then," Ian said, and something in my face must have betrayed me. He gave a pleased nod. "She's very pretty. Odd, maybe. But pretty."

"She's not for me," I said, with a rueful shake of my head.

"Why wouldn't she be?" Ian sounded outraged.

"She's young, for starters," I said, striding toward the house.

Ian matched me step for step. "She's not that young, and you're not that old."

I shot him a glance. "Sean Willis found her first, from the sound of it. She was looking at him the way you look at a new litter of puppies."

"That was bad luck. He is a handsome one," Ian admitted ruefully. "Helpful too—the women like that."

"I'm an amputee with a chain of failing restaurants," I said, reaching for the front door. "Let Jane have Sean. He'll do her more good than I would."

Ian kindly walked through the house with me, commenting on the pieces worth keeping—the antiques my mother had collected in happier days. By the time we were done, my leg ached but we had the house ready for the estate agent.

I saw Ian off before walking the three blocks to Roy's place.

Roy opened his screen door when he saw me coming down the path, his dark brow furrowed with concern.

"I didn't think you were stupid, boy, but you look like you're going to pass out from pain. Say the word and I can drive you."

"Good to see you too, Roy," I said, grasping the porch railing for support as I climbed the stairs.

"Fool boy," Roy muttered as he took my arm to help me up, but I'd known him long enough to hear the affection behind the words. We walked the short distance to his dining room table.

"I cooked," he said. "You sit down and stay there. Too much of your father's stubbornness in you."

"Funny," I said, shaking my head. "He told me once I didn't have enough."

Roy snorted and dished up lunch. A heaping serving of brisket, a spoonful of beans—I recognized my dad's recipe—and a stack of lightly dressed coleslaw.

"No corn bread? Is that what semiretirement's done to you?"

"Corn bread is for young men who don't injure themselves out of stubbornness."

"I think you'd hate my physical therapist. I'm supposed to push myself; it's how I retrain my body."

Roy harrumphed, and we both tucked into lunch. As expected, the brisket melted in my mouth, but the coleslaw took me by surprise.

"What's in this?" I asked, lifting a forkful of dressed cabbage closer to my eye.

"Pineapple, jalapeño, and enough lemon juice to keep things interesting."

"That's pretty fancy."

"Well, Austin's become a fancy town. Can't get by with cabbage and mayo anymore."

Anyone else would have thought he was grousing, but I could tell he was pretty proud of his twist on the classic.

After several minutes of focused eating, I nodded to the file folders on the table. "Talk to me about Smoky Top," I told him. "How bad is it?"

"I've been retired for the last five years, but as a shareholder, and as your dad's executor, I got my hands on the numbers. It's doesn't look good."

"Even with the coleslaw?"

"Nobody saves a business with cabbage."

I stifled a chuckle. "Words to live by."

We finished our food and wiped the sauce off our fingers before Roy brought out the papers. He showed me the accounts, the drop in profits, the loans my dad had taken out to stay afloat.

"It was so successful," I said, hardly understanding the numbers in front of me. "What happened?"

"Well, the economy, for starters. It didn't help. Cameron put a lot of work into the expansion of the locations and made a lot of money. But after he died . . ." Roy shrugged. "It was a lot for your dad. Too much. And then he got sick."

I frowned. "Sick?"

Roy frowned back. "Heart disease. Your father had a bad ticker. You knew that."

"No," I said, my breathing shallow. "I didn't."

"Have mercy." Roy shook his head. "He didn't tell you?"

"I thought he died of a heart attack."

"He did. Heart attack after five years with heart disease."

"I didn't know," I said quietly.

I didn't know because I never came home. If I had, would he have told me? Would I have noticed?

Why hadn't he told me?

"So he was sick," I said, my voice low and tired. "He was sick, and the restaurants got out from under him."

Roy nodded. "I tried to help. But I was training the kitchen staff, didn't know half of the troubles he was having. He told me some, but not all of it. One manager made off with thousands of dollars before Wallace caught it and set the police on him."

I reached for the next folder, marked *Online Reviews.*

Roy had printed off reviews from the leading restaurant review sites, and the comments chilled me. Diners from almost every location complained of slow, lazy service, orders being mixed up or forgotten altogether, dirty, dated spaces, unfriendly servers. "This doesn't sound like Smoky Top."

Roy sighed. "No. No service complaints at the flagship place—you know Wallace wouldn't allow it. But the reviewers are right about the place needing a facelift. No one likes sitting on cracked vinyl."

"At least they all say the food is good."

"Thank goodness for small miracles."

The last papers were a list of employees at each location. Five locations, six to ten employees at each—the livelihoods of almost fifty people rested in my ability to turn things around.

The thought made me sick.

The last time people had depended on me, I'd gotten my leg blown off and lost friends. While I knew that there weren't going to be any explosives in this situation, the pressure still made me jittery. But if there was one thing I'd learned in the marines, it was how to manage men and advance when things looked bad.

I spread the papers out further. "So what I'm seeing is that business is failing and changes need to be made and there are some major repairs and updates necessary but no money to do it."

"That'd be about it," Roy said, his eyes on file folders.

I turned my gaze to him. "Back in Maryland, you made it sound bad," I said.

Roy looked at me, a slow laugh rumbling out of his chest. "You always did have Wallace's sense of humor."

Did I? No one had ever thought to tell me so.

"One last thing," Roy said as he tucked the papers away. "Lila called me a few months back. Asked if there were any waitressing jobs."

"Lila? Lila asked about a job?"

"She did. If I had one, I would have given it to her. As it was, I didn't have enough work for the servers I'd already hired. Hated telling her no, but I did tell her I'd ask around."

"Thanks for telling me," I said. "Do you still have her number? I should check on her."

"Thought you might. It's inside the green file."

"Thanks, Roy."

Afterward, we took our glasses of sweet tea to the front porch, and I asked after his family. He asked about my years in service and the finer points of life with a shorter leg than I was born with.

I carried my glass inside before leaving, and he walked me down the steps. "Your car back at your place?"

"It is."

Roy scratched his head. "I'll walk over there with you. Been meaning to see what you've done to the place."

"I can walk three blocks on my lonesome," I told him. "You don't have to worry about me."

Roy grunted. "Your father told me to look in after you," he said, and I realized I wasn't going to be able to shake him, like I hadn't shaken off Ian earlier.

He filled me in on the neighborhood as we walked, telling me which trees had dropped branches in the last storm, which neighbor had a new baby or lost a loved on. He looked over the house, once we reached it, and pronounced that it was looking fine. "If you need anything," he said, as I climbed into my car, "a place to stay, a hot meal, you don't hesitate."

"I won't," I promised.

Satisfied that I meant it, he turned to walk back home.

Fancy Coleslaw

1 small head cabbage

½ jalapeño or more to taste, seeds removed (or left, if you want more
    heat), chopped fine

1 8-ounce can pineapple, juice drained into a separate container

$1/3$ cup mayonnaise

1 ½ tablespoons lemon juice

1 teaspoon pineapple juice

¼ teaspoon fresh ground pepper

Shred the cabbage, using a mandolin slicer or food processor's slicing attach-
ment. Add to a large bowl with the diced jalapeño and pineapple.

Stir in the mayonnaise, lemon juice, and pineapple juice, and scatter the
ground pepper over the top. Taste. Adjust seasoning as desired. Serve chilled,
either on the side or on top of barbecue.

Serves 6.

10

Texas is a state of mind. Texas is an obsession. Above
all, Texas is a nation in every sense of the word.

—JOHN STEINBECK

Callum

By the time I drove back to Ian and Mariah's, twilight cloaked the low hills.
The lights at the house were all on, the light pouring out the windows, painting
the property with orange and gold.

I reached for the file Roy had given me and pulled out my phone to dial
the contact number Lila had scrawled on the page. It rang several times before
the recording of Lila's voice instructed me to leave a message.

I cleared my throat. "Lila, it's Callum. I'm in town, in Austin. You've got
my number. Give me a call. It'd be good to catch up."

Afterward I found myself staring at the phone, waiting, thinking maybe
she'd simply missed the call and would call or text back. But the screen remained blank and quiet; after a moment, I slid the phone into my pocket and
headed for the house.

Even before I opened the front door, I could hear the music.

Acoustic guitar—one of them? Two? Instruments, at any rate, and the
sweetest singing voice I'd ever heard. Coming closer, I recognized the song—
Fergus O'Farrell's "Gold."

I followed the sounds to the music room. For the duration of my stay, the
room had been devoid of people, but now Jane sat on the piano bench, facing
away from the instrument as she strummed a guitar and sang. Sean sat next to

her on a barstool, filling in the chords and embellishing the melody with finger-picking.

Not a musician myself, even I could tell that they were very good. Both played with confidence, singing the lyrics to each other.

I stayed in the doorway, listening. Ian, Mariah, Nina, Celia, and Margot sat within the room, their bodies still and transfixed.

The song ended with easy laughter from Jane and Sean. Sean began to play again, picking a series of flourishes before launching into a spirited rendition of Alabama Shakes's "I Found You."

They looked flushed and happy, and if they were not in love, love waited just around the corner. I should have taken the hint.

So why couldn't I look away from Jane?

I studied her as she played along with Sean, adding counter melody with her guitar. Was it just physical attraction on my part? She made a beautiful picture, her face bright with joy, her eyes sparkling. With her fine bone structure, wide eyes, and dark curly hair, she seemed almost painterly. Not the sort of looks popular on magazine covers, but arresting just the same.

She did remind me of Lila; there was no denying the resemblance. But there was something . . . extra . . . about Jane. Almost like high school Lila, but grown and in Technicolor. Was it a fair comparison? Probably not. Lila had made her decisions and suffered when the man she chose failed her.

But Jane?

Hope still filled her eyes, especially now. Hope, but also determination and a drive for perfection. The way she played, the precision of her fingers, and the way she'd carefully brewed that cup of tea spoke of a woman with a fine sense of detail.

She was special. And judging from the way Sean sang to her, he saw it too. After his final chords, the group burst out in applause.

I joined in, striding forward and making my presence known. Sean raised a hand in greeting, and Jane smiled her wide smile, an expression I'd come to realize was uniquely hers—eyes open, taking everything in even as her smile beamed outward.

Ian gestured for me to take the seat next to him, and I obliged. "We've lucked into a home concert," he said, face pink with happiness. "Sean here brought his guitar, but who knew Miss Jane would turn out to be the surprise star?"

"Jane is excellent at everything she sets her mind to," Celia said, her voice full of warmth.

"Yeah," Margot said. "Except not yelling at customers. She needs to work on that."

Jane grinned at Margot, setting her guitar down. "She's not wrong about that," she said, shrugging off the praise.

"Have you ever set your mind to it?" Celia teased.

"I did, once," Jane said, eyes wide in mock defensiveness. "It went badly."

"But she was at the top of her class at Stanford's music department," Celia continued. "So I'd say she's a talent."

"Were you really?" Sean asked Jane.

Jane shrugged. "I can tell you anything you'd want to know about eighteenth-century chamber music."

"What other instruments do you play?" Nina asked.

Jane waved a hand. "Piano, mostly. Strings and guitar. Give me enough time, I can find my way on a clarinet. But keep me away from any of the horns."

"Bad," Margot confirmed. "Mordor bad."

"Our Ivo is taking piano lessons," Mariah noted. "His teacher says he has a wonderful ear."

"Play us something," Ian instructed, gesturing to the instrument behind Jane. "Usually it's just Ivo who plays. Four-note melodies, over and over again."

"Oh, all right," Jane acquiesced, but she didn't sound put out about it. She swung a long, shapely leg to the opposite side of the bench, lifted the cover, and placed her hands on the keys.

I'd expected something classical, the kind of show-off piece a musician might pull out as a party trick.

Instead, her fingers coaxed a series of bluesy open chords from the instrument, the melody to "The Nearness of You" slowly taking shape.

Her movements were confident, even languid. She was a musician who knew what she was doing and understood that she didn't have to show off in order to be taken seriously.

The song wound its way into my head, and I knew I'd hear it even underwater during my next lap swim.

The rest of the group burst into happy applause at the end, but I found myself wishing for just another moment of quiet to absorb the music.

A smile spread across her face, and I felt a tightness in my chest.

Mariah directed the group to slices of cheesecake on the sideboard and encouraged everyone to take a plate. Jane handed plates to her sisters, Sean, and then me. I ducked my head in thanks.

"One of these days," Nina said, "I'm going to steal your housekeeper away. This cheesecake is divine."

Celia nodded her head in agreement.

"I had an e-mail from my cousin's girl," Nina continued. "She's coming through town, some sort of event planning to get ready for South by Southwest. She asked if I had recommendations for hotels, and naturally, I just told her to come stay at mine."

"You have a hotel?" Margot asked, eyes wide.

Nina laughed. "My husband bought one, ages ago, and the sweet thing just runs along. The hotel, not my husband; he died several years ago," she clarified. "Anyway, I thought we could have her over for lunch or dinner this week."

Mariah squinted. "Do I remember her?"

"I don't know, dear. She was at the family reunion in Tulsa, the one in '08."

Mariah thought and shook her head. "I think we were in Aspen and couldn't make it."

"You'll have a chance to catch up because she'll be here for a while, organizing for the tech portion of the conference, if I remember correctly. She's the social media director for a finance start-up, something like that."

Celia's head snapped up, hard enough that I noticed, but she remained calm. "What's her name?"

"Lyndsay Stahl. Sweet girl, Lyndsay. I haven't seen her in years, but here's hoping she's got some spunk."

Sean rose from his seat. "I'd best be off," he said, and I couldn't miss the look of disappointment on Jane's face. "Walk out with me?" he asked her, tipping his head to the door. "I might get lost in the dark."

Jane's expression softened. "Of course," she said, her eyes crinkling.

They walked out together, their steps in sync.

"Look at those two," Nina said, when they were barely out of earshot. "The children would be gorgeous."

Watching them slip out the grand front door, I cringed but couldn't argue.

11

Tea! Bless ordinary everyday afternoon tea!

—AGATHA CHRISTIE

Jane

"It's so loud in there," Sean said as we stepped outside into the night air.

I cleared my throat. "I shouldn't complain. My cousin's been very generous, giving the three of us a place to land for the time being."

"One of these days," he said, "I want to hear what brought you to Austin."

"It's a long story, really. One story built into another."

He turned to me, and once again I marveled at the way his features aligned to create such a stunningly handsome face.

"How about I take you out tomorrow?" he asked. "I'll take you somewhere nice, and you can tell me all about it."

"Better be somewhere nice with a lot of food, because I'm not kidding around when I say it's a long story."

"We can always get ice cream after. I wouldn't dream of bringing you home hungry."

I smiled up at him. "No?"

"Never. How 'bout I pick you up tomorrow at seven?"

"I'd like that."

For a moment I thought he'd kiss me, but he didn't. Instead, he tipped his hat, wished me good night, and climbed into his white pickup truck.

I almost swooned. Would have, if I were the swooning type.

Instead, I walked back to the casita. My plants needed watering now that the sun had gone down, but I got distracted once I checked my e-mail and found three new orders.

Celia and Margot found me sorting teas ten minutes later. "So?" Margot asked. "What did Sean say?"

A smile stretched across my face. "He wants to take me out tomorrow. For dinner and ice cream."

"Tomorrow?" Celia asked. "He doesn't have anything to do on a Wednesday night?"

"I don't either, so I can't throw stones."

"I'm happy for you," Celia said. "Truly."

After her own heartbreak with Teddy, her words meant a lot to me. I thanked her and reached for the cardigan I kept on the hook by the door. "I'm going to water the plants, if you'd like to come out with me."

"No, thanks," Margot said. "I'm tired. I'm going upstairs."

"Is that code?" I asked. "For going upstairs to Skype with Jasmine and Emma?"

Margot paused on the stair, looking sheepish. "Maybe."

"Maybe yes?"

"I mean, it was my first real day of school and everything . . ."

"Go Skype," I told her. "But Internet off at ten thirty, okay?"

I got a nod of assent before she raced upstairs.

Celia followed me outside, unrolling her long sleeves until they once again covered her wrists. "Where's Sean taking you?"

"He didn't say, but he did say 'nice.' I don't even know that I own nice date clothes."

"You can borrow something of mine."

"Aw, thanks. For permission, I mean. I'd planned on wearing something of yours." I shot her a cheeky grin before turning my attention back to the hose bib. "I prefer having permission, though. It's better than theft." I turned the water on, letting it sputter for a moment before turning the stream to the base of the first plant. "I'm surprised you guys were able to get out tonight. I thought you'd still be a hostage at the big house."

"Keep your voice down and stop complaining. They're being lovely to us."

"They are. I told Sean as much. I just wish that loveliness meant they were a little less in our business."

Celia looked over the plants, pulling off the occasional dead leaf. "You think everyone's in your business. Your piano sounded nice. You should play more often."

"It *did* feel nice to play again." I pointed at the soil beneath the second tea plant and squeezed the sprayer trigger.

"And your gentleman friend played well too."

I batted my eyelashes. "Why yes, my gentleman friend is very refined that way," I said with an exaggerated southern accent. "But you're right—he did play well. Add that to his pro side of the list: handsome, talented, good taste in books and film . . . and music, obviously."

"Obviously."

Happiness, strange and unfamiliar, unfurled within my chest. "I really like him, Celia."

"And he's taking you out tomorrow."

I couldn't stop my grin, though I didn't try either. "He is."

Celia nodded toward my plants. "They seem happy. I think they like the sun."

"Me too. The plants and I like it here."

I watered a few moments longer, my mind wandering. A scene from earlier pinged back into my consciousness. "Wasn't Teddy doing some work for a finance start-up?"

Celia nodded. "He did."

"And their big reveal was going to be South by Southwest, right?"

"I think that was one of the plans, yes."

I waited for her to elaborate, but she didn't. "Sorry," I said. "If you don't want to talk about it, just say so."

"He's good at his job, that's all. Teddy is my past."

"And you haven't heard *anything* from him?"

"We haven't talked, no."

In this day and age of electronic media, I found that difficult to believe. But I kept my mouth shut and changed the subject.

∞

Wednesday night, I tried on every potential ensemble that could be created with our combined closets.

"You're lucky," Celia said, folding a cardigan. "You look nice in everything."

"You're sweet," I told her. "He's . . . well, he's Sean. I just want to look . . . special."

"My cardigan with the feathers would have done that for you," she answered innocently.

"I don't even know why you brought that thing."

"It looks cute on me."

I rolled my eyes. "What's disgusting is that you're not wrong. With my hair, it makes me look like one of the bad dates from *Notting Hill*."

Margot looked me over critically. "You should put some product in it. Pull it back."

"With this humidity, I think the product is a given."

"I think you look surreal," Celia said. "But nice."

"Funny. I'm not wearing the feather cardigan."

"Suit yourself."

I scanned the closet again. Part of me thought about being safe, wearing Celia's best black dress, but safe didn't appeal to me. So I reached for a brightly patterned dress instead, an easy sleeveless silk dress that pulled over my head and tied in the back. I wrapped a fringed shawl over my shoulders, and with Margot's close supervision, worked enough product into my hair to conquer most of the frizz. Any remaining strays would, hopefully, be concealed under cover of darkness.

A little fuchsia lipstick, and I threw my wallet into a tiny purse.

And waited.

Celia and Margot waited with me; it would have been foolish not to, seeing as how the casita only had two rooms—the bedroom loft and the downstairs that served as living, kitchen, and dining room. After what felt like the length of time required for a Terrence Malick film, a pair of headlights became visible at the end of the long drive to the casita.

"Either that's him," Celia noted, "Or whatever you ordered from Amazon is here." I couldn't look, not yet, but there was no denying the slam of the truck door outside.

Margot raced to the window. "Jane, he brought you flowers! Seriously, this is the most romantic thing ever."

"More than the last time he brought flowers? Those weren't half bad." I rose, peering out the window. Sure enough, a white pickup truck was parked a little distance away. Sean strolled toward the casita, and even from here I could tell he looked *good*. He wore jeans, the kind that were hand-finished by well-paid nuns, a black button-down, and a black sport coat. And the bouquet of flowers was in his hand.

I waved at him through the glass. He waved back with the hand not carrying flowers.

They were, I noted with pleasure, not the sort of flowers found at a Kroger, but a beautiful arrangement of irises—unusual and perfect.

I told him so once he made it to the door.

"Just like you," he replied, and my heart puddled at my feet again.

A wave at Celia and a giggling Margot, and we were off, with Sean giving me a hand as I climbed into the passenger seat of his truck.

"I should think about hydraulics," he said, eyes twinkling. "This truck is too tall for you."

"You could do that," I teased back. "Hook it up to a remote control."

We laughed and joked as we headed to town, crossing over the Colorado River as we headed east.

"Are you going to tell me where we're going?"

"You don't know Austin at all, do you?"

"I know it's in Texas. And it's hot, like, most of the time."

He laughed and shook his head. "You've got a long ways to go."

"The city is my oyster," I countered teasingly. "But maybe I've been waiting for you to show it to me."

"Clever girl. It's true, I know it backwards and forwards." He turned from North Lamar onto West Fifth Street. "Tonight I'm taking you somewhere with a lot of history. It's the Driskill Hotel, and the restaurant is one of the best in the city."

"I'm sure for tonight, it'll be the very best."

He grinned. "President Johnson brought Lady Bird there for their first date in '34. But it's been a destination since the twenties."

"That's amazing." I gave him a side glance. "You totally looked that up on Wikipedia before you came."

He cleared his throat. "Well now, that would be telling."

When the building came into view, I gasped. Four stories tall with lights blazing, it took up nearly the entire city block. "It's beautiful," I said, taking it in, the earth-brown exterior with elaborate white trim, pillars included. "If Celia were here, I'd bet she could tell us what architectural style it's built in. She studied architecture before switching to finance."

"Old?" he guessed. "Old and Texan?"

"Very funny."

"We'll find someone to ask."

He pulled up, letting a valet take his truck away to places unknown. We made our way through the grand front doors and turned left to the entrance of the Driskill Grill.

The maître d' met us at the front, and Sean gave his name for the reservation; a bluesy jazz combo played inside.

"What would you call the hotel's architectural style?" Sean asked the man before we set off toward our assigned table.

"Romanesque Revival," the man answered solemnly, and we followed him inside.

"Romanesque Revival," Sean repeated to me. "All these years in Austin, but one night with you and I'm learning something new."

"Wikipedia, man. I'm disappointed in your incomplete research."

He laughed, and we entered the dining room. I saw people watch us as we walked to our table, and I didn't blame them. Sean was six feet plus of all-American handsome, and my dress featured every color in the rainbow and a few new ones.

We examined our menus, Sean insisting we order anything that caught my fancy. I picked the blistered shishito peppers, the crispy soft-shell crawfish, and the osso buco for the main course; Sean picked the wild boar chops and the plate of artisanal cheeses.

"I'm not going to eat for a week," I declared as I tucked into the osso buco and Sean sliced his wild boar. His knife glided through with ease, and I marveled at the play of flavors on the end of my fork.

Afterward, we boxed our leftovers, and the server placed them in a sack for us. Sean carried the bag in his left hand, his right hand clutching mine.

"I will never forget that meal," I told him as we stepped outside. "Never ever, for as long as I live."

"I hope you remember the company," he said. "Just a little."

"Just a little," I teased, knowing I was more likely to remember the way he looked at me across our table than the taste of the peppers. By morning, the food would be a blur of *yum* while every one of Sean's smiles would remain filed away in my heart.

"Let's walk a little," Sean suggested. "It's nice out."

He took my arm, and I leaned into him with pleasure.

Was this how Celia had felt about Teddy? I considered them both, having a hard time wrapping my head around the idea. The feelings I had for Sean—they were wild and unfettered, each one welling up unexpectedly and sending me into new spirals of sentiment.

Celia and Teddy had been so . . . steady. Quiet.

Had it been love for them?

I thought I'd been in love before, with boys from school and college dates. But then our circumstances changed, and Celia and I opened the tea shop, fighting to land on our feet. There hadn't been much time for dating. Who would I have dated? Our clientele consisted of women and gay men—it was San Francisco, after all. Perhaps a savvy straight man might have come to our door in search of a woman, and if he had, he would have had options. But our world had been insular; Celia and Teddy had met at her old job.

"What do you think about ice cream?" Sean asked, interrupting my thoughts.

"In general?" I tossed him a bemused expression. "I'm in favor. I'm not angry at it."

He laughed, shaking his head. "I meant, what do you think about getting ice cream now?"

"What are we doing with it once it's gotten? Because I have no idea how I'd ingest so much as an ice cube, not after the meal we just had."

"This is really good ice cream. Local. You might make an exception."

"So you've got a specific place in mind."

"Amy's Ice Creams, the 6th Street location. It's just about a mile from here. And it's scenic," he added, pointing down the street. "We'd go past the capitol building."

"I do like taking in local sights." I turned in the direction he'd pointed. "Just to warn you, I reserve the right to sniff rather than eat."

I took a few steps before he snagged my wrist. "Where are you going?" he asked, clearly bemused.

"Ice cream?" I asked, confused. "I thought that's what we were doing."

"I was going to call for a rideshare," he answered, laughing. "Didn't think you'd want to walk."

A slow smile spread across my face. "I'll tell you something, Sean Willis. I'm a California girl. And you know what California girls do?"

"Katy Perry gave me all sorts of ideas, but I'm sure you're about to tell me."

"We walk outside when the weather is nice," I told him.

"You sure you can walk in those shoes?"

"I've made it this far, haven't I?" I looked down at my feet, clad in a pair of well-padded heels, and held a foot out. "Our feet were made for walking, and I don't wear shoes that fight that purpose."

"So much sense in one so beautiful."

I knew I shouldn't have felt *too* flattered—we'd been talking about feet, after all. But that was the power of Sean Willis. The way he smiled down at me, I felt like the cleverest, most beautiful woman in all of Austin.

Amy's Ice Creams was everything Sean promised, and more. Tub after tub of ice cream, in the most intoxicating flavors—Mexican vanilla, carrot cake, lavender chocolate, and something called "Mozart's Toddy."

As full as I was, I could feel the contents of my stomach shifting ever so slightly to make room. Because even coming from San Francisco, the city of a thousand ice cream parlors, I knew this was something special.

We ate our cones on the walk back, me with my carrot cake and molasses scoops, Sean with his dish of "Remember the a la Mode." The glow of happiness kept me warm, even while eating something frozen.

Sean cranked the heat up inside his truck, once we retrieved it from the valet. Even buckled securely to my seat, I felt dizzy with happiness.

Had I ever felt so happy? I knew, logically, that I *had,* but at that moment all those memories escaped me. All I could do was live in this moment with this man, and I couldn't think of anywhere else I'd rather be.

Sean parked his truck a little away from the casita and jumped down to help me from the passenger seat.

"I had a good time," he said, tucking my arm into his. "I'd like to see you again."

"I'm not sure," I teased, the light in my eyes surely telling him that I knew

I was speaking nonsense. "I ate so much tonight, it'll be weeks before I'm hungry again."

Sean grinned, pulling me close. "I'm sure you'll find a way."

And before I knew what was happening, he kissed me. A perfect, spontaneous kiss, warm and deep and real. The kind of kiss that confirmed that everything I'd felt had felt real for him too.

I kissed him back, of course. He was so tall, so blond, so *perfect,* never mind the fact that he tasted like ice cream. I felt myself spiral into the kiss, deeper, and pulled away a split second before I might have lost myself forever.

"You're right, I suppose," I said, my voice husky and half-breathless. "I could probably find it within myself to share another meal with you sometime soon."

"Oh really?" He gave the corner of my mouth another caress. "Sorry, I've been wanting to do that for a while."

"I minded," I said dryly. "Clearly."

"I'll pick you up Saturday night? Seven?"

I nodded.

One last kiss. "I'll see you then, Jane Woodward," he said, before returning to my side. "I still have to walk you to your door. I'm Texan like that."

12

If you are cold, tea will warm you. If you
are too heated, it will cool you. If you are
depressed, it will cheer you. If you are
excited, it will calm you.

—WILLIAM EWART GLADSTONE

Jane

I crept into the house and up the stairs to the loft. Margot was asleep and breathing heavily on her bunk. I knelt down by Celia, giving her shoulder a gentle shake. "Hey! Wake up!"

Celia groaned. "Why? What's wrong?"

"I'm home."

"I figured."

"I don't want to exaggerate," I whispered. "but he's the most perfect man ever on the face of the earth. So if you actually created him in a lab for me, don't spoil it."

She snorted and rolled over. "Okay. I won't."

"I'll let you go back to sleep."

"I appreciate that."

Naturally, we discussed the date in greater detail the next morning.

"He's super hot," Margot declared. "You should totally make it official."

"We're going out again Saturday." A smile spread across my face, and I gave Celia a gentle nudge with my elbow. "I don't know that I've thanked you properly for insisting we come to Austin."

"I imagine you should also thank me for deciding against stopping for a longer dinner that night in San Antonio the way I wanted to. If we'd come in any later, Sean might not have been there to see us and stop to help."

"You're right. You're the best sister ever. And not just because you loaned me your wrap."

"It flatters your coloring better, anyway. I'm glad you had a good time."

The look crossed her face again, the faraway look that flashed across her face every time she thought of Teddy. I waited to see if she'd say something, if there was something she wanted to talk to me about. But instead, she patted my shoulder and rose to put the kettle on.

We drank tea together, the conversation turning to a ballet studio for Margot, looking at restaurant spaces, and the fluctuations of the weather.

Everything but Teddy.

Margot picked out three dance studios to visit, and she and I made plans to visit after school. "And get doughnuts from Gordough's while we're out," she said. "Yelp says we have to."

"If Yelp says," I said, ruffling her curls before glancing at the clock. "It's time to get you to school. Are your things together?"

They weren't, so I gathered my keys and purse while she clambered back upstairs.

"Are you okay?" I asked Celia as I stuffed my feet into shoes. "You seem . . . quiet."

"I'm fine," she answered. "Want to look at some more locations today? Chad said there were a couple places."

"Of course."

Margot ran back down the stairs, backpack in hand. "I'm ready!"

I shrugged into my coat. "Let's go, kid." I met Celia's eyes. "Be back in a little bit."

Margot and I left together, but as we climbed into the truck, I couldn't shake the sense of worry for Celia.

∞

"You told them we'd be there for lunch?" I asked Celia two Saturdays later. "I'd planned on pruning the tea plants and working on new blends today."

Celia arched an eyebrow. "You're awfully whiny for someone who had yet another best date ever last night."

I took a deep breath. "I— You're not wrong. But do we have to?"

"Nina's cousin is coming, remember?"

"Ooh, the cousin." I flopped into the armchair by the window. "I forgot. About the cousin."

"Yes, well, Nina didn't."

"Mmm. Hey—when are we going to look at more tea-salon locations? I've got a bunch more orders to fill, and I'm running out of space."

"I can talk to Chad about it, see if anything new is available."

"Let's do that. Soon. The Vandermeides are being very good to us, but seriously—we need our own place."

"Yeah," Celia answered, noncommittally. I squinted at her but said nothing.

Disconcerted, I spent the remaining morning hours carefully pruning my tea plants, checking over the leaves and the soil, trimming as necessary.

The day had just begun to heat up when I heard footsteps behind me. I started and turned to see Ian's friend Beckett.

I took him in even as I took breaths to calm myself. "Oh, hey," I said. "Sorry, I wasn't expecting anyone over here." I took in his shorts and button-down shirt, his metal prosthetic leg reflecting sunlight back at me. "Can I help you with something?"

"Didn't mean to startle you," he said with a grimace. "I was just on a walk around the property."

"I'm fine," I assured him as my heart rate slowed to its normal pace.

"These are your tea plants?"

"They are," I said, plucking a young leaf and handing it to him. "That's what tea comes from—the buds and young leaves."

He examined it, running his fingers over the soft underside. "Really?"

"Yup. What makes them tea is how they're dried and oxidized."

He handed the leaf back to me. "I know these are important to you. I'll let you keep it."

"There will be more," I said with a smile before examining what I thought might be a caterpillar but turned out to be a trick of the light. "They seem to like the heat here, but I've got to be careful to keep the soil moist enough."

"I'm sure."

He stood there looking at the plants. I kept working, checking over the leaves for pests, examining the soil in each pot. But after a while, the silence made me itch. "Good walk?"

"Good enough," he said, nodding. "Sorry, I'll leave you to it."

"Are you coming to lunch this afternoon?"

"What's that?"

"Lunch? With the Vandermeides? Nina's cousin, Lucinda. Or . . . something like that."

His mouth twitched. "Lyndsay?"

"Whatever." I picked off two more dead leaves. "I'm in a rotten mood, so I probably shouldn't be in polite company."

He frowned. "Anything wrong?"

"Celia's just . . . I don't know. We were planning on getting things going with a new location pretty quickly, and that didn't pan out. I feel like we're losing momentum, and . . . I guess I'm just worried I might be the only one who cares. I don't know. I'm feeling out of my league here." I snapped my mouth shut. "This is probably very boring for you. Sister problems."

He gave a wry smile. "I never had a sister."

"No? You missed out. Sisters are the best. Though if I were a man, I might not think so."

"I would have liked a sister. My brother and I . . . we weren't close."

I'd never considered myself to be particularly perceptive—not about people, at any rate. People didn't photosynthesize. But Beckett—even I could tell that there was quite a lot of subtext in his statement about his brother.

"Celia and I have always had each other," I said softly, kneeling on the ground. Beckett followed, and I thought I detected a sigh of relief as he sat, cross-legged on the ground.

Then again, he didn't have leaves, so what did I know?

"We always had each other," I repeated, my hands busy with the foliage. "Especially after our mother died and things with our father got . . . complicated. He left . . . not so much for the usual reasons. Margot was eight, and we became her guardians. Our world turned upside down, but we did what we could for her, for each other." I hugged my knees to myself. "Enough about me. How about you? You're trying to turn around your barbecue business, right? At least, Ian said something like that."

"That's right. You know anything about the business?"

"Barbecue?" I snorted. "Nope. Not something the Bay is famous for. You might have Celia look over your books; she's a whiz. If you need to overhaul your drinks or desserts, I'm your gal." She winced. "I've also been told I'm good at firing people."

"Oh?"

"We hired seasonal staff over the summer, sometimes. It can work out, but sometimes . . . well, let's say I'm good at spotting a problem person and letting them go."

"I can't see Celia enjoying that role."

"Nope. She's a soft touch." I yanked off the last of the leaves I intended to harvest for the night, and straightened. "But if you need a hand, let me know."

"I might just take you up on that."

Callum smiled, and I noticed, maybe not for the first time, that he had a nice smile.

∞

I sat in the corner of the dining room, staring daggers at the back of my sister's right shoulder.

She sat next to Lyndsay, rapt.

And she was *talking*. Talking, to Lyndsay Stahl.

I wouldn't have minded if they'd been talking about the weather or the molding in the dining room. But I heard Celia say Teddy's name, and in that moment I felt myself freeze over.

Celia wouldn't talk to me about Teddy, but she'd talk to Lyndsay. It might have hurt less if it had been, say, Nina. Or Pilar. Or even Mariah, if Mariah would condescend to listen to such things. But in the last two hours, I'd reached the firm and irrevocable conclusion that Lyndsay was the worst.

It wasn't just Celia; everyone in the house—save Pilar—seemed enamored with her. Even Margot pulled out a few ballet steps to impress her.

Lyndsay appeared thrilled, but the thing was, she reminded me uncomfortably of the people who used to cozy up to Dad. They'd flatter him because they wanted something from him. None of Lyndsay's smiles quite reached her eyes.

For her part, Lyndsay spent plenty of time cozying up to Mariah. If Lyndsay was managing social media for a finance tech start-up, she wasn't a dummy. Silicon Valley social media was a cutthroat world.

I didn't know what Lyndsay wanted, but she wanted it hard, and Mariah was the most willing target I'd ever seen. Lyndsay asked after Ian and Mariah's four children, and when Mariah paraded them out, Lyndsay complimented them and played with them for an hour.

Which, under different circumstances, might have been charming.

But Lyndsay kept glancing at Mariah to make sure she was watching. If Mariah's attention shifted to, say, Pilar, Lyndsay's voice rose. She'd call out a child's name, toss one of the small ones into the air, or start singing a song from *Frozen*. It felt as though she'd looked up the definition of a manic pixie dream girl and intended to live it out in Technicolor.

What made it worse was that nobody else seemed to notice her ploy. Well, maybe Beckett did, but if she'd turned his head, I would have been surprised.

She didn't seem his type, not that I had much of an idea what constituted his type.

But the others? They thought she was so charming and so free and so lovely, and it all made me want to throw up.

I tried giving her the benefit of the doubt. For the first half hour.

And truly, thirty minutes of patience, from me, is generous. Lyndsay used up all my generosity—possibly a month's supply—by the end of those thirty minutes. She was so saccharine to Mariah yet barely gave Pilar the time of day. Her attention-seeking behavior was too consistent, her tone of voice too sweetly measured considering the level of dirt and hair pulling she endured.

She was undoubtedly playing a long game. I just had no idea what it was.

Beckett, lucky man, had swung through the doors looking for a bite of lunch. And then he'd swung back out, before having to make too much conversation with Lyndsay.

I edged my way to the corner, where I could pull out my phone and be moderately rude, rather than completely rude.

Nina's cousin is here, I texted Sean. *She's dreadful.*

A moment, and then a flashing notification light. *Want me to rescue you?*

I shot a quick glance at Celia. Celia would hate it if I bailed on an event with the Vandermeides.

Sure, I texted back. *And by "sure," I mean "as soon as you can, please and thank you."*

I'll be there, came the reply. *Hang tight.*

I tried and failed to keep the smile from taking over my face.

"What are you smiling about, there?" Nina called out from across the room.

"The weather is nice," I answered, as benignly as possible. "It's . . . sunny."

Celia looked over her shoulder at me, her face quizzical.

"It *is* a lovely day," Lyndsay trilled. "The colors in this room look so nice in the natural light. Did you design the room, Mrs. Vandermeide?"

I used every ounce of self-restraint to keep my groan on the inside.

The minutes crawled by until the bell at the door rang. Pilar set down her tray of sweet teas to answer the door, and moments later Sean Willis strode in, hat in hand.

He greeted everyone, working his way through the room with a series of firm handshakes and broad smiles. Sean saved me for last, placing a kiss on my cheek. "I broke speed limits," he whispered into my ear. "Did I get here in time?"

"Only just," I whispered back. "Are you giving excuses, or am I?"

"I wanted to see you—no excuses necessary." He squeezed my hand before turning back to the room. "I'm stealing Jane away," he said, his voice warm and confident. I would have done whatever he wanted, and I hated being told what to do.

Nina pressed her hand to her heart.

That, or her left underwire gave out. But she was smiling, so likely the former. "Have fun, you two crazy kids!"

I didn't dare look at Celia as we waved good-bye, half running from the room.

Pear and Earl Grey Tea Pies to Go

For the pie dough

2 ½ cups unbleached all-purpose flour, plus more for dusting the
    work surface

14 tablespoons cold salted butter, cut into ¼-inch pieces

8–10 tablespoons ice water

For the egg wash

1 egg, lightly beaten

1 teaspoon water

For the filling

4 cups pears, peeled, cored, and sliced

¼ cup sugar

1 ½ tablespoons cornstarch

1 teaspoon lemon juice

¼ teaspoon lemon zest

½ teaspoon of Earl Grey tea, finely ground

For the glaze

1 cup powdered sugar

2 ½ tablespoons strong brewed Earl Grey tea

To make the pastry, cut the butter into the flour until the mixture resembles coarse crumbs. This can also be done with a food processor, pulsing in short bursts.

Sprinkle 8 tablespoons ice water over the mixture, mixing with a fork until the dough begins to cling and form. If it remains dry, add the remaining ice water 1 teaspoon at a time—the dough should hold together without being either crumbly or tacky.

Shape the dough into two discs, cover them with plastic wrap, and refrigerate for at least an hour to allow the dough to rest.

Preheat the oven to 400°F. Line a baking sheet with parchment paper.

Prepare the egg wash, stirring together the beaten egg with the water.

In a large bowl, toss the pears, sugar, cornstarch, lemon juice, lemon zest and ground tea together.

Roll out the dough on a lightly floured surface until it's about $^1/_{16}$-inch thick. Cut the dough into 5- to 6-inch squares—you'll get between 8 and 10. Brush the edges with the egg wash, and spoon on 3–4 tablespoons of pear mixture. Place a second pastry square directly over the pear filling, and press the edges of pastry together to seal into a pocket. Use a fork to crimp the edges of the pocket, and pierce 3 or 4 holes in the top of each pie.

Lightly brush the top of each pie with egg wash. Place on a baking sheet and bake for 20–25 minutes, or until the tops are golden brown. Move the pies onto a wire rack and allow to cool.

For the Earl Grey tea glaze, mix together the brewed tea and powdered sugar with a fork. Drizzle over the top of the cooled pies and serve, or save for your next getaway—they'll keep in the fridge for up to 1 week.

Makes 8-10 pies.

13

Texas does not, like any other region, simply have indigenous dishes. It proclaims them. It congratulates you, on your arrival, at having escaped from the slop pails of the other forty-nine states.

—ALISTAIR COOKE

Callum

I was hiding, though I tried to be discreet about it. Begrudging Ian a new dinner guest was petty of me, all things considered. But Lyndsay Stahl reminded me of the women who often chased after military men, only to flit to the next guy when they found out what a military life—and salary—entailed.

No good could come from that one.

Watching Jane, I could immediately tell that Lyndsay landed on her last nerve. But as I watched Jane's gaze flit from Celia to Lyndsay, her brows pressing together with that Jane-like intensity, I knew the sight of trouble brewing.

So I wasn't surprised, not really, to see Sean's truck roll up; even less when Jane and Sean emerged from the house, hands clasped, barely containing their laughter.

But still. Still.

From my room upstairs, I could see the way she clutched his hand, the way her head tipped back in laughter.

I moved from the window, my leg aching. Today, the ghost pains shot through my calf, a calf that didn't exist. I walked to the bed and sat down.

She was happy. I should have been happy *for* her, been grateful for anything that put such a wide smile on her face.

Instead, I picked up my phone and dialed Lila's number. The line rang, but I stood up straighter when it connected.

"Hello? Who is this?"

It wasn't Lila's voice, and I could tell because it was, well, male.

"This is Callum Beckett," I answered. Did I have the number wrong? "I'm looking for Lila Branford."

"Do you know where she is?"

My stomach clenched. "No, I don't."

"Lila's missing. I'm her landlord. She skipped town and left this phone behind."

I took a deep breath. "Have the authorities been contacted?"

"Yes, sir, but no one's heard anything. And she's late on her rent."

"Where are you?"

"Austin. I manage the Casa Grande apartments."

I took his name and number and promised to be in touch. Pulling out my computer, I ran a search for Lila's name and the word "missing," and sure enough, there were local reports of a missing woman, aged thirty-three, last seen back in October.

My brain froze.

Lila had been looking for work and now she was missing. My stomach twisted as I thought of Lila as she'd been, the sun glinting on her hair, her eyes laughing, her arms over her head as she danced along the sidewalk. I thought of her after her marriage to Cameron, expensively clad, expression pinched.

Her life must have taken a very difficult turn.

I knew Lila didn't have much family to speak of. My family had been all she'd had. And now my family was just . . . me.

Maybe she had other people. I didn't know. We hadn't seen each other for years. Either way, I settled at the desk in my room and picked up my phone again.

14

What better way to suggest friendliness—and to
create it—than with a cup of tea?

—J. GRAYSON LUTTRELL

Jane

Sean and I climbed into his truck, and as we sped down the road, I found I
didn't care where we were going. Music played over the speakers, and I took
deep breaths as I felt my shoulders relax. I was *away*. Away, and with Sean.

We weren't very far away when he pulled into a long drive. "This is where
I'm staying," he said, pointing ahead to an expansive house, one not unlike Ian
and Mariah's home.

"That is massive," I said, taking in the columns, wraparound porch, and
coordinating balcony.

"It's my great-aunt's," he said. "She's elderly, and I help take care of it."

"That's good of you." I turned to look at him, enjoying the sight of his
dimples, the way his hair fell over his forehead.

"She doesn't have a lot of family," he said. "She's lonely. And she wants
me to inherit the house, so I figure if I can run the place now, I'm set for
later."

I peered out the window. "That's a lot of house to inherit."

"Perfect for raising a family, I figure." He turned and winked at me. "Lots
of room to roller-skate."

"Depends on the floors," I said without thinking.

"Pardon?"

"You know . . . the floors, if they're smooth or not." The floors of my childhood home flashed before my eyes. The travertine in the foyer, the original wood in the upstairs halls. Even after we rolled the rugs away, the way the wood ridged had made it rough going for Rollerblades. Instead, we rolled down the sidewalk, then changed into our lace-up Keds to hike back up, only to roll down again with our hands in the air.

We'd only scraped our knees a dozen times.

Those were happy memories, but I kept them to myself as Sean parked his truck inside the cavernous garage.

"Is your aunt home?" I asked as he helped me down from the seat.

"No, she's visiting friends in Highland Park. Outside of Dallas," he added, seeing my blank expression. He pulled one of my curls, grinning as it sprung back into place. "Surely you're not afraid to be alone with me."

"As long as she doesn't mind a stray visitor . . ."

"Never. She'd love you."

I didn't feel lovable, not in that moment. We walked together into the house, and I took in the soaring ceilings, but saw my old home in San Francisco instead.

Would his aunt like me if she knew about my father? Would Sean?

I'd experienced it over and over as the years had unfolded. As soon as people knew, things changed. When I left school, and Celia left her firm, very few of our friends from our former life stayed in contact. We made new friends—Celia especially—with people who didn't read the business section of any periodical, people with no connection to our former life. They knew our mother died and then our father lost his job, that we were taking care of our sister while our dad was traveling, that Celia and I worked hard to make ends meet—and that was enough. We didn't fill in any remaining blanks.

The rooms opened one into another at Sean's aunt's home. He took me to his rooms upstairs; I glanced into the space where he slept, and followed him into the one with his instruments and recording equipment.

"So you're a proper rock star. Is that what you're telling me?" I asked teasingly.

He slung a guitar strap over his head and strummed a few chords. "Do you have a thing for rock stars? Because if you do, the answer is yes."

"I had a crush on the first chair, once, in college. He was an oboist."

"You had a crush on an *oboist*?"

"He had lovely hands, played with such feeling."

"I'd respect it if he were a trumpeter."

I rolled my eyes. "Trumpeters? Drunks, every last one."

"What instrument were you playing?"

"Clarinet. But also the viola."

"That's right. You can play wind, strings, and piano. Did everyone hate you?"

I shrugged and looked away. I hadn't been extremely well liked in the music department, at least not by the other students. All the professors, however, had known me by name.

"I would have liked you," Sean promised. "Let's go outside; I'll show you the grounds."

He grabbed my hand, pulling me back out to the hallway.

"Are they particularly scenic in February?"

"I think so. And it's not cold out, anyway."

We stepped through the french doors; the bright afternoon had begun to dim, but white lights twisted in the bare branches of the trees twinkled in the last daylight.

"You're right," I said, looking around, enjoying the breeze that tousled my hair. "It's lovely."

"The lights stay in the trees year-round," he said. "My idea."

"You just didn't want to take them out after the holidays."

From his sly sideways smile, I knew I had hit the mark.

"You probably talked her into white lights, rather than multicolor," I guessed.

"She finds colored lights vulgar."

"But year-round white lights are fine?"

"She likes the lights in Paris."

"Can't argue with that."

He reached for my waist, then pulled me close before pressing a gentle kiss to my lips. "You seemed upset earlier, before we came outside. Everything okay?"

I looked up at him, at his eyes that radiated sincerity.

"It just . . . made me remember things."

"Your oboist?"

"No. Well, yes, but I don't care about that." A deep breath. "My sister and I grew up in a big old house in San Francisco. It was my mother's family's house, in the family for five generations. A long time, by Californian standards."

I gave him the abbreviated, prettified version of our life in California, covering basics but skirting details.

His hand tightened on my waist. "I'm so sorry."

"The three of us—we made it through. But it was embarrassing and hard, losing mom and the house, our respectability."

"You don't have to tell me. Not if you don't want to."

I nodded, and pressed my head against his shoulder. "We're fine. You don't need to feel sorry for us."

He snorted. "I don't see you as a victim, Jane. Anything but."

"Thanks," I said with a crooked smile. "I feel like I lost Celia, once we left California. Today just rubbed salt into the wound."

"I don't think you've lost Celia."

"She doesn't talk to me. Not like she used to. And we're *everything* to each other; at least we always have been."

He wound his fingers through mine. "I think you still are. *But* you have me too, you know."

I looked up at him. "We haven't known each other very long," I said. It was more of a reminder for him than me. I knew how I felt about him, but did he?

"Long enough," he said, before cupping my face, pulling me, my lips, gently toward him.

We kissed under the twinkling lights in the branches of his aunt's garden, and if a late winter wind blew through, I didn't notice. Not for several minutes, anyway, but even the warmth of love cannot overcome nature; Sean insisted we go inside once I began to shiver.

He made coffee with a massive Keurig, then presented it to me in a mug I recognized to be Wedgewood.

"Are you sure it's okay for me to be here? I don't want to intrude on your aunt's space."

He shook his head. "She wants me to be at home. One day, it'll be mine, after all."

I looked around. "And you'll keep it?"

He nodded. "Might not be five generations old—most of this area was built up in the nineties, after all—but it's got good bones. I like Austin. And," he added, "those floors are marble smooth. Perfect for roller skates."

"Do children even roller-skate anymore?" I asked dryly.

"Everything old is new again," he replied with a wink, pulling on one of my curls again.

"You realize I used to backhand the kids who pulled my curls in school."

"Oh?" He leaned in, running a thumb over my brow, my cheekbone, my jawline. "I'll stop if you want me to."

I lifted my lips to his. "I'll keep you posted."

He kissed me back, deeply. How coffee on his breath tasted good, I didn't know. But I already knew him to be magic.

We were interrupted by a rumble.

Sean chuckled. "Hungry?"

"That was my stomach, wasn't it?" I covered my face with my hand. "How embarrassing."

"You're not the one who should be embarrassed; I should have fed you. It's getting near supper, after all."

I smiled at the way he said *supper*.

He looked around for his keys. "Want to head into town? I know of a great little taco truck."

"Sure," I said, and within minutes we were off again, together in his truck.

Much later that night, my stomach full of tacos and butterflies, Sean dropped me off just outside the casita.

The trouble, I realized, with trying to sneak into a one-bedroom guest-house was the one-bedroom bit. Not that I'd ever tried to return home to our San Francisco apartment unnoticed, but if I *had* at least I would have had the benefit of my own bedroom door.

While Margot slept as heavily as a coma patient, Celia tended to sleep like a cat.

But, I reasoned as I reached for my key, maybe she'd tired herself out so much from her meaningful tête-à-tête with Lyndsay that she'd be dead asleep.

I slipped inside, startled to find Celia curled up in one of the two club chairs.

"What are you doing?" I blurted out. "Why aren't you in bed?"

"I could ask you the same thing," she said, blinking as she sat up.

"Sean and I were out," I answered, defensive. "You could have texted, if you were worried."

"Would you have answered?"

"Of course!" I said, stung.

She hugged her arms to herself. "I just didn't know where you were."

"Celia, we're not seventeen anymore."

"I know we're not. But we're in a new city, and it would be nice to know where you are."

"So you want me to communicate?" I asked, my voice cutting. "Share with you? Want me to tell you all about my hurts, hopes, and dreams?"

I snapped my mouth shut, trying and failing to regain control.

All I knew was that it was late, I was tired, and after she ignored me this afternoon in favor of Lyndsay the Worst, coming home to Celia the Concerned Sibling was a bridge too far.

"I'm fine," I snapped. "And I'm going to bed."

"Jane—"

"Don't worry, you won't have to tell me any bedtime stories or bring me any glasses of water. I'm capable of seeing myself upstairs."

From my peripheral vision, I could see Celia open her mouth to protest. But I used the last of my pique to shut myself in the bathroom, closing out any objections she might have made.

15

There is a freedom you feel the closer you get
to Austin.

—WILLIE NELSON

Callum

Phone in hand, I decided that enough was enough. Lila was missing, and it was
time to act. As it turned out, hiring a private investigator was not hard. Didn't
even have to go to the guy's office—I just had to pick up the phone and read
off my billing information.

"Tell me everything you know," the PI said.

His name was Clint.

So I told him about Roy, about Lila's call asking for a job, about the missing persons case.

"You should know," he said. "Some people just don't wanna be found."

"She asked for a waitressing job with the business her ex-husband once co-
owned," I told him firmly. "That's not someone who wants to disappear. That's
someone who's trying not to fall through the cracks."

After that phone call, I left the house for my therapy appointment.

It was only the second appointment I'd had since arriving in Austin, and I
was still deciding how I felt about it. I'd never seen a therapist, never paid a
person to hear about my troubles or offer counsel.

But all things considered, now seemed to be the right time to start.

My therapist, Beverly, welcomed me into her office.

"How are you, Callum?" she asked, gesturing toward the loose-springed
sofa. She wore a caftan, per usual, a pencil holding her curls back.

I sat awkwardly, unable to find a comfortable position for either leg. "Fine. Everything's fine."

"How are you sleeping?"

My jaw shifted as I looked for words. Words that might be truthful, but meant something other than the truth.

"You're not sleeping," she said, eyebrow lifted.

"I sleep some," I said.

"Trouble falling asleep?"

"Sometimes."

"Trouble staying asleep?"

"Sometimes," I said again.

"Nightmares?"

"Fewer," I said truthfully, grateful to have something positive to report.

"That's good," she said. "Are you still swimming at night?"

I regretted having admitted to the midnight swims. "I am."

"And they help?"

"They do. I can move better." Not the same—not by a long shot. But better. "And I walk during the day."

"How about social engagements? Are you seeing people?"

"I'm still staying with my friend Ian. And Ian has extra guests too, so there are more people."

"Oh? Tell me about them."

I shifted in my seat. "Ian's mother-in-law, but then she lives there most of the time. And then there's Ian's cousins." Celia and Jane's faces floated behind my eyes. "Three sisters. The older two are adults, the youngest is in her teens. The oldest is quiet, reserved. Self-possessed, but reserved. The middle sister . . . she's different."

"Different?"

"She grows tea," I said. "And she brews tea the way musicians play music. It's important to her. She's serious until she laughs, and when she laughs all you want is to laugh too."

Unless she was laughing with Sean. When that happened, I felt a little sick to my stomach.

"Do you? Laugh with her?"

"I don't know," I said. "Things are strained with her and her sister, so I guess she's not laughing as much. I guess she just looks at the world differently. She's interesting."

"Are you interested in her?"

I shook my head. "She's seeing someone else. It looks serious."

"But what about you? Are you interested?"

"It doesn't matter."

"Why not?"

"Look, the guy she's with looks like he just walked away from the casting session of a superhero movie."

She folded her arms and looked me over.

I got it. Sure, I was fit, though I ran wiry where Sean was broad. But it wasn't a matter of musculature. "Superheroes have both legs."

"Not Flash Thompson."

"Pardon?"

"Classmate of Peter Parker, Iraq war veteran. Government put him in the Venom suit; he got a spin-off series in 2011. In 2016, he got prosthetic legs." Her mouth quirked upward. "Women read comics too."

I cleared my throat. "Of course, ma'am."

"There are other people for whom I would say that yes, an amputation is a disability, but I'll be honest. I don't think you're one of them, long term." She leaned forward. "You're strong, you're athletic, and you're a fighter. I think you have more of a choice than perhaps you realize. I think you have the ability to make it simply a trait."

"I'm only connected to the ground with one organic leg."

"But you're also connected to the ground with a limb made from titanium. That's sturdy stuff, isn't it? Just . . . think about it. Some things aren't necessarily better or worse, just different."

I nodded, though on the inside I rolled my eyes. Being an amputee would never not be worse. That was all there was to it. Maybe if Beverly had fewer limbs, she'd understand.

"If you were to pursue this Jane—or any other woman—how would you do it?"

"I don't know, ma'am." I leaned into the sofa. "When I was on active duty, romance wasn't a part of my plan."

"When were you last in a relationship?"

There had been women along the years, friends of buddies' girlfriends. It had never gone past flirtatious dates. But relationships? Those took time, investment.

"It's been a while," I muttered.

But she had me thinking. Had there been anyone? Anyone other than Lila?

"When we first met, you described your relationship with your family as"—she flipped through the papers in my file—"'not great.'"

"I remember."

She lifted her eyebrows.

"I, uh, thought we were going to talk about the accident during these sessions," I said. "The war and all that."

"Consider looking at it this way," she said. "If you drop a watermelon onto a mattress from twenty feet, what do you think would happen?"

"It's going to bounce and break."

"Probably, yes. But what if it were dropped straight onto concrete?"

I didn't like where this was headed. "It would probably shatter. Don't know. Haven't dropped any watermelons from a third-story window lately."

"You might try it sometime," she said, her eyes twinkling. "Obviously this is a metaphor."

I worked my jaw, my patience wearing thin. "You don't say."

"Stick with me. Some people have lives and backgrounds that have created a protective barrier. They absorb emotional impact differently. That doesn't mean there isn't damage, but there is a difference."

"You're saying that because of my dad and my brother, I'm concrete and I shatter watermelons?"

"I'm saying it's going to hit you harder than someone with a different, more supportive family of origin."

"There is no 'more supportive.' That implies that there was support to begin with." I took a deep breath. "Look, ma'am, with all due respect, growing up with my family was tough, but others had it tougher. My dad didn't beat me or anything. I learned to be self-reliant, take care of myself—learned it sooner than my peers."

"You're not solid concrete," Beverly clarified. "You're right; you have an impressive skill set. But I do think you learned that you can't rely on people and have difficulty building and maintaining relationships."

"I've got Ian. We've known each other fourteen years."

"Which one of you picks up the phone most often?"

I frowned. Of course it was Ian. He was always the one sending e-mails while I was overseas, encouraging me to stay in his home when I came back stateside.

I hadn't, of course. Ian lived in Austin, and Austin was what I'd been working to get away from. And yet, we remained friends over the years, with him making sure we stayed in touch. Had I ever called him first?

"How many of your colleagues from your unit have you been in contact with lately?"

I thought about the e-mails in my in-box, the texts, contact requests on social media. "There have been some."

"That's good." She glanced at the clock. "Let's wrap things up today. Just keep this in mind—your father and brother didn't treat you as though you had value. But you do. And you continue to, despite the amputation, despite having to leave the marines. You matter."

Despite my resolution to remain stoic in the face of watermelons, I still felt a lump in my throat. "Thank you, ma'am. That's very kind of you to say."

∞

I drove to Roy's house and pulled into the driveway beside his Cadillac. His wife, Betsy, opened the door. "Ma'am," I said, reaching up to remove a hat that wasn't on my head. Still hadn't gotten used to being bareheaded all the time. "Is Roy around?"

"He's at the smokers, out back," she said with a smile. "He'll be glad to see you."

"I'll be glad to see him."

"You tell him I'll be glad to see him too, when he can pull himself away from all of that dead cow."

I felt my face crack into an unfamiliar smile. "I forgot you're a vegetarian, Miss Betsy."

"Mmm hmm."

My eyes darted to the backyard gate before returning to Roy's wife. "That . . . ah . . . that work out okay?"

She tipped her head back and laughed. "Are you asking how I put up with him?"

"I . . . ah . . ." I hadn't *meant* to, but . . .

She leaned forward. "It's not easy. I do pray a lot. But he's a good man, and he smokes tofu for me."

"Really? That any good?"

"You come over for dinner next week. Decide for yourself."

I ducked my head. "I'll do that, ma'am."

"Run along, now. Go find him."

Being a good southern boy, I did as I was told, following the stone pavers around the side of the porch-lined house to the gate.

I found Roy where Betsy promised I would, in the middle of tending to gigantic cuts of brisket.

He lifted a hand when he saw me approach. "What brings you to my office?"

"Your wife reminded me she's a vegetarian."

He shook his head. "I keep praying for her."

"She says the same thing about you. Do you really smoke tofu for her?"

"When you have a wife, you'll understand. Love makes you do crazy things. And . . . I like to think of smoked tofu as a gateway to smoked pork belly."

I sucked in a breath. "I could do pork belly around now."

"Couldn't we all."

"Except Betsy."

Roy chuckled.

Standing next to him, I felt a dozen questions buzzing at the tip of my tongue.

Was my dad really that detached? Did my childhood break me?

Instead, I asked if he'd join me as I looked over the books for the food ordering at Smoky Top. I'd been able to arrange for repairs and fresh paint at various locations, but the calculations involved in ordering for a restaurant were still something I was working to get a handle on.

"Of course," he said.

"I don't know anything about the restaurant business," I said. "I'm not Cameron."

Roy harrumphed.

I told him about Lila's disappearance, about the private investigator I'd hired.

He closed up the smoker, set his tongs down, and gave me an approving nod. "That's real decent of you."

Without meaning to, I stood taller. "We're all she's got left, far as I know."

As I made the statement, I thought back to my therapist's words. Who did I have left? I'd been so concerned about Lila—and rightfully so—but had I missed the fact that maybe I wasn't any less alone? I had Roy and Ian . . .

There were the guys I'd been overseas with, but so many of them had homes and wives and families, entire lives. The ones that were still alive, that is. The ones I hadn't failed.

I did my best to shrug it off, to do what my therapist told me to do, to live in the moment. A deep breath, an assessment of my surroundings. Roy's backyard, the scent of smoking beef. Betsy inside.

By the time my heart rate seemed to return to normal, I sensed Roy's gaze on me.

He didn't say a word, but I could feel him assessing my body language, my face. Did he think I might be dangerous?

Some days, I couldn't say I wasn't. At least my squirrelly sense of balance made me less of a threat than I was in my active-duty days.

"If the PI doesn't find anything on Lila, I'll look myself," I said after too long.

Roy nodded. "You're a good man."

Hearing Roy say so, it seemed almost possible.

Betsy wouldn't hear of me not staying for dinner, despite my protests that it was late notice.

"What?" she asked, eyebrows high and querulous. "You don't think we've got enough barbecue prepared?"

I couldn't argue.

The Vandermeide house was lit when I returned, and I wondered if everyone was downstairs. My heart thudded in anticipation and dread. I didn't feel up to being social any more than I had to, but if Jane was with them? I'd muddle through.

I parked in the garage and let myself in. The door from the garage dropped me into the middle of an expansive hallway.

Shrieks of laughter echoed off the stone tiles. I listened for Jane's laugh. She gave it sparingly, but when it arrived I always found it worth the wait.

None of Jane's laughter, but plenty of Nina's—not much of a surprise. The woman gave a whoop of delight when she saw me, and despite my plans to be antisocial for the rest of the night, her enthusiasm brought a smile to my face.

"Mr. Beckett! We were just eating cake, would you like a slice?"

I couldn't fathom eating anything more after my dinner with Roy and Betsy, but I knew better than to refuse. "I could eat some," I said when I was close enough to scan the room. Celia, Margot, Lyndsay, Mariah, Nina, and Ian.

But not Jane.

Was it too late to turn down cake? Even as I wondered, I knew the answer.

Mariah handed me a delicate plate of Texas sheet cake with a smile; I took a seat in one of the few remaining chairs.

"What's your sister up to tonight?" I asked Celia, who sat beside me.

Celia's face flushed. "She's out tonight."

"Out with Sean Willis!" Nina called out with a hoot. "My, those two have been joined at the hip. It's been many years since I've seen a couple so attached."

"How long have they been together?" Lyndsay asked.

"A couple weeks," Celia answered, her smile tight at the corners.

"It's a good story," Nina said. "He rescued them when their truck broke down on the freeway. Made sure they got here safe and sound."

Lyndsay pressed a hand to her heart. "That is really romantic," she said with a sigh.

"Must be romantic," Ian said. "We've not seen much of either of them for some time."

"Have they moved in together?" Lyndsay asked Celia. "That's very quick."

"No, not at all," Celia said quickly, shaking her head. "It's true Jane spends a good deal of her time with Sean, yes, and that's her right to do so. But she's also home, you know," she said, eyes wide. "We have an online tea business, and she fills orders, gets them sent out, or tries new tea blends. She's just more introverted."

Lyndsay tipped her head. "Bless her heart."

My eyes shot to Celia, whose expression I couldn't read.

I already had a low opinion of Lyndsay Stahl, but it managed to sink still lower; Celia might not know southern women, but I did. Lyndsay wasn't blessing Jane's heart. She was casting deep doubt on the veracity of Celia's words.

Anger rose in my chest on behalf of both sisters. How long did Nina's shrew of a cousin plan to be in town? I placed my cake plate on the accent table nearest my chair. "It might not be football season," I said, "but I think we can find something else to talk about rather than Jane, especially while she's not here to weigh in."

Lyndsay flushed but said nothing.

"I agree, Beckett," Nina said. "Better to wait until she can join us. I think we'd all enjoy an update about the delicious Mr. Willis from the source. And Lyndsay hasn't had Jane's tea." She leaned toward Lyndsay. "Jane makes the most delicious, authentic tea."

"That sounds . . . so nice," Lyndsay said, her nostrils flaring.

Celia finished her cake and handed her plate to a waiting Pilar. When she rose, announcing her and Margot's departure for the evening, I offered to walk them back to the guesthouse.

She surprised me when she accepted; I'd anticipated a protest that the guesthouse wasn't far at all. Margot sprinted ahead, eager to get back to her computer, Celia explained.

Celia and I walked across the wide lawn together, the lights from the house providing just enough glow to show the way to the tiny guesthouse.

"Is everything all right with you and Jane?" I asked as we crossed the lawn.

"Well enough," Celia answered.

"That doesn't sound convincing."

"I'm beginning to think we shouldn't have left San Francisco. There have been changes I didn't anticipate when we came here."

"Any luck looking for a tea . . . shop . . . place?" I asked awkwardly, trying to find the right words. It wasn't a café, at any rate. I knew that much.

Celia shrugged. "Still looking for the right place. There aren't a lot of suitable places at the moment, locations that don't need a lot of remodeling. We're looking at more locations soon, maybe we'll find something."

"You're looking for a big place, or little?"

"Little, but with enough kitchen for Jane. She needs space to be creative."

"What about you?"

She smiled. "I like the people. I'm fine as long as we have customers."

"I hope you find something soon."

"Thanks," she said, a smile spreading across her face as if the thought of that hope made her happier. "Me too. I feel like if we got back to life as it used to be—or something closer to it—things might go back to normal."

I smiled and said something in agreement before seeing her inside. But as I walked away, I questioned the possibility of it.

16

The proper, wise balancing of one's whole life may depend
upon the feasibility of a cup of tea at an unusual hour.

—ARNOLD BENNETT

Jane

The traces of the dream clung as morning light filtered through my eyelids.
Macarons. Chamomile and honey-flavored macarons. They came to me in a
dream, the way some inspirations snuck in.

I woke and reached for the tiny notepad I kept on the windowsill beside
my bed. Times like this, I missed having an actual nightstand. Using the windowsill felt like being back at summer camp. It was fine in the short term, but
at a certain point I felt that perhaps I'd aged out of the summer-camp and
bunk-bed lifestyle.

Chamomile honey macaron, orange blossom center?

I squinted at my writing. If I could read it even ten minutes from now, I'd
be a very lucky woman.

Speaking of being lucky, I checked my phone and found a morning text
from Sean.

He was amazing. Without a doubt, amazing.

These days, I spent very little time at home. Didn't want to, not really.
Cooking at the guesthouse wasn't ideal; the oven ran hot, the stove only had
two burners. And the dishwasher—which I was grateful for—was only half
size, so if I were to do any large-scale work, I'd find myself washing the larger
cookware in the bathtub.

But Sean's place?

Huge kitchen, Carrara marble countertops, oak cabinetry. It was comfortably worn-in. A real-estate agent might have advised an update, but I thought the scarred and stained counters and cabinetry gave the space character.

Sean's aunt was traveling again. I hadn't met her yet; she'd come and gone the weekend after I'd visited, this time on a trip to northern Italy. The way Sean had described her, I'd envisioned an older, more white-haired version of the woman whose portrait graced the mantelpiece, an elegant creature standing next to a dignified, mustachioed man.

But the way she traveled, I figured I had to have gotten it at least a little wrong.

Sean cared for the estate in her absence, tending to the lawn, planting bulbs, trimming back trees and hedges while they were dormant. While he worked outside, I filled orders and tested recipes, coming up with new scone mixes to offer our customers, dreaming up new tea blends. Periodically, Chad would e-mail a restaurant space, and Celia and I would discuss over text if it was worth driving by. More often than not, the answer was a disappointing no.

But at the end of the day, Sean and I would drive to the post office together, and I'd send out the day's orders.

It was cozy and unexpectedly domestic, and I loved it.

Today, a tinge of anxiety curled in my stomach as I got ready for the day. For the first time, Sean was taking me to a concert. I'd met a couple of his band mates in passing, but tonight was the first night I'd be presented at an event as the *girlfriend*.

That wasn't for hours yet though. Sean and I had plans for the day, me puttering around his kitchen while he practiced. He kissed me when I arrived and quickly took the stand mixer from my arms.

"I don't mind carrying it," I told him, smiling.

"*I* mind you carrying it," he said, setting it onto the kitchen counter.

I knew better than to argue. I set up my workstation and went to work cracking eggs, weighing out almond flour, and milling dried chamomile buds into a fine powder.

Sean perched on the barstool with his guitar, playing riffs and experiment-ing with different interpretations of songs, sometimes playing the same chorus over and over until he decided just how he wanted to do the instrumentation, where to put the pauses, where to build.

There were a few covers, reinterpreted takes on David Bowie and Aero-smith. But most of his songs were originals, ones he'd written by himself or with his friend Todd. They were good. When they played South by Southwest, I had no doubts they'd be a smash.

Soon enough, I piped out the macarons and placed them in the oven.

"Are you bringing those tonight?" he asked, plucking out a chord to accent his words. "For the band?"

I shrugged. "Hadn't thought about it. Would they even like them?"

"They're sweet, aren't they?"

"Well, sure, but if all they want is something sweet, they can go out and buy a doughnut. These are special."

"Don't you make food for people?"

"Yeah. People who like macarons. And things with tea in them."

He laughed. "So I can't have any?"

"You can," I said. "If you ask nicely. And have a documented history of liking macarons."

"I'm not sure about the documentation, but"—Sean gave a slow smile as he leaned closer—"what if I go straight to asking nicely?"

"Do you know how easy it is to ruin macarons? You'll have to make it really nice."

He closed the distance in the space of a heartbeat, likely less, his body pressing against mine, his lips persuasive.

"You don't even like chamomile tea," I murmured.

"Chamomile?" He took an instant step back, eyes crinkled at the corners. "Never mind."

"Very funny." I tugged him back, pressing a kiss to his lips, feeling the thrill of getting to touch him, to be near him.

"How did it work in San Francisco? With you baking for the customers? Did you give them a quiz before deciding if they could order?"

"If only I'd thought of that," I said, ruefully. "No, Celia and I were a team. She gave me some ideas—I'd do a daily scone, a daily tartlet, a daily macaron, that sort of thing. But I could change up the flavors. And if we had a particular hit—we could barely keep the toffee-nut chai scones in the case—she'd help me keep up with the demand. To this day, I can bake them with my eyes closed."

"Would you bake some for me?"

"Do you have toffee?"

His eyes shifted across the kitchen. "I have sugar and butter. You could make it."

"I'm not making toffee to break and put into scones," I retorted dryly. "Not today."

"There's a grocery store down the way."

"I thought you had music to practice."

"I do. I think I'm hungry."

I rolled my eyes and pressed a kiss to his chin. "Eat some lunch, then."

After time and soul searching, I agreed to take a small Tupperware of the macarons to share with Sean's band mates. I *did* want to make a good impression, after all. And the macarons had turned out really well. So well that someone else ought to eat them.

It was a little bit of an "If you make the perfect macaron but no one else tastes it, did it really happen?" sort of situation.

Going to music clubs wasn't my scene in San Francisco. I'd been too busy in the kitchen of Valencia Street Tea. So I dressed for the day in jeans and a black top and simply lined my eyes with extra eyeliner before we left.

Sean's band was playing at the Lucky Lounge, a long, narrow place with the stage at the far end. There was a giant yellow light—thing? I couldn't tell what it was, not from my vantage point. It looked like a benevolent, branded moon shining from behind the performers on the stage.

Sean disappeared into the back. I found a barstool, ordered a ginger ale with a twist of lime, and told the bartender to keep them coming. He thought I was hilarious but obliged and accepted a macaron from the Tupperware.

"That is *good*," he declared. "Your next drink is on the house."

"Thanks," I said, glad to have my own suspicions confirmed.

"You should be selling 'em."

I nodded. "That's the plan. My sister and I will be opening a tea shop. These will be on the menu, I think."

"Tea shop," he said, nodding in consideration as he pulled a pint for another customer. "I'd go to a tea shop for that."

A glimmer of hope curled in my chest, that we'd have willing customers in Austin. "I'll let you know when we open."

He refilled my glass, but the conversation ended when the band began to play. They launched into the first song, a cover to get the crowd going. And it worked—the crowd sang along. After that came a catchy original with an easy, infectious hook, followed by a song with angrier overtones and a driving downbeat.

They worked through their ten-song set efficiently, Sean pausing to introduce the band. They closed with another cover, then unplugged and dismantled with record speed. Made me think of *That Thing You Do* and Tom Hanks's character's advice to run while the crowd still liked them.

Sean came and found me moments later, after the manager cranked up Radiohead over the speakers. I hollered and wrapped my hands around his torso, damp from sweat and sound. "You were amazing!"

He bent low to give me a possessive, celebratory kiss before slinging a sweaty arm around my shoulders. "Guys, you remember Jane," he told the guys behind him, guys my eyes only just became able to focus on.

I nodded a hello, and they nodded in return, the ones closest to me proffering hands. I asked if they were hungry, holding out the macarons.

The guys nearest me each took one, politely, then nibbled at them like they might detonate.

I tried not to feel the pang of rejection; after all, Sean had encouraged me to bring them. I could very well have taken them back to Celia and Margot. Nina probably would have polished off a plate of them without blinking.

Oh well. Maybe homemade pretzels next time? I didn't know. The music-club scene clearly wasn't my world. I knew my way around a concert hall, but this?

One of the men drank his pint in one go.

Nope. Not my world.

I reached to snap the lid back onto the storage container.

"I'll take another," the bartender said. "If you're offering."

"Sure," I called back, over the music.

The bartender grinned, saluting me with the cookie before downing it in a single bite.

At least somebody liked them.

Sean and I returned to the guesthouse late, after swinging back by his home to pick up the kitchen equipment I'd left behind. He groaned, carrying it out. "This mixer is so heavy," he complained. "Are you sure you don't want to leave it here? There's room in the kitchen—for you and the mixer."

"I don't want Celia to worry," I said, recalling the argument we'd had the previous week. "If you're too tired, I can call a rideshare."

"Of course you don't need to call for a car," he said, pressing a kiss to my temple. "I'm happy to drive you."

We drove to the house. Almost all the lights on the property were extinguished for the night. "Thanks for coming tonight," Sean said as he walked me to the door. "Means a lot to me."

"You were great," I said truthfully. "I had a good time."

The second statement was, perhaps, a hair less truthful.

I caught a movement from the corner of my eye. There, by the pool. A figure in the dark.

For a moment, I wondered if there was an intruder on the property. But as my eyes adjusted to the darkness, I noticed that one of the intruder's legs didn't meet the ground. A split second later, I heard a splash.

Sean turned his head in the direction of the pool. "What was that?"

"Something must have fallen into the pool," I hedged. "Like a bird," I added. "We used to get ducks in our water feature, in California."

"Huh." He leaned in for a good-night kiss, which distracted me until he pulled away. "See you tomorrow?"

"I'll text you," I answered. "Good night."

"Good night, Jane." He lifted a hand in a wave.

I reached for the casita door, looking over my shoulder—first at Sean's departing truck, second at the Vandermeides' swimming pool.

Did Callum often swim at night? I knew instinctively that it wouldn't be too cold for him, not really. But somehow just as instinctively, I'd decided to hide it from Sean.

Why was that?

In the chill night air, I could hear rhythmic splashes. Swimming.

Callum was fine. His night swims were his own business.

And still . . .

I stepped inside my house to put the kettle on.

17

Texas is a great state. It's the "Old Man River" of states. No matter who runs it, or what happens to it politically, it just keeps rolling along!

—WILL ROGERS

Callum

One more lap.

One more.

One more.

One. More.

My arms slashed at the water as I fought to wash away the traces of the nightmare. My muscles burned as my arms fought to maintain a straight line, even as my body wanted to veer to the left.

This nightmare had the distinction of being new. The explosion itself remained the same, with a vicious twist—compliments of my mind. It was bad enough remembering the explosion, seeing Reggie's face but being too far to help. In the newest version of the dream?

I saw Jane.

I saw her sisters too and Ian with his family. They were there, and I saw them be torn apart.

I woke up with my heart beating hard in my chest, skin slick with sweat. I didn't even have to think about whether or not to go for a swim. There was no way I'd be sleeping for the rest of the night.

Since I started swimming again, I'd worked my way up to five straight laps across the pool. Tonight? I'd lost count. I simply swam until I was tired enough for the nightmare's horrific images to lose their grip.

In my mind, I could hear my instructors shouting at me, pushing me forward, yelling insults. Finally, I reached the end for the umpteenth time, grasped the rails and launched myself out.

I just made it to one of Mariah's nearby hedges before vomiting. My head swam and my vision narrowed, and I used all of my reserves to stay upright. Minutes passed; I didn't know how many. I concentrated on my breathing and waited for the world to stop spinning.

So when I saw a figure approach, a figure that looked like Jane, I thought my mind might be playing a trick on me. I squeezed my eyes shut in hopes that it might be; the last thing I wanted was Jane Woodward watching me lose dinner and dessert. I'd have to remember to take a pitcher of water out here before anyone rose, to drown out the evidence.

"I brought some tea for you," came a cautious voice, and I knew then it wasn't a figment of my imagination.

"Thanks," I croaked.

"I think you pushed yourself too hard, there. In the pool."

"Probably."

"I brought you my sleep blend. Chamomile, valerian root, bit of orange peel." She thrust the mug into my field of vision. "Rinse your mouth out, if you like."

I straightened carefully, using a trimmed topiary for balance. I took the travel mug without meeting her eyes, sipped, swished, and spat. After a deep breath, I took a sip and swallowed it that time.

It tasted . . . good. Soothing.

Another sip; I felt its warmth deep inside.

"Do you need anything?" she asked. "Did you bring a towel?"

"I— Yeah. I'm sorry." I felt my face flush with deep embarrassment. Here I was, balanced against Ian's landscaping, my scarred stump covered only by the dark of night. My towel and prosthetic waited on the patio chaise, seven feet away. To get it myself, I'd have to do the Amputee Hop in front of Jane. My cheeks and pride burned at the thought.

"My towel," I said, pointing. "And . . . my prosthetic, if you don't mind."

"Of course I don't mind," she said, returning a second later with both items. "You've got to be freezing."

I took the prosthetic first, using practiced motions to fit it over my stump. The towel, I wrapped around myself more for modesty than for warmth. "I don't register cold, not like I used to. You work as many missions as I have, cold becomes less of a problem."

"I could ask," she said. "But I don't imagine you could tell me much."

"Not much." I took another gulp of tea. "This is good."

"Is your cane outside? Do you need me to get that too?"

"No, it's okay. It's upstairs. I'm trying to use it less." Though tonight, I wished I had it. But I could make it inside, where I could use the walls for stability.

"Okay." She crossed her arms and looked away. "I was just getting home," she said, "and saw you were out. Thought you might need a cup of something."

"It's really good. Your blend?"

"My blend. It's one of the mixes I sell online."

I took another drink. "I normally don't drink tea," I said. "Other than sweet tea."

"That's not tea," she said dryly. "Not really."

"This is good," I said again, taking another swig. "You've got it online? I'll have to order some."

"Don't worry about it. I'll make up an eight-ounce bag for you tomorrow. You get the neighbor discount." She looked at the pool and then back at me. "So . . . do you swim out here often? At night?"

"Most nights," I admitted.

"Concerned about skin damage?"

I chuckled, the sensation both unfamiliar and welcome. "I don't sleep well. Not since I got back."

"I see."

In the moment to come, I expected her to say something about having a tea for that, or a pill, or some sort of fix. Instead, she shrugged.

"It's a good thing you don't get cold," she said. And that was all. "I should probably go. It's late. Went to see Sean's band tonight."

"Oh?"

"They're good. Very good, actually."

I nodded.

Jane cleared her throat. "I'll let you carry on. I just thought you could use a bit of tea."

"It's very good. Thank you." I looked down at the mug and back at its giver. "Jane?"

"Yes?"

"I don't . . . advertise my night swims."

"Didn't think so. Don't worry. I wasn't planning to gossip about it over sweet tea with Nina and Mariah."

I gave her a crooked smile. "Thanks. I know it'll be hard for you to hold back."

Her own mouth twitched. "Very."

"I'll take this with me, if you don't mind," I said, raising the mug.

"Not at all. I didn't expect you to chug it." She opened her mouth and closed it before trying again. "I hope you get some sleep."

"Thanks," I said. "Good night, Jane."

I walked back to the house then, clutching my towel with one hand and the tea with the other.

∞

"How many nights per week are you waking from dreams?" my therapist asked during our session the following week.

I did a quick tally in my head—not of nights with swims, but of nights that I woke to discover I'd slept through the night. "Four or so," I answered.

"That is a massive sleep deficit."

Her statement made me think about Jane's comment about the cold. Likewise, lack of sleep wasn't a thing that I worried about.

"I've lived with worse."

"That doesn't make me feel better," Beverly said. "I have a thought for you, and I don't want you to give me an answer right away. I think you should consider a therapy dog."

"I'm getting around just fine," I told her. "It's not like I can't cross the street."

"Hear me out. First, swimming as you have been, at night? Without anyone nearby? A little dangerous."

"I used to swim competitively," I said. "Open water, that kind of thing. It was a while ago, but I don't think Ian's lap pool poses a threat."

"Secondly, I think you could benefit emotionally from a support animal."

That I couldn't speak to. Because I wasn't emotionally disconnected enough to think I was truly emotionally stable.

"So you think I need a golden retriever?" I asked, finally.

"If you'd like a golden, I'm sure you could get one. The retrievers do make excellent therapy animals. But I had another, specific dog in mind that could be a good match."

Beverly reached over then for a manila folder that had been waiting at the corner of her desk. Leaning forward, she passed it to me. "This is Dash."

I opened the folder to see a sheaf of papers, photos paper-clipped to the top. "Dash, huh?"

The papers said he was a Great Dane—that much was obvious from the pictures—specifically a blue merle mantle. I flipped through the photos.

Dash had giant long legs, and an expression that seemed both alert and vaguely perplexed all at once. He sat in the middle of someone's yard, and I suspected that whoever held the camera also had a treat.

My brows furrowed as I got a closer look.

I looked up at Beverly and back at the photo before tossing the folder onto the low table between us. A deep breath, a moment to fight the anger welling up inside.

"You think I need a three-legged therapy dog."

"Dash had an accident," Beverly explained. "He's a service dog trained to work with people with physical disabilities."

"I can fetch and carry for myself. I don't need a horse dog."

Beverly continued as if I hadn't spoken. "After Dash's accident, he wasn't able to perform the duties his handler required of him."

Her words sunk in. "Oh."

"His handler has a new service animal, but Dash needs a place. The service organization is looking to adopt him out as an emotional support animal, to a dedicated owner who might benefit from his additional training. And if not benefit, exactly—respect it, and allow him to be useful. He's too well trained to go to just anyone and too young to retire."

"Like me."

Beverly measured her words. "There are similarities. You would understand him better than most any other placement that might be found."

"He's not in danger of being euthanized, is he?"

"Oh no, nothing like that. But his breeder and past handler are invested in Dash finding the right owner."

I stood, tucking the folder under my arm. "I'll think about it," I said.

I drove from the therapy office to my father's house. A twist of the key let me inside. I closed the door behind me and took it in. The workers were gone. It was clean.

Clean and quiet.

I walked to the dining room table, pulled out a chair, and sat, then spread Dash's dossier in front of me. There were training notes, notes about temperament, about his tasks for his handler. The handler—whose personal information had been redacted, government-style—apparently had MS and needed

Dash to retrieve items, to turn on and turn off lights, and to be a support when moving from a wheelchair and back.

After the accident, which Dash sustained while moving his handler to safety, he didn't have the stability he needed to act as a support for his handler. The handler had tried to keep going, but after two falls realized she needed a four-legged companion.

Which left Dash, trained for one purpose, out of a job.

A mess of feelings raged within my chest. Anger at Beverly, that she would present me with such a situation—a dog that served as a perfect mirror for my own existence.

But beside the anger? Compassion. Sadness. A desire to help.

I looked at the photo again. He looked kinda dopey, to be honest. But I knew just enough about service dogs to know that he'd been trained within an inch of his life.

At least, I thought, I wouldn't have to worry about him peeing on Mariah's hardwood floors.

I looked around the house. It really was quiet. I hadn't realized how accustomed I'd become to the noise in Ian's home. Despite its size, there was always the sound of a child playing or Nina laughing, one of Ian's dogs or Ian himself. There was activity. But here?

Maybe Beverly was right. I couldn't stay at Ian's forever, and if I had to stay here?

Might as well do it with a three-legged dog.

∞

I called Beverly's office the next morning and left a message with the front desk about my willingness to arrange a meeting with Dash.

One of the photographs was small, only two by three inches. I fitted it carefully into my billfold. My leg felt stiff after the previous day's driving, so I walked from my house to Roy's.

I found Roy in the back, scrubbing out the firebox of his smoker.

"Who's there?" he called when he heard the gate close behind me. "Oh. Callum, good. Grab that wire brush there and give me a hand."

I did as I was told, pulling up a lawn chair to get a better angle.

"I'm going to be moving back to my dad's place soon," I said.

"Yeah?"

"My therapist wants me to get a dog."

"That's a good idea," Roy said. "You should do that."

"This particular dog has three legs."

"Does it eat and poop like a normal dog?"

"As far as I know."

"Use your whole arm to scrub. Didn't they teach you anything in the marines?"

"Not enough, I guess." I scrubbed the walls of the firebox more. "Too bad this thing doesn't have an oven's self-cleaning setting."

Roy grunted. "It'd warp the metal at those temperatures."

"I guess I don't know as much about smokers as I should."

"You want to learn?"

"Probably should," I said, "seeing as how I own a chain of barbecue restaurants."

Roy gave a nod of assent. "Well, then. Let's get started. The key to a good brisket is a long cook time at a controlled temperature, and to do that you've got to understand the physics of smoke . . ."

18

So the small things came into their own: small
acts of helping others, if one could; small ways
of making one's own life better: acts of love, acts
of tea, acts of laughter.

—ALEXANDER McCALL SMITH

Jane

"Chad put together a new list of spaces for us to look at," Celia said early one
morning while I was waiting for the kettle to heat.

"Finally! Good! When can we look?"

"Does tomorrow work for you?"

"To look at spaces? I will make time. I'm running out of room here," I said,
pointing at the canisters and tins of tea and herbs stacked up on some new
shelves I'd put in. Even with the shelves and two IKEA carts, stock and orders
being prepped for shipment had taken over the dining area and threatened to
creep still farther. "And I can't use the kitchen at Sean's place forever."

The next morning, we stopped at Torchy's Tacos on Berkman and East
51st Street for sustenance. We ate on the edge of Bartholomew Park before
meeting with Chad.

The first space was right next to a UPS store, which I admired very much
for practicality's sake, but doubted it would lend itself to any kind of locational
romanticism.

Chad unlocked the door and let us in.

If I could have envisioned a space nearly the opposite of our space in San
Francisco, it would have been this place. I stood near the doorway and closed

my eyes. I needed to see, just for an instant, our original Valencia Street Tea row house, with the aged hardwood floor and molding around the ceiling. The light coming in through the tall paned windows in the front, the vintage sconces on the walls.

This place? I opened my eyes.

It was what you'd expect to be located next to a UPS store. The tile floors were . . . unappealing. The walls were painted a shade of beige that I'd thought had died in the early aughts. I looked up and with a cringe took in the drop ceiling.

"This is a great location," said Chad, and after that I tuned out everything he had to say.

How could we possibly set up shop in a place like that? It would take thousands of dollars to get it to be not awful; to reach a state of loveliness would take even more money. Sure, we could put the vintage bar in here, but the bar deserved better than to go on those floors. We'd have to repaint, retile—but who knew how many teacups would be broken on tile? At least with the hardwood back home sometimes they bounced.

"We could try laying down carpets," Celia suggested, as if she had read my mind.

"We could," I said, and it was true. We could. I just didn't want to.

"And we could paint." She turned to Chad. "We could paint, right?"

He nodded.

I looked the place over. Paint, tile, light fixtures—we'd have to remove the drop-panel ceiling and fluorescent lights.

Okay, light fixtures. Pendent lights. Maybe wood paneling? It would help, but again, the price tag. Mirrors to expand the space . . . the list in my head went on. "I think it would take a lot of money to get it to how we'd want it."

"It won't be like what we had," Celia said. "But I think it could be okay."

She sounded so hopeful about it that I felt myself start to lose the tenuous hold I'd had on my emotions.

The space wasn't like what we had. It was so, so much worse, from the location to the flooring.

I walked outside, and Celia followed me. "I know it's a change, Jane, but—"

"It's bad, Celia. It's a bad space. I think it would be bad for business." Once I started talking, I couldn't stop. "I hate the interior, I hate the area, and while I'm at it, I hate Austin."

"It's not that bad—"

"I think it *is*."

"It's just another change. We're good at change."

But this was different. Every other change we'd faced together, in agreement. When Dad wanted to take Margot with him, out of the country, Celia and I agreed that it wouldn't be in Margot's best interests, and we'd worked together toward a solution.

But this? We weren't working together; we were tugging at each other with competing visions of what life should look like. Suddenly Celia wanted a space in a strip mall and friendship with Lyndsay Stahl and no contact with Teddy Foster.

The person I'd always known best was turning into a person I didn't understand.

Could we survive Austin? I didn't know. My sister, my favorite person in the world, had become a person I barely recognized. And now she was giving me hopeful glances over a space in a *strip mall*.

Was this the price? Was this what I'd have to do for us to be okay? Pretend to be happy about a completely impractical space?

I took a deep breath. She wasn't going to change her mind out here. All I could do was try to hold her off and pray something better came up. "Let's keep looking," I said to Celia and Chad, who'd followed us outside. "We'll keep this place in mind. You're right," I said to Celia, digging deep for something positive to say. "The location by the park is . . . it's good."

We said little when we finally returned to the casita. I put the kettle on and brewed myself a bracingly strong cup of Irish breakfast tea. I took my tea and a couple of shortbread cookies and then shoved around tins and bags until I had a place for my teacup at the breakfast table.

A new home for Valencia Tea Company? Thinking over the day's events, looking over the chaos now, it felt even further away.

But no amount of feeling angsty would change anything. Resolved, I finished my tea and set to work.

19

Jane

"So, you've been looking at places to open a new tea store?"

"Tea salon," I corrected Sean while restraining a smile.

"Tea *salon*," he echoed, his voice set at a comedic pitch.

"And yes, we looked. I don't know." I sighed. "There are spaces available, but the foot traffic is bad, or it's too close to a Starbucks, or just plain terrible. There was a space, you know, at Hyde Park that we missed out on. I just . . ." I shook my head. "Maybe we can make one of the other spaces work. We might have to."

"How long would it take to open?"

I leaned back against the sofa at his aunt's place. "Hard to say. It would depend on where we land, on the permits, on how long it takes to get it looking right. Now that Margot's settled into school and ballet, I need to talk Celia into getting a booth at the farmers' market." I cleared my throat. "I mean, I could do it myself, but Celia's better with people than I am. Anyway, if we could start building a local clientele, that would be a good thing."

He reached for my hand and toyed with my fingers. "How important is it for you to stay here?"

My spine straightened. "What?"

"The guys and I are talking about going on tour." Sean laced his fingers through mine. "We've been registered to perform at South by Southwest for months, so we're locked into that, but we might road-trip in between."

"Oh," I said, unable to hide the disappointment from my voice

He lifted my chin with the ends of his callused fingers. "Hey. Don't look like that."

"Like what?" I asked, trying and failing to sound chipper.

"Look. I was asking because I thought . . . I thought you might want to come too."

My eyes widened. "With you?"

"Yeah."

"On the tour?"

He leaned forward, drawing me into a languid kiss. "Yes." Another kiss. "We should be touring, but I hate the idea of being away from you that long."

"Me too."

"So you'll come?"

I winced, biting my lip. "Maybe? I don't know. Margot's getting settled in . . ."

"It's just a few months. Margot's a big girl."

I lifted an eyebrow. "Margot's sixteen and moving across the country has thrown her for a loop. She hasn't had the most stable life, not with how things shook out with our parents."

"Come on. You're her sister, not her parent."

"I'm her legal guardian, actually. Celia and I share guardianship." I took a deep breath. This was new territory with Sean. "Look, it's a nice idea, but the timing is tricky, and I don't have the money to travel like that."

"You're tagging along. It wouldn't be expensive at all."

"Food, travel, hotels alone . . ."

"We'll work it out."

I squeezed his hand. "I don't want you to have to pay my way. And anyway, the timing . . ."

"What if we were married?" he asked.

My heart thudded in shock. "What?"

"Would you mind me paying if we were married?"

"I . . . I mean . . . ," I stuttered, failing at the task of trying to formulate a reply.

"Just think about it, okay?"

"Which part?" Because the tour bit seemed like less of a deal in comparison to the idea of marriage.

Had I imagined it? Had I misheard him?

But before I could attempt, say, a follow-up question, we were kissing again, his fingers entangled in my hair, and I happily allowed myself to become fully distracted from the topic at hand.

In bed that night, my thoughts returned to Sean's proposal. Me, a roadie? I snorted and rolled over onto my stomach, trying to picture myself in a band T-shirt, nose ring, and ironic tattoo.

Or *Almost Famous*-style, heart-shaped sunglasses.

That would be a solid *no,* times four. But still, I hated the alternative. I hated the idea of months apart. Especially now, when things between me and Celia were so weird.

As much as I wanted to get away from it all, leave with Sean, I knew the truth. I couldn't leave my sisters yet, no matter how much they drove me crazy. Sean and I would be fine. We'd talk, we'd text, and when he got home, we'd pick up exactly where we left off.

The next morning at ten, the FedEx truck arrived, and rather than stopping in front of the Vandermeides' for their near-daily Amazon shipment, it rolled up to our door.

Celia paused from her work at the sink, dried her hands on the nearest dish towel, and peered out the window as the deliveryman hauled a large, flat rectangular box from the truck.

"Did you order something?" Celia asked from the window.

I shook my head, choosing not to leave my perch in the makeshift living room's one chair, where I'd been perusing a plant catalog.

A knock soon sounded at the door, and Celia persuaded the deliveryman to set the awkwardly shaped package just inside.

"What is it?" I asked, finally succumbing to curiosity. Catalog set aside, I rose to inspect the delivery label.

"It's . . . it's from Teddy," Celia said, her face pale.

Margot's face appeared over the loft railing. "Teddy? Teddy sent something?" She raced down the stairs, arms flailing. "What is it?"

"I have no idea," I called back, "But it's in a very large, very ungainly box." I tested the weight of the box. "And for the cost of shipping, he might as well have flown out himself, first-class."

Celia didn't reply, only reached for the box cutter and began to slice through the packing tape that held the ends together. Within minutes, she'd dismantled the box and cut carefully around the layers of foam and bubble wrap.

We stared at the contents in a mixture of awe and disbelief.

Our windows. The windows I thought of when I couldn't sleep, the ones that had once been in our tea shop in San Francisco. I ran my finger over the familiar wood casing, tears coming to my eyes. I felt like I'd just been unexpectedly reunited with an old friend.

The white of an envelope caught my eye. I plucked it from its perch, taped to one of the window panes. "'Dear Celia, Jane, and Margot,'" I read, my gaze flickering up to Celia and back down to the handwritten text. "'Phoebe is elbow deep in modernizations of the row house you rented from Atticus. These windows were removed last week to make way for energy-efficient ones. As they were about to be discarded, I thought the three of you might want them for your own purposes. If not, feel free to discard them yourselves.'" I looked up at Celia in disbelief. "Discard these windows, with that glass? As if! I suppose no one told Phoebe they'd probably be worth something, else she would have sold them to the highest bidder."

Celia's mouth gave a grim twist. "No doubt."

I returned to the letter. "'While I'm sure you'll have windows of your own in your new tea salon, I thought these might serve a decorative purpose.'" I leveled a gaze at my sister. "Just how much HGTV did the two of you watch together?"

"Enough editorializing." Celia plucked the letter from my hands.

I crossed my arms. "I'm glad he sent the windows, but I shudder to think what else Phoebe is throwing away. If she gets rid of that molding, so help me . . ."

"'I suspect,'" Celia read, "'that given the opportunity, Jane would happily take ownership of every discarded scrap.'"

Margot snorted. "He's right, you know."

I shrugged, unable to argue. I would have made a mobile from the doorknobs, given the materials and opportunity.

"'Rest assured,'" Celia read on, "'the molding and flooring have stayed and have been restored to a pleasant sheen.'"

"That's something, at least," I said, irked that Teddy should know me so well. "Well? What else? Did he say anything to you?"

"The letter is addressed to the three of us," Celia replied. "The rest is a note about how he hopes the glass survived the trip and he hopes we're all well."

I ran a fingertip down one wavy pane. "We could hang them, you know. Use them as space-dividers? We'd have to have the right mounting, so they wouldn't fall, but it might be interesting."

I tried to picture them inside the first location we'd visited that morning. They took the edge off, a bit, though that flooring . . .

One step at a time.

I rested a hand at the top of the wooden frame. "It was very nice of him to send them."

"Yes," Celia agreed. "It was."

"I wish he'd brought them himself," Margot said. "I've gotten better at poker. I could probably beat him at least once."

I turned to Margot. "Where did you learn poker?"

"Nina taught me. I can do Texas Hold'em too."

I shook my head and turned back to Celia. "How did he know where to have them shipped?"

"We've exchanged a few texts. E-mails."

"You've exchanged texts," I repeated dumbly. I shouldn't have been surprised. Shouldn't have been. But considering she'd never mentioned such a thing, it wasn't a response I'd been prepared for.

"Well," I said, after clearing my throat, "it was very thoughtful of him to have them shipped to us."

"Yes," she agreed. "We probably don't want to leave them here. Why don't I go to the main house and see if Callum might help us move them to the back?"

"Yes," I answered. "Good idea."

Clearly, the subject of Teddy had come to a close.

Callum arrived a few minutes later, his back straight and his gait purposeful; I could tell by his stride that he appreciated being called upon to help.

Within minutes, we'd moved each heavy window panel out of the entryway. Rather than stack them in the back as planned, Celia decided to leave two in the living room and placed two upstairs, leaning against the walls. The glass reflected extra light; the shine lifted my spirit as well as Celia's, while the chance to labor for a cause visibly brightened Callum's stoic demeanor.

I offered him a cup of iced tea once we'd finished moving furniture.

"I'm having a barbecue at my dad's—at my place," he said, while I poured the tea into a tall glass. "I'm inviting everyone I know here in Austin to come. The Vandermeides, you and Celia—Sean too, if he'd like to come."

"That's the house you inherited, right?" I asked.

He nodded. "I've been with Ian because it needed repairs."

"And Ian insisted," I guessed.

A soft chuckle. "That too. At any rate, the house is ready and I'll be moving."

"Oh." The news settled uncomfortably in my head. "Really?"

"It's sitting empty. I can't stay at Ian's forever."

"Of course," I said. "Where is it?"

"It's in Hyde Park."

"Oh . . ." My eyes widened. "Is it older, then?"

"It is. But it's been renovated a couple times."

"And it's nice?"

Callum smiled. "It's spacious. Big kitchen, big yard, big sunroom—big pool."

At the mention of a pool, my shoulders unknotted. He'd have a pool. He'd be able to swim. "That's good." I nodded. "The kitchen. The pool."

"And if my therapist has her way, I'll have a dog."

"Really?"

He gave a wry shrug. "I guess."

I laughed at his response. "How do you feel about dogs?'

"I guess I'll find out." He took a long drink of the tea. "This is good. So that's two kinds of teas you've given me that I've liked. How many does it take until I can call myself a tea drinker?"

I couldn't hold back a smile. "That's entirely up to you. I can bring some to your barbecue, if you like."

"I'd appreciate that," he said, his face easing into a smile.

He had a good smile, the kind that transformed a face.

"My pleasure," I said, and I meant it.

20

I didn't drive eleven hours across the state of Texas to watch my cholesterol.

—Robb Walsh

Callum

On Tuesday, I agreed to meet Dash, the Great Dane. The three-legged Great Dane, to be precise.

His foster caretakers arranged to meet me at Ramsey Park, at the picnic tables near Burnet Road. I'd come prepared with treats, having stopped at the Tomlinson's off Lamar on my way from Ian's. The employees had advised me on my purchase, a bag of dried lamb lung pieces. I thought it sounded ghoulish, but both employees assured me that lamb lungs were a totally normal, highly desirable dog snack.

I handed them my credit card, then continued north on Lamar. It was only a meeting, I rationalized as I drove. Maybe I wouldn't like the dog; maybe the dog wouldn't like me. After all, I hadn't had a dog since I was a kid. It was a mutt that idolized my brother Cameron, despite the fact that Cameron could seldom be bothered to give it the time of day.

Maybe I didn't have good dog energy, and dogs could sense it.

Despite the time it had taken to select the treats, I arrived early. I parallel parked along Burnet, climbed from my car, and waited.

Waited long enough to feel conspicuous, a lone man sitting at a park picnic table with a bag of dog treats. The weather had spiked to seventy-four degrees, and I'd found that as a civilian I liked the freedom of shorts and webbed sandals whenever the weather permitted. Here in Austin, that had translated into most of the time. As a side effect, though, my titanium prosthesis remained visible.

When the caretakers arrived, we recognized each other immediately; after all, how many people would be bringing a three-legged Great Dane to an amputee at the park on Tuesday afternoon?

Dash ambled next to them. Ambling was the best word to describe his stride, which was smoother than I'd expected. There was a bit of a hop in the back—he was missing his right hind leg, but it was followed by steps so relaxed that it simply became a gait that wasn't awkward as much as idiosyncratic.

I shook hands with the humans and bent down to greet Dash—though not far, because his head came to the base of my rib cage.

We all sat down at the picnic tables while the caretakers explained Dash's routine, diet, and habits.

Dash waited patiently, but after a few minutes he rose, positioned himself to my left, and sat down again. And after yet another moment, he rested his chin on my knee.

His caretakers watched, mouths agape.

"He spends so much time on duty," one said, "he doesn't usually approach people. He's not wearing his vest. He knows he's off duty, but still . . ."

I looked down and then reached with a cautious hand to stroke his neck.

Dash gave a great, contented sigh.

I patted his neck. "I suppose that's it then."

The day of the barbecue, I woke up feeling . . . happy? Was it happiness? The feeling seemed too manic around the edges for true happiness, but then, I reasoned, I hadn't felt happiness for so long that it was likely I might not recognize it when it happened.

I rolled over and spied Dash on the floor, sprawled across the gargantuan dog bed his previous handler had sent with him. It looked like an overstuffed twin mattress, and I wondered—not for the first time—if such a thing existed for humans.

Dash heard my movements and tipped his head to look up at me.

I smiled at him; he yawned and clambered to his feet, only to give a great stretch that started at his front toes and ended at the tip of his tail.

Stretch completed, he blinked at me, waiting for his first request. His care-takers explained to me that while he was retired as a service dog, he'd spent his life thriving on being useful. Without tasks, they said, he'd grow listless and anxious.

They shared ideas of things I could ask him to do for me. I'd protested, saying that I didn't *need* those things, but they waved their hands. It wasn't about what I needed; it was about what Dash needed. He thrived on service, and the accident hadn't taken that out of him.

"Okay, buddy. Pants," I said.

Dash's ears perked, and he trotted to the shelf inside the walk-in closet, where a folded pair of sweatpants waited.

His jaws spread wide, but he took the pants with the gentlest of bites, car-rying them to me with his tail held high. I held out my hands, and he placed the fleecy pants onto them before dropping into a sit.

Waiting. There was no help for it.

"Slippers," I said with a sigh.

Dash bounced over to where I'd left my slippers. He brought them to me one by one, and sat contentedly while I slid my right foot into one. He sat, fascinated, while I attached my prosthesis. To make him happy, I fitted the slipper over my prosthetic foot.

I rubbed his neck. "Good boy. Let's find some breakfast."

We walked downstairs together, his toes clicking on the hardwood floors. I made a mental note to look for some rugs, something that would give Dash some traction.

I measured out the kibble for Dash and placed it into his food stand;

among other things, I'd learned that Great Danes often needed to have their food and water elevated. Once Dash was taken care of, I used my dad's coffeemaker to make a very large pot of coffee.

A little after midnight, I'd started the brisket. While I'd spent more time away from the smoker than Roy would have preferred—taking a few hours at a time to sleep—I'd watched the fire and temperature carefully. In another few hours, it would be done in time for the barbecue.

I prepped the coleslaw, giving it a chance to chill. For dessert, I had fresh peaches that could go onto the grill and be served with ice cream.

Roy and Betsy arrived first, each carrying bags of food: corn bread, baked beans, and cheese fritters.

"That is a big dog you got there," Roy said, eying a seated Dash. Even seated, Dash was undeniably tall.

In the kitchen, Roy examined the brisket. He poked at it with his index finger before tearing off a corner. He chewed, swallowed, and nodded. "Not bad."

"No?"

"Could be more tender. Did you watch it all night?"

"Dash was tired. Had to get him inside, and he gets lonely."

Roy's eye glinted. "I see." He clapped me on the back. "Not bad. You'll have to lose more sleep if you want it to be better, but I don't imagine this crowd will complain too much."

Betsy swatted her husband's shoulder. "Roy. Be nice."

"Perfection requires more than nice," Roy said.

"I know, dear. You've said so many times."

"Thanks for bringing the sides," I told them both. "Everything looks great."

He waved a hand. "The corn bread's mine, but the baked beans and cheese fritters were all Betsy. She wanted to make sure there was enough food."

"Roy!" Betsy swatted him again, rolling her eyes. "I can't take him anywhere; he's telling all my secrets."

"I'll order out if we run low," I said with a chuckle. "But I'm not worried."

Ian arrived at noon with Mariah, Nina, and the kids in tow. The kids ran straight to Dash, who sat and waited patiently while they reached up for his ears and stroked his back.

"My!" exclaimed Nina as she took in the house. "This is lovely! And such a nice day out—are we eating alfresco?"

"We are," I said. "There are tables, chairs, and loungers on the back porch."

Celia arrived with Margot and Lyndsay; ten minutes later, Sean's white truck pulled up and Jane jumped out of the passenger side. She opened the cab door; Sean arrived just in time to open it the rest of the way, reach in, and retrieve the jugs of tea she'd brought along. Jane looked mildly annoyed that he'd intervened but didn't stay peeved long. Instead, she reached into the truck again and pulled out a small box.

Sean nodded as he approached. "Hey, man," he said, and I had to bite back a sarcastic response. "Nice place you got here."

"Thanks," I said, following his gaze and taking in the house. In a neighborhood that looked like rows of dollhouses, the house I'd inherited from my dad dominated the block. He'd had ostentatious taste, and I'd inherited the results. But it wasn't bad looking—I had to hand him that. With its double-decker wraparound porch, the upper one screened in, it was a good-looking place. And with the ceiling fans throughout, also functional.

I smiled at Jane as she came near, though I could feel my smile fade when I got a closer look.

Her lips were fuller than usual, her cheeks rosy.

She looked like she'd been thoroughly kissed. The realization hit hard. My thoughts raced toward the idea that she could look like that if I kissed her, that her eyes might shine at me the way they shone at him.

But. But she wasn't mine. She wouldn't be. I blinked and pasted a polite smile on my face. "Thanks for coming," I told her. "And thanks for bringing the tea."

"You're welcome," she answered, and her face flushed lightly. "I brought a Texas sheet cake too. Texas sheet cake squares."

"Worried I'd run out of food?"

She laughed. "No. I just made them as an experiment. Trying to fit in with the natives . . . you know."

I looked down at it. "Jane?"

"Yes?"

"Did you put tea in it?"

She tucked her lower lip beneath her teeth. "Would you believe me if I told you there isn't?"

"Nope."

A pause, and then a confession. "I put black tea into the cake. Like I said, it was an experiment. It's okay if you don't like it. I just made it and, I mean, even Margot has a limit about how much cake she can eat. So it's okay. I just brought it in case someone else might eat it."

I raised a teasing eyebrow. "You're not an altruistic food sharer?"

"No." The laugh continued. "I'm really, really not. It's one of my larger character flaws. I bake for myself. Feeding people isn't even secondary."

"Third-ary?"

Her smile turned impish. "Maybe fourth-ary. I don't have much of an altruistic streak, sad to say."

"I'm not sure about that." I'd seen how fiercely protective she was of Celia, the way she watched out for Margot, how she slipped food to Ian's kids. His dogs followed her around, knowing she was a soft touch. But I also knew her well enough to know that she'd argue if I tried to pursue the point.

She looked up at the house. "It's a nice place. And you've got good timing, you know."

"Oh?"

Her gaze darted to where Lyndsay stood, examining the shrubbery alongside Mariah. "You know that Ian offered for Lyndsay to stay at the house for the immediate future."

"He did mention that, yes." While I would miss Ian—and the substance and regularity of Pilar's meals—missing out on having Lyndsay's visits didn't upset me.

"Bullet dodged then," Jane said, the corner of her mouth twitching.

I wanted to kiss that twitch, I realized in a rush. Not a V-E Day kiss, not now, just a small claim on the corner of her lips that twisted with rueful amusement. Instead, I nodded in agreement and took a step backwards. I was the host, and Jane had Sean, and kissing a guest at random wouldn't have been gentlemanly.

I distracted myself by offering the group a tour through the house, then listening to Nina's appreciation of the space and Mariah's suggestions for home décor as we went.

Lyndsay compared everything she saw unfavorably to Mariah's home; the light was good, yes, but maybe not as good as Mariah's home. I would have tuned her out altogether, but listening to Jane mock her proved too entertaining.

"It is a very nice kitchen; I like the vintage appliances," Jane commented once we stepped inside. "I think Mariah's kitchen has more electrical outlets though."

Celia elbowed her sister in the ribs.

Jane cleared her throat. "What do you think, Lyndsay?"

Lyndsay squinted as her eyes roamed the kitchen walls. "I think you're right, Jane. You could probably add more, Callum. If you think the house's wiring could support it."

"It's been rewired," I said dryly. "You could run a hair salon in here, if you wanted."

"I'd like to see that," Ian said with a hoot. "I'm hungry, Beckett. Where'd you hide the brisket?"

I'd wrapped it in foil and stashed it in my oven, per Roy's instructions. Within minutes, we'd broken out the paper plates, and everyone started heaping piles of food on top.

The atmosphere livened with the scent of food. Once each guest had a loaded plate, I served myself and followed the group to the porch.

Just as I crossed the threshold, I felt my phone buzz in my pocket. I stepped backward; my phone rang so rarely, it was worth looking at the screen to see if I recognized the caller. My breath caught in my chest when I saw the number—it was the private detective, Clint something-or-other, the one I'd hired to look for Lila.

"I, um, I gotta take this."

I met Roy's questioning gaze but no one else's. I lifted the phone to my ear, striding away as I answered.

Texas Sheet Cake with a Black Tea Twist

For the cake

2 cups flour

1 $^2/_3$ cups sugar

¼ teaspoon salt

5 tablespoons cocoa powder

2 sticks salted butter

1 cup strong black tea

½ cup buttermilk

2 eggs, beaten

1 teaspoon baking soda

1 teaspoon vanilla

For the icing

1 $^3/_4$ sticks butter

5 tablespoons cocoa powder

6 tablespoons whole milk

1 teaspoon vanilla

3 ½ cups powdered sugar
½ cup finely chopped pecans

Preheat oven to 350°F.

In a medium-sized mixing bowl, stir together the flour, sugar, and salt.

Melt the butter in a saucepan over medium heat. Once melted, add the cocoa and stir. Add the tea, and let the mixture boil for about 30 seconds. Remove from heat and pour over the flour mixture. Stir gently to combine.

In a smaller mixing bowl—ideally one with a pour spout—stir together the buttermilk, eggs, baking soda, and vanilla. Pour the buttermilk mixture into the flour and chocolate mixture, and stir until just combined.

Pour the batter into an 18 x 13 sheet cake pan; you can also use two 9 x 13 pans. Bake the cake for 20 minutes, or until the top is firm and a cake tester comes out clean.

While the cake bakes, prepare the chocolate icing. Melt the butter in a saucepan over medium heat. Add the cocoa, stir, and allow it to boil for 30 seconds before removing the saucepan from the heat. Whisk in the milk and vanilla, and then the powdered sugar, one cup at a time. Keep whisking until all the ingredients have been added and incorporated, to prevent clumps.

Once the cake has finished baking, remove and immediately pour the icing over the top. Use a spatula to spread the icing over any bare spots.

Sprinkle the chopped pecans over the top. Allow the cake to cool 5–10 minutes before slicing into squares.

Serves 24.

Note: Twenty-four servings is a lot. This recipe can also be halved. Also, if you don't have buttermilk on hand, replace the buttermilk with ½ cup whole milk and ½ teaspoon white vinegar or lemon juice. Allow the milk and vinegar/lemon mixture to stand for 10 minutes before using.

21

Honestly, if you're given the choice between Armageddon or tea, you don't say "what kind of tea?"

—NEIL GAIMAN

Jane

I watched, perplexed, as Callum strode away, leaving his plate of food behind on the kitchen counter. Why the food bothered me so much, I wasn't sure. It made sense not to carry it with him, if it was an important phone call. Maybe that was it—it *had* to be important, deeply so, for him to leave like that.

"Whatever could that be about?" Nina wondered out loud.

"I'm sure he'll be back and explain everything," Ian reassured her.

Ian was only partially correct. Callum did return, but only to say he was leaving.

"I'm sorry," Callum said, his face pale and tense. "Please, stay and enjoy the food."

"I can lock up," Roy offered, "if you don't think you'll be back before tonight."

Callum nodded. "That would be helpful, yes. I don't know when I'll be back."

"What?" Nina clasped her hand to her heart. "Where are you going?"

"Dallas," Callum answered. "I have . . . business. In Dallas."

"Immediate business in Dallas?" Nina shook her head. "Surely not, it's a Saturday, and both of us know Smoky Top doesn't extend to Dallas. Out with it—what is this really about?"

"Mother!" Mariah exclaimed, stark horror written across her face.

Nina continued, undeterred. "Beckett, slow down. It can't be as bad as all that. Sit down for lunch, leave tomorrow night, be there first thing Monday morning when the banks are open. If, that is, it's truly a business matter."

Mariah placed an anguished hand over her eyes.

Callum's response came swift and certain. "I wish I could. I'm sorry. I really do have to leave."

Dash, who'd sidled up to Margot, picked up on his master's anxiety and whined in concern.

"What about Dash?" Celia asked.

Margot's hand shot up. "I volunteer as tribute!"

"Yes," I agreed. "We'd be happy to watch Dash."

"He's welcome in our kennels as well," Ian assured him.

I leaned over to Ian. "Best of lucking wresting him from Margot," I whispered.

The mention of Dash caused Callum to slow down, just the slightest bit. "Dash. Yes." At the sound of his name, Dash rose and nudged his master's hand. Callum petted him absently, and I wondered if he even realized it.

"We'll watch him," I said. "Celia will make sure he eats."

"I'll walk him every day," Margot promised, eyes full of excitement. "Every day, twice a day."

My heart squeezed as I remembered how much Margot had wanted a dog when she was thirteen. With me and Celia in and out of the shop, we'd had our hands full with Margot herself, let alone a dog. She seemed to like Ian's dogs well enough but had clearly fallen in love with Dash.

Roy rose. "If you're leaving, I'll pack a lunch for you that you can eat on the road."

Callum's shoulders relaxed, just slightly. "Thank you, Roy. I appreciate that."

Roy left for the kitchen then, and Callum left to pack. The military must have trained him in the art of packing a bag in twenty minutes or less, because he returned shortly after to say good-bye and apologize yet again.

He had a duffle in one hand and an oversized dog bed and canvas bag in the other. "Dash's things are in here," he said, lifting the bag. Margot jumped up to take it from him. "There's a binder in the bag that his foster parents gave me. It's got instructions for his food and routine. Just give him some things to do. He likes that."

Margot nodded solemnly. "We'll take very good care of him."

Stress still creased his face, but he smiled at her. "I know you will, Ace." He gestured to the bag again. "His vet's number is in there too, in case of emergency, and you can call or text me as well. I'll have my phone."

"Dash will be fine," Nina said, standing to wrap him in a tight hug. "I don't know what's going on, not exactly," she said softly to him, but not so softly that Celia and I couldn't hear. "But I have my suspicions. And if it's to do with *her,* then I wish her well. Let me know if there's any way I can be of assistance."

We called out our good-byes and wished him well; minutes later, his car pulled out of his driveway and he began his mysterious journey north.

Roy and Betsy excused themselves to the kitchen, and maybe it was the lack of Roy's watchful gaze, but Sean, seated at my right, cut a glance toward me. "That was awkward."

"It sounded like a true emergency," Celia said, her voice firm. "I hope everything's well."

"If it is an emergency, of course. And if not—if he just needed to shrug out of hosting duty, then I plan to eat all his food in his absence."

"Sean!" I exclaimed, horrified.

"What? It's not like anyone would consider Callum Beckett some kind of social butterfly."

I didn't even try to hold back my sarcasm. "You think he'd leave his dog behind with an instruction binder if he were just going out for ice cream?"

Sean crossed his arms. "Still, you'd think the guy could have finished his lunch."

"I wonder what it could be about?" Lyndsay asked. Her appetite didn't seem to be the worse for wear, since she'd already made a second trip to the kitchen.

When it came to the food, though, I couldn't blame her. Callum had provided an excellent spread. The brisket was tender, the coleslaw tangy, and the cheese fritters were addicting.

I promised myself I'd go for a run when we got home, even though I wasn't a runner in the slightest.

Margot finished her food in record time. "Can I take Dash outside?"

Remembering that the yard below was fenced, I gave my assent and watched as the two of them loped down the hallway for the back door Callum had shown us earlier. Moments later, I could hear her running Dash through a list of commands she must have found in the binder, as well as her praise as he completed each one.

Roy and Betsy lingered in the kitchen, attending to their inherited hosting duties, and with my food finished, I found my curiosity getting the better of me. With Nina seated to my left, all I had to do was lean a little in her direction.

"What did you mean?" I asked. "When you were saying good-bye to Callum?"

"What I said—about how I suspected it was about *her*? Well, I might be right; I might be wrong. But I am almost always right about these things. I imagine it's to do with Lila Williams."

"Who's that?" I asked.

"You could try to be discreet, mother," Mariah suggested pointedly.

"Lila was Callum's sweetheart," Nina continued, blithely ignoring her daughter. "They dated when they were young. But they parted ways after high school, as young people do, and she married his older brother."

"Ooh, intrigue," Lyndsay said, leaning forward. "Did she break his heart?"

I couldn't stop my eye roll. Celia caught it and elbowed me in the ribs.

I elbowed her right back.

Nina carried on. "Yes, but not as bad as Cameron did hers. They had a terrible marriage. Cameron carried on with nearly every waitress he ever hired."

I grimaced. "That's awful!"

"Oh, it gets far worse. He used her family's money, you see, to help expand the business. When he divorced her, he cut her off and left her with nothing."

"Texas is a community property state, isn't it?" Celia asked.

"It is," Nina said.

I frowned. "And she couldn't fight it in court?"

"Couldn't afford to," Nina said, shaking her head. "Cameron moved the bulk of their resources into the company, you see. Sneaky son of a biscuit eater."

Mariah's eyes widened. "Mom!"

Nina kept talking. "Beckett hasn't mentioned Lila, not since he's been back, but I know she fell off the grid a while back."

"How on earth do you know all this?" Mariah asked, crossing her arms.

"Oh, well, Ian has known Beckett a long time. And"—she held her hands up—"one of the hostesses at Smoky Top is a very good friend of mine."

"That's hardly reliable information, really, Mother."

"Also, Cameron's attorney's paralegal attended my mah-jongg club."

"Mom, that is confidential information!"

"Oh, it's all water under the bridge, darling. And Cameron's been dead for years, so statute of limitations and all that."

Mariah squinted at her parent. "I don't believe that phrase means what you think it means."

"Well, I've always believed our Beckett has carried a torch for her, but he's been overseas all this time. Until now."

"So you think he went looking for her, now that he's back?" Lyndsay asked. "How romantic!"

"Let us hope so, chickens. Beckett deserves some happiness in his life."

Mariah changed the conversation to football then, and while the others joined in with enthusiasm—because, Texas—I lost interest within minutes.

But my thoughts lingered on Callum, his brother, and poor Lila Williams. Was Callum still in love with her? What was Lila like? Had he been pining for her all these years? For some reason, the questions needled me.

Disconcerted, I squeezed Sean's hand for reassurance. I looked up at him, but he was staring off into space. I squeezed his hand again, and his head snapped back toward me. "Sorry, what did you say?"

"Nothing, not yet."

He glanced around. "When do you wanna get out of here?"

My first thought, to my shame, was that I hadn't yet heard all the gossip from Nina. What if we left and she dropped another tidbit of Callum's past? But no sooner had the thought crossed my mind than a torrent of embarrassment replaced it. "We can leave," I said quickly, before he might have a chance to read the thoughts on my face.

"I'm sure you two lovebirds have other places you'd like to be," Nina said with a smile and only a slight waggle of the eyebrows.

I felt the room's eyes turn to me, and my face flushed. "I . . . um . . ."

"I can take care of Margot and Dash," Celia assured me.

I glanced outside, where Margot and Dash were chasing each other on the back lawn, Margot's face flushed and rosy, her curly ponytail turning into a halo.

"Since the host has other places to be," Sean said smoothly, interrupting my thoughts, "we'll be heading to our next scheduled activity."

There was something about the way he said it that sounded . . . suggestive. My face flushed an even deeper shade of red.

We said our good-byes and slipped out; I said little as I buckled myself into Sean's truck.

Sean was quiet too as we drove. The sound of the road and the music unspooling from the stereo speakers filled the silence. After a few moments, he stopped at a light and turned to gift me with a smile. "How about dessert?"

That smile—that smile could turn me into the biggest pile of mush. "Sure," I said, finding myself smiling back.

He took me to La Pâtisserie, where we filled a box with more pastries than I believed possible to eat in a single afternoon. From there we drove to the riverfront, where we walked hand in hand.

The morning's clouds had cleared off; the sun warmed my face, and a soft breeze teased my curls.

Sean offered me bites of whatever he was eating; I teasingly refused to reciprocate until he pulled a face. We walked and laughed, and after a mile, Sean tugged my hand, leading me behind a leafless tree. "I love you," he said, his eyes taking in my entire face as if he was trying to memorize every curve and crevice.

I happily tipped my face up to his, kissing the lips that had turned serious. He tasted of lemon and white chocolate. He kissed me back, his hands pulling me close.

We pulled away just before the kiss became too heated for a public park—but only just. I looked up at him, breathless. "I love you. You make every day better."

He pulled a curl from my forehead, twirling it between his fingers before tucking it behind my ear. "You make the sun shine brighter."

"Back atcha," I said, grinning. "But just when did we get so mushy?"

He exhaled, but didn't release his hold on me. "I just want you to know how much I love you." He breathed kisses on my cheeks, my eyelids, and a last reverent kiss on my lips before resting his forehead against mine. "Let's go back to my place."

I pressed a light kiss onto his lips. "I can't. I should get back. I promised Celia we'd look at some more restaurant spaces today with the real estate agent."

A kiss to my jaw. "You can't reschedule?"

"With an hour's notice? No."

"You're a good sister."

"I try."

Sean pulled me close again, his kiss making my head spin. He pulled back with a groan. "I don't want this to end."

I laughed. "I promise you can come see me tomorrow, and I'll be more than happy to kiss you then."

He squeezed my hand, and we began the walk back to his truck.

∞

Chad took us to three more locations, each of them drearier than the last. There were reasons they hadn't been snapped up yet. At the final one, even Celia seemed disheartened. Back at the casita, I cheered myself by sending an e-mail out to our mailing, baking a fresh batch of scones, and listening to Margot play with the Great Dane.

I snapped a picture of them and sent it to Callum. I didn't receive a reply, but then, I didn't expect one either.

I took another picture, this time of the scones, and sent it to Sean. I expected a reply to that text, and yet I didn't receive anything but orders for the rest of the night. Even heartened by the orders, I found myself sleeping fitfully.

The next morning, though, I had a new text from him.

Those look good, it said. *I'm on my way.*

I grinned and typed out a reply. *I'll check and see if there's some left.*

"Sean's coming over!" I called out to Celia.

She stepped out of the bathroom, toweling off her hair. "I promised Mariah I'd look at wallpaper samples this morning, so I'll be out of the way."

"I'm not kicking you out," I told her.

She gave a half smile. "This casita's barely big enough for the three of us, let alone four. Don't worry about it."

"Want to take some scones over? There's plenty left over, if Mariah doesn't mind day-olds."

"I'm sure she'd like them."

"I'll put a plate together," I said, twisting my hair into a ponytail. As I walked to the kitchen, I passed the spot where we'd left the old windows, the ones Teddy had sent.

"Did you tell Teddy thank you from us?" I asked, pointing at them.

"I sent a note," she said.

"And?"

She smiled sadly and shook her head. "It is what it is, Jane. It's fine. It's nothing."

I felt my chest, my mouth, fill up with words. It wasn't nothing—I was sure it wasn't. But she'd finished dressing and slipped on shoes. All I could do was hand her the plate of scones.

Margot and Dash watched Celia walk across the lawn to the big house. "How long are you and Celia going to be fighting?" Margot asked, her brow furrowed with concern.

"We're . . . fine," I answered. It wasn't a lie, if you used the word *fine* broadly enough. "Why would you ask that?"

"There's a weird vibe between you," she said. "Since we left home."

"Mmm," I answered, giving her hair a gentle stroke. "Moving to Austin has been a shift, but Celia and I are fine."

Her lips pressed together. "You're like my parents, you know. My weird sister parents."

"Thanks," I said dryly. "Does that make you our weird sister daughter?"

Margot didn't crack a smile; that's how I knew she was really and truly anxious. I resolved to do better. I would leave Celia alone about Teddy. I would stop caring that she wasn't confiding in me.

I reached out and put an arm around Margot's shoulders, pulling her close. "It's okay. Sometimes change is hard to navigate, but that doesn't mean we don't have each other's backs."

"What happens?" Margot asked. "If you married Sean, or if Celia and Teddy got back together—which I totally think they should—what happens to me?"

It was a perfectly valid question, one that Celia and I had danced around when she and Teddy started getting serious. But at the time, we'd been comfortably settled in San Francisco. I'd assumed that if Celia and Teddy married, Margot and I would move into the house next door or the attic above them, whichever was more affordable.

Probably the attic.

But we'd all known and loved Teddy, so the question hadn't warranted asking. We'd known that Margot's well-being was something he would have been concerned with too.

"Neither of us is getting married anytime soon," I told her, taking a sip from my mug of tea.

"Sean looks at you like he wants to make out with you all of the time."

Only the purest self-control prevented me from spraying my mouthful of tea across the front window. "Um, thanks?"

"He's totally into you."

"Again, nobody's getting married in the immediate future." I felt guilty saying it, though, knowing that Sean had impulsively mentioned the idea. "But even if that changed, you're ridiculously important to both of us. We'd figure out something and make sure you're happy with it."

"You wouldn't send me away? To live with Dad?"

"No, honey," I said, giving up the pretense of a casual discussion in order to wrap her in a tight hug. "Never. Not even if you begged to go."

It must have been something that had troubled her for a while, because rather than shrugging out of the hug, she let me hold her tight.

We stood there until Sean's truck rumbled up the drive; I lifted a hand in greeting but didn't let go of Margot.

She sniffed. "Sean's here."

"He is."

"Do you want me to take Dash for a walk?"

"Sure, if you want. But you don't have to leave the casita if you don't want to."

"Nah," she said, removing herself from my arms the way I'd expected her to minutes before. "You guys might start making out."

"We . . . I . . ." I just closed my mouth. "We've never kissed at the casita, not once."

"Ew! I don't want to hear about it."

"You brought it up!"

Margot straightened. "I'm taking Dash out."

"Don't forget the bags," I said. "Or Mariah will never forgive any one of us."

Dash had long since positioned himself by the door, his alert ears having heard the words *Dash, walk,* and *out.* I supervised Margot as she clipped on his leash and checked the bag dispenser that attached near the handle and then walked outside with her to meet Sean.

Margot waved at him and he waved back, grinning his patented Charming Man grin. If he could only bottle that smile, he'd be a millionaire.

I wrapped my arms around his strong torso. "Good morning," I said, grinning up at him. "Margot's taking Dash out so she doesn't accidentally witness us kissing." I raised myself up on my tiptoes to plant a peck on his jaw. "It's nice to see you."

He held me close, then pulled away while holding my hands in his. "Let's go inside," he said. "I need to talk to you about something."

"Oh, sure," I said, and when he held the door open I stepped through.

We walked to the living room, a journey that required about three steps. Sean led me to one of the club chairs, and he sank into the one opposite me.

The lines of his face were taut and serious. He didn't look like himself. He looked like a stranger.

My brain whirred as I tried to anticipate whatever Sean might have to say. Was it bad news? I had no reason to believe so. I thought of the time we'd spent together the day before, and my heart warmed all over again. His blue eyes studied my face, blue eyes I trusted without reservation.

Maybe . . . Was he?

We were facing each other, his face solemn. He couldn't be . . .

He couldn't be asking me to marry him, could he?

Technically, he'd already asked, but was he more serious about it this time? My thoughts instantly raced back to my conversation with Margot.

"Jane," he said, holding my hand in his. "I— The band and I are leaving."

"Oh," I said, my heart giving a flip. We hadn't spoken again about the prospect of me going with them. If he was leaving sooner, I didn't understand what it meant. "You're leaving on tour early? Did you get new gigs or something?"

"Yeah." He looked down. "We're making Nashville our home base."

"So . . . you're not planning on coming back to Austin? You're *moving* moving?" My mind spun. "I mean, Nashville makes sense, but what about your aunt?"

"She's fine," he said quickly.

"Okay." That didn't match with what he'd said in the past. "When are you leaving?"

"Tonight." He squeezed my hands. "Listen, Jane. I'm going to be gone, and things . . ."

In that moment, I honestly believed he was going to ask me to come with him. As he spoke, I was puzzling out the logistics of how I could follow, how I could leave Celia and Margot, for just a little while, to be with Sean. Maybe it would be fine? A tour wouldn't last forever, and maybe if Sean and I were in Nashville, Celia and Margot would come too. I was only a split second away from nodding my head and telling him that yes, of course we would figure it out. For a breathless moment, it felt completely sane and reasonable.

But I paused. I sucked in a breath, and Sean filled the void. "Things have been great. We've had a lot of fun together. But it's just been fun, right? We were never going to be serious." He gave a facsimile of the smile I knew best, but his eyes didn't meet mine.

Another breath; his words filled my lungs and spread throughout my body. I tried to catch his gaze, look into his eyes, but he kept his gaze firmly fixed on the tiled casita floor.

I exhaled slowly, my mind weighing his words against all his actions. The scales tipped wildly, desperately out of balance.

A dozen emotions fought to rise to the surface, but I shoved them down deep.

Something was wrong.

"I don't believe you," I told him simply. "I'm not a fool, and I don't know why you're saying these things, but I don't believe them."

His face remained impassive. "It's the truth. I'm sorry it's difficult for you."

Those sentences were even less believable, and I hoped for his sake he had no designs on acting. "Did something happen? What aren't you telling me?"

"Nothing happened," he said. "It's just time for me to move on. Nashville is better for the band. More venues, better proximity to labels."

My feelings began to rise to the surface. I wrapped my arms around myself to keep them tucked away for just a few moments longer. "I hope it works out for you."

He met my eyes then, his gaze softening. "Thanks."

"One of these days," I said, "I hope you can tell me what's really going on."

Another string of denials, each more half-hearted than the next. I barely paid attention to the words. The pain would come, I knew it, but I didn't want him here when it happened.

"I have online orders to fill," I said, before remembering that I'd texted him with scones in the first place. "Do you want a scone for the road?"

He looked at me as if I'd just offered very nicely to slice open a vein for him. "No, no, I'll be fine. Thank you."

And then he left.

I watched him leave, watched until his truck disappeared from view. Once he was gone, I walked straight to the kitchen and threw all of the remaining scones into the trash. Every repressed question and emotion rose in my chest, a massive tsunami of feeling that stole my breath and tore hard at my heart. I sank to the kitchen floor, a sob bursting from my lips.

The only good thing about Austin had just walked out of my life with his head held high.

22

Like most passionate nations Texas has its own
history based on, but not limited by, facts.

—John Steinbeck

Callum

Where are you off to? Very worried, let me know if you need anything.

Lucadia had a litter of puppies this morning. Nice litter, good-looking pups. Let me know if Dash needs a buddy.

Are you planning to be back next week? Planning a birthday party for Mariah, no stop left un-pulled.

Seems that Sean boy up and broke up with Jane and then moved to Nashville. Between you and me, I think you need to come back and give her a nice shoulder to cry on, you know?

Of all the texts I'd received from Ian, his most recent one took me off guard. Sean had left? For Nashville? I breathed deeply, but no amount of oxygen in my lungs made me want to kill him less.

I'll be a little while longer, I texted back. *Watch out for her for me.*

A buzz. *I'll watch out, but I think you'd do a better job.*

Somehow, I doubted that the loss of Sean would suddenly send Jane into my arms, but I had to shove those thoughts away as I pocketed my phone.

I'd be home soon enough. For now, I needed to use every ounce of knowledge I had about American bureaucracy. Knowledge, charm, and if I needed to play the wounded vet card, I would. Come hell or high water, I was getting Lila out of Mexico.

"I found her." That was how the investigator began the conversation when he'd called that Saturday afternoon.

He'd followed the trail Lila had left since the divorce—out of Austin, out of San Antonio, and into New Orleans, where she'd gone through a string of boyfriends. A bad breakup sent her back to Austin, when she'd asked Roy for a job. Her friends were only too happy to tell Clint about how the men had taken her attention, her money, and her pride, until she'd met one who seemed to be the real deal. He had charmed them, one and all.

Lila and her charmer moved in together, and after six months went on a vacation to Cancun.

During that vacation, everything had gone wrong. They'd been mugged, lost their credit cards, phones, passports. They made it back to the hotel, where Lila's boyfriend had enough cash to make calls and contact family members for help. Her paperwork stalled, and he told her that he set her up with the room for two weeks. He promised he'd expedite her departure once back on American soil.

He didn't.

And as it turned out, he'd paid for just one week instead of two, and when Lila realized it, she had to make a deal with the hotel management to work in exchange for staying in a room that needed repair. She'd been making trips to the consulate on her days off, but had made little headway through the chain of bureaucracy.

Also, she was pregnant.

That's how the investigator, Clint, had said it, toward the end. After he'd painted a scenario in which Lila had lost everything, was barely surviving.

She'd been able to use the hotel computer, usually reserved for guests checking their travel itineraries, to e-mail the man who'd left her behind. He'd e-mailed back that he couldn't help and then disappeared.

The few relatives she had tried to get help from had flaked on her, and she'd been too ashamed to contact me.

When I hired Clint, I told him to do whatever it took to find her. So he'd flown to Mexico, gone to the hotel, and asked around until he found her in an ill-fitting uniform, inventorying cleaning supplies. By the time he called me, he'd set her up at a new hotel, made sure she had whatever she needed. And unlike the man who'd brought her in the first place, he didn't leave.

I took the first flight to Cancun and felt my whole body exhale when I finally saw her. She looked older; we both did. On the way, I'd wondered if maybe I was still in love with her, the way I'd been when we were young.

As she hugged me tight, crying, she thanked me for sending Clint to find her.

I hugged her back. "You're family," I told her. "I'm sorry I wasn't here for you sooner."

And that was it, I realized. She was family. I was desperately glad to see her, but I didn't feel the same electric pull toward her that I felt about . . .

About Jane. There was no denying it, not anymore. I was in love with Jane.

Jane, who'd been in love with Sean Willis, the very man who'd abandoned my sister-in-law in Mexico, pregnant and alone.

∞

Later, Clint and I walked around the corner to a bar recommended by the hotel's front desk. The PI was younger than I'd anticipated. Over the phone, his weariness had read as age. In person, he appeared to be only a few years older than myself, though his eyes had the same haunted looked I'd seen in soldiers who'd seen too many years of combat.

"I can't thank you enough," I told him once we'd settled at the bar and ordered drinks; the least I could do was to buy the man a beer. "Not just for finding her, but taking care of her afterwards. Please, tell me what I owe you."

Clint took a swig of his drink. "The flights, the hotel, I'll give you receipts. The rest? Don't worry about it."

"Look, man, I don't want to put you out. Lila told me about how you brought her hot meals and fresh clothes."

He shook his head, taking his time before responding. "It's not a happy business, what I do. It needs doing, most of the time, and it pays the bills. But I don't get to help people, really help them. I get to tell them that their partners are cheating, that their friends are stealing from them, that their birth parent died of a drug overdose ten years ago. I don't get to be a hero, is what I'm saying, and for the last week I've gotten to do that." He lifted a hand. "I'm good. I bought a nice lady food and clothes. I don't need to be reimbursed for it."

I nodded. "You're a good man, Clint."

"Nah. Not really. She's had a lot of tough breaks."

"You read up on my brother?"

Clint cocked an eyebrow. "Were you and he close?"

"No," I said. "Lila didn't deserve what he did to her. Those years took their toll. She doesn't have a lot of people left."

"She's gonna need a lot of friends around her."

Clint's tone was protective, challenging. I studied his expressionless face, wondering. Did he—did he have feelings for her? Nina would have thought so, if she were here. But then Nina detected romance in the unlikeliest of conditions.

"I'm going to make sure she's taken care of. My brother, the divorce de- cree—I wasn't around to do anything about it. I regret that."

"If a guy wants to be a dirtbag that much," Clint said, "he generally won't listen to anyone else. He doesn't strike me as being the listening kind."

"He wasn't," I answered simply. "I just wish I'd been around."

Clint nodded at my leg. "It's hard to defend your country and your family at the same time. You did what you could."

Maybe. I'd also been hiding from the life I'd left behind in Austin. Rather than say so, I took another drink.

"I also found the guy who left her here," Clint said. "If you're interested."

I set my bottle down, harder than intended. "Sean Willis?"

"Sean Willis," Clint repeated with a string of insults, not a single one unwarranted.

"Unless he lied to a friend of mine, he's in Nashville."

"You know him?"

My jaw tightened. "Yep."

Clint gave a low growl.

"I'll make sure he pays child support," I said.

"Just as long as he pays," Clint answered, and I knew he wasn't limiting payment to that monetary support for his unborn offspring.

I thought back to the day I'd gotten the call. Everyone had been there. Nina being Nina—I thought back to her words as I left. *And if it's to do with* her, *then I wish you well. Let me know if there's any way I can be of assistance.*

Had Lila's name come up after I'd left the room? *Discreet* wasn't a word I'd ever apply to Nina.

Did Sean hear Lila's name and run? I considered the possibility. Was he that much of a coward? Even as I asked the question, I knew the answer. After leaving Lila behind, running away and leaving Jane was far from out of the question.

I'd seen them together, seen them too many times. I'd seen how he'd looked at Jane, as if she'd hung the moon. I'd seen her in moonlight myself, and I wasn't about to rule out the possibility.

Well, Sean had run away to Nashville to escape his sins, leaving Jane behind. He'd already begun to pay.

The next several days were spent hacking through the paperwork and bureaucracy necessary to arrange Lila's travel documents. There were calls and e-mails and ultimately contact with our shared congressional office. Clint stayed as well, saying he was due for a vacation.

Despite calling it a vacation, he made nearly as many calls as I did, calling in favors to get Lila's case expedited as quickly as possible. After two weeks, the color had come back to Lila's cheeks. Her shoulders relaxed, and her familiar old smile crept back.

Clint and I made sure she ate; he watched her like a hawk, and I didn't begrudge him his feelings. He didn't say much, but his actions had declared his intentions to be deeply honorable.

"He bought me vitamins," Lila confessed to me one day. "Lectured me on the importance of folic acid."

"He's a good guy."

"So are you. I forgot y'all existed," she admitted wryly. "I shouldn't have, but I did."

"There are a few of us."

We sat at the edge of the hotel pool, an activity she'd confessed was a recent favorite. "When I worked at the last hotel, I wanted to swim so badly and couldn't."

"There's a pool at my place," I told her. "And you can swim there every day, if you want." I kicked my one leg in the water, feeling the swoosh of the water between my toes. "I want you to know that you'll always have a place with me, at the Hyde Park house."

Lila began to shake her head. "Cal, I couldn't . . ."

I cut her off. "You could and should. I'm also going to have papers drawn up to give you part ownership of Smoky Top."

"No," she protested, but I held up a hand.

"It's what Cameron should have done. The way he treated you—it shouldn't have happened, is what I'm saying. I just want to make it right."

Lila lifted a foot, sending a spray of water skittering across the pool surface. "I shouldn't have married him. Maybe I got what I deserved."

"Nobody deserved that. There are four bedrooms at the Hyde Park place, far too much room for me and Dash."

She smiled. "I love that you have a dog now."

"He'll love you. You can stay as long as you like."

"I'll pay you rent, once I have a job."

"If you want," I told her, deciding in that moment to set it aside in a fund for the baby.

She leaned back on her arms and looked at me sideways. "How come you're not married?"

Heaven help me, I thought of Jane. I sent up a prayer for her; who knew how she was faring in the wake of Sean's mess. If I hadn't been in the middle of a conversation with Lila, I would have sent Ian a text asking after her.

"There *is* someone," she said, squinting at my face. "I'll be. Cal Beckett, in love at last."

I felt my face flush, entirely without my permission. Lila saw it and hooted.

"Cal's in love," she repeated, shaking her head. "What's she like?"

"First off, it's complicated," I told her, only to be met by a magnificent set of rolled eyes. "Secondly, she's been in a relationship until recently, and I don't think she even looks at me that way."

"Why not? Look at you!" More rolling of the eyes.

"And third . . . I don't know," I said, hedging.

"Tell me about her."

A smile tilted my lips. "At first, she reminded me of you."

"Shut up."

"She's about your height, curly hair like yours."

"You have a type."

I shrugged. "You're . . . a little more easygoing."

"I've never been called easygoing in my life. How neurotic can she be?"

"Single-minded, I think is more accurate. She cares about things, little things, more than anyone else might, but when she explains it she makes you care too, or at least see why she does. She won't like someone—or something— because she's supposed to, but when she does it's with her whole self."

"You're in love with her."

I shrugged.

"So what's the holdup? Why haven't you swept her off her feet yet? And don't say your leg; that's stupid."

I shot her a wry glance. "Not entirely stupid."

"Completely stupid."

"Lila . . ."

"I'm not saying what you've been through is easy, Cal. I'm sure there have been repercussions that I can't even imagine. But if she doesn't fall for you because of your *leg*? That's her fault and not yours."

"She was seeing a guy," I told her, choosing my words carefully. "A guy she thought the world of, and they were dating until recently."

"They've broken up though?"

"They have."

She shook her head. "If I were less selfish, I would send you back to the States to go get her."

"I'm not going anywhere."

"And I'm not letting you. Like I said—*if* I were less selfish. I'm not. I'm not letting you out of my sight until I'm back stateside. And when I get back? I'm going to kiss the tarmac, like the pope."

"The pope kissed the tarmac?"

"Every country. It's a thing."

"Really? Why?"

Lila heaved a sigh. "I'm not Catholic, how would I know?"

"This conversation has taken a very strange turn."

"Whatever. What's her name?"

I hesitated, but saw there was no help for it. Not if she was moving back to Austin, into my house. "Jane. Jane Woodward."

"She sounds very sensible. Are you sure she has a sense of humor?"

The sound of Jane's laugh came to mind, and I smiled at the memory. "I am."

"Well, I hope we get back soon. You've wasted too much time on me."

"Never," I told her. "Never a waste."

She tipped her head. "Who's watching that dog of yours?"

"The Woodward sisters," I admitted, feeling my face flush all over again.

"You've got it bad."

I sighed in defeat; there was no arguing, because she wasn't wrong.

23

Don't trade our love for tea and sympathy.

—Jars of Clay

Jane

News of my breakup with Sean spread exactly as quickly as I might have guessed, knowing our relations as I did.

Celia found me that afternoon, still on the kitchen floor in a sad puddle of my own tears, clutching at a stoic yet confused Dash. She asked what was wrong, and I felt my mouth dry out. The words could barely pass from my lips. Sean was leaving for Nashville; we'd broken up.

She frowned, her brows furrowed in confusion, and I realized she was making a lot of the expressions I'd made at her when she and Teddy had broken up—except that she hadn't been a puddled mess on the floor.

I cried for two weeks.

Truly, I felt as though my brain had ceased its ability to function. I filled Internet orders . . . and cried. Watched Celia leave to look at properties . . . and cried. I baked . . . and cried.

In the morning I would reach for my phone to check for a text from him and . . . nothing.

No texts.

No texts, notes, e-mails, phone calls. We went from seeing each other nearly every day to *nothing*.

Nothing at all.

I wondered about him. Was he settled into his new place in Nashville? Did he miss me anywhere as much as I missed him?

Without Sean, I missed San Francisco more than ever. I missed the sense of being home. When orders came in from our regulars, I found myself tucking small notes into the packaging, notes about hoping all was well in the Bay.

I dreamed about our old shop. Simple dreams, nothing notable other than the location. Austin felt even more alien than before.

Celia hovered close, bringing me foil-covered dinner plates from the big house. The three of us watched Paul Feig comedies and laughed, and I'd tuck the spare laughter into my heart to hold me until I could sleep.

Margot traded bunks with me so that I could sleep with Dash next to my bed. If I woke in the night, the sound of his sleepy snuffles soothed my anxiety until I could fall back asleep. If I reached for a paw during the night—or, one time, his nose—he didn't mind.

After two weeks, I agreed to go to dinner at the big house with Celia and Margot. I'd had hopes, beforehand, that perhaps Lyndsay wouldn't be there and the breakup might go unremarked upon.

My hopes were in vain.

"I never liked him," Lyndsay said when she saw me. "He seemed unreliable. You're much better without him."

"I don't know what that boy is thinking," Nina said after giving me a bracingly tight hug. "Anyone could tell he was in love with you. Does he have commitment issues, do you think? Was he unloved as a child?"

"I don't know," I told her honestly.

"Those musicians, they don't always know what they want. Believe you me, I spent my fair share of time with musicians in my day."

"Your husband?" Margot asked. "Was he a musician?"

"Producer. Less exciting, more stable."

"Google Michael Hennings," Ian said with a nod. "The man has a Wikipedia page. Nina too."

"There's no need to send people to Google," Mariah admonished her husband.

"No need to be ashamed of it, either," Nina told her daughter, and I knew then I was listening to a very old family argument. "The music money did very well for us; it paid for Wellesley like you wanted."

"I spoke to Charlie earlier today," Mariah offered, smoothly redirecting the conversation. "Charlie is my sister, you know," she informed the rest of us before continuing. "She and Pierce have finished building their lake house, and she floated the idea of having us all over. And she invited everyone," Mariah added, nodding to me and Celia, as well as Lyndsay. "Charlie loves a full house."

"Really?" Lyndsay asked, eyes wide. "A lake house? That's so kind!"

"Charlie is a born hostess." Nina beamed in pride. "Voted 'most sociable' at her sorority all five years running."

"Perhaps," Mariah added, "if she'd been less sociable, she might have graduated in four years. But Charlie hates to be rushed at anything."

"Leave your sister alone," Nina admonished. "Mark my words, each one of her sorority sisters has gone off into the world, every one of them a contact for the future. At any rate, she and I spoke as well. She's putting the finishing touches on the lake house and suggested we come out for a visit at the end of the music festival." She shook her head. "I get so confused these days, with the music and the technology and the film. But Michael's company sends me tickets by the fistful every year, of course, and I thought to myself, what a fun thing that would be for our young guests!"

"Really?" Margot gaped in surprise. "That would be amazing!"

"You have school part of that time," I reminded her, fully expecting an eye roll. She did not disappoint.

"I spoke to a friend of mine," Nina continued. "One of the women at the label that Mike used to work with. She was telling me about an artist they're promoting during the festival, and I told her about my young friends opening a tea shop, and we agreed that it could be a good fit. I vouched for your scones, heaven knows how many of them I've eaten!" She waggled a finger at us. "Vicki is too busy to come sample, so she's trusting me on this one, and I trust you won't let me down."

It was Celia's turn to gasp. "Oh, Nina!"

"Don't thank me! The success of your shop will be thanks enough. I love seeing strong women succeed and so does Vicki. But"—she raised a playful eyebrow—"should you also attract the eye of a good man while we're there, I can't promise not to be thrilled."

The promise of a catering gig at South by Southwest did indeed lift my spirits. But more than that? I knew Sean's band would be playing there. I knew—*knew*—that he had to be miserable. He *had* to be missing me. I remembered the way he didn't meet my eyes. Nina's statement had gotten me thinking. Was it really as simple as a difficulty with commitment? That day by the river, he'd told me, told me that he would always love me.

That kind of sentiment didn't evaporate in twenty-four hours, did it?

So maybe . . . just maybe, I could try to see him while he was in town. Try to find out if there was anything left in that sentiment, anything left worth clinging to. If there wasn't, that was an entirely different bridge to cross. But if there was? It would be worth it. He was worth it.

With the catering gig and the promise of seeing Sean, I set to work.

First, we sent a thank-you box to Vicki with a selection of my favorite tea blends and scones, cream scones I knew would be just as delicious the second or even third day, if wrapped well. I packaged it up with printed tissue paper and overnighted it to Vicki's office in Nashville.

Vicki had, in turn, sent us a copy of the musician's album.

Celia and I listened together. Ruby Lou Shaw was an up-and-comer, and from the opening bars, I knew why Vicki was excited about her. The sound was light and catchy, with a variety of skillful instrumentation. There were ukuleles that would have sounded cliché if they hadn't been paired with lyrics so contrastingly cynical. There was a mandolin, two nice piano tracks, and a violin. The album included videos of Ruby performing, and we watched, rapt, as Ruby easily shifted from one instrument to another even while singing a complicated run of lyrics.

We'd had a conference call with Vicki and Nina that morning, and the biggest decision to come out of that was the plan to focus on iced teas.

Iced teas were different from my normal standard, that was for sure. Because, while it wasn't hard to have a large variety of tea leaves on hand to brew for a customer, the very temperature of iced tea prevented spontaneity. There were some teas that could be brewed strong and then iced, but others would turn bitter if oversteeped.

The solution was simple, just different for us. We'd prepare a selection of iced teas that we could serve quickly out of oversized carafes.

"What if," I said, "we offered, say, four teas for people to choose from? I can make four different blends."

"That sounds good," Celia agreed.

I widened my eyes. "And we can name them after the songs."

"Vicki will love that!"

I reveled in her approval. Since I'd broken up with Sean, things between Celia and me seemed . . . not back to normal, but easier.

"How about something black with lots of vanilla in it, a green tea with citrus . . ."

"That's always nice."

"And then a chamomile and hibiscus blend—just a touch of the hibiscus—and a peppermint."

"What about sweetening?"

"I'll just prepare a simple syrup, make it optional."

We matched tracks up to the teas, and then set to work planning pastries.

"Let's do miniature pastries," Celia suggested. "Something easier to eat in a bite or two."

"You're right." At the tea shop, we'd always kept a section of the pastry case reserved for miniature versions of some of our larger offerings. They were perfect for people who only wanted a small bite of something decadent.

I looked over the notes I'd taken while we'd listened. "In the third track, she mentions caramel popcorn. What about a salted caramel tartlet with a caramel popcorn garnish?"

"I like that, write it down. She mentions strawberry as a color in that other song—a strawberry tartlet?"

"Easy peasy." I wrote it down too. "I think two tartlets is a good amount. Let's do a lemon bar, those are always good. And maybe goat cheese and pistachios on puff pastry, for something savory."

"Perfect."

I smiled; for a moment we felt like *us,* and even if it was just a moment, I determined to hold it close.

Mini Strawberry Tartlets

For the crusts

1 ½ cups all-purpose flour

½ cup confectioner's sugar

¼ teaspoon fine sea salt

9 tablespoons cold unsalted butter, cut into small pieces, plus more
    for the tartlet pans

1 large egg, beaten

For the filling

1 cup mascarpone cheese

½ cup crème fraîche

2 tablespoons honey

2 teaspoons vanilla bean paste

1 pound strawberries, hulled and sliced

Lightly flour a work space to knead the dough. A wooden cutting board, pastry cloth, silicone mat, or even a clean countertop will work just fine.

In a medium-sized bowl, whisk together the flour, sugar, and salt with a fork. Sprinkle a third of the butter pieces over the flour mixture, toss, and repeat until all of the butter has been added. Using your hands, rub the butter into the flour mixture. Continue to mix until you have clumps of butter the size of small peas and others the size of rolled oats.

Pour the beaten egg over the butter and flour mixture, and use a fork to stir and work it into a shaggy dough that just holds its shape.

Turn the dough out onto the prepared work space, and knead it lightly, only a turn or two to incorporate any runaway flour.

Divide the dough into two discs. Place each dough between two large pieces of plastic wrap. Roll to $3/16$-inch thickness, tuck the edges of the plastic around the dough, and refrigerate for 30 minutes.

Butter the tartlet pans. Place a teaspoon or so of butter onto a paper towel and use it to spread the butter over the surface of the pans.

After 30 minutes, remove the dough from the refrigerator and plastic wrap, and press into the tart pans. Refrigerate the dough inside the tart pans for 30 minutes.

Place the oven rack at the center, and preheat the oven to 375°F.

Cut pieces of aluminum foil to fit over the tartlet crusts, butter them, and press them, buttered side down, over the frozen crusts, pressing tight to seal.

If you're using a tart pan or pans with a removable bottom, place a layer of foil on the rack underneath, to catch any melting butter that may leak out.

Bake the crusts for 10–15 minutes or 15–20 if you're using a full-size pan instead of smaller ones. Remove the pans from the oven, and discard the foil from the tops of the tartlets. If any of the crusts have puffed up, use a spoon to encourage them back down. Bake for another 5–10 minutes, or until the crusts are golden brown. Remove; when the crusts are cool enough to handle safely, use a sharp knife to trim the tops with a sharp knife.

While the crusts are cooling, stir together the mascarpone, crème fraîche, honey, and vanilla bean paste. Spoon the mixture into a quart-sized plastic storage bag or pastry bag.

To assemble, carefully remove the shells from the pans. Cut the corner of the plastic or pastry bag, and pipe the cream into each shell, leaving just a little room at the top. Evenly distribute the sliced strawberries, placing them vertically in the cream. Serve immediately.

Makes 12 mini tartlets, 4 medium-sized tartlets, or 1 large tart.

24

Tea is quiet, and our thirst for tea is never far from
our craving for beauty.

—JAMES NORWOOD PRATT

Jane

Nina's last act of irrationally generous benevolence was to set us up in the pent-
house suite of the Tribeca Grand Hotel, two blocks from the Austin Convention Center.

Margot begged to join us. "It's just not fair!" she wailed. "South by Southwest is so cool, and you get to stay in a hotel!"

"You've got school until next week," Celia told her. "Mariah and Pilar have
very kindly offered to drive you to school and ballet."

"Pick two events," I suggested. "Two events that don't clash with school
and ballet. We'll make sure you can go, and then you'll come join us during
spring break."

This mollified her, at least for a time. But as I looked around the hotel
room, I knew that once we brought Margot, she'd never want to leave.

"Here you are, chickadees," Nina said as the porter showed us into the
largest hotel room I'd ever seen—even before our father's fall from grace. "So
much more convenient this way."

I couldn't reply. I was too busy gaping.

"This is too lovely," Celia said. "Truly, we would have been fine driving to
and from each day."

"Nonsense. There have to be some perks of owning a hotel, don't you
think? Trust me—with the traffic, the parking—no. And certainly not with

your foodstuffs. There's a full kitchen in here—double oven, subzero freezer, I don't even know what. But I imagine you can do whatever baking and preparation you'd like to do here. At any rate, it'll be easier than trying to do it out of Mariah's guesthouse."

She had a point. Ian had offered the use of their kitchen, but I hated to get in Pilar's way.

"Whatever you need, chickadees, just call the concierge. They'll arrange everything."

Celia and I exchanged glances, but promised to take full advantage of the hotel's services. Arguing with Nina was like betting against the house; the house always wins.

What to do with Dash during the duration of the festival proved a challenge; in the end, we elected to bring him with us. Margot hadn't been happy about it in the slightest. But she'd be staying at the big house during our absence and be with us over the two weekends we'd be gone. Mariah had delicately made it clear she didn't relish the idea of having yet another dog in the house, much less one three times the size of her three-year-old, Arabella. Our last resorts, Roy and Betsy, were out of town, visiting their grandchildren in Texarkana.

So Nina, ever generous, offered for Dash to come and stay with us at the hotel, where he would have plenty of room and a dedicated valet to take him on walks.

Dash bore the change in scenery nobly, watching from a generous distance as we baked and scurried around the kitchen. In truth, I was happy to have him. In the days since Sean had left, the oversized galoot of a dog had been a comfort, ready to sit as close to me as physics would allow.

Just as at home, we placed his bed next to mine and carried on.

∞

I texted Sean the first night, letting him know I was at South by Southwest. I sent the text and waited.

No reply.

After two hours, I felt my nerves begin to vibrate. He'd always been quick to text back. Quick with a flirtatious reply and some variation of a smiling face.

I sent a second text the following morning. *We're at the Tribeca Grand Hotel,* I said. *It'd be nice to see you.*

We were in and out most days, going to one party after another with Nina. Not shockingly, she had a steady stream of friends to visit. More surprising was exactly how well connected she was. App-release parties folded into panel discussions in which Nina knew—and often had pet names for—half the panelists.

After a panel about threats to women on the Internet, we walked to the Grove for a late, light dinner. There were people everywhere, disappearing into establishments and spilling out of them. The music portion of the festival hadn't started yet, but that didn't stop musicians from playing in the streets anywhere they could find space. For that short time, Austin seemed to have a few hundred town troubadours on retainer.

The next afternoon, we met in person with the organizer of the party we were catering and finalized our plans.

Celia and I baked and prepared, and I tasted and tweaked the teas until I felt the blends were just right. By three on the afternoon of the party, Nina arrived at our door to roust us from the hotel room, insisting that we'd baked enough and had to get out and live a little, see the sights.

She was right, at least, about the fact that we'd overbaked. Otherwise, a herd of longhorns couldn't have dragged me away from the oven. But at this point, preparation had become excessive, to the point that even I knew enough had to be enough.

And so when Nina arrived, we were shooed away from the kitchen and told to primp. Celia being Celia, all she needed was a spritz of dry shampoo, a dab of lip gloss, and a gentle mist of perfume before emerging from the bedroom looking—and smelling—like an angel from heaven.

Me? I needed a shower and enough conditioner to convince my curly strands to hold hands and make friends, as well as fresh clothes that weren't dusted with flour.

The dress code at the festival I found perplexing at best. While I imagined things would tilt toward funky and relaxed later on, the tech portion seemed to skew to hip business casual. After all, people were here to network. Network first, and if the street noise after dark was any indication, drink by the gallon after.

With that in mind, I twisted up my damp hair before pulling on a black jersey wrap dress. I made it interesting with a rose gold necklace I'd picked up from a boutique in San Francisco, and finished my face off with black eyeliner, mascara, and a shimmery rose gold lip cream.

I emerged from the bedroom to find Nina in the sitting area, Lyndsay by her side.

"You look so nice! I look so underdressed next to the two of you," Lyndsay said, opening her arms so we could get a better look at her own ensemble, which was perfectly chic in its own right, just a little more casual.

I opened my mouth to say something snarky—hadn't decided what yet—but Celia beat me to speech.

"You look perfectly dressed for the weather," Celia said.

"I think all of you look wonderful," Nina said. "Let's get out and find some nice men to admire you, shall we?"

Lyndsay, having found an easy target for her latest compliment fishing expedition, stuck close to Celia, isolating her from the group as we made our way out of our hotel and onto the street.

As we walked, I found myself looking for Sean. Even though he likely hadn't arrived yet, I scanned passersby for a man with his height, stride, and golden head of hair. And I didn't stop looking, not really. Not once we entered the Austin Convention Center, squashed into the elevator, or stepped out onto the rooftop.

There were lights everywhere, and model waitresses in snug branded T-shirts passing out drinks and hors d'oeuvres.

Not surprisingly, Sean wasn't anywhere to be found. I'd seen him with his iPhone—he wasn't a tech guy. But all my subconscious looking meant that my eyes landed on a familiar angled bob, one that had occasionally haunted my less pleasant dreams.

Where there was one, there was likely the other . . . if I could just duck behind Nina to hide . . .

"Jane! Celia! What a pleasant surprise!" Jonathan's voice boomed over the heavy dance beat.

Busted.

We turned in unison to face our former landlord and his wife, and I couldn't stop the flush of resentment that covered my cheeks. "Phoebe. Jonathan. Hi." I cleared my throat, which had grown clogged with unspoken words. "What brings you here?"

Phoebe's expression shifted from dismayed to smug. "My brother," she said. "This is all for him, of course. We're very proud."

I shot a look at Celia. She stood very still, her face pale but lovely.

"Your brother?" I asked. Whatever would Teddy be doing here? This wasn't his scene, though to be honest, it wasn't ours either.

"Yes," Phoebe said. "We're here to support him. This new venture is, of course, very exciting."

I thought Nina had said this was an app launch, but I could have misheard. "How is he involved?"

"He wrote the algorithm, of course. He's so sharp; we're very proud."

"He—" I squinted, and then it began to dawn on me.

"There he is!" Phoebe raised a slim arm to hail her brother as if he were a cab. "Rob!"

Rob. Not Teddy. I knew I couldn't look at Celia without being indiscreet, but she was close enough that I could reach for her hand and give it a gentle squeeze without Phoebe noticing. Phoebe's attention, after all, remained fixed on a brother I'd forgotten she'd possessed.

Rob approached the group, grinning at the group of us. "Hello, ladies," he drawled without any hint of irony.

"Rob," Phoebe said, clearly pleased to be able to show off the family's technological prodigy. "This is Jane and Celia. They used to lease space from us, back in San Francisco."

I tossed a confused look at Celia after smiling at Rob. Had they never met? At any rate, it was the strangest introduction I'd ever heard—it was a feast of conveniently omitted facts.

"It's so nice to meet you," said Lyndsay, who held out her hand in a manner that almost could have been considered professional if she hadn't cocked her hip so far to the side. "I work with Teddy."

"Do you?" Rob took her hand in the spirit in which it was offered.

Did she? I shot a look to Celia, but Celia's impassive face rested on the meeting of Rob and Lyndsay.

Lyndsay nodded, her eyes wide. "Not in the same department—I've been consulting with his team though." Her gaze flicked to Phoebe and Jonathan. "I understand the two of you own some early twentieth-century buildings in the Bay Area. Is that true?"

Where was she getting this? Had Celia told her? Teddy?

"We do," Phoebe said, oblivious to my growing state of bafflement. "It's just a small part of our real estate portfolio though. Most of our holdings are quite modern."

Lyndsay pressed a hand to her heart. I didn't miss Rob's eyes following, specifically at the area between her hand and her heart.

"Teddy always spoke so highly of you and your business acumen," Lyndsay continued.

I could barely contain an eye roll. If Teddy had said anything of the sort, I'd give up tea and devote my life to the cultivation of coffee beans.

But Lyndsay's shamelessly sycophantic lie only caused our former landlords and their Silicon Valley Lothario of a brother to be drawn in nearer. She had Phoebe laughing at an attempt at a joke before departing with Rob to the throng of dancers.

I looked longingly at the door. Nina had brought us, and it would be rude to leave the party. If only staying didn't mean being near Phoebe.

∞

The morning of Ruby Lou Shaw's concert, I woke up an hour before my alarm went off. I was wide awake; there was no point in trying to go back to sleep.

Not when there was so much to do.

I dressed in a print cotton dress I'd ordered from ModCloth two years before. The dress looked like it had come from one of the early seasons of *Mad Men,* but managed to be both comfortable and functional, with deep pockets and a cheery floral print that hid food stains. I tied my hair up and applied red lipstick to my mouth. It wasn't my usual look, but it *was* on brand for Valencia Tea Company.

Dash set off on a walk with his valet of the day, and Celia met me in the kitchen. We checked off the items on our individual to-do lists before loading up the oversized metal food carts we had in our room for this purpose. By the time we finished loading them with the carafes of iced tea and baked goods, we had to lean hard to push them out of the room.

Nina arrived with extra hired help just then, and we made a slow procession to the service elevator and down to the ground floor.

The event wasn't more than five blocks away; I felt funny taking a van for the trip, but it made more sense than pushing the food through the festival crowds.

Vicki met us at the door to the space, and I admired her handiwork. It could fit a crowd, but the stage had been set up with Persian rugs on the floor and side tables with beaded lamps and a couple of houseplants.

We set up our goods, using the pastry cases that had been delivered that morning. I was glad to see that the serving area had been set up with bar space in mind, meaning we had sinks and plenty of counter space.

Celia opened up one of the containers of tartlets and offered one to Vicki. "That's so good!" she exclaimed. "I'm very pleased. I think you'll be a hit." She chewed a moment longer. "I'm going to make a plate to take back to Ruby. She'll appreciate this."

I nodded, opening boxes to pull out a selection of the prettiest offerings for Vicki to take back to the greenroom, as well as a cup of the chamomile tea.

The next hour was a blur as we set up. It felt good to work like this again, me and Celia side by side. I'd forgotten how well we could negotiate a space and anticipate each other's thoughts and requests.

"Wait!" I said, just when it looked like we were ready. "The business cards."

"Yes!" Celia reached into one of the canvas bags, retrieved the box of cards, and set a stack out for people to take. And then there was nothing to do but wait.

Soon enough, concertgoers began to pour in. They were dressed for the weather but also to make a statement.

Also? They were all thirsty.

Celia and I worked fast, pouring iced tea, snapping lids over the cups, and jamming colorful straws into them. We handed out plenty of pastries, but the drinks were by far the most popular.

"How are the teas holding out?" I asked Celia. "I took Vicki's estimate into account and made more, but . . ."

"I think they had a bigger response than expected. We're running low on the black tea."

"No, really?" I turned around, and she was right.

Vicki rushed toward us. "How are you girls doing? What a turnout!"

"It's great," I told her brightly.

"Show's going to start in ten," she said.

When she left, I spun around to Celia. "Okay. We need a plan."

Celia nodded in agreement. "We can't run out of tea."

"Nope. Nope, we cannot." I looked over our prep area. We had an ice maker, but no way to boil water. "My kingdom for an instant hot water faucet."

"Your kingdom is a set of potted tea plants," Celia observed, mouth twitching in a smile.

"Yes. But there's got to be an industrial kitchen in a place like this. If I figure out how to brew more, can you hold down the fort here?"

"You have more tea?"

"It's me," I told her, feeling confident and a bit manic all at once. "I always have more tea."

I'd packed an emergency stash. But my spirits sank as I realized I hadn't packed tea bags.

One problem at a time.

I found a member of the hotel staff and talked my way into the empty kitchen the floor above us. Working fast, I filled pots with water and set them to boiling. While they heated, I found the hotel's hot water pitchers and—most importantly—the cupboard full of coffee filters.

A little clever folding, and I fashioned tea bags. I dropped one into each pitcher.

The staff member was visibly nervous by the time I filled the pitchers. "They have a reservation for this space in twenty minutes," he said, clearly regretting having helped me in the first place.

"I just need five," I told him, hurrying but taking care not to spill water. Once the pitchers were full and loaded onto yet another cart, I pushed them down the hallway and back to the elevator.

When Celia saw me, her shoulders sank in relief. "I just poured the last of the black tea."

"I'm glad that's what I made. If everyone had decided to switch favorites, this would have all been for nothing."

"Is it done steeping?"

"I sure hope so," I answered.

We didn't have to wait long to find out. Celia put a smile on her face for the next patron. I poured the hot tea over a cup full of ice just as Ruby Lou started her next song.

Which, ironically, was about living life in a hurry.

But the tea looked like it had brewed nicely, and I handed it to Celia with pride.

Afterward we were tired and discreetly sweaty, with a full tip jar and far fewer business cards.

"It was wonderful!" Vicki told us as we cleaned up. "Amazing turnout, and y'all didn't bat an eye. I appreciate that kind of preparation."

We thanked her and sent her off with a box of leftover pastries.

"Hey," I said to Celia, wrapping an arm around her waist. "You were awesome. This was fun."

"If I was awesome, you were a rock star," she said, hugging me back.

"I love you, Cee," I said, and wished in my heart we could stay in that moment forever.

∞

The day of Sean's concert, I woke up with butterflies but without a return text. I was going to go; Celia hadn't even tried to talk me out of it. With everything that had happened, I needed to see him—even if it was with him on stage and me camouflaged in the middle of a crowd.

Later that night, we stepped into the Cedar Street Courtyard together, Celia and I. Nina promised to join us shortly; the booker at Cedar Street was an old friend of hers, and she waved us on before lagging behind to catch up with him.

My heart pounded as I looked around, trying to spot Sean. The band's equipment was on stage, but I couldn't see any of the band members.

"Look at this place!" Celia said, tilting her head back to take it in. The courtyard really was that—hemmed in on both sides with buildings, one of them covered in a thick layer of ivy. There were balconies on either side as well and two trees in between.

I searched the crowd for any familiar faces, for Sean but also for his band mates.

After several long minutes, the music over the speakers stopped and those very faces took the stage, instruments in hand. Sean walked out last, and the crowd's screams grew louder.

He looked completely the same and yet different at the same time. I recognized his T-shirt, his favorite faded CBGB shirt that happened to cling to his arms just right. But in the weeks since I'd last seen him, his hair had grown longer, and there was a shadow of a soul patch on his chin.

My heart ached to look at him.

Sean winked at the girls in the front, his attitude somehow both flirtatious and bashful. He gripped the microphone in a practiced gesture, adjusting it just so. "We're the Bandwagon Rebels," he said, with a nod toward the band behind him. "We're originally from Austin, and it's good to be home!"

Another cheer from the crowd.

"You guys are lucky: we've got a surprise," he said, leaning his body far enough away from the mic to strum his guitar as he spoke. "We've got a guest tonight, someone you might be familiar with. And if you're not? You will be. Ladies and gentlemen, Sofi Grey!"

Amid another ear-splitting cheer, a young woman took the stage with them. Sean caught her hand and tugged her close, adding, "My fiancée!"

The din that followed must have finally succeeded in producing deafness, because while I could see everyone clapping and hollering, I couldn't hear any of it. I heard Sean's words, I heard my own heartbeat in my ears, and that was all.

Celia pulled me close. "We can leave," she said. "We can go back to the hotel. We can do whatever you want."

I couldn't respond. The drummer kicked off the beat, the backup guitarist strummed the opening chord, and the bassist plucked a low, resonant pair of notes. Sean joined in, adding the picking he was known for; Sofi played with him. They faced each other, playing together as if it were a duet, like they were the only ones in the room.

It was like watching Reese Witherspoon and Joaquin Phoenix sing to each other in *Walk the Line*.

I stood there through their set, motionless as if my arms and legs had lost functionality. Celia stood behind me, and I could feel her gaze. Everyone swayed and jumped and danced to the music, people bumping into each other and us—hands, elbows, torsos, feet.

After four songs, they launched into the song I knew was their concert-ender, a barn burner meant to get everyone hyped for the next act, but still sharp and catchy enough to linger through the next band's performance.

The band rushed forward to take their bows before exiting to make room for the next act; and that's when my limbs seemed to fill again.

With slow but steady steps, I made my way forward, weaving through the crowd. The scents of sweat, cheap cologne, and body odor filled my nose, and any jostling I'd received earlier was now multiplied.

The guys reemerged from a side door minutes later, their faces grinning and triumphant. They spilled out, accepting high fives and catcalls from the restless crowd. Sean led the pack, soaking it in. His stride was loose and his head high, and he nodded at people as he moved past.

Until he saw me, that is.

When our eyes met, he stilled. Froze, really.

I became stronger. I walked up to him and tipped my head until I could meet his gaze.

I knew those eyes; I knew everything about his face. How could a face so familiar look at me as if I were some random woman? A woman he hadn't met on the side of the road, a woman he hadn't spent hours with, a woman he hadn't asked to go with him on tour?

Only weeks ago, he'd woven his hands into my hair and told me he loved me. And now he was *engaged*?

Did he have a brain tumor?

My eyebrows tipped in confusion. "I texted you," I said. "I wasn't coming to the festival here for you. Nina brought us, we catered a . . . thing. But I texted. I thought we could . . . we could talk."

He said nothing; I wasn't sure if he was breathing.

"Won't you say something, Sean?"

The question came out as a breathy plea, and I heard the desperation behind it. I knew everyone else had too, the way people either averted their gaze or stared unabashed.

"I'm sorry," he said finally, his voice stiff. "I got a new phone."

"You got a new *phone*?" I heard the pitch of my voice raise an octave, felt Celia's hand on my arm.

In my peripheral vision, I could see the guys behind him—each one looking like they wished they could dissolve into the floor.

"I've got a new life now," Sean said. "I'm getting married."

His voice was wooden. If there was any joy to be found in his new circumstances, I couldn't hear it in his words.

"I didn't come here to harass you," I said, suddenly tired. "I thought . . . thought you might want to see me."

"Sorry, Jane," Sean said, glancing over his shoulder at his new fiancée. "I've moved on."

"Right."

My eyes filled with tears then, and Sean's face grew distorted. I couldn't seem to get a deep breath; the air was too hot and too heavy to breathe.

Sean moved past, and even over the noise I could hear him murmuring to Sofi. "Ex-girlfriend, sorry," he told her. She accepted it with a shrug and only the briefest of glances. His band mates followed after, ducking their heads, faces flushed with embarrassment.

When the arm—Celia's—reached for me again, I didn't resist. I let it pull me, lead me back to the street where the air was only a little cooler.

I swayed on my feet. Celia led me to a bench, and Nina found us moments later.

"I just heard!" she exclaimed with a gasp. "Our Sean, engaged to Sofi Grey! After such a short time, I wouldn't believe it if I hadn't heard it from my good friend Terese Taylor. There was a bidding war among the labels to sign Sofi, you know. Not Mike's label, they're too sensible for that. But Whippoorwill Records made her a wealthy woman, and they're in talks with Sean's band too, and it sounds like they'll all be leaving on tour soon." Nina gave a wistful sigh. "I do miss the touring life. Waking up in new cities, meeting new people . . ."

"We need to get her home," Celia said firmly, wrapping one arm around my waist, her opposite hand on my shoulder. "Home, the hotel, whatever is fastest."

"The hotel then," Nina answered. "Let's be quick before the gossip gets worse. You know how people are."

I could barely breathe by the time we got back to the hotel. Nina and Celia helped me to the bedroom, where Nina squinted at my face. "I don't like her color, not at all."

"You're white as a sheet, Jane," Celia said.

It took everything I had to try to form a sentence. "I . . . can't . . . breathe." The weight on my chest squeezed at my heart and my lungs, and spots danced before my eyes.

Nina reached for my wrist; at first I thought she was holding my hand in a gesture of comfort, but when she pronounced my heart rate to be concerningly high, I realized she'd been feeling for my pulse.

"You're having a panic attack," she said calmly. "My daughter Charlie used to get them, poor love. Best you can do right now is wait it out."

Celia sat next to me and squeezed my hand.

My thoughts raced. Sean was gone. For good. He'd be spending his life with Sofi Grey, a successful musician whose father probably wasn't an international laughingstock, who probably had a perfect relationship with her sister, and—I imagined—was also aces at folding a bottom sheet to look like a top sheet.

Was she smarter than me? A better kisser? More fun? Had he asked if they could tour together, and she enthusiastically agreed, without reservations?

Probably all of the above.

I didn't buy Sean's line about a new phone number, not for a second. And it wasn't as if somehow I'd become unreachable, gone off grid.

No, the choice to shut me out had been deliberate.

I'd thought Sean and I meant something to each other. Up until tonight, a part of me had believed that he'd travel, he'd think, he'd come back to me. I'd believed that maybe I mattered to him, that our relationship had mattered to him.

Tonight had just proved exactly how irrelevant I'd been all along.

I woke with Dash snuggled next to me—a feat he could achieve here, since the room featured a king-sized bed. I wrapped an arm around him and held him close, leaning forward to get a whiff of him. He smelled of dog, of shampoo, of comfort.

Callum was seriously lucky. Or unlucky, considering that I wasn't sure I'd be able to give Dash back.

When I could talk myself into it, I rose and showered, changed into fresh clothes, and twisted my hair up before stepping out of the bedroom.

Celia stood in the kitchen, kneading dough. "Hey! There you are." She gave the dough two more turns before setting it aside and dusting off her hands. "How are you feeling?"

My eyes filled with tears again, and a fresh sob escaped from my throat.

"I'm sorry. I'm so sorry." Celia wrapped her arms around my torso and held me tight.

Dash padded out of the bedroom to join us, ambling closer until he could sit and lean against the two of us.

I hung on to Celia's hug, enjoying the moment. It had been so long since we'd felt so close.

"Breakups are awful," she continued. "I get it. Everything will be okay."

And then . . . her words watered the seed of resentment, and I felt an ugly blossom bloom deep inside my chest. I pulled away. "How can you say that?"

Celia's eyes widened. "What?"

"How can you say that you get it? That everything will be okay? Sean—he was the only good thing about being here in this awful city. He wasn't just my boyfriend, he was my *friend,* and he listened to me and talked to me and . . . trusted me." An awkward hiccup.

"When Teddy and I broke up—it was awful. I understand."

The ugly bloom unfurled its petals even farther. "You can't understand, Celia! I saw you when you and Teddy broke up. This is nowhere near the same."

Celia stared at me.

"Look," I said, trying to calm down. "I get it. We've both had breakups. This one—this was more than a breakup." I ran a hand through my hair. "I followed you, Celia. I followed you to Austin because I thought it's what you needed. And then we got here, and you shut me out. You talk—you talk to *Lyndsay.*" I all but spat the name out. "The Celia I knew would have agreed very politely that she's completely asinine. But now you talk to her and you don't talk to me, and the only person who does talk to me is this guy, this wonderful, kind, sweet guy who shows up exactly at the right time, and he shared thoughts and his dreams and gave me a place where I felt like I almost belonged."

"Jane—"

"And then he left! Like he woke up that morning, and everything we had didn't matter and never had, and then weeks later I find out he's engaged? That's not a garden variety breakup. It's, like, a breakup wrapped in a betrayal, served with a dash of"—my voice caught—"indifference. I didn't matter to him."

Celia's eyes filled with tears. "I . . . I don't know what to say."

I wanted to tell her to be my sister again. To be the person who trusted me back.

The words sat on the tip of my tongue, but I couldn't force them out. What was left of my pride had already been shredded by Sean; I didn't have it in me to beg my sister to be my friend again. My real friend, not a person standing with me in a hotel kitchen offering platitudes.

So rather than be the one to beg again, I disappeared back into my room.

25

I done drew the line. Just like the Alamo. You're either
on one side of the line or the other. I don't want to
ever leave Texas again.

—BUM PHILLIPS

Callum

Lila very nearly kissed the tarmac, but two things stopped her. First, the fact
that we disembarked onto a jet bridge that took us straight to the terminal.
Secondly, it occurred to her that placing her lips to the floor was a sure way to
catch a strange disease and pass it on to her child.

But Lila, ever creative, struck a compromise. She retrieved four paper towels from the women's restroom, placed them on the floor, and kissed those
while I snapped a picture.

"This doesn't feel crazy at all," I told her.

"I'm glad you agree with me," she retorted.

The drive home was quiet; we'd spent enough time together in the last
weeks that I could tell when she was growing tired and needed to rest again.
When we reached my house, I carried her suitcase inside and took her straight
to the guest suite.

"You don't mind if I take a nap right now?" she asked, eying the bed
greedily.

"I'd be offended if you didn't." I pulled my house key off the ring. "I'm
going to go see my friend Ian. Here's a key to the house if you decide to go ex-
plore the neighborhood later."

"Won't you need it?"

"I have the spare downstairs. Call me if you need anything, please. The house phone is in the kitchen."

"I'm fine."

"There are a few dry goods in the pantry, but I'll leave cash downstairs if you want to call for delivery."

"I'm fine," Lila insisted, sitting on the bed and pulling her legs up. "I'm going to nap now. Go away."

"If you—"

"Go away, Callum!"

I ducked as a slip-on shoe sailed past my ear. "I forgot you played softball. You can still pitch."

Descending the stairs, I realized my ears were listening for Dash's soft taps. He'd barely been with me more than a couple of days—and I'd been gone far longer than that—but I missed him in the house. Was it the silence of the house that made it worse?

I thought about it as I drove to Ian's.

Quiet, for me, was a new phenomenon. In the military, there's little solitude and less quiet. Same in the hospital. And Ian's house, though sprawling, usually hummed with some activity or other—the children playing, Pilar's housekeeping, Ian's pack of dogs, even Mariah herself as she attended to the household.

Never mind the guesthouse with the Woodward sisters, though that was a different matter entirely.

But my house? It didn't yet feel like my house. It looked like a spiffed-up version of my childhood memories, as if a storybook good fairy had waved a wand and cleaned it up.

Having Dash had taken the edge off the quiet, and without him I felt myself rattle more than usual.

Pilar answered the door, then ushered me in while chiding me for not letting myself in. "You're family," she said. "I had to leave my kitchen to come get you."

"I missed you too," I told her.

She harrumphed, but patted my arm.

"You're back!" Ian rose from his desk when he saw me.

"I should have called," I told him, but Ian shook his head.

"Of course not; glad to see you." He sat back in his chair and threaded his fingers together. "So? What can you tell me?"

I took the chair opposite his desk, along with a deep breath, and gave him the condensed version I'd worked out during the flight. I left out the identity of the man who'd left Lila in such straits, focusing instead on Lila's return and the aid I'd received from Clint.

"That," Ian said, "was more of an adventure than any of us anticipated. Lila's well, then?"

"She is. She has an appointment with a doctor this week."

"Good, good. You'll let us know if she needs anything?"

"I will," I promised, though I knew that taking care of her myself had become a point of family honor. My brother had gotten her into this mess, and I needed to undo the damage.

I shifted in the chair and changed the subject. "Anyway, I thought I'd stop by, say hello, and pick up Dash from the Woodwards."

"You've been gone so long! You won't find him here—or the Woodwards, either. No need to panic," Ian assured me before I could say anything. "They're all fine, at least as fine as can be expected. Nina put Jane and Celia up at her hotel for the duration of the festival, and they took Dash with them."

"They did?"

"Nina made sure he's got a valet taking him for walks," Ian said, as if relying on a hotel valet for walks was an experience every dog endured. "Young Margot has been with us, though she's at a concert with her sisters before the end of the festival. Tonight, we're headed to Charlie's lake house. You're coming, aren't you?"

"I . . ."

"What am I saying? Of course you are. Bring Lila with you."

"I'll check with Lila."

Ian leaned forward. "Jane's going to be there. Nina might have to tie her up, but she's determined for Jane to have a good time." Ian's gray eyes narrowed at me. "You are still interested in Jane, aren't you? Or have you decided on Lila, now that she's back?"

"Lila's like a sister to me," I told him. "Jane . . ."

"She's single now."

I opened my mouth, closed it, and thought for a moment before trying again. "I might be in love with her. Hard to say. But she deserves better than someone who doesn't know."

"Just come to the lake house. At the very least, she could use a friendly face."

"I— I'll think about it," I said. "When are y'all headed to Charlie's, again?"

"Tonight—she's hosting us for dinner."

"Tonight?"

"You said you'd think about it!"

"I have some accounts for the restaurant I should go through—"

"Bring 'em with you."

I looked at my old friend, his eyes as eager as Dash's at dinnertime. "There's not a lot I can say that's going to let me off the hook, huh?"

Ian leaned forward. "Beckett, if I thought it was in your best interests to stay home, of course I'd want what's best for you. But you've been through a hard time, and you need to blow off some steam. And it just so happens, we're planning a trip to my sister-in-law's place and the woman you're in love with is going too. How is this a bad plan?"

"When did you turn into a yenta?"

Ian's face turned sad. "When my best friend returned from overseas convinced he was broken beyond repair and destined to be alone for the rest of his life."

His words landed like grenades, one after another, each one aimed at the center of my chest. For a moment, I couldn't breathe. I couldn't breathe because he'd just put into words everything I had been afraid to say aloud since returning to American soil.

"She's special, Ian," I said, finally. "And it'll take a special man to be with her. I'm not sure I'm up to the task anymore."

"Beckett—"

"I'm not strong enough."

Ian sighed as if he'd just aged several years in a single breath. "Just come to the doggone lake house, Beckett. You can have an existential crisis while you watch the sun set over the lake."

I looked at my friend, the pleading in his eyes. I knew I hadn't been easy since I'd gotten home. I hadn't been easy *before* I'd come home. Yet he'd included me in his life, pulling me into his orbit, patiently waiting and hoping.

If he wanted me to go to the lake house, I'd go to the doggone lake house.

I took a deep breath and shook my head. "Why do I get a feeling that you're going to hold my dog hostage until I agree?"

Ian's mouth twitched. "The thought occurred to me."

"I'll come," I said. "Can't let Dash think I don't care about him."

"We wouldn't want that. To be honest with you, I don't think he's suffered too much with the Woodward sisters. Nina said that he's been sleeping with Jane."

Jealousy flashed through me. Jealous of my own dog?

I needed to get a grip. "I'm glad Dash has been taken care of," I said, making every effort to sound like the reasonable adult that I was supposed to be.

"Don't forget to see if Lila wants to come too. You know Charlie, the more the merrier. She invited Lyndsay to come along too, but she's taking a few days to sightsee historic San Antonio with Jane and Celia's former landlords."

"What?"

"I don't understand it myself. Seems Jane knew the wife's brother well, or maybe Celia. I'll ask Nina. Anyway, they asked Lyndsay if she wanted to go see San Antonio with them." Ian leaned back in his chair. "At any rate, if we managed to bring more people than Charlie has room for, she'd sooner construct a new wing before turning anyone away."

"Right," I said, though my brain considered the inherent conflicts involved if I brought Lila. If Jane were there too, that might be unnecessarily difficult, for both of them. Given time, I suspected they might make friends of each other, but with Lila pregnant with Sean's baby and Jane fresh from her own breakup—a trip to the lake house seemed unwise.

"I'll talk to Lila. She may not want to travel anymore right now, and she's got a doctor's appointment coming up." I rose from my chair. "I'll be in touch."

Next, I drove to Roy and Betsy's. As I pulled into their driveway and looked at their house, with its welcoming front porch, I realized something. I had people. Ian's family, Roy and Betsy, Lila—not the family I'd been born into, but family just the same, in their own way. And maybe they'd mostly been there all along, and I hadn't seen it. Hadn't let myself see it.

As I parked, I resolved to do better. If they were my people, I wanted to be one of their people in return.

Betsy greeted me at the door with a hug. "Did you just get back?"

"I did."

"Glad you're home. We just got back too; saw the grandbabies in Texarkana."

I admired several photos she'd taken with her phone before she rousted Roy in from the garage. Roy groused all the way inside. "I'm trying to build you a smoker," he said, removing his welding helmet and smock. "I can't finish it with these interruptions."

"I missed you too," I told him and was rewarded with a smile.

"How's that Lila?" he asked, and within minutes we were seated around their table with glasses of iced tea and warm corn bread, the latter nearly drowning beneath a layer of warm butter and honey.

"She has cameras on you," Roy said, pointing at his wife. "That's how she knew to have the corn bread ready."

Betsy swatted her husband's arm. "Oh, stop."

"When you're not around, it's just water and unseasoned beans around here."

"He missed you," Betsy told me. "When we weren't with the grandbabies, he was walking around hangdog, worrying after you."

Roy shook his head. "I don't know where she gets this."

"Lila's fine," I told them and provided the same retelling I'd given to Ian. "She needs some R&R, but I think she'll be all right."

Betsy breathed a prayer of gratitude.

"I'm thinking of heading to Ian's sister-in-law's place on Canyon Lake for the weekend. Lila's resting at my house. If she doesn't want to be there by herself, I was thinking that maybe she could stay with you two? If it's not an inconvenience."

"Of course not!" Betsy exclaimed. "We've got a whole guest bedroom, it's very nice and cozy. With our boys all grown, I'd love to have her."

"We'd be happy to have her, even if the boys were here," Roy said. "Set your mind at ease."

I explained that I told Lila I'd make her a rightful part owner in the restaurants. "I know she'll be looking for work," I said. "Though with the baby . . ."

"First things first. Do you think there's something in the office she could handle?"

"I'm sure there is," I said. "She studied business in college, same as Cameron."

"Then you can create a job for her and set her up on payroll and benefits, maternity leave, that sort of thing. One step at a time."

"Right." I exhaled.

"Don't you worry," Roy said. "It'll all shake out."

I nodded, wishing I could be so sure.

∞

After enjoying a second slice of corn bread, I said my good-byes to Roy and Betsy before making the short drive home.

I found Lila at the long farmhouse table, enjoying a slice of pizza.

"Don't get me wrong," she said. "There's pizza in Mexico. But American pizza?" Her eyes rolled up. "You know how sad it is to be pregnant and craving American pizza and not to be able to get any?"

I took a seat next to her. "I'm glad you've got it now. Good nap?"

"Very." She finished the end of crust she'd been eating and nudged her plate away. "Listen. Clint called."

"Oh yeah?"

"He offered me a job."

That wasn't what I'd expected. "Really?"

"His admin is moving away—military spouse, you know how it goes."

"I do."

"Anyway, he asked if I'd be interested, and I said yes."

"You have options," I told her. "I was just talking to Roy about where to put you at Smoky Top."

"For now at least, I could probably do both. I can do accounts, if they need doing. And the ordering—it's what I used to do, and I was good at it."

"I didn't realize you used to do the ordering."

"Until Cameron realized it would be easier to have an affair if I wasn't around on-site, yes."

I winced.

Lila shook her head. "Not your fault. Anyway, between the two, I should be able to afford a place of my own."

"Of your own? Are you sure?"

"I am," she said. "When I was young, I trusted Cameron to take care of me. And then Jake and Ben and Frankie—"

"Frankie?"

"A rebound. Don't judge. And then there was Sean, and we both know how that turned out. My point is that I've relied on too many men to take care of me when I need to be taking care of myself. And it's not that I don't appreciate you—I do. To the moon and back. It's . . . it's just a thing I need to do for me, and I think I need to do to prove to myself that I can be a mom."

"You'll be a good mom."

Lila gave a wobbly smile. "I don't know about that yet. Maybe if I get to a point where my life doesn't read like a cautionary tale."

I leaned forward on the table, palms to the surface. "It's not that I don't believe that you can do whatever you set your mind to. Could you just promise me, please, that you'll come to me if you need anything?"

She gave a wide, brilliant smile. "I promise. And I probably will. I don't think I'll have my act together fast enough not to need you at some point."

I took a deep breath, her words sinking in. A part of me wanted to argue, but the wiser part of me knew not to. If she was stepping forward after all these years, I wasn't about to get in her way.

"Okay. Okay." Another breath. "The other thing I was going to tell you is that I—we—have been invited to Ian's sister-in-law's lake house for the weekend. Or the week. It's open like that."

"Is she going to be there? Jane?"

I felt my face flush, and from the widening smile on Lila's face, I knew that my tan hadn't camouflaged it. "Yeah, she'll be there. I'm supposed to pick up my dog from her there, at least that's Ian's plan."

"Then the last thing you need is to show up with me. I'll sit tight here; I'm fine. You go enjoy your lake house." She spoke the last two words with an upper-crust drawl.

"It's not like that," I protested, but she only laughed.

"You have to remember, I used to be a part of that world. Feels like a lifetime ago. No, you go and have a good time. Catch up with Jane. Sweep her off her feet. There's a lake, isn't there?"

"Canyon Lake is technically a reservoir, but yes," I answered dryly.

She leaned forward. "What you need to do is go for a swim, you know, in your clothes. Somewhere where Jane can see you."

"I don't understand where this is going."

"Make sure you're wearing a white shirt, that's the most important bit. Go for a swim, and only walk back to shore when she's looking."

"In my clothes."

"Trust me."

"That is the most ridiculous thing I've ever heard."

"Every woman swoons over a man walking out of a lake in a white shirt. It's a universal truth."

"I doubt that. And Jane would think I'd lost my mind."

"You won't know unless you try."

"I hope you're amusing yourself."

Lila reached for another slice of pizza. "I am, thank you very much. Just do something, Cal. If you love her, don't let her slip away."

Southern Skillet Corn Bread

1 ¼ cups coarse-ground cornmeal

³/4 cup flour

¼ cup sugar

1 teaspoon sea salt

2 teaspoons baking powder

½ teaspoon baking soda

¹/3 cup whole milk, at room temperature

1 cup buttermilk, at room temperature

2 eggs, lightly beaten, at room temperature

1 stick butter (8 tablespoons), melted

2 tablespoons butter, at any temperature

To serve
Salted butter
Honey

Preheat a 9-inch cast-iron skillet in a 425°F oven.

While the skillet is heating, whisk together the dry ingredients. In a separate bowl, stir together the milk, buttermilk, and eggs. Make a well in the dry ingredients, and pour the wet ingredients into it, folding them together. Add the 8 tablespoons of melted butter.

Remove the skillet from the oven (make sure you've got excellent hand protection—it'll be hot!), turn the oven down to 375°F. Use a spatula to spread the remaining 2 tablespoons butter around, coating the bottom and sides. Pour the batter into the skillet, and bake for 20–25 minutes, or until the corn bread is lightly browned and a tester comes out clean. Allow to cool for 10 minutes before serving.

Cut into squares or wedges, and serve with lots of butter and honey.

Serves 8.

26

I must say as to what I have seen of Texas, it is the garden spot of the world.

The best land and best prospects for health I ever saw and I do believe it is a fortune to any man to come here.

There is a world of country to settle.

—Davy Crockett

Callum

I drove out to Charlie's place myself, though Ian had offered to drive. He understood when I explained that I needed a vehicle in case Lila had an emergency. I knew she'd have rolled her eyes at my show of caution, but it seemed practical.

Besides, it would be nice to drive back myself with Dash as copilot.

I left later than intended and hit traffic leaving town. By the time I arrived outside Charlie's sprawling "cabin," a fleet of cars was parked in the circular driveway. The evening was warm, and laughter spilled over the edge of the balcony.

"Oh, look, Beckett's here!" came Ian's voice.

Several voices rose in tandem, and I took the stairs as quickly as possible to find their source.

Charlie met me by the door; I may not have seen her for years, but she looked unmistakably like her mother—open features, broad smile, and a ready—if verbose—welcome.

"Captain Beckett! So glad you've made it to our little cabin! Come right in and make yourself welcome. We're just out having an evening snack. Can I get you something? Sweet tea? Coke?"

"I wouldn't turn away a Coke, thank you, ma'am," I told her.

"I'll get one for you right away. And leave your shoes on; we're on the balcony."

She talked, I followed—and listened as she told me about how glad she and Pierce were to finally get to use the lake house, how they'd been in town too long, and the city just got to her. And especially with the new baby, it was so important for them to get away from it all and bond.

I congratulated her on their new arrival, and she answered with a broad smile that made the resemblance to Nina even more apparent. "We're very happy, of course, and Pierce is thrilled to pieces. Bowie is napping, but he'll be up soon enough. He'll want to meet you, of course."

"How old is he?"

"Thirteen weeks." Another smile. "He's such a love."

If Bowie was anything like his mother or grandmother, I didn't doubt that he really would want to meet me, despite his tender stage of development.

We rounded the corner together, and I saw the open french doors leading to the patio.

"Beckett! There you are!" Ian rose from his rocking chair. "I thought maybe you'd gotten lost."

"Between the front door and the patio?" I asked, joking, as Dash trotted over to lean against me. I bent over to rub his face and ears. "Hi, buddy," I said, enjoying the way his eyes and tongue lolled in pleasure. "Missed you."

"It's happened before," Charlie said, handing me a bottle of Coke—a glass bottle—from an oversized bucket of beverages and ice placed on a nearby wrought-iron table. "Help yourself to the taco bar; the shrimp is in the chafing dish. Pierce whipped them up tonight. He's so handy in the kitchen."

Celia lifted a hand in greeting. "Good to see you, Callum. I hope your trip went well."

I saw Jane then, seated next to her. I could feel my heart in my chest as I took her in. She looked—I could hardly wrap my head around it. She looked like herself, just less of it. Less present, less vibrant.

"Hello, Jane," I said, my voice careful and controlled. Kind too, I hoped.

Jane started and looked up at me, as if she suddenly noticed I'd entered the room. "Oh. Callum. Hello." She glanced at Dash and back at me. "Glad you're back," she said. "Dash missed you."

"Not from what I heard," I said, smiling while I continued to give Dash the pets and attention he was convinced were overdue. "Thanks for looking after him," I told her, glancing at Celia and young Margot to include them in my thanks.

"He's kind of the best dog ever," Margot said, and from her expression I suspected she didn't consider me worthy. And maybe I wasn't, but I was awfully fond of him, even after such a short time.

"Dash is a very good dog, and I love dogs. Ours is around here somewhere, probably sneaking a nap on the sofa." Charlie's eyebrows knit together. "You know, Ian might be right about the entryway. We should really think about trying to shorten the path from the front door to the patio. Pierce, honey, do you think if we knocked out the wall in the dining room—"

"No more construction, Charlie." Charlie's husband Pierce cut her off before she could continue her mental takedown of the house's interior.

"But Beckett here—," Charlie protested.

"Survived the walk in one piece," Pierce said, though his eyes widened as he noticed my prosthesis.

I stepped forward, offering my hand. "Callum Beckett. I don't think we've met."

"No, but I've heard a lot about you. Pierce Palmer." He gave me a solemn nod as we shook hands.

"Nice place; thanks for having me."

"Of course. It's good for this place to get some use." He looked around, wrinkling his nose.

"It's a very nice home," Celia said, her voice assuring.

"You were smart to buy on this side of the lake," Mariah said, stretching out on the patio chaise. "It's an excellent investment."

"Oh yes," Charlie answered, nodding, "The neighborhood is very good. Though there are several good spots around the lake. I heard yesterday that that singer—Sofi Grey? She just bought a place across the lake. You can see it from here; it's that pretty white one over there."

Jane, who'd been drinking a cup of water, choked and spluttered.

"Sofi Grey?" Nina pressed a hand to her chest. "No!"

All eyes turned to her. Charlie's jaw dropped; she hadn't expected her mother's response. "No?"

"Sofi Grey is the fiancée of Jane's no-good ex-sweetheart, Sean."

"No! Really?" Charlie's eyes were the size of dinner plates as she turned to Jane. "What's he like?"

Jane's body went rigid. "I'm not sure I knew him at all."

"He is very handsome," Nina said. "Like a young Robert Redford."

"I thought he looked more like Chris Evans," Margot piped up before Celia shushed her.

"Ooh, yes," Nina continued. "Very blond, very handsome, but he left poor Jane and became engaged to Sofi Grey in a matter of weeks! Extremely suspect, if you ask me."

Nobody had, but that seemed beside the point.

"Do you think she's pregnant?" Charlie asked, eagerly.

Jane leapt from her deck chair. "I have a headache," she said, picking up her plate. "I need to lie down."

"Oh!" Charlie suddenly realized that discussing an ex-boyfriend's engagement and potential family in front of Jane might be in poor taste. "I'm so sorry. Truly. And really, I don't like Sofi's music; honest I don't. And now that I know, I don't even want to look at her house. Pierce?"

"Yes?" Charlie's husband didn't even bother to cover the dread in his voice.

"We must plant some trees. Nice, tall trees, so we won't be able to see Sofi's house at all."

"That might ruin the view," Pierce said. "Which might ruin the point of a lake-view house."

"I'm just tired from the festival," Jane said, this time resting her hand on Charlie's arm. "I'll be better after I lie down."

"Oh yes, of course. Do you remember where your room is?" Charlie asked. "I really should have signs made. Like a hospital."

"Or those colored track lights," Pierce suggested, his tone sarcastic.

Charlie's face lit. "Ooh, yes, those would be better!"

At that moment, a thin, static-y squawk emitted from somewhere near the drink bucket.

"Ooh!" Nina clapped her hands. "Bowie's awake!"

Both Charlie and Pierce crouched down to put their faces near the baby monitor, which I realized had been positioned next to the beverages.

"Is he awake?" Charlie asked breathlessly.

Pierce's eyebrows knit together. "Might have been a fart."

"Pierce! We say 'toot' here."

"I don't know if you noticed, but that's a boy in there. Girls may toot, but boys fart."

"I can't believe we're having this conversation—"

Bowie must not have believed it either, because his next cry was unmistakably just that.

"Definitely awake!" Nina stood up. "I can go get him."

"Let's go together," Charlie said, clasping her mother's hand as if they were going to go off on an adventure. "And we'll make sure Jane gets to her room." She turned to me. "Be sure you make a taco; they're delicious."

I caught Jane shooting her sister an "Is this real?" look, but Celia wasn't looking at her—she was looking out onto the lake.

Whatever had happened while I'd been gone, the sisters seemed more disconnected than ever.

Shrimp Tacos with Cilantro Crema

For the shrimp
1 ½ pounds shrimp

2 ½ tablespoons dried oregano

2 teaspoons dried thyme

1 teaspoon dried lemon peel

1 teaspoon salt

2 teaspoons fresh ground black pepper

5 tablespoons olive oil

2 whole chipotle chilies in adobo, chopped fine

4 teaspoons adobo sauce

Cilantro crema
1 ½ cups lightly packed fresh cilantro leaves

4–5 tablespoons freshly squeezed lime juice

3/4 cup sour cream

½ cup mayonnaise

For the tacos
6-inch corn or flour tortillas

2 cups cabbage, shredded or chopped

In a medium-sized bowl, mix together the oregano, thyme, lemon peel, salt, and pepper. Set aside.

Place the shrimp in a colander; rinse and clean, deveining and removing the tails. Pat them dry with paper towels. Toss shrimp thoroughly with the spices. Keep refrigerated until ready to cook—up to a day.

Mix the crema dipping sauce by whisking all ingredients together. If it's too tart, add more mayonnaise.

Heat oil, chipotle peppers, and adobe sauce in a skillet over medium-high heat. Use tongs to place shrimp, about 10 at a time, into the pan, allowing enough room for each to rest on its side. Cook for approximately 1 ½–2 minutes per side, or until the shrimp becomes opaque and lightly pink. Continue to cook in batches until all of the shrimp are cooked through.

To assemble the tacos, layer the shrimp over the shredded cabbage, and drizzle the crema on top.

Serves 6.

27

Tea should be taken in solitude.

—C. S. Lewis

Jane

As soon as the door clicked shut, I took a deep, rattling breath. I shouldn't have come. I should have insisted on being dropped off at the casita or taken a cab or walked the eleven miles back from the hotel.

First, I didn't feel well. It only made sense that after being surrounded by swarms of humanity, I would catch a bug.

Second, it might not even have been a bug. With the hours I'd been putting in and the heartache over Sean, my body might simply have decided to mutiny.

I pulled painkillers from my purse first and made sure to down an entire glass of water. It hadn't been a lie. I really did have a headache.

With a sigh, I lay down on the bed and pulled the coverlet up to my chin. I wished I had Dash next to me. I missed his doggy smell, the snuffly sound of his breathing. It was right for Callum to have him back, and yet I wondered idly if it would be possible to steal him. Maybe Callum wouldn't notice the loss of his hundred-and-twenty-five-pound dog.

For an hour I dozed off and on. I'd dream about Sean and the concert—and then I'd wake up. Over and over again.

My headache didn't lessen; instead, it seemed to be laughing at the painkillers I'd taken.

I opened my eyes and rolled back over. The sky had darkened; I couldn't hear the party outside, but I knew they were out there. Lurking. Socializing. I was hungry but didn't want to make the small talk that going out for a snack might require.

How hard would it be to order a pizza and have it delivered to the back door? This house had to have a servant's entrance, right? Those were the questions in my head when my phone dinged. I reached for it, blinding myself with the brightness of the screen.

It was an e-mail. I sat up and turned on the light beside the bed so I could read the screen without squinting.

The e-mail was from Sean.

We hadn't ever e-mailed. Weeks together, we'd sent things over instant message or text, more often skipping both because we were together in the same room.

He'd used the contact form on our ordering website, the one I'd made for our online tea business. Never mind I hadn't blocked his number on my phone; he'd sent me an e-mail.

Through a contact form.

The thought alone chilled me, and my anxiety only rose as I read.

Dear Jane,

Thank you for coming to see the band at South by Southwest. Your support means a lot.

I got the feeling after the concert that we'd gotten wires crossed about a few things, and I'm writing to clear them up.

Your friendship meant a lot to me while I was staying in Austin, but I didn't plan on settling there. I hope I didn't lead you to believe differently, and if that's the case, I'm sorry.

We had a good time together, and I enjoyed hanging out.

Since meeting Sofi, though, my life has changed. Not just the engagement—haha—but I never knew I could fall for someone the way I did for her. I hope you find someone like that.

Maybe it's just my imagination, but I just didn't want to leave you with the impression that our friendship was more than friendship, you know?

Just wanted to make sure we're still cool.

Have a good life, Jane Woodward. Take care.

—Sean Willis

I read it twice, three times, in disbelief. The fourth time I read it, I realized that his e-mail address read Sean.Sofi@gmail.com.

A knock sounded at my door. "Jane?"

Celia.

I rose and opened the door.

"I just wanted to check on you," she said, but her words stopped and her eyes widened.

"What happened?

In answer, I shoved the phone into her hand.

Celia looked at me, looked at the phone, and then looked back at me. "Sean sent you an e-mail?"

"He did."

She squinted at the phone. "He e-mailed you from Sean.Sofi@gmail.com?"

"Yup."

"Sorry. I'll stop . . . wait." She looked up again. "He thanked you for your *support*?"

"Keep going."

"He wants to make sure your wires aren't crossed?"

"Celia—"

"I'll keep reading—*he never knew he could fall for someone the way he did her*? He doesn't want to leave you with the impression that there's more be-tween you than there was? He hopes you're *cool*? What is he, sixteen? And he wishes you a good life? What is going on?"

"He doesn't love me."

Celia arched a brow. "Yeah, and the pope is Protestant."

My eyes flew open at the acidity in Celia's voice. Was anger the first sign of some sort of shellfish allergy? I'd never heard her speak ill of anyone.

"Of course he loved you," Celia continued, shaking her head. "I saw the way he looked at you; we all did. Honestly, Jane"—she bit her lip—"I was waiting for you to tell me that you guys were engaged."

"We talked about it. Around it. He never—he never exactly proposed." I pressed my hand to my forehead. "He told me they were going on tour, and he asked me to go with him."

"He asked before he left? What did you say?"

"I didn't. He changed the subject." Well, we were kissing, but close enough. I squinted. "I just— Clearly, he's moved on. He's engaged to Sofi, whatever. It's just confusing. The day before we broke up, the day of the barbecue at Callum's? He . . . he told me that he loved me."

"Because he *did*."

"He told me that he loved me, that I made every day better." I wrinkled my nose. "And then he came over the day after to tell me he was leaving for Nashville."

Celia folded her arms. "Well, I still think he loved you. He might be a sociopath, but he loved you."

"That . . . doesn't exactly make me feel better."

She sighed, and her voice softened back to its usual Celia register. "I feel like . . . like maybe he's manipulating you. That e-mail—it's all lies. He never knew love until he met Sofi?" The edge returned. "Look, Jane. He's lying, and making it seem like this is all in your head. That's gas-lighting; that is not okay. He feels bad about breaking up with you, but rather than apologize, he's trying to twist reality into something that it's not."

"Maybe he was lying," I said, suddenly feeling the need to shower, to wash the entire relationship off. "Maybe all of it was a lie."

"I . . . I have a hard time believing that. He'd have to be a really good actor." Celia pointed to the phone. "That e-mail was pathetic. I don't think the sort of person who could write that e-mail would be capable of convincing all of us how he felt about you. It makes more sense that he loved you and he's trying to cover it up." She glanced at the phone again. "Badly. Never mind the e-mail address."

"It doesn't make sense."

"No."

It made about as much sense as Celia and Teddy breaking up, to be honest. Two people who clearly loved each other suddenly parting ways as if it hadn't meant anything at all.

"I don't know what to think anymore," I said. "I'm going for a walk."

28

He wanted to live where there was space and clean air and a bloke could get a good start in life without people looking down their noses at him, and Texas was the place, so he'd heard.

—LEILA MEACHAM

Callum

I didn't know how many guest rooms Charlie had at her little "cabin," but I had a room to myself—myself and Dash. It was plenty comfortable, but I couldn't relax. The air crackled the way it did when there was a thunder-and-lightning storm coming, so when the skies lit and the clouds rumbled, I wasn't surprised.

If the weather had been better, I would have tried for a swim. But with the storm outside, I decided to sit in the oversized armchair and catch up on paperwork for Smoky Top.

With Roy's help, I'd begun to feel like I had my feet under me. I understood the broader, if not finer points of smoking brisket. I'd spoken to two of the ranchers who supplied our beef and, with oversight, our ordering costs had come down.

I knew there would be personnel changes coming up next, but for the time being, things were looking up. Not that Dash thought so—he was sprawled on the bed, casting me baleful glances. It was after midnight, and Dash wasn't impressed with my insomnia.

The first time the knock sounded, most of it blended into a roll of thunder.

The second time it didn't, and Dash lifted his head as I rose to open the door.

What I'd expected was Ian coming to make sure I had towels or a book or a water dish for Dash (in truth, he'd been happily helping himself to the toilet water in the en suite bath, and after ensuring that there wasn't any bleach treatment in the tank, I'd allowed him to enjoy the presence of a ready water supply apt for his size). Instead, Celia stood on the other side of the threshold.

"Hi," she said, her face strained and anxious. "Did I wake you?"

"No, I've been working. What's wrong?"

"Jane," she said, and at the sound of the name, I ushered her into my room and closed the door behind her.

"What happened?"

"Sean. He sent her an e-mail . . . it was bad."

"The e-mail was bad, or her response was bad?"

"Both? I mean . . ." Celia searched for words. "She read it calmly and went for a walk."

"Oh."

Dash sneezed, and I winced at the amount of Dash-drool now sprayed upon Charlie's guest bedspread.

I looked back at Celia. "Okay. So, Jane went for a walk. Did something happen when she got back?"

"She hasn't come back," Celia said in a soft voice. "I'm worried."

My eyes widened. "She's out in the storm? When did she leave?"

"About ten."

"Did she take her phone?"

Celia shook her head. "She left it behind. The e-mail came in on her phone. I think she didn't want to take the e-mail with her. That was around nine thirty."

Jane, out for two and a half hours in the middle of a Texas storm. My body went cold, but I managed a nod. "Okay. I'll wake up Ian, maybe Pierce, and the four of us, if you're willing—"

"Yes," she said, simply.

"We'll go look. Take your phone; we'll take flashlights."

"Okay."

"We'll find her."

Celia nodded.

I could read the worry in her eyes—anyone could have. I knew there was nothing I could say, and I wasn't going to try.

Because the worry in her eyes probably looked like the worry in mine.

Ten minutes later, Ian and Pierce had joined us in the search. Ian and Celia walked the neighborhood, while Pierce and I took the lakeside path, each of us starting off in opposite directions.

At the house, Nina, Mariah, and Charlie waited up, keeping watch in case Jane returned, or if the household's only sleepers, Margot or Bowie, woke up.

I scanned the path and the terrain as I walked, my gaze frequently straying to the lake. The water reflected the dark sky, rippling beneath the stormy winds.

What if she'd somehow fallen in?

If only I had my military-issue night-vision goggles. Or ten minutes in a helicopter with an infrared camera. I could have used them, but after starting down the path, I had a thought about where Jane might have gone.

After all, there was a white house across the lake, owned by one Sofi Grey.

I hated that Sean still held any power over her. Hated that I hadn't said anything that would have dissuaded her affections, hated that it probably wouldn't have improved the matter.

But as much as I hated the situation, hated myself, hated Sean, none of that would help me find Jane. So I focused on the path, watching for Jane's small form.

Lightning zipped across the night sky, and rain began to pour. I walked on. My leg ached, but I walked on. As the sock grew wet and chafed against my stub, I walked on. If there was one thing I had learned in the marines, it was that I could keep going, in almost any circumstance.

My heart thudded in my chest, and I felt rivulets of rain down my neck and back.

Ahead, I saw a pier. Squinting, I tried to make out the shadow I saw at the end. The closer I came, the more the form took shape. And the more it took shape, the more I recognized Jane's familiar silhouette. I hadn't realized until that moment how much I knew her, that even from hundreds of feet away I could see the way she stood, the tilt of her head, and know her at once.

I called her name, but even as I called I knew she wouldn't hear. The wind blew in my face, carrying my voice away and far from earshot.

Still, I worked to pick up my pace, sweat mixing with rain.

The closer I came, the more details I could see. The rain had soaked through Jane's hair, and likely her clothes. How long had she been standing out there?

A bolt of lightning, two, and then the roll of thunder just overhead; it sounded like the roar of a fighter jet. The storm was close.

More thunder. I wanted to call to her, but I knew I wouldn't be heard. Still, as if she could have heard my footfalls, she turned my direction.

She turned, but in that instant, a bolt of lightning struck the pier.

I heard Jane's shriek. I didn't know how, but I heard it. And I couldn't do anything but watch as she lost her balance and fell into the lake's dark waters.

"Jane!" I yelled again, futilely, my legs picking up their pace, keeping time as I counted the seconds. She wasn't coming back up.

"Jane!" I yelled once more, her name tearing out of my chest.

If only I knew the lake better; if only I had the gear. I tried to remember what I knew of the area, what had been mentioned in passing. I knew this section was deeper than the rest.

I struggled into the water, unused to swimming with my prosthetic leg attached, my body absorbing the pain. I knew how to do this, to shove the pain into a place in my brain that didn't care.

And then I was under, swimming, searching. The flashlight was water resistant, but I didn't know how long I had.

This was just a mission, I told myself. I had been on dozens. If I didn't have a light, my eyes would adjust to the dark. I could go a long, long time between breaths.

I swung the light from side to side, searching, even as I made my best progress through the water. It wasn't my old body—but this one was tougher. More stubborn. And the stakes were too high to think about.

Right, left, right, the light cut through the darkness as I searched.

And then I saw her.

She was unconscious, her body sinking, her hair floating like a cloud around her face. The water wasn't very deep, but that didn't mean it wasn't dangerous.

With renewed energy, I fought through the water to reach her. Closer, closer—and then the light went out.

It doesn't matter, I told myself in the darkness. *You saw where you were going. Just find her.*

I closed my eyes, relaxing, allowing my hand to drop the flashlight. It was easier to reach her without it; in my mind, I focused on where I'd seen her, on my body in the water, on each stroke, staying straight and true in the water. In my mind, I measured the distance.

When I opened my eyes, she was there. A hand's breadth away.

One more kick, and I had her. I wrapped my left arm around her and relied on my good foot to plant into the lake floor, and my good leg to propel us to the surface.

It had to be about seven, eight feet deep. Too deep for me to stand, but not so deep that we didn't reach the surface in a hurry. Holding tight to Jane's torso, I could feel her unconsciousness.

Fast. I had to be fast.

I swam toward the pier, and then along it until I could touch and use the ground to hoist Jane onto the hard surface. I climbed up after her as fast as I could. Her head lolled to the side. Leaning over her, I rested my ear next to her nose. No breath.

I'd done this before: CPR and first aid in the field. I'd been there for members of my unit, for friends. It was part of the job.

But this? I bent over to breathe air into her mouth, but I could feel the tentacles of panic squeezing my chest even as I compressed Jane's rib cage beneath my hands. One cycle, two.

I replayed her fall in my head. She'd gone under and not come back up. Had she given up? Decided to rest under the water like the heroine of a Victorian novel? Had something happened, and she'd lost consciousness during the fall?

I blew into her mouth a third time, being careful with her ribs as I compressed.

And then her body shuddered beneath my hands, and her eyes flew open. She gasped and coughed at the same time, choking on the water as it worked to leave her body.

She rose unsteadily on her knees, and I braced her with my hands so she didn't topple from the pier a second time. She vomited then, and I held her hair as her body expelled the contents of her stomach and coughed the lake water from her lungs.

"Just breathe," I told her. "Even if it's little breaths, get all the oxygen you can get."

She looked at me then, wide-eyed, swaying gently. The motion must have caused her pain; she winced and reached gingerly for the back of her head.

"I— It hurts," she said, her voice hoarse.

Out of habit, I reached for my phone to call for help.

And then I laughed, rocking gently until my weight rested on my tailbone.

"What?"

"My phone. It was in my pocket."

"Oh no!"

"No. No. It's the least, very least, of my concerns. Other than the fact that it means I can't call for help or use the light to look at your head." The thoughts sobered me up fast. "We have to get you back. Can you walk?"

"I think so," she said, and we struggled together to stand upright.

But she doubled over again, the shifting of her body sending whatever remained in her stomach onto the pier.

"Climb on my back," I told her.

"What if I throw up on you?" she asked, weakly.

"It's happened before," I told her truthfully.

"Your leg—"

"It's fine. I used to carry packs that weighed twice as much as you." That statement stretched the truth, and she knew it, but I crouched down, and she eased onto my back.

She didn't weigh that much—enough to be counted as a real, solid woman on my back, but not more than I could carry.

But she wasn't wrong that my leg was being taxed well beyond what any physical therapist or physician would ever recommend or allow. So much of it hurt that I couldn't tell what it was doing, but from the sharp, stinging pain coming from the surgical site, I didn't think it was anything good.

It could wait though. If they had to take more of my leg off, let them have it.

Jane couldn't wait though. Jane needed to receive real medical attention as soon as possible. That thought alone kept me going as I walked the long miles down the path along the lake, back to the lake house.

29

The sky in Texas is the most amazing sky in the
whole country, I think, like you can see more sky in
Texas than you can see anywhere else in the world.

—IDINA MENZEL

Callum

I staggered through the Palmers' downstairs patio door, half dragging Jane. It
wasn't a pretty moment. Nina leapt to her feet when she saw us. She threw the
doors open and ordered Mariah to call for an ambulance, while Charlie called
the other members of the search party.

Celia made it back first, gasping when she saw Jane. "You're bleeding?
What happened?"

"Slipped on the wet pier," Jane answered wearily. "It was stupid. And I
think I hit my head."

"You're not sure?"

"I blacked out."

Nina put a hand on Celia's arm. "Don't worry, the ambulance is on its way.
Charlie, dear? Bring your warmest blanket downstairs."

Charlie, phone still pressed to her ear, nodded and jogged upstairs.

"Do you think we could drive her instead?" Celia asked, softly. "Our in-
surance ended last month. Margot's covered still, but Jane and I . . ."

"Don't worry about it," Nina told her. "I would pay for a fleet of ambu-
lances, twenty times over."

"But—"

Nina ignored her, turning her attention to me. "Beckett, sit down."

"Yes, ma'am." I sat heavily, every muscle shouting at me in the process.

Charlie returned with blankets and towels, which were handed to me and Jane. "Thank you, dear," Nina said. "I'm going to turn on the fireplace. It'd be nice to warm them up before the EMTs get here."

Jane waved a hand. "I'm fine; I don't need a hospital."

"You almost drowned," I said, my voice overloud.

Pierce and Ian returned then, their footsteps heavy in the entryway. "You've got her?" Ian asked as he entered, catching sight of the lake-soaked Jane. "She nearly drowned?"

"Calm down," Jane told them, but no one listened.

I rose from my seat. "Hand me your flashlight, Ian."

"Here you go. Lose yours?"

"In the lake." I shone the light into Jane's eyes. Her pupils contracted, but not fast enough. "You're still concussed," I told her.

"I'm fine," Jane protested. "Someone just help me upstairs. I'm sure I'm fine; I just need to sleep it off."

Just then, Margot came down the same stairs. "What's going on?" she asked, her eyes squinting from the light. "Jane?"

"I'm fine, honey," Jane said, holding her blanket tight.

I remembered I had a blanket in my hand, and I absently wrapped it around myself. "You're not fine," I told Jane. "You're going to the hospital."

"But—"

"You nearly died!" I shouted.

Margot burst into tears then, followed by Jane and Celia, and I realized the enormity of the mistake I'd just made.

Yelling at a man in the field? In my line of work, it saved lives.

Yelling at a woman who'd been through a traumatic experience in front of her sisters? Not wise. Looking at their tears, knowing I'd caused them, I felt like the lake scum that clung to my shoe.

Nina stepped in, her shoulders squared. "We're all very concerned for Jane, but she's here and well because of Beckett. The hospital is nonnegotiable." She turned to Margot. "If you'd like to come, dear, you can ride with me. Go get your jacket."

Nina left Ian, Charlie, Pierce, and Mariah with a list of instructions of things to find and pack, and by the time the EMTs arrived at the door, Nina, myself, and the Woodward sisters were prepared for a trip to the hospital.

EMT Joe looked Jane over swiftly and agreed with my assessment of a concussion and the value of having her seen. He still heard water in her lungs. "That may need to be aspirated," he said with a grimace.

Celia asked to ride along in the ambulance, and the EMTs agreed.

Jane protested the gurney, but they ignored her, placed a brace around her neck, and carried her away.

The sight sent a chill through my body. *She's fine. She'll be cared for. She's safe,* I told myself, setting aside the blanket and reaching for my car keys.

"Sir." The youngest EMT lagged behind. "I'd like to examine your leg."

I shook my head. He was young, this kid, his uniform too big for him, his skin smooth, and his face full with the last traces of baby fat. "I'll be fine."

"Sir, it looks like you've bled through your sock." He pointed at the sock I wore that covered my stump.

Sure enough, dark red had seeped into the fabric, fabric already soaked by rain and lake and sweat.

Celia, standing in the doorway, looked over her shoulder. "Is everything okay?"

"It's fine," I said through gritted teeth. The EMT looked at me expectantly, waiting for me to remove my prosthesis and sock.

I would have died before letting Jane see it. Celia—I didn't like that either. Not now, not ever. But she walked back, and the EMT waited.

"Can I wait," I said, "and let them check it out at the hospital?"

"It's a long ride," he said, his feet shifting. "And I have to. It's my job. I have to make sure everyone's been attended to."

"But—"

"Callum," Celia said, in that soft voice of hers. "Please, let him look. I'll leave if you want me to, but please."

I sighed, reached over, and unclasped the prosthetic harness before removing the sock.

Sure enough, carrying Jane had taken its toll. The scar had reopened; it was hard to say how much.

The EMT blanched, but recovered. "I've never seen this happen at an amputation site," he said as he set about cleaning and rebandaging. "Did you put a lot of pressure on it?"

Literally, metaphorically, yes. I mumbled some sort of reply.

"This is going to need real stitches," he said. "It's cleaned now, and I packed in gauze to slow the bleeding, but you should have it looked at."

"I will."

"Tonight."

I took a deep breath. "I'll follow the ambulance."

The EMT straightened. "Sir, I don't recommend that you drive."

"I can drive," I began to say, but stopped when Nina strode back into the house.

She paused in the foyer, taking in my newly bandaged stump and the very anxious EMT. "Beckett? What's wrong?"

"He needs stitches, ma'am."

I glared up at him. Kid probably just violated HIPAA or something.

She looked at me, looked at him, and looked at me again. "I'll drive you, or you can ride in the ambulance."

Ride with Jane? The idea held some merit. I'd be able to make sure they were taking care of her. But I knew Celia would do that as well. My leg was screaming at me, and the last thing I wanted was for Jane to see me like this.

"I'll ride with you," I answered.

∞

Despite my expectations, Nina remained quiet and focused during the drive. "I have to watch carefully," she said. "My eyesight."

"I could drive," I told her.

"I don't think that sweet baby EMT wanted you to."

I snorted and looked out the window. "It's too soon for him to be away from his mother."

"When I was young," Nina said, her voice wistful, "firemen and paramedics were handsome and strapping."

"Did this group not meet your expectations?"

She sighed. "No. Such a disappointment."

I stifled a laugh. "Is it regional? Maybe we should try again in San Antonio."

Nina sat up straighter. "Maybe." She looked at me. "Jane is going to be fine."

This time I fixed my eyes on the dash. "I had a buddy. We got him in time, rescued him. He seemed fine. And then he went to bed and never woke up." His face flashed before my eyes. "Secondary drowning. There's enough water in the lungs that the lungs become irritated and swell up. We got him out of the water and breathing, but he didn't make it."

"Jane's in good hands. I'll bully anyone who tries to give her half-hearted medical treatment—you know I will."

I smiled at that. "I believe it. They probably have your photo posted at every hospital in Texas."

"And Oklahoma," she added, "after Mike passed on. I'm probably on some nursing board's watch list." She reached out and patted my leg. "She'll be fine."

We were silent the rest of the way, both listening to Nina's stereo and praying that Jane would pull through safe.

30

A crisis pauses during tea.

—TERRI GUILLEMETS

Jane

Celia held my hand when I woke up at the hospital. "When did I fall asleep?" I asked, struggling to sit up.

"Hold still." She rose, gently pressing on my shoulder to encourage me back to my reclining position. "You feel asleep during the CT scan."

"Ah. Convenient. How did it go?"

"They didn't tell me, but since you're here and not in surgery, I'm optimistic."

"Oh good." I wrinkled my nose. "My lungs hurt."

"You tried to breathe water. That doesn't work."

"Noted."

"Jane," Celia started, then paused for a moment, her face frozen as her brain decided how best to phrase her next words. "Callum said you fell off the pier. And you didn't come back up."

"Lightning hit the pier. It was stupid," I told her. "I shouldn't have been out there, in the storm like that."

"So it wasn't . . . intentional?"

"Intentional? You mean—" Her words sunk in. "You mean, did I intend to drown myself?"

"You were very upset."

"Never," I said, my tone uncompromising. "Never ever. I was upset. I shouldn't have been on that pier. But I wasn't trying to kill myself."

Celia's eyes squeezed shut. She looked harrowed, and I hated what I'd put her through. I reached with my hand, the one without the IV, and clasped her hand. "I'm so sorry. It was an accident; it was stupid. It might not always seem like it, but you and Margot are the most important people in my life. I wouldn't give all that up because I was upset over a boy."

Celia squeezed back. "I'm glad. I'm . . . I'm sorry. I'm sorry for how things have been the last few weeks. I can't . . . I don't even know how to explain . . ."

"No." I shook my head. "You don't need to explain. It doesn't matter. Not enough for us to not be friends again."

Celia exhaled a sob. "I messed everything up. I should never have brought us to Austin."

"You didn't mess everything up. Or if you did, I was messing things up alongside you as well as I could."

Celia laughed, and I continued. "Austin's growing on me," I said, resigned. "Maybe it's Stockholm syndrome."

"Or breakfast tacos?"

"I do like the breakfast tacos," I admitted.

Celia opened her mouth, closed it, and then tried again. "It's none of my business," she began cautiously.

I rolled my eyes. "You're my sister *and* my best friend. Also my business partner. There's enough overlap that I'm pretty sure it might also be your business."

"It's . . . it's just . . . It's Callum," Celia finally blurted out.

"Callum?" The memories came rushing back, only jumbled and nonsensical. I really must have had a head injury, because what I did remember didn't make sense. "You might fill me in on how I got back from the lake, because I'm not sure I've got it all straight."

"I don't know all of it," she said. "But he pulled you out of the water and resuscitated you."

My eyes flew open, and I touched my hand to my lips. "Resuscitated? Like . . . ?"

"Like what?"

"Like with his mouth?"

Celia cleared her throat. "It's the best way to get oxygen into drowning victims, since he didn't have a set of bellows on hand."

"Very funny," I said, though I couldn't help but wince when I heard the words *drowning victim*. "So what you're telling me is that I am the proud recipient of Callum's cooties."

Celia pressed her lips together. "It's not funny."

"A part of me is still twelve," I said. "It's a little funny."

"You're not allowed to make jokes yet. Last night was—"

"It was serious, I know." I folded my hands primly. "I'll try to be more appropriate. Is there any ice water?"

"There are some ice chips over here, they're half melted. Your throat hurt?"

I nodded.

"Just rest," she said.

I took a sip of the icy water; the temperature felt good and terrible at the same time. "Where's Margot?" I asked.

Celia tipped her head toward the corner of the room, and I sat up to peek. Sure enough, Margot sat curled up in the corner chair, her sweatshirt wadded into a pillow.

"Nina tried to talk her into going back to Ian and Mariah's, but she wasn't about to leave. Nina," she said, "has been really great."

"What else happened?" I asked. "How did I get back to the house?"

"Callum carried you."

I felt myself grow very still. "He can't have."

"He did."

"But his leg." I stared into Celia's eyes, waiting for her to tell me she'd made a mistake, that it somehow wasn't true.

She only stared back, her eyes sad but certain.

"Is he okay?" I asked, my voice small. "Callum? Is he okay?"

"I think he reinjured himself, some."

"Where is he?"

Celia shook her head. "He was treated in the ER and released. But I imagine he's around here, somewhere. I doubt far."

"He doesn't . . . You don't think . . ." I didn't know how to put the thought into words, and even if I did . . .

Because if he did, if Callum somehow cared for me? I didn't deserve it. I didn't at all deserve it.

"I'm tired," I said, ashamed to meet Celia's gaze. "You should go home—or the lake house, whichever is closest. Get some sleep. Drag Margot with you."

"Nope," Celia said, leaning back in her chair. "I'm staying put. You rest, though. You haven't slept a lot, since . . ."

"Since the breakup? Not a lot, no." I glanced back at Margot. "You don't have to stay. You'll sleep better at the casita."

"No I won't. And Margot's sleeping just fine."

"What if I can't sleep while you're in here?"

Celia's face turned serene. "Count sheep."

I counted sheep until Celia fell asleep. One of the benefits of a sisterhood like ours is knowing your sister's breathing patterns. If she takes a breath every second, she's lightly asleep. Every second and a half? Deep sleep.

When she'd reached deep sleep, I climbed, slowly, carefully, off the bed.

Thankfully, I wore three hospital gowns, one of them backwards, so I wasn't at risk for a sitcom moment, but I still reached for Celia's discarded woolen sweater and draped it over my shoulders. I slipped my feet into the ill-fitting but dry slippers the nurse had left behind for me, and then quietly wheeled my IV stand beside me.

Maybe my gut was wrong, but Celia had said Callum was nearby.

Not a single nurse stopped me, which was good, because I didn't feel like an argument, not this time, especially while dragging an IV stand like a recalcitrant dog.

I walked out the double doors to what I assumed was the waiting room, and sure enough. There was Callum, asleep, his head tipped straight back against the wall.

I took a seat next to him, carefully; every one of my muscles ached. By the time I'd made it safely into the seat, I looked up at him only to find that he was awake and looking back at me.

"Hi," I said, suddenly feeling shy. Shy and a little self-conscious. I cleared my throat. "I don't remember everything, but I remember enough to know that I need to thank you."

"No, you don't," Callum said, his voice pitched low.

"You okay?"

"I'm fine."

I glanced down at his leg, the one with the fresh bandage. "Hmm."

"I'm fine," he repeated.

"Thank you. And . . . I'm sorry."

He shook his head. "You have nothing to be sorry about."

I snorted. "Nothing, aside from being out for hours, long after dark, in the middle of a storm without a cell phone, flashlight, or even a pack of matches. It was stupid. And then I stupidly went out onto a wet pier, and"—I looked down at my lap, ashamed—"I shouldn't have needed rescuing in the first place."

"You were upset."

"I could have stayed home and colored."

"Colored?"

"You know, those adult coloring books, the ones with the teeny flowers. I could have done that." I paused and chewed my lip. "I recognize I'm rambling."

A small smile tilted his mouth upward. "Just a little. How are you feeling?"

"I'm fine."

He looked me over, taking in my bedraggled appearance, complete with the IV. "Hmm."

"I'm fine," I repeated. "They're pumping me full of electrolytes, since I went and swallowed a bunch of lake water."

"Lungs hurt?"

"A little."

Callum turned until he faced me squarely, raising an eyebrow.

"Okay, fine. I didn't know my lungs could feel like this." I started to laugh, but the space of a painful breath turned it into the beginning of a sob.

And that baby sob felt like my lungs were being torn apart. Suddenly, the sense of needing to cry over the night, over Sean, over my own stupidity—all of that was eclipsed by my lungs reminding me that they'd been full of lake rather than oxygen.

"Hey," Callum reached over, putting his hands on my shoulders. "Take it easy. Close your eyes. Focus on your breath."

I couldn't. But I could focus on his voice. There was something about it, something about the pitch or the rasp, I couldn't tell. His voice sounded like full-leaf Assam tea tasted. As I listened to his voice, my breathing evened and the dark swirl of emotions dissipated into a fog that I could, at least, see through.

When my breaths felt close to normal, rather than uneven stabs in my chest, I opened my eyes. Callum was right in front of me, his dark eyes fixed on my face, his face lined with concern. He was looking at me, and I realized, now that I could breathe, that I didn't want to look away.

"Thanks," I said, my gaze still fixed on his face. Once I realized I'd been staring, though, my face flushed and I glanced away. "I tried to get Celia to go home, but she's stubborn and won't listen to me."

That tilted smile again. "Hmm."

"You should go. Go sleep. This can't be comfortable for you."

"I used to sleep outdoors, on rocks."

I had to cover my mouth to stop from laughing—it would hurt too much. "On rocks?"

He nodded. "When I was deployed, it happened."

"So you'd look around for a giant pile of rocks and pick that spot out for yourself?"

He folded his arms and leaned back. "If I didn't know better, I'd say they can take that IV out. If you're sassing me, you're not feeling too bad."

"The sass makes me stronger."

"Good." He nodded toward the IV pick on my hand. "And leave that in there. You don't want any complications." His gaze found mine again. "I thought you'd died because I wasn't fast enough."

"I'm sorry. I'm sorry, and I can't say it enough," I told him, my heart full of despair. "It was stupid and emotional and I'm . . . I'm old enough to know better. Margot's old enough to know better." My eyes squeezed shut.

"It's partly my fault," Callum said, his voice dark and low.

"What?" I tipped my head to look at him. "No. Not at all. The opposite, actually."

"I didn't tell you." He leaned forward, lacing his fingers together. "My sister-in-law, Lila? She was dating a guy, six months ago. He took her on a trip to Mexico. Her documents, cash, and credit cards were stolen, and she couldn't reenter the country."

"Oh no," I said, even as I wondered why he'd decided to tell me now. "But you brought her back, right?"

"I did. She was in a bad spot, and she's not in the clear yet. The guy just left her there. And she was pregnant." He looked at me then, his eyes full of sorrow and compassion and something else, something I didn't understand. "Jane, it was Sean."

"What?"

"Sean and Lila were together. He left her in Mexico."

"Oh." I blinked once, twice. Three times. "He—*oh*."

And suddenly, the pieces fell into place.

How Sean had been preoccupied after Nina told the story about Lila, how he'd taken me out on our romantic adventure before breaking up with me. He hadn't been going to Nashville for his career; he'd been running away. Running and running hard and making me feel like it had all been in my head.

He'd been living with his aunt, and now he was with Sofi—who knew exactly what was motivating him. But he'd pretended that it was all for his career, all for love, and never a breath about how deeply he'd failed someone he'd professed to care about. Sure, he'd hurt me, but Lila, pregnant with Sean's child, abandoned in Mexico?

The last bit of me that was still in love with him—that bit gnashed its teeth at the thought of another woman sharing intimacies with him, carrying his child. The part of me that railed in anger felt doubly justified for believing him to be the lowest of the low.

And the rest of me? It just felt . . . tired.

"Lila's okay?" I asked Callum, steering my thoughts back to the present.

"She'll be fine."

"She should make sure Sean pays child support."

"I'm on it. Me and the PI who found her."

I nodded. "Good." I bit my lip. "I was really in love with him."

"I know. Everyone did. And from the spectator's seat, it looked like he loved you back."

"But the love of a terrible person, what's that worth? How did I fall for someone with that kind of . . . absence of character?"

"Sometimes we fall for the wrong people."

"We?" I looked up at him. "You ever fall for the wrong person?"

"I was in love with Lila, a long time ago."

"Oh?" A strange stab of jealousy struck my chest. That, or a bit of lake moisture that hadn't made it out of my lung.

"But she married my brother, and I realized that we were needing and wanting different things. She's important to me," he said, clarifying. "But sister-important."

"That makes sense."

"Speaking of sisters," Callum said, "does Celia know you're out here?"

I shook my head. "I, ah, snuck out."

His mouth tipped upward, forming that increasingly familiar hint of a smile. "You don't say."

"I also stole her coat."

"Looks good with your gown."

"Thank you," I said, my voice prim.

"Instead of telling everyone else they should sleep, you could get some sleep yourself."

"I could." I looked back at him. "I wanted to thank you first. For everything."

"It was nothing."

I stood up carefully. "It was everything," I said. "At least it is to me and Celia and Margot. When I get back home to my kitchen? I'm making you a cake."

31

That's right, you're not from Texas.
But Texas wants you anyway.

—LYLE LOVETT

Callum

The hospital released Jane after a battery of tests, an adjustment of her electrolytes, and several hours on oxygen. Her CT scan showed the sort of mild swelling expected from a concussion, and the chest X-ray didn't observe any concerning debris in her lungs.

Still, the doctor provided literature about warning signs for complications. Celia tucked it into her purse.

Nina decided it would be best if we all returned to Charlie's—after all, a long visit had been planned, and Pilar had been granted time off while the family vacationed. If Jane and Celia returned to the lake house, a team of well-intentioned friends would be available to help.

Jane groused about feeling like a nuisance, but Nina waved her off.

If I'd been aware of Jane before, that awareness had multiplied exponentially since her near drowning. As we drove—Nina behind the wheel, Jane in the front passenger seat—I watched the rise and fall of her shoulders. I listened to her voice, ears tuned to any hint of rasp or cough.

Back at the lake house, I watched for signs of weakness or fever.

I tried to be subtle about it, of course. But I realized I hadn't been subtle enough when Nina brought me a cup of coffee midafternoon.

"If you're going to play sentry," she said, "you'll need coffee." She shot Jane, sitting across the room, a significant glance.

I accepted the cup as casually as possible.

"How's your leg?"

It burned like the fires of Mordor. "It's fine."

"Do you need to take something for it? To ease the pain?"

If only. "I don't like the painkillers," I told her truthfully. "I don't like how they make me feel."

Nina sighed. "And I'll bet the over-the-counter ones don't do anything for you."

I snorted without thinking, and then excused myself. "No, ma'am."

"How about one of the kolache Charlie picked up from 7 Grams this morning?"

"That sounds very nice, thank you."

"Thank *you*," she said, and bustled off toward the kitchen to bring me back a pastry.

She brought one for me and one for Jane, who looked like she wanted to escape the house altogether.

"Is that a Danish?" Jane asked, examining the offering.

"It's a kolache," Nina said. "Czech immigrants came to central Texas during the mid-1800s, and they brought kolache with them. The ones from 7 Grams are my favorite."

Jane took a bite. "It's like a brioche donut. Celia? You should try this."

Celia came and tasted; I could see the wheels turning inside Jane's head.

"It's good," Celia said, taking a second bite. "We could do this. What do you think, a two-rise dough?"

Jane took another bite. "I think three. It's really good."

"I'll bring you more," Nina said, and Celia blushed, realizing she'd eaten half of Jane's.

"I'll tell you what," Nina said. "You girls put kolache in your pastry case, and you'll never want for business."

Charlie entered the room. "That's true; I'll drive miles to get to my favorite ones."

"They're too sweet," said Mariah, but nobody listened to her.

"It's very good," Jane told Nina and Charlie. "I'm sure you can find them in the Bay Area—you can find anything—but I haven't had one before."

"Really?" Charlie asked, her eyes wide. "That's so sad."

Jane tore off a piece of the sweet bread edge, and held it close to her face.

"Is there something wrong with it?" Charlie asked.

Jane squinted. "I'm just examining the crumb structure."

"You can tell a lot about a bread from the crumb structure," Celia explained. "Jane's a better baker—"

"Shut up. You're an ace baker," her sister retorted without breaking her focus on the piece of bread. "The person who baked this knew what they were doing. It's well baked, good rise. Good color, nice loft." Jane looked to Nina and Charlie. "What kind of flavors do they come in?"

"Oh, all kinds," Nina answered. "Apricot, cherry, chocolate . . ."

"Pineapple, raspberry and cream cheese, or just plain cream cheese."

Celia raised her eyebrow toward Jane. "I think you've got some creative license."

Jane brightened. "Sounds like it! I like the idea of raspberry and cream cheese. I think it would be nice with a black tea."

Celia leaned forward. "I think so too."

The sisters sat there, smiling and contented. They looked more relaxed together than I'd seen them since their arrival in Austin. I could see the ease between them and understood Jane's distress when it was gone. For both their sakes, I was glad to see them happy.

Jane yawned. "I'm beat, and I slept badly at the hospital, on account of being in a hospital. I'm going upstairs to take a nap."

I sat up, alert, and Dash did likewise. I didn't like it. If she took a nap, I wouldn't be able to keep watch. But Dash . . .

"Want to take Dash with you?" I offered, giving his neck a pat and hoping my voice sounded casual.

Jane met my gaze with a mischievous smile. "So he can alert you if I've stopped breathing or fallen in a well?"

"Is there a well upstairs?" I asked innocently. "I hadn't noticed."

"There *is* a water feature," Charlie said with a wince. "But I don't think it'll cause any problems."

"I don't think so either," Jane said brightly. "But I'm happy to steal Dash away."

Hearing his name, he ambled up and walked toward her to get his ears scratched. "You want to be stolen away," she cooed at him. "Don't you?"

Dash's tail swished hopefully.

"Go on, you," I told him, and he followed her up the stairs.

Raspberry Cream Cheese Kolache

Dough

2 3/4 cups whole milk

3 packets (21 grams) active dry yeast

½ cup warm water

1 teaspoon sugar

2 sticks unsalted butter

1 cup sugar

3 egg yolks

3 teaspoons salt

2 teaspoons orange zest, grated

7–9 cups flour (more or less)

Egg wash

1 egg, beaten

1 teaspoon milk or water

Cream cheese filling

24 ounces (3 8-ounce packages) cream cheese, room temperature

½ cup sugar, plus more to taste

3 egg yolks

1 tablespoon vanilla extract

2 ½ cups fresh raspberries

Heat the milk on the stove in a heavy-bottomed saucepan over medium heat, stirring frequently. Once the milk has begun to bubble at the edges and starts to steam, remove it from the heat and allow to cool.

Prepare a large mixing bowl for the dough as it rises; wipe the sides down with olive or vegetable oil, and set aside.

In a glass measuring cup or bowl, stir the warm water and yeast together. Sprinkle the 1 teaspoon of sugar over the top, and set aside in a warm spot to bloom.

In a stand mixer, cream together the sugar and butter on high speed for 3–5 minutes, or until pale and fluffy. Lower the speed to medium, and add the egg yolks one at a time, mixing until the yolks are well incorporated. Add the salt and orange zest. Scrape down the sides as necessary.

Add the yeasted water and 1 cup of the flour, and stir by hand with a wooden spoon until incorporated. Making sure the milk is cooled to 110 degrees or lower (if you touch it and it's body temperature, you're just fine), add it and stir gently. Add the flour, a cup at a time, and stir. Continue to add as much flour as you can handle while stirring with a wooden spoon.

Turn dough out onto a floured surface, and knead in enough of the remaining flour until the dough feels moderately soft. Continue to knead for five minutes, until the dough feels smooth and elastic.

Place the dough into the prepared bowl, and turn the dough to get a light coat of oil all over. Cover the bowl with plastic wrap or a tea towel, and allow to rise until the dough has doubled in size, about 1 to 1 ½ hours.

Punch the dough down, knead it a few times and return it to the bowl. Cover, and allow to rise another 1 to 1 ½ hours, or until it's doubled in size again.

While the dough rises, beat together the cream cheese, sugar, egg yolks, and vanilla. Separately stir together the beaten egg and milk/water for the egg wash. Chill the filling and egg wash until ready to use. Line two baking sheets with parchment paper.

Once the dough has finished rising, preheat the oven to 375°F. Punch the dough down a second time, and divide the dough into egg-sized portions. Place them, 6–8 to a baking sheet, and let the balls of dough rise for 1–3 minutes. Shape each kolache, poking a hole into the middle and stretching it to form a significant well in the middle. Brush the kolache all over with the egg wash, and then spoon 1 tablespoon of the filling into the well. Repeat until each one is filled.

Bake the kolache in batches until golden brown, about 10–15 minutes. Remove from oven and allow to cool on a wire rack. Place 3–4 raspberries into the cream cheese center of each kolache. Kolache are best enjoyed warm.

Serves 30.

Note: Feel free to mix up the toppings! Any kind of berry will work up top, or bake them with apple pie filling (bake 1–3 minutes longer) or chopped chocolate in the center (bake 1–3 minutes less).

32

Rainy days should be spent at home with a cup
of tea and a good book.

—BILL WATTERSON

Jane

I woke up feeling like there was an elephant on my chest. In the past, that expression had always sounded particularly hyperbolic. Why an elephant? Why not "a small child" or "a large dog," or even "a horse"? Why go straight to elephant? I'd posed the question to Celia, once, and she'd just laughed at me.

But now—a giant immovable weight on my chest; I could barely breathe. *I could barely breathe.*

Awareness crawled in. If I couldn't breathe, something was terribly wrong. I tried to sit up, but—elephant. Never again would I make fun of the people claiming the presence of pachyderms on their person. While trying to adjust my body, my hand hit something warm and solid.

Dash.

"Dash," I told him, hating how hoarse and out of breath I sounded. "Get help."

I could see the instant that Dash as a companion ended and Dash as a service dog began. His eyes flew open, and he sprang up in a tangle of long Great Dane limbs. He went for the door, and pawed at it—if it had been one of the long-handled ones, like the ones at the casita, he would have opened it in a heartbeat. But they were round, cut glass affairs—stylish, but impossible for a dog without opposable thumbs.

Dash whined, shook himself, ears flapping. And then he leaped against the door, throwing all hundred-plus pounds at it, and barked.

He barked until help came—Celia and Margot and Nina, but Callum first with panic in his eyes.

"What's wrong?" Callum asked, kneeling beside my bed.

"Chest. Hurts." I rasped. "Hard to breathe."

"You're going back to the hospital," Callum said, in the voice that I assumed he had used in the past to order troops. "Now."

I nodded.

Celia pressed a hand to my forehead. "You're burning up, Jane."

If I thought about it, I was also freezing cold and my limbs ached. All that paled in comparison to how difficult it felt to fill my lungs with oxygen.

Callum reached behind me and helped me to sit up. "Nina's calling an ambulance. They'll get you hooked up to oxygen again. Margot, can you find Jane's purse?"

Margot's thin voice answered in the affirmative.

"Perfect. Put her phone and charger into it, okay?" He turned back to me. "You're going to be okay."

I tried to look up into his eyes, but he was busy helping to ease my feet back into the shoes I'd kicked off.

"Dash is a good dog," I rasped.

He looked up then. "Yes, he is."

"Thank you for sending him upstairs with me."

His gaze shuttered, though he brushed my hair from my face. "You're going to be okay."

And that's when I realized exactly how dim I'd been. He'd sent Dash with me for this reason—and I'd made fun of him for it. But he'd worried about me, and he'd turned out to be right.

Too right.

"You'll be fine," Nina said. "But Charlie?" Nina addressed her younger daughter, who gaped from the doorway. "Best you and Pierce take Bowie home. If this is pneumonia, you don't want him catching it."

"Pneumonia?" Charlie's eyes were wide. "Oh. Yes. We'll do that."

My eyes squeezed shut. My own stupidity may have endangered Nina's grandson.

Celia sat next to me, wrapping her arm around me. I shut my eyes and shut out the world until the paramedics arrived at the house for the second time.

Celia rode with me in the ambulance again. The EMTs had fitted an oxygen mask over my face; I couldn't speak. Not that there would be much I'd be motivated to say. Little more than "I'm sorry, I'm sorry, I'm sorry" over and over.

At the hospital, they wouldn't let me fall asleep, even though it was all I wanted in the world. Well, I would have accepted a time machine. But I had to answer questions and rate my pain and be poked and prodded all over again. Another X-ray, this one showing pneumonia in both lungs.

Once they had me back in a hospital bed, IV antibiotics pumping into my system, I finally managed to close my eyes and shut out the world and the mess I'd made, if only for a little while.

33

Texas will again lift its head and stand among the
nations. It ought to do so, for no country upon the
globe can compare with it in natural advantages.

— SAM HOUSTON

Callum

While Nina took Margot with her to find something for dinner, Celia and I
waited while the doctors ran tests on Jane. The risk of sepsis was mentioned;
there was nothing to do but wait and pray.

If my leg didn't ache so badly, I would have paced as well. That the EMTs
had to put her on a stretcher and carry her out again filled me with shame. I
should have been able to do it. But I couldn't.

It was an irrational shame, but I felt it just the same.

I couldn't pace, so I tapped. I leaned forward, leaned back, and fiddled
with my fingers until Celia rested a hand on mine.

"Thank you for waiting with me," Celia said.

"You don't have to thank me." I'd long grown tired of being thanked so
often. "I wish I could do more." I looked at Celia and took a deep breath. "The
truth is, I'm in love with Jane."

Celia gave a sweet smile. "I know."

I coughed, low in my throat, and looked away. "Everyone knows."

"That may be true. Not Jane, though." She leaned back in her chair. "I
think you'd be good together."

"I'm going to talk to her. When she's better." I shook my head. "I'm— I can't— I wish there was something I could do. Something I could get, someone I could bring. Something that would make it better."

"Take her a cup of real tea when she's awake next," Celia advised. "That'll go a long way." She sighed. "I should call my father."

"Where does he live?" Ian hadn't said much, only that he wasn't so much a fan of their father. For Ian, that constituted harsh rebuke.

"He's in Montenegro, I think. It's complicated. We don't speak often; we're not close."

It didn't take much prodding; a few questions, and Celia explained their father's past, and how it had affected the three sisters. Knowing their history, Jane began to make more sense. I hadn't thought it possible, but it made me admire her that much more.

"You've been through a lot together," I said, when the story finished at the present date. "A lot of families would have scattered after something like that." Mine certainly would have. "Margot is lucky to have you."

"We've always been close. The last few months have been hard, but after last night, I felt like we were on the road back. We were good today."

The panic in her voice sent my own despair spiraling. But I took a deep breath and reminded myself that I wasn't in charge.

"I'm hopeful," I said after a long moment. "I think you'll be good tomorrow too."

∞

We waited for hours, going long stretches without word. The fever was high, they said, and though they were pumping her full of antibiotics, she had yet to show significant improvement.

"Right now," the nurse had said, "what she needs is time and rest. Until the fever is under control and her lungs clear up, she's in critical condition."

Nina came and went, finding food, finding coffee—finding *better* coffee— and tracking down the gift shop. Everywhere she went she took Margot, who trailed after her like a lost puppy.

They'd been by recently and shared food, but Nina announced that Jane needed flowers for her room, and that she and Margot would visit a florist shop or two to find something satisfactory.

Someone who didn't know might have thought Nina shallow, but I knew better. I knew she was keeping Margot busy and out from underfoot. Celia wouldn't leave the hospital, but that kind of waiting would have been too much for Margot. Instead, Nina created an endless series of tasks and errands, like a never-ending scavenger hunt as the sky darkened.

Celia hugged her arms to herself as she sat on her upholstered waiting-room bench. "I need to figure out what to do about Margot."

"I'd be happy to put her and Nina up in a hotel," I told her. "You too, if you'd go."

"I won't. Can't."

"You could rest for a little while, come back."

"But what if . . . while I was gone . . ."

"I would call you right away. But I understand."

I understood because I knew I wasn't going anywhere either.

"You're right, a hotel for Nina and Margot is probably the most practical." She gave me a grateful smile. "Thank you."

I shook my head. "Don't thank me anymore. I've been thanked enough for three lifetimes."

She arched a fine blond eyebrow. "I'll be the judge of that."

I chuckled. It reminded me of something Jane would say. Did Jane realize how similar she and her sister could be?

Twelve hours. That's how long it took for Jane's fever to break, for the hospital to adjust her antibiotics until one of them began to obliterate the infection in her lungs.

When we could see her, Celia and Margot rushed in, each one taking a hand. Nina and I followed.

"I'm okay," Jane croaked. Her skin was still waxy, her color somehow too pale and too high at the same time.

I wanted to hold her hand to reassure myself of her presence, but it wasn't my place.

"You weren't okay!" Margot grasped her sister's arm, hours of pent-up feelings written all over her face.

"Shh." Jane squeezed her hand. "I'm here. I'm okay. I'm pumped so full of antibiotics I won't poop for a year."

Nina hooted; Celia suppressed a smile.

Margot's eyes widened. "Callum's right over there," she whispered.

Jane gave a resigned nod. "He's a grown-up. I'm sure he's heard about such things."

Margot gave a shocked giggle, and I realized that Jane had managed to get her sister to laugh, rather than cry.

Celia spoke then. "Nina's here too. She and Callum have taken very good care of us. All three of us."

"I'm not surprised," she said. "I'm baking you both cakes," she told us, her voice straining to reach a higher volume. "Cakes for life, at this rate. Be prepared. Buy a treadmill."

While her tone was upbeat, I also heard the undercurrent of emotion underneath.

"One cake is plenty," I told her. "We're just happy you're on the mend."

"Speak for yourself, Beckett!" Nina pressed a hand to her chest. "I've tasted Miss Jane's kitchen handicrafts, and I'm not a strong enough woman to try to change her mind. All joking aside, though," she said more seriously, "we're very blessed to have you healing, dear. Also, I like chocolate."

"Chocolate you shall have," Jane promised. "Once I can stand up without falling over."

"Take your time, my dear. Rest up."

The nurse came in then. "I agree with the 'rest up' part," she said. "I think Miss Woodward needs to start that rest about now."

Margot looked mutinous, and Celia didn't look like she planned on being cooperative, either.

But Jane yawned and nodded. "I still feel terrible," she said. "I'm sorry, guys. I'll be better company tomorrow."

"We're staying at the hotel next door," Nina said. "And I think this time Celia and Beckett should come back with us."

"You should," Jane said, pulling Celia's hand close. "Get some sleep."

"And a shower," Margot muttered under her breath.

"Come back tomorrow," Jane said. "And if you bring me real breakfast food, I'll love you forever."

I made a mental note of that.

She squeezed her sisters' hands good-bye, and they in turn kissed her cheek and forehead. "My forehead's gross," Jane protested. "I can't wait until I can get a real shower. I feel like the lake is still coming out of my pores."

Nina patted her shoulder, and Jane thanked her yet again.

I nodded to her before I followed the others.

"Thank you," Jane said. "Thanks for watching over Celia."

"It's my pleasure," I said. What I didn't say was how much I wished I could stay and watch over her.

But Margot did have a point. I knew I needed a shower and a change of clothes.

"I'll see you tomorrow," I told her instead. "Rest well, Jane."

34

Tea, but the strong stuff. Leave the bag in.

—Toby Whithouse

Jane

I woke up the next morning, and as my eyes focused I remembered where I was. The ICU, because of the double pneumonia. The pain in my chest had eased, and the fever had abated, but I still felt . . . terrible. I opened my eyes wider.

My mouth felt so dry.

"You awake, there?"

I tipped my head to the side and saw Callum sitting in the plastic chair next to me. "Hi."

His face relaxed into a warm, real smile. "Hi."

"How'd you get in here?" I asked.

"Celia told the staff I was family yesterday. Nina too."

I couldn't argue with that. "Whatever test exists to create family status, I think you both passed a while ago."

"They're still sleeping at the hotel. I came to see how you were doing. You hungry? You mentioned wanting a big breakfast last night."

"That was more to give them something to do." I thought for a moment, and focused on my stomach. "Nope. Not hungry."

"Thirsty? I found some tea."

My eyes widened. "You did?"

"I'll be more specific," he said. "Your sister found tea in your purse, and I found hot water and insulated cups."

"That tea in my purse keeps coming in handy. I'm glad I restocked." I reached my non-IV hand out. "Hand it over, mister."

"Tell me if you need a straw."

"A straw. As if." But the cup was heavier than I was prepared for, and only Callum's quick reflexes kept me from giving myself a baptism of hot tea. I blushed. "Thank you."

"Of course. You've got it?"

"I have it, thank you," I said, my flush not fading at all. I took a sip, and the crisp, clean taste of green tea filled my mouth. "This is perfect." I squinted. "This tea—it's loose leaf. How did you . . ."

He folded his arms. "I begged coffee filters off the nurses. Stapled them together to make a bag."

"Did you, now? I wish I could have seen that." I told him, slowly, around sips, about how I'd had to make last-minute tea at Ruby Lou's concert. "That tea was loose too. I need to start carrying bags around." I gave a tiny shrug against my pillow. "Feels like a very, very long time ago."

"You used coffee filters at the concert too?"

I gave a half smile. "I did. Tied them with string. For someone who doesn't know how to make coffee, I use a lot of coffee filters."

"You don't know how to make coffee?" His eyebrows flew upward, incredulous.

"I don't drink it. Why should I know how to make it? It's like asking a vegetarian to know how to roast a chicken."

He laughed, and I enjoyed the sight. His face—so often appearing stern, broadened and crinkled when he laughed.

I gave the tea another sip and realized I was starting to wear out already.

He must have been able to tell, because Callum reached for the cup and set it aside, onto the small sliding tray that clipped to the hospital bed. "You should rest," he said. "But I know it can be boring when you're in bed for any length of time—especially for someone like you."

"What do you mean by that?"

Callum gave a soft laugh. "You like to stay busy, that's all."

I sighed. "True enough. Though at the moment, I don't feel like being busy at all."

"You'll feel better. How's the fever? Still gone? You look flushed."

I cleared my throat. "I'm not sure."

Actually, I was pretty sure my blush wasn't at all fever related.

"Well, I brought a book. When I was young, there was one week when my parents were away on vacation in the Bahamas, and Roy and Betsy were watching us. I fell ill with the chicken pox, and when Roy was off work, he'd read to me while I rested."

I smiled up at him. "That's a wonderful story."

"I felt better, and I think the book did the trick. So I brought it with me." He reached into his jacket pocket and brought out a beaten paperback.

Peering at it, at an angle, I just managed to read the title.

The Princess Bride, it read.

I pursed my lips together.

Callum Beckett? *The Princess Bride?* I'd read the book ages ago, enjoying the author's sly fictional narrative about "abridging" the "original." And it looked as though I was about to enjoy it a second time. Callum flipped through to the first page and began to read. "'This is my favorite book in all the world,'" he read, his voice deep and even, "'though I have never read it. How is such a thing possible? I'll do my best to explain . . . '"

35

Tea! That's all I needed. A good cup of tea. A
superheated infusion of free radicals and tannin.
Just the thing for heating the synapses.

—RUSSELL T. DAVIES

Jane

"How are you feeling?" Celia asked for the fourth time that morning.

"I am well," I answered, working hard to stay patient. She did, after all, have my best interests at heart. "How about this: I promise, cross my heart, to tell you if I need to rest."

"That would be more believable if you hadn't fainted last week."

I winced. "I should have known you'd bring that up."

In truth, my recovery had been much slower than I'd hoped for. I tired easily and sometimes had difficulty catching my breath. The experience was frustrating because after such close encounters with death, I was eager to get on with life. And as far as I was concerned, that meant getting serious about opening a tea salon here in Austin.

While I rested, I prepared my heart for a location that would do in the meantime. For a place to start out in, while we waited.

But this morning, while I weighed tea for orders with *Parks and Recreation* playing in the background, Celia took a call from our leasing agent. I couldn't hear what he said, but I could see her body shift in anticipation, excitement radiating from her pores.

When she hung up, she clapped her hands together with glee. "There's a new space! It's not even listed yet; Chad found out about it through a contact. We can take a look at it today, at noon. Jane—it's in Hyde Park. On Duvall!"

"You're kidding!"

Celia's face split into a smile. "Not even kidding."

"Shut up!" I rose as fast as I could—though not my top speed—and hugged her tight. "You said noon?"

"Yes!"

"Aw, that's too bad. I have my canasta group at noon."

Celia laughed and swatted my arm. "Shall we plan on getting tacos on the way?"

"Was there any question?"

At noon we pulled up in front of the property in question. "It's not officially listed yet," Chad said, and I could see why. People were still coming and going, carrying out furniture and equipment.

I knew the feeling. And I felt guilty, in that moment, for being so fast on the scene to scoop up a place after the death of someone's dream.

I've been there, I wanted to say. *I've been in your shoes.*

But . . . life went on, I realized as I looked around. For better or for worse, life had continued. Leaving San Francisco hadn't ended me, or me and Celia, and now we were here, on the precipice of good things.

This location still wasn't quite as magical as the first one we'd seen, before we'd arrived in Austin. But there were some friendly plants around the building, a patio for outdoor seating, and parking spaces not only in front but also behind.

Celia squinted across the street. "Is that a Smoky Top over there?"

I made a show of casually peering in that direction. "Oh, I guess so."

Celia looked back at me. "Huh."

"Never a bad thing to have barbecue nearby," Chad remarked, oblivious.

"No," Celia agreed blandly. "It's not."

With that bit of knowledge out in the open, we turned our attention to the space itself. In truth, I braced myself for the interior to be dreadful.

While it didn't hold a candle to the architectural grace of our San Francisco location, it wasn't bad. The tiles were faux stone, in a nice dark green with blue and gray undertones. The walls were covered with what I surmised to be twenty-year-old wallpaper but would be easy enough to take care of.

The orientation of the space was similar to our last location, which meant that the marble-topped bar had a very natural placement within sight of the front door. I glanced up and found a drop ceiling. As far as I was concerned, the drop tiles would go, and we'd embrace exposed ductwork like true hipsters.

Maybe I'd even grow a moustache.

We walked into the kitchen together, taking in the space—most of the appliances and equipment had already been sold off, but the space had an efficient flow.

I turned to check in with Celia. "What do you think?"

She turned to me, her face carefully arranged. "I think it could work for us."

"Good," I told her. "I totally agree."

Chad looked gobsmacked. "You do?"

Celia's eyes widened. "Really?"

I nodded. "I think we should do it."

Celia squealed and threw her arms around me, her momentum sending us spinning across the floor.

I grinned, hung on tight, and spun with her.

"I can't wait to put up new wallpaper, and we can put shelves on the wall. Can you imagine?" Celia asked as she drove. "Being able to put in wall shelves up high without worrying about an earthquake?"

"You trust customers not to break their cups?" I asked.

"I'm sure we'll lose a few, but I think it'll be fun."

"Then we'll do it. I'm excited about the office space. It was that or take out the TV to put in more shelves at the casita. Once we open," I continued, "it might be worth hiring someone to fill the orders. Margot can do it after school, some of the time, but the kid's gotta get outside." I paused, and then continued. "I've been toying with an idea; I'm not sure what you'll think about it."

"What is it?"

"A tea subscription box. Every month, we'd send a selection of teas—or people could pay extra to pick their own—and a bag of scone mix or something. Maybe spend a bit of extra money having the boxes printed with local artwork." I looked over at Celia, my lip caught between my teeth.

"I think it's genius," Celia said. She glanced at me, and then back at the road. "You have good instincts."

"Thanks," I said, my sister's approval filling me with a warm glow. "I think you do too."

"Speaking of good things," Celia said, her voice turning coy. "You and Callum?"

My face turned the brightest shade of red. "Yes?"

Celia waited, raising an eyebrow when I didn't continue. "It's like that, is it?"

"I . . . I don't want to jinx anything," I admitted. "By rushing in."

"I see," Celia said, a smile tugging at her lips.

"He asked, if I was well enough, if I could come by Smoky Top today. Help him manage some of the employee situation."

"Oh?"

"Figuring out who to fire, mostly."

"Oh," Celia said again, this time on an exhale. "That makes so much more sense. You'd be really good at that."

"I feel like I should be offended, but I can't muster enough effort to get there."

"Really!" Celia protested. "You're good at handling that sort of thing. Much better than me."

"It's kind of hilarious, sometimes, how good you were in the finance world, all things considered."

Celia shook her head. "I wouldn't have lasted there forever. I'm good at what I do. I've enjoyed helping Ian with his accounts. But that world wasn't for me. The suits, the attitude—no. I'm happier doing this."

I reached out and squeezed her hand. "I'm glad."

"What about you?" she asked, her eyes full of concern. "I don't . . . I don't know that I've ever thanked you. Not properly. You gave up school so that we could have the tea salon. It was your idea, and you were right. So right. But are you happy?"

Celia's question made me stop and think.

"I'm happy we finally have a new location," I said slowly. "And I'm happy to be here with you, and happy that Margot is settling in. There have always been things I've wanted to do, to learn. I still want to finish my degree; that's important to me. But you and Margot, you two matter more. And"—I pictured the almighty mess of teas on our tiny table—"I like this. I'm good at it. It's not what I would have chosen at nineteen. It's good to have dreams. But sometimes dreams change, or take different forms, or you go down a path and realize that while it's not the beach, you really like the forest." I squinted at Celia. "That's really deep, you know. I hope you appreciated my profundity."

"Very much so." Celia squeezed my hand. "I just want to make sure you're happy."

"I am, I think. I'll be happier still when we have our own place. But we're all together right now, and that's the thing that matters most."

I drove to Smoky Top later that afternoon, the one kitty-corner to our new space. Walking inside, I found myself feeling shy as I looked around for Callum.

The hostess seated me and I waited, stacking the tiny tubs of whipped butter. I was working on making a bridge with the hand-wipe packets when he came around the corner.

He stopped at the door first, and flipped the Open sign to Closed before he approached my table, a smile on his face.

I looked up at him, feeling my breath catch. "Hi," I said, sounding weird and out of breath. I looked down, saw my tower of table accoutrements, and flushed. "Sorry, I'll put these back in their places."

"Don't be sorry," he said, sliding into the booth on the bench opposite me. "I did that all the time when I was a kid."

"Yeah, but the operative word in that sentence is *kid*."

"Give it up if you want, or level up to being able to make something with the sugar packets."

I grinned at him, and he grinned back.

We just sat there, at the back booth of the Hyde Park Smoky Top, grinning at each other like happy idiots.

"I really appreciate your willingness to give me a hand around here."

"Not sure how helpful I'll be," I said, managing to close my mouth right before I could say, "but it's the least I can do."

If there was one thing Callum hated, I had learned, it was any sign that I might feel beholden to him. So I said nothing, just smiled with my lips closed to keep the words inside.

One by one, that afternoon, I met with each member of the staff, looked over the slim personnel files, asked a few questions.

"Do you like your job?" I asked each one. "What would you change around here? Who deserves more responsibility? Who do you think is a poor fit?" And one by one, they either told me—or told me more by how they evaded answers.

Afterward, Callum and I ate banana pudding and discussed each staff member.

"Well," I said, "I think Latisha and Ramon are super sharp, and Latisha should probably be your front-of-the-house manager. It sounds like Asher needs to be fired yesterday. With more training, I think Yolanda and Hector could be really strong."

"You think?"

"You might double-check with Roy—I feel like he'd know things—but I think so. It's ultimately your call, though."

"You'd think that after running a company of marines, this would be easier."

I shrugged. "Civilian life is different. Different kinds of variables."

He ran a hand over his face. "You got that right."

"I think firing Asher is going to do a lot for this location."

Callum dipped his spoon into his pudding. "Want to go out with me this weekend?"

The sudden change of subject set me back, but not for long. "Yes."

"Good." Another spoonful. "There's a Balmorhea concert, Saturday night, at the Empire."

"Oh?" My eyes widened. "I love Balmorhea!"

"Thought you might do."

There was nothing to do but sit and grin at the man.

He really had wonderful eyes. Large and dark, rimmed with eyelashes so long I wondered if he'd caught flack for them when he was on active duty.

Realizing I was staring, I dropped my gaze down to the bowl in front of me and cleared my throat. "Can I, um . . . steal your recipe for banana pudding?"

His mouth quirked into an easy smile. "I don't see why not. Recipes are in the kitchen."

"Yeah? Give me the fifty-cent tour?"

"Happy to."

We stopped in the kitchen first, where I swore to Monroe, the chef on duty, that I would only use the recipe for personal use.

Callum showed me the smokers afterward, and then led the way to his office. He stopped dead in the doorway before I could see inside.

I stepped beside him, just far enough to see the woman sitting behind the desk.

"Oh, hi," I said, putting two and two together very quickly. "You must be Lila. We haven't met yet."

She was pretty, very pretty. And pregnant.

She was Callum's first love. And now she was carrying my ex-boyfriend's baby.

This could either be really complicated—or really, really simple.

"I'm Jane." I stuck my hand out, stepping forward so she wouldn't have to rise from the chair to shake it. "I'm sorry we didn't get to meet sooner; I've been sick."

Lila studied my face as if she wasn't entirely sure how to respond.

"Anyway," I continued, in a rush, "I'm glad we've finally gotten to meet."

"Yes," Lila said, in an exhale. "I'm glad too."

"You should come over for tea. Come meet my sisters. Here"—I reached for the pen and stack of sticky notes on the desk, and scrawled my number onto it—"is my number. Text me when you're free."

"I'll do that," Lila promised, taking the piece of paper. "That would be nice."

"I'm really glad you're back in town," I told her, tucking my hands into the pockets of my jeans.

"Thanks. Me too."

I smiled and raised a hand in farewell before backing out, hopefully ending any chance of saying something truly awkward.

Callum said something to Lila I didn't hear and followed me out.

"Are you . . . ," he started, but I turned around and gave a broad smile.

He was doing a good, honorable thing, and the last thing I wanted was to make any of it more difficult than necessary.

I thought highly of him. And, I realized, I wanted him to think well of me.

"I'm fine," I told him. "I'm fine, and I think . . ." His hand was inches from me, and I touched his fingers with mine. "I think you're really great."

He studied my face, still, like he was afraid to breathe.

Or maybe that was me.

I cleared my throat. "I need—I need to go. I need to get Margot from ballet."

"Can I pick you up Saturday? For the concert?"

"Yes! Yes, of course." I looked up at him, and felt the inevitable flush cover my face. "I'm looking forward to it."

His lips tipped in a slow smile as he studied my face. "Me too."

"Thank you for the banana pudding recipe."

He gave a low chuckle. "Anytime."

36

The sage in bloom is like perfume
Deep in the heart of Texas.

—Hank Thompson

Callum

I walked Jane to her truck and watched her drive away before walking back inside the restaurant and to the office.

To Lila.

She lifted her eyebrows when she saw me. "So?" she asked. "Did I ruin everything with you? I'm sorry; I completely forgot she was coming by today."

I sank into the chair opposite the desk. "No. Not ruined. We're going out Saturday."

"Everything's okay?"

I thought of the way she touched my hand, the way she looked up at me. If my memory of those last few moments was accurate, we were more than okay. "Yeah," I said. "It's fine."

She leaned forward. "You're blushing again."

I leveled a gaze at her. "You're taking this whole sisterly thing very seriously."

"Someone has to."

"Haven't seen you for a few days. The new apartment is working out for you?"

"It is! The neighbors are nice; I like hearing the kids play outside."

"You know—"

"Yes, I know I can stay at your place. Trust me when I say that I don't think you need me around, not right now." Lila gave a nod. "I'm glad she has you. She's a lucky girl."

"Don't go running ahead of things. She just agreed to a first date, that's all."

"Sometimes, that first date is just a formality."

I laced my fingers together. "Speaking of, how's Clint?"

This time, Lila's face colored. "Just fine."

"That formality date go okay? What are you up to, four formality dates?"

"Shut up," she said, with a smile on her face.

"I'm glad you're happy."

She folded her hands over her belly. "I didn't think I'd ever get to be happy. It's nice to be wrong." She looked up at me. "I hope you have a good date."

That unfamiliar feeling, hope, spread in my chest. "I hope so too."

37

Surely a pretty woman never looks prettier than
when making tea.

—MARY ELIZABETH BRADDON

Jane

Picking up Margot took longer than usual, on account of her inability to leave her newfound circle of friends. I watched them chat away amiably, pleased that she'd found her people.

Once I got her inside the truck, she was full of news about the upcoming spring ballet and the costumes that were planned and how there was a boy at school who'd been particularly attentive lately. The latter topic kept us busy until we reached home. When we arrived, Margot barreled inside to video chat with said friends, the ones she'd said good-bye to only moments before. I was hardly out of the truck myself when Nina came flying out of the big house and across the lawn.

"Jane! You'll never believe it. Where's Celia?"

Celia must have heard the commotion, because the door opened and she stepped outside. "Is everything all right?"

Nina raced up to us, clutching her phone in her hand. "Lyndsay! She sent me a passel of texts, not thirty minutes ago. Remember how she went and toured San Antonio with Jonathan and Phoebe Foster? She's eloping, right this minute, with Phoebe's brother Rob."

"What?" I asked, wrinkling my nose. "Lyndsay and Rob?"

Really, come to think of it, the two of them made sense together.

"That's what the texts say. Apparently she was seeing Rob's brother, Ted. But he'd just gotten out of a long-term relationship"—Nina wrinkled her nose—"and wanted to keep it quiet."

I forced myself to breathe in and breathe out. "She was seeing Ted? Before she met Rob?"

So help me, if I ever saw Teddy again, I'd murder him with a tea strainer.

"Yes! Discreetly and long-distance, I suppose. But she got tired of the distance, met Rob, and the rest is history." Nina pressed her hands to her heart. "It's so romantic."

"Romantic," I echoed woodenly. "Well, that's . . . that's very nice for them."

"I'm headed to town. I thought I'd buy them a wedding gift, something silver. Do young people use silver anymore?"

I wasn't capable of enough thought to formulate an answer.

"Depends on the person, I suppose. Lyndsay might like it," Celia said.

It would be shiny, so I imagined so.

"I'll go and see what I see. Don't let me keep you." Nina patted my cheek and then Celia's. "You two are so pretty. I'll bet that when you've got your tea shop open, you'll have a line of men out the door, coming for tea and a look at you both."

"I've always wanted to serve tea in a zoo," I quipped before we said good-bye and walked inside.

I closed the door behind us and leaned against it, trying to catch my breath. "Lyndsay and . . . Teddy." I looked up at Celia.

She wouldn't meet my gaze.

"This didn't surprise you," I observed. She was upset, yes, but shocked? I didn't see it. "You knew about them."

Celia took a deep breath, and exhaled until her shoulders slumped. "Lyndsay told me."

I squinted at her. "Lyndsay . . . told you?"

"Yes."

"So, this whole thing is supposed to be a deep, dark secret, and Lyndsay comes to Austin under—let's be honest—the thinnest of pretenses, and the one person she tells is you? Teddy's ex-girlfriend?" My eyes widened. "She was warning you off. The snipe. And then when he wasn't advancing the relationship fast enough, she bailed for Rob. I might not be happy with Teddy, but that's not a lateral move."

"She confided in me about seeing Teddy, asked me to keep it quiet," Celia said. "And I agreed."

"But why? After all, Teddy had already broken up with you."

"But he didn't," Celia answered simply. "I broke up with him."

"You—what?"

"It was Dad's scandal. We loved each other, but his superiors made it clear that as long as we were together, he wouldn't advance."

"That promotion," I said. "The one he didn't get."

"Right. He should have, but he didn't. He told me it was fine, told me that he'd been thinking of quitting and going to seminary."

My brows lifted. "That's a switch. I bet Phoebe loved that."

Celia tipped her head. "No. It was creating problems with his family, and my presence was creating problems for him at work."

"So why didn't he just leave?"

"It was a big decision; he'd been wrestling with it for months. And after things went so badly with the shop and Jonathan and Phoebe, and he did . . . nothing, I knew we couldn't be together anymore. Marrying him would mean that Phoebe would be my sister-in-law, and whatever the Fosters wanted, or his job wanted, would come first." She shook her head. "I couldn't do that."

"So you broke up with him."

"Not just because I was mad. I loved him," she said simply. "I still do. And Dad's scandal was holding him back at work, at the job he couldn't convince himself to leave. He wasn't able to make a decision, so I made it for him."

"Oh, Celia. And then Austin . . ."

Celia ran a hand through her hair. "It was far away. It seemed . . . it seemed like the best option, to be far away. Not just for that," she continued in a rush. "I hated that after all these years, we were still Walter Woodward's daughters. At some point, it would have touched Margot too. So we had to go somewhere, and Ian offered the casita. It seemed to be the right thing." She hugged her arms to herself, and her voice grew thick with tears. "In hindsight, I realize . . . I was running away and dragging you and Margot with me."

I crossed the room to her then and wrapped my arms around her in a tight hug. "You know that we would follow you across the world, right?" I pulled back so I could see her face. "I'm so sorry about you and Teddy. I was so terrible to you about it, especially after Sean . . ."

And then we were crying together and hugging and crying some more. "I should never, ever have kept it from you," Celia said. "Never ever. From now on, I'm telling you everything."

"Yes! It's nothing but TMI from here on out," I promised, heartened by the laugh my statement elicited. "I love you, Celia. You and Margot are the most important people in the world to me."

"I love you too, Jane. You're my best friend. I can't believe—I wish—I'm sorry—"

"Stop apologizing and hug me," I told her. "We're going to be fine."

Callum picked me up for the concert Saturday night, and I left with Margot's hoots ringing in my ears. Nina waved at us through the window of the big house. I think I saw Ian give us a thumbs-up.

If I'd felt like dating Sean had happened in a fishbowl, going out with Callum made it thirty times more intense.

I looked up at him to find him grinning back, and felt . . . complete bliss.

So I waved back at Nina and Ian.

The concert was lovely, and I was excited to hear my favorite song of theirs, "Lament," which, for the sadness of the title, was lyrical and peaceful.

Callum leaned over, his lips next to my ear, and his breath warm on my cheek. "The guy on guitar and keyboard is really good."

My face flushed. "He is," I agreed, though it was difficult to pay attention at that moment.

I was lucky that the music was so soothing, because my heart was already beating so fast that something up-tempo might have sent me back to the hospital.

Not long ago, I was thinking of being with Sean Willis forever, and then that house of cards had come crashing to the ground in a heap. And now here I was with Callum, listening to one of my favorite bands, sitting so close I could feel him breathing.

This was the man, I reminded myself, who had rescued his former sister-in-law, who had fished me out of a lake, who had read to me in the hospital.

Never mind he was an American hero.

After Sean, being out with someone felt crazy. But when that someone was Callum?

It still felt crazy. Just . . . good crazy.

We'd eaten dinner beforehand, but the butterflies in my stomach seemed to have worked their way through it, because my stomach rumbled as we walked to Callum's Jeep. I didn't say anything, but Callum must have heard it because we stopped by Torchy's on the way home. "It's a good night for a taco," he said simply. "Or three."

Afterward, we pulled up at the casita quietly; all the lights were off. It was a warm night, with just a soft breeze. A perfect night—and I didn't want it to end.

Callum tipped his head toward the pool. "I brought the book with me," he said. "Want to sit poolside and read a little more? Unless," he rushed to add, "you're tired. That's fine too."

The dark hid just how broad my grin was. "I'd like that."

As we walked to the pool, slowly—his leg healing, my own stamina not yet recovered—I took account of the seating options. Deck loungers, deck chairs, and strung between two of the trees, a hammock.

"How about the hammock?" I asked.

He cleared his throat. "Good idea."

We climbed in carefully, the initial swaying slowing as we found a comfortable spot. We were side by side, and while my arm wasn't around him, nor his around me, his body felt warm and pleasant beside me.

As we settled, a thought occurred to me. "How exactly are we meant to read out here? It's a little . . ."

He chuckled. "A little dark?" He reached inside his jacket. "There's this device called an e-reader, and it's got a handy little backlight."

"Look at you being clever."

With a little work, he found where he'd left off reading and began to read again. "'She was outside his hovel before dawn. Inside, she could hear him already awake. She knocked. He appeared, stood in the doorway. Behind him she could see a tiny candle, open books. He waited. She looked at him. Then she looked away.'"

Listening to his voice, curled up next to him, I felt both more relaxed and more alive than I'd ever felt. I listened as Buttercup told Westley how she felt about him, and how he'd slammed the door in her face. And how the next day, he was packed to go and find his fortune, but not before telling her that he loved her and had all along.

He read until I felt so relaxed that I seemed nearly boneless.

Somewhere in there, we'd shifted positions. His arm had come to be beneath my neck, so that my head rested in the crook of his arm, my hand on his chest.

He smelled good, like spice and trees.

After a while, when his voice had begun to grow rusty from reading, he turned off the e-reader and put it back inside his jacket.

"This is nice," I said. "Thank you. I know I keep thanking you, but you've given me so much to thank you for."

"It's nothing," he said. "I enjoyed spending the evening with you."

There were so many other things to be said, they hung around us like fireflies in the dark.

I shook my head. "It's not nothing."

"Jane—" He pushed himself up to a near-sitting position. As much as one could in a hammock. "The truth is, I've—I've cared for you for a long time. We haven't spent a lot of time together, so it's hard to say if it's love. Maybe it is. I don't know." He took a breath and exhaled hard. "But I didn't do anything for you because I'm altruistic. I did it because I didn't want to be without you."

"Oh," I said, because that was all I could manage. Every other word had fled from my mind.

"You don't have to say anything. I know it's been a difficult time for you. But I thought I should be honest."

I looked up at him. "I— I'm not sure I believe that."

He started to protest, but I held up a hand and continued. "If you say you love me, I believe you. I do. But I don't believe that you weren't altruistic. If it had been Celia or Margot, or Charlie or Nina, wouldn't you have gone out looking for them too? And done everything possible to bring them back?"

He didn't answer.

"Ian told us about your last battle overseas. You rescued people. Not as many people as you wanted but as many as you were able. You help people. All kinds. It just happens that some of the people you really care about have needed your help in a big way, and I, for one, couldn't be more thankful." I rested a hand on his chest. "You have a hero's heart, Callum."

Callum reached for my hand and cradled it with his own. "Thank you, Jane," he said, his voice deep and husky.

I gave a slight nod, my words gone.

But I wasn't silent because I was overwhelmed with feelings—well, I was, but it wasn't just that. I was silent because he held my hand so gently in his, and with our faces very, very close together, I was silenced by my own curiosity.

What would it be like, I wondered, to kiss Callum Beckett?

As I wondered, our eyes caught and held. I couldn't look away.

Callum cleared his throat. "As I said. I recognize that you've endured a time of significant emotional upheaval. But"—his voice grew hoarse—"I would like to kiss you. If you're not ready, it's understandable—"

He was going to keep talking, and there was only one thing to do. I used my elbow as leverage against the hammock fabric, and closed the small distance to kiss him.

Just a light kiss; more like a brush. That's all it took get him to stop talking.

Up close, he smelled wonderful, but the feel of his lips beneath mine was even better. The feeling was so heady, so overwhelming, I could have stopped there and been content.

But not Callum.

In the space of the smallest breath, the moment shifted from me kissing Callum to Callum kissing me. Kissing me deeply.

Kissing me with joy and fear and reverence, each emotion taking precedence before shifting to the next and back again. His fingers wove into my hair, drawing me close, every caress a question.

I answered every question with a caress of my own.

Kissing Callum was like finding a favorite thing I hadn't known I was looking for. But now that I'd found it, I didn't want it to ever end.

Just as I thought my heart would burst, Callum gave my lips a last caress before brushing kisses on my cheekbones, my eyelids, all while rubbing the base of my neck gently with his thumb.

"I should be gentlemanly," he said, his eyes searching mine, "and walk you to your door."

"Oh. Right." I swallowed. "Sure."

Neither of us moved.

"I'm going to show my hand," he said, "and tell you that I'm afraid that if I leave you and go home, I'll wake up to discover this never happened."

I smiled up at him. "If it would make you feel better," I said, "we could make plans to do this again tomorrow."

He stroked my hair, twirling a curl around his finger. "Don't play coy with me, Jane Woodward. I don't think my heart could take it."

"You're not wrong. It's been a"—I searched for the right word—"tempestuous time. I have a lot of sorting to do. Celia and I are finally back on the right footing."

He smiled. "I'm glad."

"And Margot's still settling, and we're pressing on with the tea shop. But even with all of that, I think this, right here, is very much worth following up on."

"This?" He leaned forward again, pressing a new, sweet kiss to my lips. "Right here?"

I kissed him back, enjoying the mix of kissing and laughter. "Yes," I answered. "This right here."

He laughed then, a full-hearted laugh, swinging himself around and off the hammock gracefully. "Come on," he said. "Let's say good night so that tomorrow we can say hello."

38

I will tell you. I was going to. I just need tea.

—Joanna Trollope

Jane

"So," Celia said over the breakfast table the next morning. "Either you had a good date last night or you had a facial, because you're glowing."

"It was a really good date," I said, feeling my cheeks turn pink.

"Margot," Celia asked sweetly, "does Jane look like she's blushing to you?"

Margot closed the fridge to look, and then burst into cackling laughter. "She *totally* is!"

"Tease me now," I told them. "When you're both in love, I won't hold back."

Celia sat up straighter. "Speaking of being in love, you'll be pleased to hear that while you were cavorting on your date last night—"

I snorted. "We were hardly cavorting."

"You wouldn't be blushing so hard if there wasn't any cavorting," Celia pointed out.

"There might have been a little," I admitted primly. "Some."

"You were making out," Margot crowed.

I raised my eyebrows at Celia, but she ignored me.

"I created an online dating profile last night," she said. "And tomorrow, I have a coffee date."

"Coffee?"

"It's casual," Celia said. "If he's worthy, we'll go to tea."

I laughed, and reached out to grasp her hand. "Good plan. I hope it goes well."

"Yes," Celia answered. "I just wish . . ."

"Not over Teddy yet?"

Celia swallowed hard. "Not quite yet." She gave a tremulous smile. "But I need to be. It's time."

∞

Within a matter of days, we had a signed lease and keys to the new space. Celia and I spent our days setting up the salon and getting things ready. We ordered the sign that would hang outside the door, proudly announcing Valencia Tea Company.

At last.

Ian, Roy, and Callum, along with a few staff members from Smoky Top, helped to get the marble-topped bar into place.

"Hello, love," I said, running my hand over its cool, smooth surface. "It's nice to see you."

"I see," Callum teased. "I thought it was just me, but it turns out you're friendly with your countertop too."

I spun and wrapped my arms around his neck before pressing a kiss to his lips. Mostly because I wanted to, a little because it was the fastest way to stop him from teasing me any further.

Roy carried a box in. "That Lyndsay Stahl girl stopped in the other day, at Smoky Top," he said, setting the box on top of the bar. "This one's labeled 'teapots.'"

"There on the bar is fine," I said, glancing at Celia. Her eyes were downcast, preoccupied with the placement of our vintage cash register.

"She was there with her new husband," Roy continued. "Didn't know she'd gotten married, but congratulated the kids. Gave them dessert on the house."

"Good," Callum said, catching the look on my face.

I'd told him the story of Lyndsay and Teddy and Celia, and he'd shaken his head. "I don't understand," he'd said at the time, "how any sane guy would date Lyndsay after Celia. Your sister's a class act."

I had agreed wholeheartedly.

Celia was quiet for several minutes after Roy left, but by the time we began to unpack the teacups, her smile had reappeared.

"We won't put the shelves up until after we've redone the wallpaper," I said. "But I think it's going to look really good."

Celia hugged me, resting her chin on my shoulder. "I agree."

We settled on a pretty black-and-white print paper from Graham & Brown that featured pen-and-ink blossoms, tree branches, and butterflies on a white background. It somehow straddled the line between modern and old-fashioned, which perfectly suited our concept.

Three days later, the rolls had arrived, and Celia and I were up to our elbows in wallpaper paste and loving every minute.

"It's going to look really good," I said, "with the hanging windows."

"Is it blasphemy to say I like it more than the paper we had in San Francisco?"

I considered the question. "I don't think it's ever wrong," I decided, "to love what you have more than what you had."

"That is very wise," Celia said. "It would sound wiser if you didn't have paste on your nose."

We were laughing together, mostly at my attempts to wipe it off with the back of my arm, which left even more than I'd had in the first place, when the bells over the door rung behind us.

My first thought was that Callum had come to visit. But when I heard Celia's intake of breath, I realized I was wrong.

"Celia," said Teddy's voice. "Hello."

"Hello," she said, turning around fully.

I set down my paper and brush. "Hi, Teddy."

"Hi." He gave me a careful smile.

If seeing Sean again had been strange, seeing Teddy again was even more so. His hair had grown long enough to dust his collar, and he was wearing shorts and a T-shirt, which was the most dressed down I'd ever seen him. But he still looked like our Teddy, right down to the way he couldn't tear his eyes away from Celia.

"It's nice to see you," I said. "How . . . how did you know where to find us?"

"Oh. Yes. I subscribe to your newsletter," he said. "And you just sent out the mailing talking about how you found *the* place."

"Ah," I said. "That makes sense."

It was clever, actually. But what didn't make sense was what he was doing here.

"Jane," he said, after a moment, "I'd like to speak to Celia for a few minutes."

Celia took a half step closer to me.

"I don't think so," I said, raising my chin. I wasn't trying to be mean, but after what Celia had been through, he'd lost his one-on-one privileges with my sister. "Not without her say-so, at least."

"Whatever you have to say," Celia said at last, her voice hoarse, "I'd like Jane to be here."

"Right," he said, glancing down at the floor. "Yes. Understandable." A deep breath, and then he looked up at us again.

"Congratulations on acquiring Lyndsay Stahl as a sister-in-law," I said, my voice as dry as one of James Bond's martinis. "Congratulations, apologies, potayto, potahto. Our friend Roy served her at the Smoky Top recently." I paused. "I hope you weren't deeply disappointed. The two of you were dating, right?"

"Er, somewhat. Lyndsay and I caught up a bit," he said, "after Celia and I broke up."

"You were rebounding."

"More or less."

I shot a look at Celia, a look that meant *more,* but she wasn't looking at me. I shifted my attention back to Teddy as he stammered on.

"Lyndsay and I dated a long time ago, in college," he said, "and we reconnected over LinkedIn. But she came out here and spent time with Rob, and it seems that they hit it off."

He cleared his throat. "I'm not surprised, to be honest. Rob's start-up went public the day before. It made a lot of money."

"So . . . now you're here," Celia breathed.

Teddy took a step forward. "I don't know what I was thinking. I was lonely, and I missed you. I was tired of missing you. And Lyndsay liked me."

"I liked you," Celia said softly.

They stood there, each watching the other's face so carefully. I felt certain both of them had forgotten I was even there.

"I understand why you broke up with me," Teddy said. "I had a choice, and I should have chosen you. I should have chosen you without a second's hesitation." He took a deep breath. "If you don't want to see me, I understand. But I wanted to see you and tell you that Lyndsay and I, well, that was never a thing, not really. And I also quit my job."

Celia's eyes widened. "You quit your job?"

"I left without notice, actually. Spent a lot of time thinking and packed up my desk. I've always wanted to go to seminary, and I'm going stop second-guessing myself and do it. I've applied to Dallas Theological Seminary and Fuller too. And if they don't accept me I'll apply to others. Talbot. Western. All of them."

There were quite a few more, but I knew better than to open my mouth at such a time.

"You were right about me," he said. "I should have been stronger. So I'm going to do better, and that means applying for seminary. And"—he paused—"I thought I'd show up and see what would happen if I begged you to give me a second chance. I love you, Celia."

As it turned out, he didn't need to beg. He just needed to be brave.

Celia rushed across the room to him. "I love you, Teddy!" she said, throwing her wallpaper-paste-covered arms around him.

And Teddy, for his part, clearly did not care. He held her tight, and in no time at all, they were kissing. I suddenly saw Margot's point about making oneself scarce when one's sister and her boyfriend were in the midst of a romantic moment.

I snuck out the back door and leaned against the alley wall.

Celia was happy.

Margot was happy.

And me? I might have been the happiest one of them all.

Epilogue

When tea becomes ritual, it takes its place at the heart
of our ability to see greatness in small things.

—Muriel Barbery

Six Months Later

I turned off the Open sign in the window of the tea shop and turned around
to face the assembly. More specifically, Celia, Teddy, Margot, and Callum.
"Everyone take a seat," I said. "And help yourself to a scone. I made them fresh
this morning and saved them."

"Even though we ran out of scones at three o'clock today," Celia clarified.

"Those were regular scones," I said. "These are special scones, with im-
ported French butter. I don't make these for just anyone."

Celia snorted, but I pressed on.

"Celia and I have called a family meeting because," I said, "there are going
to be some changes."

"Wait," said Margot, taking the seat next to me. "Teddy and Callum aren't
family. Not, you know, 'legally,'" she said, adding air quotes.

"Margot," Teddy said, "I've asked Celia to marry me."

"Really?" Margot squealed, her cheeks squishing her eyes until they were
small but glowing. "When? Can I be a bridesmaid? Can I do the flowers? Is
Jane going to bake everything?"

"We haven't set a date," Celia answered. "And of course you'll be a bridesmaid. I thought the three of us could do the flowers together, and the food logistics are still under consideration."

"I'm baking everything," I told Margot. "Don't worry."

"What if you were just a bridesmaid for one day?" Celia asked me. "Have you considered that?"

"Of course I considered it," I retorted. "But I can do both."

"Teddy lives in Dallas," Margot interrupted. "Are you moving to Dallas?"

"That's the plan, yes," Celia said, nodding. "At least while Teddy's in school. We want to come back to Austin when he's done. Plant a church."

"Oh," Margot said, noticeably more sober. "So . . . I'll stay with Jane at the townhouse."

Callum reached under the table and squeezed my knee. "Yes," I said.

This was harder than I'd expected.

"Callum asked me to marry him," I said in a rush.

Both of my sisters stared at me, wide-eyed, their ensuing questions—*what, really, when*—stacked on top of each other.

"Why didn't you say anything?" Celia asked, looking from me to Callum and firmly back to me. "I . . . I thought . . ." I knew what she was thinking, that we'd promised not to keep secrets from each other.

"I thought it would be easier to tell you both when we were all together, making plans," I said. "And he just asked me."

Celia turned a sharp stare to Callum. "When?" she demanded.

Callum held his hands up. "Yesterday. I couldn't stop myself."

I turned and arched an eyebrow at him. "Did you try?"

He winked at me. "Not really."

"You've known since yesterday?" Celia reached over, picked up a scone, and lobbed it at me. "You knew for twenty-four hours, and you didn't say anything?"

"Those are special scones! Don't throw them!" But I picked one up and tossed it at her.

Margot reached out and picked up a broken piece of scone. "These are really good," she said in a small voice, tucking the crumb into her mouth. "You probably shouldn't throw them at each other."

Celia straightened. "Margot's right."

"She is. Look," I said, turning to my younger sister. "I was only a couple of years older than you when we lost the house we'd grown up in."

Margot nodded. "I remember that house."

"I loved that house, and after Dad sold it I felt completely unmoored. So it's really important to me that you know that Celia and Teddy and Callum and I all love you. You have a room full of weird sister-brother parents, okay?"

"This is starting to sound like a cut scene from *Chinatown*," Teddy murmured.

"She knows what I mean," I said, haughtily. "Don't you, Gogo?"

Margot nodded.

"If you wanted to come to Dallas with us," Celia told Margot, "we'd love to have you. That's one option."

Margot wrinkled her nose. "But won't you be, like, honeymooning and stuff?"

I waved a hand. "There's going to be lots of honeymooning going around. It can't be avoided, but"—I paused to take an anxious breath—"we'll work it out. You're important, Margot."

"What your sister is trying to say," Callum cut in, "is that we realize that this is your senior year of high school and that you may not want to relocate again. I have my house here, and there's lots of room—including the finished attic."

"Which has air-conditioning," I added.

Callum nodded. "It does. We'd love to have you. But I know that Celia and Teddy would love to have you too. The choice is up to you."

I squeezed his hand in thanks and held my breath. By now, I had a well of tears just under my eyelids, threatening to spill.

When Callum asked me to marry him, I was ecstatic. I loved him. We loved each other. We were going to be together.

And then I remembered Margot and Celia's recent engagement and the conversation I'd shared with Margot so many months before, in that short window when Sean and I had been serious.

Also known as that time when Sean had asked me to marry him so I'd consent to being a roadie.

So as happy as I was about the prospect of being with Callum, I'd immediately begun to worry about Margot. She'd already been uprooted, moved across the country, and moved from the casita into an admittedly much more spacious three-bedroom townhouse.

Callum had offered to move into the townhouse, but I was enough of a pragmatist to think that maybe—while honeymooning—we might all appreciate the extra room.

And then I began to panic that Margot might choose the adventure of following Celia to Dallas. Losing Celia to Teddy—I could handle it. Almost. Mostly. I could deal with it, as long as I had a steady dose of texts and calls and silly photos paired with the promise of returning to Austin.

But losing Celia and Margot, both at once? My heart squeezed at the thought.

Sitting at the table, I waited for Margot to speak.

Callum squeezed my hand and leaned over to whisper in my ear. "Don't forget to breathe," he murmured. I squeezed his hand back.

"It's okay if you want to take some time," Celia told her.

"No," Margot said. "It's okay." She looked to me and Callum. "You guys are keeping Dash, right?"

"Of course," Callum answered, a smile on his lips.

"And Celia will come visit? And I can visit her?"

Celia and I both nodded. I couldn't speak.

"Then I'll stay with you and Jane," Margot said at last.

I exhaled in a whoosh, leaning over and wrapping my arm around her. "I love ya, kid."

"I love you too," she said, and I knew she meant it.

"And it's okay that you're only staying for the dog."

"I don't think it's just about the dog," Callum said, but I was crying now, and laughing, and hugging Margot, Celia too, and Callum. And all at once we were standing and hugging and crying. I didn't know where my arms ended and anyone else's began, and I didn't care.

Celia might be leaving, but she'd be back. And maybe Margot would leave us someday. But we loved each other. And we were together now, and we'd be together again, and that's what mattered most.

I opened my eyes to see Celia's face across from mine, on the other side of Margot's shoulder.

"Hey, Celia," I said, finding my voice.

"What, Jane?" she answered back

"I'm really glad we came to Austin," I told her. And I meant it from the depths of my heart.

Pumpkin Scones with Chai Glaze

½ cup canned plain pumpkin

2 tablespoons whole milk

1 egg

2 cups all-purpose flour

Scant cup sugar

1 tablespoon baking powder

½ teaspoon salt

1 teaspoon cinnamon

½ teaspoon nutmeg

¼ teaspoon cloves

¼ teaspoon ginger

6 tablespoons cold butter, cut into very small pieces

For the glaze

1 cup powdered sugar

2–3 tablespoons whole milk

For the chai glaze

1 cup powdered sugar

3 tablespoons powdered sugar

2 tablespoons whole milk

¼ teaspoon black tea, very finely ground

¼ teaspoon cinnamon

1/8 teaspoon nutmeg

1 pinch ginger

1 pinch clove

Preheat the oven to 425°F. Line a baking sheet with parchment paper.

Whisk together the pumpkin, whole milk, and egg. Set aside.

Stir the flour, sugar, baking powder, salt, and spices together in a large mixing bowl. Using your hands, rub the butter into the flour mixture until the mixture resembles small peas.

Fold in the pumpkin mixture, stirring until a shaggy dough forms.

Turn the dough out onto a floured pastry cloth or silicone baking mat. Knead the dough for a couple of turns, and then form it into a long rectangle, about 3/4-inch thick. With a large knife, cut the dough into three squares, and then cut each square into two triangles.

Place the scones onto the lined baking sheet, and bake for about 15 minutes, or until the scones are lightly browned on top. Allow to cool fully.

To prepare the glaze, stir together the milk and powdered sugar. Brush over the cooled scones. For the spiced glaze, stir together all the ingredients. To pipe over the scones, you can use a pastry bag and a tip, or simply spoon the glaze into a zipper storage bag and cut the tip of one corner off. Drizzle over each scone in a zigzag pattern; allow to set before serving.

Makes 6 scones.

Readers Guide

1. *Jane of Austin* borrows much of its plot and characters from *Sense and Sensibility,* but there are references and character elements from other Austen works as well. Which did you notice? Which were your favorites? Discuss what Austen character you would most like to see in the modern era.

2. Much of the story revolves around the relationship between the sisters. How did you relate to Jane and Celia's communication challenges? Which sister's approach to conflict or change do you relate to more, and why?

3. Jane and Celia have career and relationship options today that *Sense and Sensibility*'s Marianne and Elinor Dashwood didn't have during the early nineteenth century. What social constraints still exist that compare to Austen's era?

4. Callum's psychological challenges due to his family history and his professional experience have real, lasting consequences. Discuss what you imagine as Callum's future with Jane, in his BBQ business, with Dash, and for his well-being. How have you experienced animals connecting with humans under emotional duress?

5. Jane falls for Sean Willis soon after meeting him. Do you think she would have felt the same way if she remained in San Francisco? If she and Celia weren't emotionally distant? How do you think her situation affected her response to Sean?

6. A common thread in Jane Austen novels is the revealing of a person's true character. Which characters in *Jane of Austin* are revealed to be different than expected?

7. Both Jane and Callum struggle to find a sense of home. Why do you think it's so important to them? What makes it a challenging search?

8. Margot is an important part of Jane and Celia's relationship. How do you think Jane and Celia's story might've been different if not for their role as Margot's guardians?

9. For a long time Callum doesn't see himself as worthy of being someone's hero. Why do you think that is?

10. Tea and baking play a big role in how Jane relates to other people. She takes care of her loved ones through tea. What are some of your favorite nonverbal of expressions of love?

Acknowledgments

In writing this book, I owe a deep debt of gratitude to many people, all of whom I'm extremely grateful for.

This book wouldn't have happened without my editor, Shannon Marchese, for many reasons but the biggest of which is that she came to me with the title. It was a fun challenge coming up with a story to go with it, and I'm so thankful for the opportunity.

I'm perpetually thankful for my agent, Sandra Bishop, who is a class act and a stand-up lady, and handles my panicked moments with aplomb.

Many, many thanks to my friend and line editor Rachel Lulich, who always has sharp observations and worthy notes and manages to make them and make me laugh at the same time. That is not a simple task, but I'm so glad for it. She also dug up the quotes about tea from *Doctor Who,* which made all the difference.

Many thanks to Laura Wright and her team for polishing the manuscript and getting it book-worthy. And thanks to Kelly Howard for the gorgeous cover.

I'm so thankful for the smart writers I get to call friends—Kara Christensen and Sarah Varland, for listening and brainstorming when necessary.

Many thanks to my Street Team, for their enthusiasm in all things, including recipe testing! Bakers Becca Peterson, Courtney Clark, Dani Redican, Michelle Brown Jinnette, and Sarah Varland have been endlessly helpful, and I so appreciate their willingness to try new things.

I'm also very thankful for my many Austin advisors, most notably Jamie Lapeyrolerie and Allison Pittman, as well as Mindy Feather, Elisabeth Greene, and Sara Duncan Lisberger. You guys are all awesome, and because of you, I ate all of the tacos at Torchy's while I could.

Thanks to Nöel Chrisman for assisting with the naming of Valencia Street

Tea, and to Patti O'Connell for answering questions about how Callum would use his cane.

Many thanks to the fine folks at 7 Grams Coffee House and Bakery, who told me everything I needed to know about kolache, and to Janell Teach, who offered her expertise during my own experiment with making yeasted dough in general, kolache in particular.

Thank you to Google, for making it possible to map out where everyone went and analyze the street views of everywhere from Hyde Park to Valencia Street. It makes my job easier.

I would like to thank the security guard at the Austin Capitol building, for making sure I got to see everything I ought and then giving me a Junior Texas Highway Patrol sticker when it turned out I needed to head out because of time constraints. I still have it and will cherish it always.

Many thanks to the ladies of the Portland Heights Ladies Hat Club, for their support of me and my books over the years. You're fabulous, one and all.

Lastly, many thanks to my family for their support over the years—both the family I was born into and the one I married into. And speaking of marriage, many thanks to my husband and sweetheart, Danny, for the encouragement, trips to Starbucks, and hard work that makes *this* work possible.